Fling Club

ALSO BY TARA BROWN

The Devil's Roses
Cursed
Bane
Hyde
Witch
Death
Blackwater
Midnight Coven
Redeemers
Betrayers

The Born Trilogy
Born
Born to Fight
Reborn

The Light Series
The Light of the World
The Four Horsemen
The End of Days

Imaginations
Imaginations
Duplicities
Reparations

Blood and Bone
Blood and Bone
Sin and Swoon
Soul and Blade

Crimson Cove Mysteries
If At First
Second Nature
Third Time's a Charm
Four Crimson Corners
Hang Five

The Blood Trail Chronicles
Vengeance

Vanquished
Valiant

The Seventh Day
The Seventh Day
The Last Hour
The Earth's End

The Single Lady Spy Series
The End of Me
The End of Games
The End of Tomorrow
The End of Lies
The End of Love

The Royals Trilogy
A Royal Pain
A Royal Affair
A Royal Wedding

The Lonely Duet
The Lonely
Lost Boy

Puck Buddies
Puck Buddies
Roommates
Bed Buddies
Baby Daddies

Stand-Alone Novels
Lost in La La Land
My Side
The Long Way Home
First Kiss
Sunder
In the Fading Light
For Love or Money
Sinderella
Beauty's Beast
The Club

Fling Club

THE SERENDIPITY SERIES

TARA BROWN

SKYSCAPE

SKYSCAPE

Text copyright © 2018 by Tara Brown
All rights reserved.

Published by Skyscape, New York

www.apub.com

Amazon, the Amazon logo, and Skyscape are trademarks of Amazon.com, Inc., or its affiliates.

ISBN-13: 9781503903852
ISBN-10: 1503903850

Cover design by Eileen Carey

Printed in the United States of America

THE RULES OF FLING CLUB

RULE ONE.
If he doesn't belong to the country club,
he doesn't belong in your pants.

RULE TWO.
Never say the *L* word, unless it's *loser*.

RULE THREE.
No reheating a sister's old leftovers.

RULE FOUR.
Hos before bros; whoever sees him first gets him.

RULE FIVE.
See rule four; don't try to date a brother without permission.

RULE SIX.
Minimize couple's time. This isn't courting, it's socializing.

RULE SEVEN.
Act like a lady in the streets and freak in the sheets.

RULE EIGHT.
We don't pay. Go Dutch and you're out.

RULE NINE.
Protect yourself. That means your body and your reputation.
Know where the camera is.

RULE TEN.
Everything has an expiration date. Playtime ends August 31.

Chapter One

BETRAYAL 101

Cherry

Hey, Cait, I am so sorry to pull the plug at the last minute, but I've really made a connection with Griffin. We're—I bit my lip as my cheeks flushed, and I contemplated what else to say in my text. What Griffin and I were and where we were going.

Was it too early to speculate?

Was I jinxing it by thinking or texting about it at all?

Even worse, how was I ever going to back out of Fling Club without becoming a social pariah? Fling Club had been my entire life every summer since I was fifteen.

Cait Landry wasn't going to take my resignation lightly. Not only because she didn't take anything lightly, but also because I was a founding member, and this was our last year.

Our last year of Fling Club.

My last year as a Paulson Academy alumna, hosting the summer events in the Hamptons.

Fling Club, or *slut club* as my brother, Andy, called it, had been a tradition now for six summers. Six summers of girls running the show, running the boys, and ruling the shore.

But this would be my first summer going against the grain. Going rogue.

Because I was breaking the fundamental rule, one that had been in place from the start: anyone who left the group was cut. And while I didn't want to be cut, and hated the thought of doing that to my mother, being single for selection wasn't an option.

I was in love. Or falling into it at the very least.

I bit my lip harder and watched the suburbs fly by as the commuter train carried me closer to Boston and Harvard and Griffin.

Griffin.

My boyfriend.

My first real boyfriend.

This was the first time I felt like my life was coming together.

Griffin was my reason for skipping out on my final summer of Fling Club. My reason for smiling randomly and blushing inexcusably. My reason for risking possibly being friendless and disowned by my mother.

I got lost for a second, dreading all the horrible things Cait might do to me, before reminding myself that my commitment to Griffin mattered more than one season of parties and superficial fun and conditional love from a parent. Griffin was real world; he was real life. He was my future.

And maybe other couples would invite us to do whatever it was couples did. Maybe couples had better summers than singles, or maybe Cait would accept the fact that I was choosing to be in a serious relationship and show some respect.

Maybe.

A lot of maybes.

A lot of dread.

And yet I knew the moment I saw him I wouldn't care. I would find the strength to finish this text, and it would be settled.

I smiled to myself, excited that my fling from last summer had come back into my life to share an amazing six months. Not to mention that he was the sort of person my parents approved of. My mother would have to give me that if I were booted from Fling Club.

Griffin was already one of them—us. From a wealthy East Coast family with connections and the right kind of expectations. I didn't have to sneak around or pretend to date someone I didn't even like. I didn't have to have the conversation my friend Betsy just had, essentially a coming out of sorts. No, I didn't have to worry about that. Griffin ticked all their boxes, and mine.

I put away the phone and fantasized about surprising Griffin until the train ride was over, then hurried for the Uber I'd arranged to meet me at the station.

When the driver dropped me off on Ware Street, at the apartment building Griff lived in, my stomach fluttered the way it always did just before I saw him. I sighed and headed inside, wondering what this summer would bring. I knew where I imagined it going from the moment he told me he loved me.

Griffin was a second-year law student, so I assumed our life would start in New York, maybe separate apartments in the beginning. I could work in marketing, and he would work for his uncle. Then we'd get married and move to a house and have kids, and we'd get a vacation home near our parents and, of course, be part of the country club. Me, running our lives and taking care of kids and going to the spa and hosting dinner parties and helping with galas and fundraisers. Him, working hard to become a partner in his uncle's firm and needing me to do everything for him.

He already needed that. He was busy and disinterested in menial details like what to wear or whom the fundraiser was for or where the sheets came from.

He needed me. And perhaps, in a way, I needed him.

I liked being a "we." I liked fitting into the crook of someone's arm. I liked the way he snored when he was stressed and that he preferred me to do my homework next to him, so he could help. I liked feeling that I was more than just myself when we were together. There was safety in being with him and not having to stand on my own.

My marketing degree was never going to be as prosperous as his law degree, especially when we had kids. I knew that. I liked it. There wasn't pressure for me to decide my entire future. To some extent, I could ride on the coattails of his. And while it was the least feminist thing ever thought by a modern woman, I didn't care. I was content. I could worry about my future later, when I knew myself better.

As I climbed the stairs to his fourth-floor walk-up, each step felt like a door opening and a boyfriend box being checked off.

Romantic, check.

Smart, check.

Handsome, check.

Connected, check.

Rich, check.

Driven, check.

Safe, check.

I opened the door with the key he'd given me this week when I needed to drop off his dry cleaning, as he'd had a bachelor party to go to and needed to rush from school to the party. The key to his house. His beautiful apartment with the spaciousness of a loft that was so rare in these older buildings.

But the blush from the mental checklist and the pitter-patter of my hopeful heart fell away as I stepped inside.

A sound.

A moan.

A rustling of blankets.

The annoying squeak of that headboard.

A grunt.

A foot sticking out of the white thousand-thread-count sheets I'd just picked out.

Blonde hair.

A sapphire clip holding the tussled tresses halfway up.

A pearl necklace—real pearls.

Manicured fingers reaching back, clutching blankets and sheets.

A long, slender, tanned back arching.

A sapphire ring that looked too much like Kate Middleton's.

My eyes darted from the custom-made Kate Spade phone cover on the granite counter to the Chanel handbag on the floor below it to the cream Diane von Furstenberg dress on the floor, and stopped at the way Griffin's toes were clenching when they poked from the sheets.

My lips parted to scream, but she beat me to it.

She—*God, why her?*—screamed out in ecstasy, and I backed out.

Leaving the door ajar.

The key inside it.

My heart on the floor.

I ran down the four flights of stairs, unchecking each box until I was empty, my chest aching and pounding.

I swallowed the acidity of my hate and fled to the street, to the safety of being away from them both.

My boyfriend and my friend.

No.

No.

No.

Neither of them were *my* anything.

Cait, the ringleader of my life, was not *my* friend. Friends didn't have sex with their friend's boyfriend. On sheets you bought.

But as much as her pretending to be my fake socialite friend was awful, his pretending to love me was worse.

I gagged and fought back tears, speed walking on shaking legs and wobbling heels to the corner of Ware and Broadway. Flashes of flesh and sounds of wrinkling sheets and squeaking headboards clouded my mind, and the next thing I knew, I was sitting on a bench outside a media arts studio.

Something brought me out of the haze I was in: a sound. Unable to place it, I blinked and stared at the concrete in front of me.

"You getting on, lady?"

"What?" I glanced up to find a bus driver and an open door. I blinked again, unsure what he meant.

"You getting on the bus?" he asked rudely.

"Yeah." I got up, staggered to the door, and climbed aboard. I slipped my heels off and padded down the aisle barefoot to a seat before slumping into it and staring out the window.

I didn't check where the bus was going. I rode it until somehow, magically, it ended up back at the train station, the place where I started. The place where, just moments before, I'd had a heart full of hope and a checklist that was complete. I'd gone in a full circle and yet ended up back in time. Single. Lost. Alone.

Holding my shoes and what was left of my composure, I wandered to the tracks to wait. I didn't bother checking the time or my messages. I didn't check my heart to see if it was even in my chest, still beating, or if I'd left it behind on the floor of Griffin's apartment. I didn't realize how much of me I'd given him until now.

I paced and contemplated until nothing made sense.

Then I called my brother.

"Hey, Cherry. Look, I can't talk—"

"Cait's sleeping with Griffin," I blurted out, cutting off whatever excuse he was about to make.

"What? Who?" It took him half a second to connect the dots. "Oh, shit, seriously? How do you know?"

"I just caught them." My words had turned to a whisper. I was ashamed of my former friends for betraying me, and of myself for having been so naive. I knew Andy would call me stupid and tell me I deserved what I got for dating a shithead like Griffin, and that I was a sheeple like Mom and Cait, and—

"Oh, Cherry. I'm so sorry. Neither of those asshats deserves you."

That reaction, I didn't expect. Andy's kindness broke me. Angry tears flooded my eyes, and before I could help it, I was blubbering with rage in front of a platform full of strangers. I'd called Andy because I needed his sarcasm to toughen me up and put me on the defensive. I needed to be strong, like him. But instead he gave me tenderness, something I couldn't handle at the moment.

"You're lovely and sweet and kind. And you would never do something like that to anyone. Not even an enemy. Not even a whore like Cait. She's such a phony bitch. I'll come get you; tell me where you are."

"I—I'm going home. I'm at the train. I feel sick." My words were coming out in gasps.

"Screw them both. Let them have each other. I never liked that idiot. He's like Mom and Cait. He thinks his blue blood earns him the right to everything—clearly. They're selfish people, Cherry. Selfish and stupid and blind. I'm glad he showed his true colors before you got too invested in him."

Not wanting Andy to know I felt as invested as I could be, I stayed silent while he shouted and ranted all the things big brothers said to sad little sisters.

"I should beat the piss outta him! Want me to kick his ass? I'll go find a couple of friends and we can make sure he doesn't show up for—"

"No." I sniffled. "I just—" What did I want?

"Listen. Go home and take a hot bath, drink a bottle of wine, and try to get some sleep. I'll come get you in a week. We'll go to New York and get trashed, and you—"

"Sleep!" I snapped, finally losing the hold I had on my ferocity as his words landed. "You think I could sleep right now? I'm not Mom, Andy. I can't just take something and coast through shit like this."

"Okay, don't sleep. Try eating a whole sheet cake and plotting their deaths. I don't know. He's a douche and she's a bitch. They aren't worth the energy you're putting into being pissed off. I've never understood how you were friends with her. Or part of her slut club. Which, by the way, she only started because Wendell cheated on her with that chick from Derby. It's ironic, because then she turns around and does this to you."

"What?" I paced the cold concrete, lost on what he was talking about. He'd said too much too fast, as always.

"Cait started that stupid Fling Club to ensure no guys got away with double dating chicks all summer. You remember Brom Wendell, the guy she dated after she and I broke up? He was seeing Cait for a couple of months, but I guess he was screwing around with a girl he met at Derby behind her back. That summer, Cait founded that club, protecting her own interests by controlling the dating scene in the Hamptons for the entire season. Hell hath no fury, and all that jazz."

"Andy, I don't care why she started it," I groaned, wiping my eyes. "I don't care that some asshole cheated on her in high school. I care that she's currently sleeping with my boyfriend. I care that they were fucking on my goddamn sheets. The sheets I just bought and—"

"Cherry, take a breath. If you're crying, you're losing it."

I heaved, realizing I was blind with rage and tears.

"If you can't get past this with a simple cake, then I don't know what to say. If I ever make the mistake of falling in love again, it'll be with some girl in a different financial bracket. This is why we don't date our kind."

"Yeah, great advice now!" I spit my words, feeling the fury building.

"Don't lose control! You're in public, and you're a Kennedy for God's sake. We don't lose it in front of strangers. Plus, you'll be upset you didn't cry in the shower like a winner."

"Shut up!" I hated him sometimes.

"Cherry, getting upset and ruining your summer is pointless; you're the only one who suffers. They'll win. They'll ruin your last summer before college is over and the real world hits. Don't let them do that to you."

"What should I do then?" I burst again, sobbing.

"I don't know. Maybe take her down. Get revenge. Just whatever you do, don't go back to that moron, Chatsworth. The guy's an asshole."

"I won't." I sighed. "I can't talk about this anymore. I'll text you later."

"Trust me, eat the cake. It will make you feel better. Do that before you do anything else. My friend Angela swears by it." He laughed bitterly and hung up.

But I didn't focus on the cake or the bath or the wine. My mind was stuck on the one thing Andy had said that was useful, on repeat.

Get revenge.

And I would.

Chapter Two

A Family Affair

Cherry

A week later, I stared at the boxes, contemplating how long it would take for the movers to load them up and hoping I still had a few hours before Andy arrived with our chauffeur. I needed to run to the coffee shop with my laptop and post the help-wanted ad my little sister, Ella, had insisted our plot required.

Pacing, I tapped my finger against my lip, finalizing what the ad would say. Ella hadn't given me all the details, but she assured me what she had in the works would ruin both Cait and Griffin. And she was merciless when it came to the upper crust. She was merciless period. It helped that she hated Cait, the mean girls, elitist attitudes, conformity, and being born with a silver spoon. Anarchy was her ultimate goal.

My phone vibrated on the counter behind me, no doubt another message from Griffin.

My cold and concise breakup text hadn't been well received. I wasn't sure what Griffin would say or think, being dumped by text after six months, and so soon after I'd said "I love you" back. But I didn't care.

From what I could tell, he was crushed, devastated even, that this end had come out of nowhere. He was legitimately surprised that I could possibly not want him. Considering I broke up with him the day after I caught him cheating, I really thought he'd be capable of putting two and two together. I wondered if he didn't suspect that, just maybe, I'd discovered that he was sleeping with my "friend."

Apparently he was not as bright as I'd ever given him credit for.

No, instead he acted like he was the one who had been wronged.

Frankly, from the moment I sent the breakup text, I forced myself not to care what he thought or how he felt.

Growing up in a world where arranged marriages were still a thing, I'd promised myself I wouldn't ever be that girlfriend, fiancée, or wife. The one who quietly looked the other way. The one who pretended things were perfect, smoothed her dress and her hair and all the wrinkles on her face. The one who lied to her reflection when she whispered that it was just sex; it meant nothing. A common problem when business was the focus of the joining families, and not love. No, growing up I knew I was surrounded by many self-important men who used sex as a reward for success or a way to blow off steam, or even as a rebellious act against the system they kept perpetuating.

I also was never going to be like my father, suffering through a loveless marriage for the sake of appearances.

"Cherry?" A voice I knew called from the hallway to the open door of my apartment. "Are you ready or what?"

"Andy?" I scowled, unsure why he was here so soon. He wasn't supposed to be here for hours.

"No, your conscience has started sounding like me." Andy lifted an impatient eyebrow as he got to the door of my apartment. "We've been waiting for ten minutes. I texted you before we left Harvard. I got finished early. Hans is downstairs with the car. Let's go."

"I didn't realize you were coming so soon—I missed the text. You guys go on ahead. I'll take the train." I winced, not wanting him to know why I was staying behind. "I'm not done packing up."

"Looks like you're done. Or is it that you're not ready to leave here, being so close to Boston?" Andy's eyes narrowed. "Have you gone to see him? Or agreed to see him? Christ, you're not taking him back, are you?"

"No! I don't care about Griffin." It was only a little lie. "I'm just not ready to go home yet."

"Why? What's going on?" He stepped closer, coming into the foyer of the apartment and closing the door. "Don't lie." He knew me too well. "What's that look in your eyes? Something's wrong."

"Nothing." I swatted at him.

"Spill, now, or you won't leave the apartment alive." He used the bossy tone I didn't enjoy.

"Honestly, it's nothing."

"Cherry," he warned, lowering his voice even more.

"Really, it's nothing. I'm just going to take your advice is all." I didn't know how else to say it.

"Which advice? Some of it's pretty bad." He tilted his head skeptically.

"The uh—revenge advice." My words became a near whisper.

"Oh, that advice." He cringed. "That was bad advice. Ignore that. Did you try cake? We can go get some cake now and eat it in the car on the way home."

"No. God, I don't want cake. Dessert doesn't solve everything. It's like you want me to get fat."

"Who are you, and what have you done with my sister?" he said seriously.

"Shut up." I stepped back as he reached for my arm. "I'm going to take Cait down, Andy. She's done ruling over my life and everyone else's."

"How do you propose doing that?" he asked dubiously.

"I have a plan." I said it confidently, as if I'd come up with it on my own.

"What plan?"

"I'm going to make her break all the rules of Fling Club. Publicly. I'm going to humiliate her and ruin the stupid club altogether." I whispered, not even wanting the walls to hear this. "I'm thinking about finding a scholarship student from a community college and paying him to date her for the summer while he pretends to be a wealthy European. And then, I'll be able to prove that she's a fraud and a bully. I just need to slip down to the café and use the Wi-Fi to post the ad."

"Genius!" He burst out laughing and clapping. "Fucking genius! I love it. When do we start?"

"We?"

"Oh, I want in on this. It's brilliant. How did you think of it?"

"Well, Ella pointed out that Cait always goes for guys who show an interest in me. She takes them every summer, which we all know she does. It's part of the sick little game we all play as the cost of being popular and liked by Cait: pretend to have interest in a guy, let Cait take him, then go for the one you actually want. Griffin was the first one she didn't go after publicly, but she betrayed me behind my back. It wasn't a game this time, though. He's my boyfriend—was my boyfriend. Not some fling. Anyway, all I have to do is make the guy I choose hit on me in front of her—"

"Seriously, Cherry," he interrupted, "this is the best idea you've ever had." A wide grin cracked across his face as he beamed at me. "But forget the community college; go for the gold on this one. Nothing pisses the rich elite off more than MIT. We'll go there. Find some middle-class nerd and make him the handsome prince for the summer." He started to laugh. "Oh, God, this is good. I always thought you had some sharp edges in you; I'm glad to see they're finally poking out."

"Well, ugh . . . it was actually Ella's idea," I offered weakly, wishing I could take credit for it.

"Right." He said it like that made more sense. "I guess I should have known. She has the darkest soul of anyone we know."

"Besides Cait."

"That's assuming Cait has a soul at all." He chuckled again. "When did you talk to Ella?"

"On the train after I talked to you. I called and asked what would be the one thing that would ruin Cait Landry. She instantly went for the Fling Club."

"Slut club, Cherry. Call it like it is."

"How is it a slut club, moron?" I snapped back, still a little protective of the club and adverse to that word in all its connotations. "The girls pick one guy for the summer and take him to all the festivities. How is that slutty? And why aren't the guys slutty? If slut club were a thing, it would be filled with egotistical men who like to play ladies. Not the reverse."

"It rolls off the tongue smoother than *ball-buster club*." He rolled his eyes. "Come on. I'll make up an excuse for Hans to make a quick pit stop at MIT so you can post on the community Post-it board."

"The what?"

"The Post-it note wall." He said it like I should know.

"What's that?"

"Seriously? You all-girls-school chicks are deprived." He grabbed my arm, handbag, and cell phone and dragged me from the apartment as the movers passed us in the halls. "I get that it's not as necessary to have a Post-it note wall here at an all-girls college, what with the lack of hormonal teenagers and diversity in gender. But surely you've heard about them out in the real world?" He side-eyed me with his usual big-brother shittiness.

"No, I haven't. And we have a few guys here, FYI. This is the real world, dick. Just because we don't drug each other and dry hump at parties doesn't mean we aren't having fun." My tone grew defensive just as his got aggressive. It was our brother-sister dance.

"Dry humping is the stuff of life, Cherry; you ladies are missing out. And don't try to tell me some of the girls aren't dry humping."

"Andy!"

"What?" He poked my arm. "It's true. Anyway, back to the important stuff. All you do is post something on the Post-it wall, and someone will answer your note. It can be anything: a bottle of wine you recommend, a rant, help wanted, or a for-sale item. Sometimes we have poetry on ours, or people bitching about professors, or students ass kissing, or TAs being annoyingly passive-aggressive." He laughed at that one, like maybe he'd left a few of those messages himself. "People can answer by either sticking a Post-it note to your original post and making a chain, or they can text the phone number or email address you've left behind. It's like old-fashioned communication in an era overburdened by technology."

"That sounds weird and archaic."

"Look at you, using big-girl words! Well done." He nudged me. "It is archaic—that's the point. It's ironic and anonymous. But I think your best bet is to advertise the position there. It'll be simple. You write the note and leave an email address; that way you don't have to keep coming back to Boston to check the wall for a chain of responses. They'll email you, we'll set up some interviews, and Bob's your uncle."

"What?"

"Nothing. One of my TAs is British. He says it a lot."

"What are you talking about?" He drove me insane with his random shit.

"The Post-it wall."

"I know that. I mean the rest of it. Can you focus on one thing at a time?"

"Too fast for ya? I can slow it down."

"Shut up, Andy." I was already emotionally exhausted before he got here; ten minutes of him and I was ready to nap.

"On the note, you need to write that you're looking for a guy to make a fool of someone. Specify that it's a revenge plot so the guy knows what he's signing up for." He opened the limo door for me and grinned. "I can't believe we're finally doing this."

"Finally doing what?"

"Finally destroying Cait."

"Jesus." I scowled. "How much thought have you put into your own revenge plot against Cait?" I feared the answer.

"More than you can imagine," he offered, then shut my door.

Cait had broken Andy's heart years ago. They'd dated early in high school until he found out she was also seeing a guy in Italy. He'd hated her ever since, and of course hated Fling Club from the moment of its inception. Being one of her exes meant no club member in our part of the Hamptons would be allowed to touch him. It was a rule. While no one outside of the club knew the actual rules, but the guys we dated started to guess after a few seasons. Some rules were more obvious than others.

Andy got in on the other side, grinning. "We're going to have to be picky when it comes to our selection. We need someone who can be made handsome enough that Cait will want him. Have you seen the guys at MIT? They're not exactly used to interacting with members of the opposite sex, if you know what I mean."

"Since when are you a specialist on hot guys?" I laughed for the first time since walking in on the freak show in Griffin's bedroom.

"I have no issue admitting a guy's hot. It's called self-confidence. And the guys at MIT are known for brains, not brawn or chiseled jaw-lines. It reminds me of troll hall back there." He pointed at my school.

"Andy!"

"What?" He ignored me and carried on. "It's a shame we're asking some smart guy to dumb it down for the summer. I don't think Cait cares about brains. In fact, I suspect she prefers her men without them."

"Present company included," I teased.

"She cheated on me, so I doubt it. It was probably because I was too smart."

"And modest, but you tell yourself whatever you need to." I rolled my eyes.

"I will. Anyway, you're going to have to glow up some geek. Do you have a plan for that?"

"No. I never thought about the makeover much. Ella just said I needed to find a guy who was middle class, attractive, in need of money, and had a moral compass that pointed south. Or who was at least morally flexible."

"He definitely needs to despise the elite if he's going to be able to resist falling for Cait. She's rich, gorgeous, confident, and sexy. He needs to know his one job is wooing the ice queen without falling for her."

"That's true." I cringed, realizing that might be impossible for any guy. "Maybe—"

"Trust me, this is why we tell him the truth—all of it. No guy deserves to go into this blindly. Keeping him from her evil clutches and not having him turn on us will be my job. I'll befriend him and keep him on the straight and narrow. Mom's been nagging me to come home early and house-sit, so he can stay with me. This way we don't have some stranger in our guesthouse."

"I don't think I can do this." A wave of nausea hit me as the car got smaller and the temperature rose. I hadn't even considered what would happen if our mystery man turned on us and Cait crushed me. What if I ended up the big loser? Again. Who was I kidding, I couldn't go up against Cait.

"Really?" Andy lifted a dark eyebrow. "You don't think you can get revenge against the girl who pretended to be your friend while she slept with the first guy you ever loved?"

"I did-didn't." I couldn't even say it.

"Okay. Fine. Stay in denial. We can just go home, and you can continue being her little bitch, and when she chooses the guy you like again this summer, you can roll over for the seventh year in a row. Shit, maybe you can just introduce them and give them permission to bang behind your back." He leaned in, hissing in my face, "Is that what you want?"

"No."

"I have spent half my life watching that hateful witch use and abuse you. She's made you her little whipping girl. You and all your stupid friends. She doesn't say *jump*; you bitches just hang around jumping all day in case she wants you to. I never imagined we'd get you out from under her. Now that you see what a terrible person she is, surely you can't want to go back to that life?" He was impassioned on the subject, more than I'd ever seen him.

"No." I admitted it. I admitted to myself she had been cruelly abusing me for years. That I had done things because she was the queen bee and I was a worker bee.

"Good, because it's depressing to watch your sister lose herself when the girl she worships tells her she isn't good enough. Between Cait and Mommy dearest, you've been a vapid waste of flesh for years." He'd hit below the belt. But maybe I needed a painful blow.

He was right. I couldn't let her win. Not this time. Griffin wasn't the first boy Cait had stolen from me. He was just the first one I cared about. "I can do this." I mustered fake strength and pretended I was like Ella, that I didn't care what anyone else thought or did.

"It's going to be easier than you think. Trust me. You have me, and you have Ella." He sat back, plotting so loud I could almost hear it. "And that's as good as making a deal with the devil. You need to find some of that savage redhead strength all the other gingers have." He laughed at his own joke.

It wasn't easy being calm, even in my own head, but by the time we got to MIT, I'd come to terms with the fact that Cait was going down.

My brother was brilliant and strangely good at acting. He was going to make a killer lawyer and an excellent coconspirator this summer.

My sister was an evil genius hell-bent on destroying the hierarchy that we were created and raised by.

And I was considered the good girl. No one would ever see this coming. Not from me at least.

Who knew that plotting Cait's demise would be the thing that brought my siblings together in such a way?

Suddenly I felt strong and confident. I slipped my sunglasses on, realizing that I needed to not be recognized.

This was it.

Let the games begin!

Chapter Three

Teachers and Traitors

Ashley

My fingertips still ached from typing the last of my final projects for the semester, even though it had been two days since I'd handed them in at the last minute, like always. Fortunately most of my professors were also last-minute people—honest ones who felt no shame in sharing that this was also their working habit. Being raised by two professors, I knew the hidden practices that most of them got away with, and their desperate need for a spark under their asses to get them going.

My mother was worse than my father, though both procrastinated until the very last second, then burned the midnight oil to complete whatever paper they were working on. My mother swore that all genius came in the wee hours of the morning when sanity was lost and the light was too dim to be distracted by details. And if I was being honest and unbiased, her work was better than my father's. The rawness of it held poetry that my father's didn't.

I would never tell either of them that. She was smug enough, and his poor Scottish pride would never last through the insult. I'd be tried for treason and forced to submit to questioning, driven to the point of insanity while giving examples of her superiority.

No, that secret would go to the grave with me.

"You ready?" my roommate asked, holding up his controller.

"Yeah," I said, contemplating calling my parents before we started an epic journey into the world of the undead, led by a corrupt man bent on redemption. *The Last of Us* was not the normal way college-aged men spent their last few days in dorms. But we weren't ordinary guys, and end-of-year parties held no interest for either of us.

Jack, my roommate, was the picture-perfect version of a nerd and avoided all social settings at all costs. Human interaction made him sweat unnecessarily. And I couldn't be bothered to care what self-exploitive bullshit was happening on campus. Which wasn't a big deal; the other students in my program didn't really like partying. Instead of cock-size contests or beer-chugging events, we robotics engineering students had our own version of underground fun, and it was by invite only.

"I'm gonna ring my parents before we start. Get any potential interruptions out of the way." I grabbed my cell phone and stalked out to the hall for some privacy.

"Okay. I'm just going to load it and get us rea—" Jack shouted as I closed the door, cutting him off.

The phone rang after several seconds, as if stretching its reach just a little to get all the way across the pond.

"Hello?" My mom sounded tired for it being early in the evening.

"Hiya, Mum."

She lowered her voice. "Darling, how are you?"

"Is everything all right?" My body tensed, waiting for bad news. A new thing for me. I'd never been a pessimist, but the last few months had been hard.

"Och, yeah. Everything's fine." Her tone suggested she was lying. "How was end of semester?"

"Fine."

"And how's wee Jack?" I knew she grinned when she spoke of him, always calling him *wee* like he was a little Scottish girl.

"He's good. He's heading back to Connecticut tomorrow, and I'm going to Providence the day after." It would be weird, my parents not being there.

"Did you find something for the summer?"

"Not yet, but as soon as I get home I will. I'll check the Post-it note board here tomorrow to see if anything came up. There're always summer school kids looking for someone to do their work under the guise of tutoring or whatever." I half smirked saying that to her.

"Ashley Michael Jardine!" she gasped.

"Who's that?" My da's voice popped up in the background. "Ya on the phone again?" he teased.

"No one!" she hissed, no doubt feigning anger for effect.

"Then who ya yammering on at?" He sounded gruff, as always.

"Oh, it's that son of yours. Being a brat." She conceded and handed him the phone.

"Son?" my dad barked into the phone. "Where ya at?"

"School, Da. How ya feeling?" I closed my eyes and tried so hard to sound normal, indifferent.

"Right as rain, lad. Your mother's still a feisty wee thing, though. We've only been here two months, and she's already trying to have the traitors come round for tea."

"Oh, come on, Da. Ya know you're in the land of Shakespeare. You have to let her win a little. And just because they're English doesn't make them traitors." I chuckled, feeling elated that he was pulling her chain again.

"I'll tell you"—he raised his voice, working at getting a rise out of her—"no bloody self-respecting Scot would ever consider themselves a Shakespearean expert." He laughed, then lowered his voice. "Now have ya got a filly you wanna bring round when ya come for a visit?"

"No. I have too much going on this summer." I didn't want to say that I had to find a job. I couldn't make him worry about me. He was a proud man, and being one of the walking wounded wasn't easy for him. He hadn't been unemployed in thirty-five years.

"Not too busy to come ho—here to this godforsaken place?" He'd nearly called it *home*, though it was to me. And Mom. He was the only one who fought it.

"Not too busy for that," I assured him.

"Right, well, I'll be expecting some of that smoked meat when ya come. Here's your mother." He handed the phone off without saying *love you* or *goodbye*. He was unconventional like that.

"Don't listen to him," she scoffed. "He's loving it here. Been round to the teahouse every bloody day. He's eaten more finger sandwiches in two months than I think he's eaten in his whole life." She lowered her voice again, obviously sneaking off. "If ya cannae come this summer, he'll understand. We both will."

"If he needs me, I'll be there. Especially if things don't go so well for him with the meds. Love ya, Ma. Take care of him. And don't be too hard on him. He's never been sick before."

"He's an old ox, and I'll do what I like," she snapped, but I knew she was taking better care of him than anyone could have. "Chat soon; don't let it go too long. And don't stay up all night playing video games. Go outside. Breathe fresh air."

"Love ya," I repeated, needing to get off.

"Love ya, Ashley. Behave yourself. Bye, dear." She hung up and I sighed. It was going to be a weird summer, no mom or dad around, no robot wars, and no fun. I needed to earn as much as I could. Dad might not have wanted to admit it, but he needed me here, to work and help out. They'd gotten me through the first three years of school; I could help them get through the hardest year of their lives.

Putting my game face back on, I turned and entered the room, smiling when I caught the glare coming off Jack. "My mum says hi."

"Did she call me wee again?" He rolled his eyes behind his thick glasses.

"She did," I teased, and sat down, taking the controller for my turn.

"Well, tell her I said hi back next time you talk to her."

"I will." I started the game. "Let's do this."

We left our troubles behind, or tried to at least, and entered the world of the undead, ready to kick some serious butt.

Chapter Four

The Wall

Cherry

The Post-it wall was exactly what I expected, and yet I was still stunned when I saw the sea of yellow, pink, and blue notes.

It was almost creepy, like a real-life version of a Facebook page.

Random thoughts: *When I eat cooked peppers, I get heartburn. WTF?*

Strange questions with no answers: *Who keeps turning out the lights in the girls' bathroom by the coffee house lounge?*

Different questions with answers linked to them, like the chain Andy had talked about:

Where is Professor Moon?

He ran away and joined a circus.

He's Mrs. Moon now.

He got demoted to Harvard.

And then there were the random messages that I didn't understand. Equations and coded messages.

My hands were sweating as I lifted my fingers to grab a Post-it note from the stack on the table. I chose yellow; it just seemed right—official. Like pink was too cute for this moment and blue wasn't business enough.

As I stared at the blank paper, my mouth went dry.

I'd never done a mean thing in my life. I'd tormented my brother and sister, but this was a whole different level of cruelty. This was manipulating someone's emotions. This was Cait's territory.

Doubts and second-guessing flooded my brain, forcing me to let go of the Post-it note and back away.

"I knew you'd pussy out. Honestly, I'm not even ashamed of you anymore." Andy stormed across the hall and snatched a pink Post-it note. He wrote and spoke the words at the same time. "Seeking young man to participate in a revenge plot. Position pays well—very well. Must be willing to live on location and forgo scruples while pretending to love a pretentious woman. Must hate rich elitism. Email vengeanceisours@gmail.com for more information."

"Andy!"

He ignored me and glanced at the wall, tilting his head. "This won't work." He started rearranging the Post-it notes, tearing some down and moving others around until there was a blank space in the middle. He placed our note smack-dab in the center of the frame and stepped back, folding his arms. "That's better."

"You sure about this?" My insides were tense, desperately screaming at me that this was a bad idea.

"Stop being a little bitch, Cherry. Try to remember that deep down, you're related to Ella and me, and this is exactly what Cait deserves." He beamed at the Post-it note that was almost blinding me with its brightness. "It's a revolution. You need to break free from her and the hold she has over you."

"I'm no one's little bitch," I offered weakly.

"That's my girl." He patted me on the arm, then pulled, dragging me away before I could change my mind.

The ride home to New York was painful.

Andy rode up front with Hans, telling him about his last semester, like our driver gave a shit about second-year law school and Andy's chances of passing the bar and his internship.

I sat in the back of the limo, deleting pictures from Instagram and Facebook and every other site I'd used to brag about being in love.

Love.

What a joke.

Sitting back, I sighed, staring out the window.

I hated it, but Andy was right. I was a pushover. Not just with Andy or Ella, but with friends and our mother. I was Cait's doormat. She wouldn't even have given a second thought to sleeping with my boyfriend, because she didn't think anything of me. Nice, sweet, moronic Cheryl Kennedy.

Years of Cait's mental abuse needed to end. I wasn't just doing this for myself. I was doing it for every young woman who'd let Cait slither under her skin and control every aspect of her life.

My phone rang, interrupting my imaginary crusade. I glanced at the number, unsure of it, and answered. "Hello?"

"Jesus, Cherry. What the hell?"

"Griffin?" Wincing, I closed my eyes and lowered my voice. "Whose number is this?"

"I get a text, a fucking text, after six months? I know you're a college girl, but this is beyond childish. You can't even call me and tell me it's over? Or God forbid, come to my house and—"

"I did!" I snapped, almost spilling the beans. "This isn't a good time, Griffin. I can't talk about this right now." I didn't want Andy to hear me.

"No, Cherry, we need to talk. You . . . you need to explain this to me. One minute you're planning our entire summer and possibly future together, and the next you're breaking things off with a cold fucking text and you won't answer me? What changed?" He sounded angry, like he had the right to be. "Is it because you want to do Fling Club?"

"I told you, I can't talk right now." I turned my face to the back of the limo, speaking into the corner and praying Andy didn't hear me. "I have to go."

"You owe me an explanation! You need to get your ass over to my house—"

"I owe you?" And that was the end of my hold. It was the end of nice, sweet, moronic Cheryl Kennedy. She died in the limo on the ride home. Some parts of her died, at least. "I owe you?" I gasped, spilling it all out, all at once. "Have you lost your mind? I have done nothing but be the perfect girlfriend." Words formed in my mouth and brain, but I tried to stop myself, choking mostly. "I came to your house—I bought you those sheets—I bought them, you fucking asshole! You were lying on your bed."

"What?"

"I saw you—!" I hissed too loudly, earning a look from Andy and cutting my sentence short. I wanted to ask why it had to be one of my friends. No, she wasn't my friend. She wasn't my friend, and he wasn't my boyfriend. "I can't believe I told you I loved you."

"Cherry—"

"No! From now on, you'll leave me the hell alone. I never want to see you ever again. Goodbye, Griffin!" I hung up the phone and shuddered as all the awful feelings I was preventing from slithering out of me fought against the confines of my closed mouth.

"What was that?" Andy glanced back at me.

"Nothing. I'm fine," I lied, swallowing it all back down before the burning in my throat became angry tears and confessions and desperation. "It was a wrong number." It was easily the worst lie I'd ever told. There was no way he and Hans had missed any of the conversation.

"Okay." Andy gave me a look, one that suggested that we would talk about it later.

I turned away from the worry in my brother's eyes. Him caring about me broke me more than anything. Between Andy and Ella, I was going to have to channel my grief into anger before we got home. I finished deleting pictures, chanting inwardly that I was over it. I was practically over it.

I would be over it very soon.

One day.

I would be over it one day.

But not today.

Today, I could be angry and bitter, and focus on how I was going to go from being Cait's little bitch to making her mine.

Chapter Five

NOT OVER IT

Cherry

"Seven guys, and all of them can meet up for an interview this week." Andy held up his phone as he strolled into the front sitting room of our town house. "We'll pick one and be at the beach in a week." He was too excited about this plan. He and Ella were texting every half hour with a new twist to add. I, on the other hand, was scared, and I didn't even know all the details yet.

"Yeah, sure. Fine," I agreed, hoping we could stop talking about it. My excitement had waned.

"Did Griffin call again?" Andy scrutinized me.

"No," I lied. He'd been calling all day from different numbers, trying to explain his way out of it. It was like listening to a politician try to get out of trouble. It started with "It wasn't me" and worked its way to "It might have been me, but I was very drunk," then ended at "Whatever you think I did, it didn't mean anything, and I still love you."

I love you, but I accidentally had sex with another woman . . . because that's not a big deal. Since I hadn't told him whom I'd seen him with or what I'd seen, his guilt was obviously chipping away at him, because he'd confessed to a lot of things other than sleeping with Cait. In fact, he didn't confess about her at all.

"You're not meeting him, are you? If he even thinks about coming by, I will kick his ass in the foyer." Andy snarled and headed into the kitchen, shouting back at me, "And Hans says he's in as well. Hans hasn't kicked anyone's ass in ages. He's due."

"Fine," I muttered, but he was already gone, off to make Mary, our chef, angry by messing up her kitchen to prepare his own nachos. She didn't get that he was trying to do her a favor by cooking his own food, the same way he didn't see that she worked because she needed the job.

My phone vibrated, making me dread looking at it. Seeing my mom's number wasn't that much better than seeing Griffin's.

"Hey, Mom." I tried to sound sunny.

"Hello, dear, it's Mommy." She started our conversations the same every time, still not getting the whole call-display thing or the fact that I'd already said her name. "I tried calling Andrew, but he isn't answering, again." She sighed, like whatever she was calling about was on par with a real-world emergency. "Marcia and Robert Weinberg's head of household took ill and they haven't had time to replace her, but they're leaving for Europe for a month. You know how strange they are about staff living on the grounds."

"Okay." I was lost on why the hell she needed to tell me this. It was her thing, overexplaining to the point that you forgot why she called in the first place and ended up just agreeing to whatever it was she was about to ask.

"They'd like Andrew to stay there for the month to care for the house while he's home. Can you make sure your brother calls me back? I'd hate to ruin their trip with needless worrying about who's at their house."

"Sure."

"Are you all right?" Her tone changed ever so slightly, signifying that she suddenly cared. Any normal person would have missed it, the subtle shift in inflection. "You sound distant."

"Yes, I'm just trying to get everything organized from the year." I didn't even know what that meant, but it was the first thing that popped into my mind.

"Okay, dear." She didn't care what it meant. "See you when you get home. And don't forget to tell Andrew I need him to call me ASAP, please." She said *ASAP* in a fierce way and hung up. She never said goodbye, like we lived in a TV show or a movie.

Who didn't say goodbye?

Texting my brother to relay the message from Mommy dearest, as if I were his secretary, I sauntered into the formal living room and plunked onto the sofa as commotion came out of nowhere.

"Cherry?" My name was shouted in a hubbub of girls' voices and quick footsteps on the stairs. "Oh, there you are!" Sarah came rushing in with Cora, Erica, and Laura hot on her tail. My girlfriends from home unexpectedly burst into the room, spewing emotion and gossip.

"Oh my God, I am so sorry. We just heard about Griffin!" Erica dropped to her knees in front of me. "We came as soon as we heard you were back in New York."

"Are you okay?" Laura asked as she sat next to me on the sofa.

"We grabbed gelato, in case you weren't—okay, that is." Sarah held up gelato from the Italian bakery down the road.

"Sorry, Cherry," Cora offered softly.

"Thanks, girls." I nodded, trying to keep my cool. These were also friends of Cait's, the same way I was, so I had to be careful. Keep my cards close, as my grandma always said. "I'm okay. I swear."

"What happened?" Erica asked the question I dreaded. "Why would you ever dump Griffin?"

"Tell us the truth," Laura blurted.

"What have you heard?" I asked carefully. I hadn't even told anyone we broke up.

"I heard he was banging someone else, and you walked in. My sister has a thing with Carl, and he said your brother called him, flipping shit and asking him to help beat the piss out of Griffin." Sarah opened the gelato and handed me a spoon. "Which of course Carl would love to do. He hates Griffin. I don't know why."

"Oh." I took a deep breath and grabbed the spoon to scoop a large bite of spumoni gelato, our favorite. I'd have to remember to thank Andy for his "chivalry" later. "Then I guess you know the story."

"Carl hinted it might have been Cait," Laura offered as she took a big scoop. She was bold, but even she didn't look me in the eyes when she went fishing. We all feared Cait, even when she was eighty-five miles away at the beach.

"I don't know who it was. I didn't see her face, just her on top of my naked boyfriend. Blonde hair. Tanned skin. Thin girl. French manicure. That's all I can confirm."

"No wonder Carl assumed it was Cait. That describes her to a—"

"Clearly it was her, you dummy!" Laura blasted Cora.

"Oh." Cora flushed.

"What a bitch. I can't believe—" Erica paused. "No. I can believe. Sorry this happened, Cherry."

"At least now ya know he's not worth it," Cora offered quietly.

"Yeah, at least you didn't fall head over heels and start planning the engagement." Laura nudged me.

"Right. But I don't know if it was Cait. Honestly, it could have been anyone. Cait and Griffin don't even really know each other that well. His family has never been one that she thought worthy." I spoke carefully, not wanting to ruin Andy and Ella's plan. I shoved a big bite of gelato into my face, ignoring my blushing cheeks. Something Sarah didn't miss.

She offered a slight smile—a knowing one. "No matter who the girl was, he was your boyfriend. He should have treated you better."

"You're right." I agreed with Sarah and defended Cait, forcing the words from my lips. "Whoever the girl was is inconsequential. A stand-up guy wouldn't do that. And even if it was Cait, she shouldn't have been invited to sleep with my boyfriend."

"Cheers to that!" Sarah clinked her spoon with mine. "It doesn't matter who she was. It matters that he's a dipshit."

Sighs filled the room as relief hit. I wasn't going to start drama.

I was letting them all off easy.

No one would have to pick a side or pretend to hate Cait for me, while outwardly acting like her friend so they could have lives this summer.

Had it really come down to it, I imagined Erica, Laura, and Cora would be my friends in the end. None of them were fond of Cait, even though they couldn't admit that.

But Sarah would struggle with it.

Well, all of us would struggle with it.

All of our summers relied on Fling Club.

So, instead of having the hard conversation, we ate gelato and laughed, pretending all was well with the world. We planned our summer flings, teased each other about possible candidates, and skated around the giant elephant in the room.

But in spite of the lightheartedness, my heart was kind of broken, and Cait was at least partially responsible. I pretended it wasn't her for the sake of peace, even if she was a whore-face who lied and cheated and stole and everyone knew it. Everyone knew it long before this incident. And she always got away with it.

She was getting away with it right now, and I was helping her.

For the moment, but not for long.

Cait was going to get hers. And the visit with the girls was exactly what I needed to stoke the fire in me and bring out the rage.

After they left and I closed the door to the town house, Andy gave me a curious scowl from the hallway. "So, no one plans on skipping slut club this season?"

"Nope." I almost beamed. "I played it perfectly. Even you would have been proud of me. I acted like it wasn't Cait who betrayed me. I sold them all on the 'hos before bros' mantra like Ella said to: that it didn't even matter who the girl was, that Griffin was really the one at fault. It will be business as usual in the Hamptons this summer."

"You did it? You actually convinced them you weren't pissed at Cait?"

"I think so. If anyone is skeptical it's Sarah, but I can manage her. She drinks too much to be an issue."

"Then let's move on to the interview portion of this plan." His eyes glistened with devious excitement. He was enjoying this way too much. But then again, I was starting to have some fun myself.

Chapter Six

RICH PEOPLE

Ashley

"Where ya headed?" Simone, the girl in the dorm next door, asked, leaning on the doorframe and sounding like a Canadian. Everyone I'd met from Vermont did a little.

"Off to an interview." My lips lifted at the thought of the job description.

"Back home?" She twirled her hair.

"No, in New York."

"Holy shit, what kind of job?" She sounded surprised and impressed. I couldn't imagine her look if I told her the truth. She was naive, hadn't had a lot of exposure to the world.

"Not really sure. Something to do with working for the wealthy in the Hamptons. I happened upon a job on the Post-it wall, and it promised to pay well. I shot them an inquiry, and they asked me to come for an interview."

"Man, good luck. All the way to New York, then back to Providence? You didn't want to find something closer to Boston?" She said it like she was hopeful. "You could stay with me while you look. I have a sofa bed in the place I'm subletting for the summer."

"No, this one pays incredibly well. I need to give it a try." I shrugged. "You know how the wealthy are."

"Not so much," she said flatly.

"They're crazy and outlandish about how much they offer for services. They don't understand actual costs." I smiled as I grabbed my bag. I had only the one large suitcase; everything else had gone home to Providence a couple of weeks back when I'd been there to check on the house.

"Hope it does pay well for all that traveling." She rushed me, hugging tightly and pressing her body into mine. "See ya in the fall," she whispered, too close to my face. This wasn't the first time she'd come on to me, but I hoped it was the last.

"Right, you will." I pushed her back carefully, forcing her to a comfortable distance from me. "Have a great summer, Simone."

"You, too, Ash." She sighed as I shrugged my backpack on and rolled my suitcase to the front door.

Outside the weather was cold, weirdly so. I climbed into my Uber and sat back, worried about the money I was spending to go to New York, but intrigued by the job. The ad had been strange: bitter, off putting, and written on pink paper. As if a blunt or borderline rude girl had written it, or a guy pretending to be a girl. I wasn't sure which.

The email address had been even stranger. But the pay was beyond what I could make helping undergrads skate through their classes: twenty thousand dollars to spend the summer in the Hamptons pretending to be someone I wasn't—a rich someone I wasn't. They hadn't even given me all the details yet, which meant they were hiding something. And that had me intrigued.

It didn't sound hard. It sounded weird; there wasn't another word for it. Maybe *bizarre*. Essentially some rich people wanted to buy me for a lack of morals and a willingness to play along.

At the point I was at in my life, I had decided some things were worth more than morals and self-respect. If this job was going to pay that much money, and offer me room and board and spending money and possibly the opportunity to go home to see my dad, before . . . then I couldn't turn it down.

Seeing my dad was worth more than morals.

Helping my mom out with finances was worth selling my soul to do.

Spending the last summer before school in the company of other people might even be good for me.

Even if these were the type of people who made it easier to remain in the company of avatars.

All I could do was hope the gig wasn't illegal.

There were some things I couldn't take back and that weren't for sale. I had lines—maybe not morals, but integrity. I couldn't sell that.

No matter what.

Chapter Seven

Interviews

Cherry

"So where do you normally summer?" I asked one of the questions Andy had written down.

"Summer?" The prospect, a nerdy guy named Marcus, sounded confused. "I work for my parents' shop all summer and stay in my old bedroom. Sometimes I go to the movies or the odd Comic-Con if I can get there."

Sweet Jesus save me from this moment.

"Comic-Con." I nodded but knew I sounded bewildered. I was lost.

"Have you ever had a girlfriend?" Andy muttered, distracted by the girl ordering at the counter.

"In junior year, there was a girl on the mathletes squad with me. We held hands a couple of times." His cheeks flushed. "Why is this important?"

"Oh, it's just that the job entails seducing someone who could spear you and eat you alive—"

Andy cut me off. "Mostly being able to put the moves on her."

"Cool. I can do that." Marcus nodded, a little too confidently for the level of skill he was rocking. Cait would never even contemplate him. And if she did, she would chew him up and spit him out in no time.

I kicked Andy subtly under the table and sipped my cold brew.

"Well, we'll be in touch. We have your email." Andy stood, offering the guy a hand.

"Oh, uh, okay." Marcus got up and shook Andy's hand, clearly squeezing and trying too hard. "Nice meeting you both." He sauntered off, pausing like he wasn't sure which exit to take.

"Dear God," I whispered.

"The second guy wasn't so bad."

"Are you kidding? He was awful," I scoffed. "He told that same story about band camp three times. Like dating Cait will be anything like playing the flute."

"Okay, that was bad. But he could have been made attractive. He wasn't a complete loss in the looks department." Andy was reaching, and we both knew it. I didn't even have to respond. "No, you're right," he lamented. "He wasn't the one. If the next guy doesn't work out, we might have to resort to some actor from a Broadway production."

"Off-Broadway, you mean," I grumbled. Two days of this had been a wash.

"Off-off-Broadway." Andy sighed, cracking his neck and stretching.

"Right," I groaned. Even the cold brew wasn't keeping me invested in the whole thing. I was dreading the next interview.

"Can you do me a solid and get me a brownie, please?" He handed me a five and glanced at his phone. "I'm just gonna check my emails again and see if this next guy is even showing up."

"I guess. But you're sharing it with me."

"No." He handed me another five. "Get your own. Sharing with you means I don't get any."

"Fine." I snatched the money and went to the lineup. Waiting for the lady in front to finish her order, I got lost gazing at the various baked goods. The brownie was delicious, but so were the raspberry buns. I leaned into the glass case and inhaled, trying to get even a hint of them.

"If you're trying to decide, get a raspberry bun. They're amazing. Worth every calorie," a guy said quietly from behind me. "We have one of these franchises in Boston, and I absolutely love them."

"Yeah, I've had them before. They're my favorite." I glanced back, pausing when I took in his face. He was cute in sort of a scruffy way.

"The amount of cream cheese icing on them should be illegal," he said with a moan, not perversely, but like someone truly enchanted by the buns.

"I'm sure cardiologists everywhere would agree with you." I smiled at him, noting that I still felt a little whisper of guilt looking like that at another guy.

"Oh, aye." He smiled, chuckling. The way he said *aye* sounded foreign, but I couldn't place his accent.

"Can I help you?" the girl behind the counter requested impatiently.

"What?" I turned.

"What do you want?" she asked, irritated by my very existence, or her own.

"Two raspberry buns, please," I ordered, panicking, then stepped to the side so the guy behind me could order.

"Oh, look at you." The guy chuckled. "Getting two buns. Throwing all caution to the wind. Everyone respects a girl who gambles with her arteries. Enjoy them. While you can anyway." He grinned. "Before the cardiologists win," he said, before smiling wide at the barista. "I'll have the same. Two big buns are better than one." He winked at me, taking my breath, and any comeback I could have made, away.

"Certainly." The girl behind the counter grinned back at him, not even a hint of the rudeness I received evident.

"Enjoy," I managed to mutter like an idiot. I took my plates and sauntered back to my table.

"What the hell?" Andy glared at the bun as I handed him his. "Brownie, Cherry. I said brownie."

"They were out," I lied, and nestled back into my seat, excited for the bun and the possibility Andy wouldn't eat his and I could have it too. He hated cream cheese, and I had a serious sweet tooth that never got enough action and was at max capacity for stress and discomfort. My favorite time to eat.

"Whatever. I think our guy's here, anyway. NASA shirt." He waved at someone behind my back. "You must be Ashley." Andy stood and offered a hand.

Ashley? He had said *guy*, hadn't he?

I spun, stunned that the cute raspberry-bun guy was our next interviewee. He didn't look the part, based on recent experiences. For one, he was taller, and two, he had just more of everything. While he had the thick black-framed glasses, unkempt hair, and a nerdy T-shirt like the others—this one said "NASA"—there was something about the way he held himself that was altogether different. Underneath his T, he was filled out, like he exercised. And he stood taller, sure of himself. He didn't slouch or try to shrink inside his own body. He didn't mind being seen or even stared at, if the girl behind the counter was any indication. And he flirted outwardly, confidently.

"And we meet again." Ashley grinned, and my stomach tightened. He had perfect teeth framed by plump lips, but some serious coffee stains to go with his coffeehouse scruff.

"Yeah." I sounded moronic.

"And you must be Andy?" Ashley spoke again with what seemed to be a subtle accent.

"Yes. This is my sister, Cheryl. Have a seat. I see we have the same pastry." He glared at me and sat again as Ashley did. Only I remained standing, confused and momentarily stunned.

This was our geek?

He just wasn't right.

And yet he was perfect.

He could glow up.

There was potential in the canvas, for the first time out of all the interviews.

But also for the first time, I didn't want this one to take the job. He was too cute.

I could tell right off the bat that he was funny and charming, and it would be wasted on Cait. She didn't deserve any of it, even if Ashley would just be putting on an act.

"Cherry, sit!" Andy barked.

I obeyed, oddly, still stuck on Ashley's smile and the way his dark eyes narrowed like he was amused from behind the glasses.

"Cherry?" Ashley smirked. "That suits you better than Cheryl."

"Uh, thanks." I lifted my cold brew and sipped.

"So, tell me about this job." His eyes dazzled, like Andy's. Like he was already game for some shenanigans. And he was the sort of guy who said *shenanigans*.

I observed them as Andy went totally off script with this one. He didn't ask questions like he had of the others. Instead he rehashed the disgusting particulars of my ex-friend, Cait, and her betrayal with my ex-boyfriend, giving all the dirty details. It was hard not to be embarrassed that Ashley was hearing it. That he knew my sad little secret. As if this were a flaw in me and not in Griffin and Cait.

I mentally slapped myself and repeated that old Cherry was dead. I was here now and taking names. Getting even . . .

Ranting internally, I tore off a piece of the bun, devouring it as if eating were the same as going to war. I chewed and told myself that Cait was obsessed with me. That with any guy I even glanced at, she slithered between us and weaseled her way onto his lap. I reminded myself that Griffin had been lying and wooing and charming me from the beginning. Saying and doing all the right things, but breaking all those promises behind my back.

"Easy, tiger. Try chewing." Andy spoke to me, drawing my attention to the fact they'd finished speaking and were now both staring at me.

"What?" I blinked as Ashley lifted a napkin and reached for me.

"You have a bit of icing there." He wiped and smeared, proving I had more than a bit on my face.

"I think you might be wearing more than you ate, Cherry." Andy rolled his eyes.

"Shut up, Andy." I snatched the napkin and wiped my own face.

"Yeah, Andy." Ashley defended me, but mockingly. "She's got a broken heart. Girls with broken hearts are allowed a bit of icing on their faces." His smile made attempts at soothing things I wasn't ready to have healed.

"I don't," I blurted, lying. "I don't have a broken heart. I'm fine."

I wished it back in my mouth the moment it left. It was the sort of lie everyone could sense but no one called out. Their eyes simultaneously filled with pity.

"I'm going to hit the bathroom." Andy got up and walked away, leaving us in the awkward silence he normally took up.

"Anyway, you're interested in the job?" I tried to fill the gap.

"In what?" He leaned forward, offering me that grin. The one he'd given the rude girl at the counter. The one that made me feel like he wasn't the sort of geek I was expecting. He was smooth. Just like my brother. Smart and witty and fast.

"In the job," I muttered back, oozing a quality of my own that was neither charm nor icing. I knew my brother long enough to know not to trust his womanizing ways. He might come across as a big nerd, but he always got the girl. I had to show disinterest, even polite disinterest.

"Yeah." He didn't sound certain.

"Even with all the dirty details?" I couldn't believe he'd be interested. I couldn't believe anyone would be.

"If I'm being honest, it's a bit of a reach for me. A little offside to trick some girl as a revenge plot. I can't imagine a world where that stupid Fling Club exists. It sounds ridiculous, even if you can't tell us the rules. And what self-respecting guy would want to be in on this? What a pathetic way to spend a summer. Some lapdog for a rich girl." Ashley chuckled, sounding like my brother while my cheeks lit up, again. "But it's your money and your mission, and I am in need of a job, so it seems like a win-win?" He perked up, sounding more sure again.

"What do you normally do for the summer?" I didn't want to talk about Fling Club. I knew I would have to, but seeing it from another person's point of view wasn't very flattering to us members.

"My family spends summers together back home. I usually get a job at a local coffee shop. Something casual and easy, and then I do a lot of odd jobs in electronics. This summer will certainly be different." He sat back, chuckling and folding his toned arms while staring like he was analyzing me.

Fortunately Andy came back, rescuing me. "And where were we?"

"I was just telling Cherry here that I think this Fling Club is distasteful." He gave me a look like he was challenging me to defend it.

"Oh, you have no idea. I've always been outside of it, looking in. I don't really know how it works; these girls are tight lipped about the rules. But from what I've gathered over the years, it's as bad as it gets. They try to use that whole 'hate the game not the player' mentality."

"Yeah, that's what I was picturing."

"Only maybe they wear cotillion dresses while throwing gang signs and playing tough girls." Andy burst out laughing, slapping Ashley on the arm like he might have known what cotillion was.

"Exactly!"

I almost excused myself and left as they shared a series of bromantic moments that included lumping all us rich girls together as the witches of the East Coast. Man-eaters of the worst sort.

Granted I was part of the club, but I'd never played a guy or eaten a man.

I couldn't vouch for Cait or maybe a few of the others, but my close friends hadn't either. It was honestly just for fun. Even if I was now questioning my version of fun.

As they laughed too hard at their own jokes and got along like brothers, I had to ask, "Do you guys know each other?" It came out a bit harsh.

"No," Andy scoffed. "But I'm pretty sure we'll get along just fine sharing a space this summer."

"Like minds." Ashley nodded, no longer laughing.

"Hey, I have an idea," I interjected with mock enthusiasm. "Why don't you guys just date each other and live happily ever after? Interview time is over, or should I say, playtime is over? We'll be in touch, Ashley. Thanks for coming."

"Oh, come on, Cherry. He's got the job. Firstly, he'll never be a sap for Cait's charms, and secondly, he's got the intelligence we're looking for. Shevaun's going to have a blast with him." Andy laughed again. "I'm just sorry I have to miss it."

"Miss what?" Ashley asked.

"Your makeover. We have to have you looking international. Someone Cait won't be able to resist."

"You aren't staying for that?" I asked, nervous about being alone with Ashley.

"No. As much as I would love to stick around, Mother dearest has volunteered me to housesit for the Weinbergs. I'm all in this week, and then you'll have to do next week, Cherry. I'll have to go back to New York with Dad. You'll stay at the Weinbergs' the whole month, Ashley. I'll say you're a friend from Oxford who's over for the summer to hang and help out. You'll be able to come and go as you please." Andy beamed. "After that, we'll move into the guesthouse at our parents' and continue the fun."

Our plan to ruin Cait was fast becoming Andy's own personal plan for the best summer of his young life.

"Sounds sharp. So, who is Shevaun?" Ashley wasn't beaming when he asked. He sounded nervous. "And what kind of makeover?"

Andy's dark eyebrows formed into peaks like an evil queen's as his eyes narrowed in delight. "Just wait. You're gonna love it." He winked at me.

I suspected Ashley wasn't going to love it. In fact, I knew he was going to hate it. His NASA shirt told me everything I needed to know about his sense of fashion. That and his near unibrow.

This was going to be amusing, for sure—only not for him.

Chapter Eight

THE TOWN HOUSE

Ashley

"You sure you don't mind me staying straight away?" I asked Andy as we strolled back to the town house alone. Cherry had left ahead of us. When Andy had suggested I start the job immediately, Cherry had seemed unnerved.

I couldn't believe she was part of the job. The redhead had caught my eye the moment I walked in, and as I'd watched her drool over the dessert counter, I started salivating as well, only not over the pastries. It was disappointing she was one of them, the rich elite. Not my type, that was for sure.

"It's better this way. Cherry can bring you up to speed on the devilish intricacies of our world, especially dealing with Cait and all her wondrous qualities."

"Cait." I inhaled sharply, noticing the nerves filling me up with every step we took. "So, what level of wondrous are we talking?"

"The most wondrous." Andy lost all his humor. "My sister is one of her minions; they all do whatever Cait wants. If she says something's cool, it is. And they all try to emulate her. None of them think for themselves. She barks, and they come running like little sheeple."

"And how does she keep them under her thumb like that?" I scoffed that some spoiled princess could hold so much power. I was secretly looking forward to disabusing her of that notion.

"I don't know. One summer she was just Cait, my girlfriend, and the next she was running the entire shoreline. Girls who attend Paulson from out of state stay all summer long to be part of the festivities. It's bizarre," he said with a hint of something, regret maybe.

"You dated this girl?" Disgust and an instant loss of respect hit me. I didn't even hide it in my tone.

"I did, for a while. We were much younger then; it was years ago. She was different and I was shallow." He shrugged. "My dad jokes that I ruined her, but honestly, she sort of ruined me." He laughed, but I could hear the bitterness in it all as he continued, "Cheated on me."

I was starting to see his true motives for wanting to get revenge against Cait. Andy wasn't just this great older brother rescuing his sister; he wanted payback for himself too.

I didn't know how to feel about any of this. Andy was obviously a cool guy, the kind of guy I would hang out with, and I was trying not to let his privilege taint my opinion of him.

"After a while I began to see that she did me a favor. I had been one of the in guys up to that point. After she dicked me over, I saw everyone—and this whole world we belonged to—in a different light. It changed me. For the better." He said it like we weren't plotting revenge and scheming like mean girls, and then he said the most important thing he could. "And honestly, if it weren't for Cherry, I wouldn't be doing this. I wanted revenge against Cait, of course. But I'm a man now, not a schoolboy bent on destruction. I just need to get my sister's self-respect and confidence back. I need to show her what the world looks like outside of the snow globe, just like I found out."

"She wouldn't be able to do that on her own?" I asked as we rounded the corner of Fifth Avenue, a place where addresses mattered almost as much as breeding.

"No," he said breathily. "She's spent her life being brainwashed by our mother and the society we belong to. She doesn't stand a chance. She goes to Wellesley for God's sake. She's a doormat, and if I don't save her now, she'll end up the wife of some asshat like Griffin. The fact that she hasn't already taken him back is a miracle. If I have to stoop to Cait's level to bring her down and rescue my sister, then so be it. I'd do far worse for her." He almost sounded like he owed her.

Some, not all, of the respect I'd had for Andy when we met seeped back in. He wasn't entirely disgusting. And this plan wasn't completely self-serving. And because of that, I wasn't exactly selling all my morals to make enough money to pay for a trip to see my dad and help with bills.

We rounded the corner at East Sixty-Ninth and walked past a couple of the old mansions before he stopped at one of them. "And we're here." Andy held out a hand, suggesting the brick four story was his house.

"Is this a joke?" I glanced back down the road toward Fifth Avenue, seeing the park, and started to laugh. "Oh, you're this rich." I didn't quite understand what level of wealth we were discussing. Seeing Cherry, the vacant but drop-dead-gorgeous debutante, was one thing; seeing the mansion half a block from Fifth Avenue was another thing altogether. They'd seemed so normal at the bakery. I thought maybe they lived in a nice apartment in the city worth ten million or something. Not this. This house had to be worth almost a hundred million dollars.

"Well, I'm not this rich." Andy laughed. "But my dad and my grandpa, yes. They're this rich." He slapped me on the back. "Time to assume your character and start using your accent."

"Right, I actually have an accent. I use the American one to stop the questions about my accent." I started using my normal accent.

"Oh, brilliant. Then I guess the only acting will be pretending you're part of this world. That's what you're getting paid to do, after all. Don't make too much eye contact with the staff; don't do any of the things I do. Let them serve you. It's easier than trying to explain how you disagree with having employees run your life or the need to have a house this size."

"That should be easy," I joked. "How long has your family owned this house?"

"Over a hundred years." He opened the front door, and I tried not to be the mouth-agape, eyes-wide-open, "fresh off the turnip truck" bumpkin I apparently was. But it was difficult.

The foyer glistened with white-and-black-checkered marble floors and carved columns in the doorways. The dark walnut staircase leading up to the second floor was as wide as my bathroom back home, possibly my dorm room, and so glossy I could see the light reflecting off it.

The walls were white and high, ten-foot ceilings at least, with several doorways leading off the massive square room. There was not much furniture besides two sizeable beige Queen Anne chairs and a shiny round black marble table standing on a stunning royal-blue rug. There was artwork, though, I would guess originals, all pictures of abstract flowers done in grays and beiges with a slight bit of blue on each of them. It was as if they were commissioned for the room.

We were greeted by a man with a suit and a friendly smile. "Good afternoon, Master Andrew." He nodded, almost bowing.

"Richard, how are you?" He offered the man his hand. "This is my good friend, Ashley Jardine. He'll be staying with us for the week and then coming home with us to the Hamptons. He's here from Oxford."

"Very good, sir," Richard said, uncomfortably taking his hand back and tucking it behind his back so as not to shake my hand.

"Nice to meet you." I smiled, noting his accent was from Kent. I knew the area well. I contemplated saying something but figured the rich wouldn't make idle chitchat with the help.

I tried to cover up my what-the-fuck face as we made our way to the second floor.

Glistening walnut floors and a massive main-floor living room with several conversation pits and two fireplaces. The dining room looked like something from a castle back home. The kitchen was white and easily the size of the main floor of my house. Everything was clean and shiny and new in a way that suggested it was made over every morning.

"Holy shit," I whispered accidentally.

"Take it all in. Get used to it," Andy muttered back.

"I don't think I can." I gave him a look. "This is insane."

"Yeah, wait until you see the beach house." He sounded dismal.

All my self-doubt and worry about taking this job came rushing at me. The room narrowed and widened, and I closed my eyes for a second, taking a deep breath.

I was out of my league, way out.

"Oh, you're here." Cherry strolled into the living room, her red hair and porcelain face both striking compared to the room. She added vibrancy, and yet there was a cloud over her. If we'd just been two people in a coffee shop, buying glazed buns, I might have sat with her and asked her out and tried my best to win her over with charm and intelligence. I would have been nervous about what she was thinking under those stormy eyes and her pained expressions. I would have imagined she had all sorts of deep ideas and felt more than mere mortals. Her eyes suggested battles and wars waged inside her.

But my worst fears were confirmed the moment we met.

She was the job. She was a rich snob. One of *them*. A vapid socialite who looked pretty and did what she was told.

Still, something in me wanted to see what she really cared about under that exterior. I had to rein myself in, remind myself that the temptingly beautiful redhead wasn't ever going to be my type. She was a spoiled rich girl who played with men's hearts. And those stormy eyes were a lie.

Not that it mattered. I was the staff. She represented everything I disliked in a girl and a human. She was hiring me to trick someone else, take them down a couple of pegs, as if she and her brother were the authority on what was right or wrong.

No, she was never going to be the kind of person I could hit on. Not if I wanted to look myself in the eye. Or worse, look my mother in the eye.

Chapter Nine

Proper Gentlemen

Cherry

Sitting at the men's salon, waiting for Ashley to finish getting his make-over, I busied myself by answering texts that contemplated the list of hotties Cait had compiled in the chat we had going on Facebook. I tried being the old, phony me, acting excited about whom I would distract myself with over the summer, but it wasn't happening. Instead I ended up on Griffin's Instagram page, scrolling through his photos. He still had all the ones of us up. Pictures of me smiling like a fool. The fool I was and just didn't know it at the time. His newer photos were weird, dark and random.

There was one of an alleyway, like where he might have peed after a late night at the bar. It looked like he was in Boston, meaning he was still there, as the picture was posted yesterday. The newest picture was of choppy seas and a gray sky. It would have been a cool picture if an asshole hadn't taken it.

Curiosity got the best of me. I wondered if he and Cait were still seeing each other. I went to his contact in my Messenger and checked his location, flinching when I saw that he was in New York. In fact, the little red pin appeared to be a couple of blocks from me. The phone recalculated and showed it getting closer and closer.

"No." My stomach clenched as I wondered if he was looking at my location and coming this way, or if it was by chance? He went to this salon when he was in town. But why would he be in town now? He said he wasn't coming home until a full week after me, and I had only been in New York for four days. Today was my first day alone with Ashley; it was already tough enough. Adding Griffin would really be the icing on the cake.

Getting increasingly uncomfortable, I turned my location services off and sat awkwardly in the leather chair, no doubt looking like I wanted to run away. Sweat formed on my brow, and uneasiness crept around inside me.

What did I do?

What if he was coming here?

I couldn't face him.

And how could I explain being at a men's salon?

Who I was waiting for?

I couldn't tell him who Ashley was or why we were here together or how we knew each other.

I decided to leave and meet Ashley back at the house, but as I was about to get up, Griffin appeared in the mirror across from me, walking through the front door. My entire body clenched with dread. I gripped the seat and pretended not to see him and act casual, even if sweat was glistening on my brow for no reason. The air blasting in with him was frigid. We'd had the worst spring on record for temperature.

"Griffin, darling, how are you?" Norma, the front desk girl, squealed as she rushed over. She hugged him and gushed, "Do we have you on the books today? How did I miss this?"

I leaned forward slightly to get a better view of their interaction in the mirror.

"No. Just here to see Cherry." He forced a smile, but his dark eyes darted in my direction as his body straightened, as if the hug she was giving him was completely foreign to him.

"Oh, of course. Silly me. We see you next week, don't we?" She giggled and sauntered back to the counter. Watching how she fawned all over him made me wonder how much of her he'd already seen. No wonder he was so awkward in front of me. They'd likely been having sex too. Maybe that was why Andy liked this salon so much; it was full service.

"Can we talk?" Griffin asked me as he stepped around the foyer, suddenly becoming a real person instead of a mirror image.

"Not a chance."

"Is—" His eyes darted around the salon. "Is Andy here?" He sounded nervous, almost. Griffin didn't do nervous. His voice didn't tremble, and he didn't get emotional. But he was close.

"Go away. I said no." I shook my head.

"Look, Cherry?" he pleaded. "You need to hear me out."

"I don't, actually." I wished I had a magazine or a friend or a task I could pretend to be busy with. All I had was my phone—the very phone I'd been pretending I wasn't holding all day as he called and texted nonstop.

"Cherry, please." He lowered his voice, begging. He was close to making a scene, something he wouldn't care about, but I didn't want Norma the blonde bumpkin to know any of our business. Salons were gossipy, and this one was the most popular for men traveling in our circle.

"If I give you one minute, will you leave me alone?" I conceded.

"No." He offered a sad stare. "I need more than that. I need you. I miss you."

"You now have forty seconds." My voice cracked. It was going to betray me along with my eyes. I almost never cried when I was sad and almost always cried when I was pissed off.

"Cherry, come on." He opened the door and held it for me, letting in more of the cold spring air.

"And . . . you're down to thirty seconds," I huffed, then got up and stomped past him, barely containing my fury. My fingers dug into my palms, and my jaw trembled with all the things I wanted to say. Things I would likely not say. I usually bit my tongue.

"I'm not going to beg for forgiveness; I know you're never going to forgive me." He started smart at least. He was right about that. I was never going to forgive him. Ever. "But if you could just give me a second chance. A fresh start. A new relationship as new people. I would be different. Don't forgive old me, but give new me a chance. Please." He stepped close to me, flooding my nose and memories with the scent of him. I loved the smell of him. It was home and soft kisses and—no!

He smelled like Cait now. She'd tainted him.

"No." I stepped back, but his legs were longer, so he was able to take a second step and press my back into the wall behind me as his torso pushed into my chest.

"Cherry." He looked down at me, his dark eyes swimming with emotion, something I had a hard time resisting. "I love you. I made a mistake. There are no excuses. I will never be sorrier than I am right now. Please, give me a second chance. Let me be your fling this summer so I can prove to you I've changed. This breakup has changed me. I never realized just how much you meant to me until you left."

"No repeats, Griff. You can't be my fling."

"Fuck the rules."

"You mean fuck the rules so you can fuck other girls?" I mocked him with bitterness dripping from me. I was mentally chanting all the things I needed to remember as he stared down into my eyes.

"Cherry, please don't do this." He lowered more, like he might kiss me. I inhaled, catching a strong whiff of him. He was intoxicating and yet disgusting. "I can be different," he repeated, whispering as he bent to kiss me. "Don't do this."

"Do what exactly?" I shoved him back. "Get some self-respect and stop letting you treat me badly?" I stepped to the side, breaking from his attempt to hypnotize me. "Stand up for myself and defend my own honor? Something you should have done instead of betraying me." It was happening. I was saying all the things I wanted to. It felt foreign, but I kept going. "What else should I do, just roll over? Just let you sleep with other girls? Just look the other way? Is that the girlfriend you want? A doormat who pretends it's just sex and doesn't bother about the details? You want to date someone like our moms? You want me to have my own affairs and live with the fact our life is faked for the world and we live as roommates?"

"No! That's not what I want!"

"Just stop!"

"No, I want you." He lunged forward as a voice broke our private moment.

"Cherry?"

I glanced past Griffin to where a god stood before me. It was the moment Clark Kent became Superman in those ridiculous movies Andy always made me watch.

I exhaled everything, losing all my fury and rage.

I forgot my name and Griffin's reason for being near me.

I took a step toward Ashley, letting him suck me in like he was the light at the end of the tunnel.

"Who are you?" Griffin moved in front of me, cutting my fantasy short by knocking the wind from my sails and blocking my view.

"I might ask you the same thing," Ashley responded, sounding like he was annoyed.

"I'm her boyfriend," Griff remarked, folding his arms and stepping in front of me even more. "You're him, aren—"

"Ex. You're my ex-boyfriend, Griffin," I managed to say as I pushed past him, choosing the light in front of me.

The light was dressed like a proper boy now. He wore a Tom Ford Japanese felt officer jacket and straight-fit black corduroy jeans, with a tight white T-shirt and Blundstone boots.

But it wasn't just the clothes; it was the fit body and toned arms and perfect haircut and the separation of his eyebrows.

No more straggly, greasy hair or coffee-stained teeth. No. They were bright white and almost blinding.

His face was clean shaven, so much so that I wanted to rub my hands over his cheeks and smell his aftershave.

Without the glasses, his dark eyes were stormy and menacing. I could almost see the clouds moving in them as he focused on Griffin.

"So, you're the dipshit?" Ashley chuckled.

"Cherry?" Griffin warned me with his tone.

"This is Ashley," I offered, almost laughing with nerves.

"And what are you doing with him?" Griffin's eyes narrowed. "Is this the guy she told me—?"

"I'm not really one to kiss and tell, friend. But I will say I think you should leave the lady alone." Ashley winked at Griffin but squared his shoulders, looking taller and wider. More like a door Griffin wasn't getting past.

"This is why you ended it so suddenly? Cait was right. Instead of telling me you were seeing someone else, you made this all my fault." Griffin's eyes were on fire, and his words were lava. "You slut! I fucking knew it. I knew there was another reason you broke up with me!"

"Whoa!" Ashley barked, cutting him off and stepping forward.

I pulled him back, shouting my defense. "I didn't even meet Ashley until after we were through! Unlike you, I like to close one door before I open the other!"

"And that's that. Door's closed." Ashley nodded. "We're done here. It was not nice meeting you." He wrapped an arm around my shoulders and spun me, heading to the sidewalk. His accent was fully English now. He was doing his Oxford act perfectly. He never wavered and went back to being an American, not since he arrived at the town house.

"Are you kidding me right now?" Griffin shouted, and grabbed my arm, sending me stumbling to his side. I staggered in my boots and barely caught myself. He spit his words at me. "I deserve a fucking explanation!"

"Wrong." Ashley pulled his arm back and swung, connecting with Griffin's cheek, making a horrid sound. Griffin stumbled back, and part of me wanted to run to him, but I didn't. I stayed with the light. I let the light wrap an arm around my shoulder again, pulling me into him. "You stay away from her. I won't tell you again." He turned us and walked up the sidewalk, squeezing me. "You okay?" he asked softly.

"Yeah." I wasn't. I was shaking and confused on a lot of issues. The warm nest Ashley's arm made was one of the issues. As we rounded a corner, I pulled away, hugging myself. "I can't believe him."

"He's a prat. What did you ever see in him?"

"I don't know." That was also a lie, but I didn't want to say the truth. I didn't want to say that he checked all the items on my list. It didn't even sound okay to my own ears anymore.

After what just happened, I was starting to think I needed a new list.

We rounded another corner, and Ashley cringed. "Sorry for that," he offered, not sounding very sorry at all. "Not very gentlemanly to fight in front of ladies."

"I'm not sorry," I muttered, holding myself. I knew I sounded weak. It wasn't just that; I was also incredibly embarrassed. I wasn't one to cause public outbursts and men to fight. Guys didn't grab my arm and drag me around. This was all new and upsetting.

We walked, and my stomach ached with the feelings I had. Seeing Griffin punched didn't bring me satisfaction; honestly, it was devastating to see someone hurt him. But it was as if Ashley, being a near stranger yet more gentlemanly than Griffin had ever been, shined an obvious glare on Griffin, exposing his flaws.

What had I been thinking dating someone like Griffin?

He was horrid.

My attraction to him had faded along with my resolve to never forgive him. Everything I once felt for him, the good and the bad, waned, getting lost in the dissolving feelings.

With every step I took toward home, I left another piece of my sadness on the street, like a breadcrumb trail that stopped short in the middle of the city because I ran out of sorrow.

By the time we'd arrived home, I'd run out completely.

Chapter Ten

DON CORLE-ELLA

Cherry

"I still can't believe this is just your city place." Ashley turned in a circle when we got back to the house. "This is insane. I also can't believe people live like this," he joked. At least I assumed he joked. "Do you have more money than the Rockefellers?"

"My parents do well—my father does, at least." I didn't want to say *old money* or *blue bloods* or anything else. I didn't want to bring up the country club or the rest of it, but I knew I would have to eventually. At some point in the next couple of days we were going to have to talk about the club and how life among the rich worked. "I want to thank you again, for defending me."

"The guy's a wanker." He said *wanker*.

"Are you English, by the way? I realize I don't know much about you when you already know so much about me."

"No, Scottish. Jesus. Easy on that one. Most Scots don't take lightly to being mistaken for Brits," he joked, and his eyes did that dazzling thing again, but now with his eyebrows separated and his teeth glistening white and his glasses gone, the whole expression was different.

Where it made my stomach tight before, now it took my breath away. He was beautiful.

"But your accent; it's English. And before when we met it was American?" I tried to understand.

"It's a long story, which is why I use the American accent when I meet people. I'm tired of the story." He sighed, staring at the house.

I stared at him.

He could have been a model.

He was handsome before this moment, but now . . . groan . . . he was perfect. I almost sighed out loud but reminded myself that regardless of his fighting for my honor, he was essentially the same person as Andy. Same breed of nerdy womanizer and haughty asshole. He'd already mocked me with my jerk of a brother, lumping me in with all the other "rich girls." The problem was that Ashley was a much hotter version of Andy. And not related to me. So being annoyed didn't change the fact I was slightly smitten with his looks. Slightly more than slightly.

Seeing how attractive he was, I wanted to laugh manically, knowing Cait was going to fall for this one hook, line, and sinker. But I also dreaded him being around her. What if he fell for her too? What if all I accomplished was finding Cait another guy to ruin?

No, I couldn't think of that now.

"So, we should get to know one another." I tried to smile, hating the chill in the air. With Andy gone, I wasn't entirely sure how to steer the conversation.

"Yeah, that sounds like a plan." He sounded indifferent, not excited about getting to know one another at all.

"What are you studying?" I knew he was an engineering student.

"Robotics." A one-word answer.

"Cool. Where do you think you'll work after school?"

"NASA." And another one-word answer.

"And are your parents in America as well, or the UK?"

"UK."

He wasn't going to make this easy.

"Oh, they're not in the States anymore?" I felt like a reporter.

"My parents moved to America to work at Brown. They're literature professors." He spoke like an American again. He wasn't kidding, he could turn it off and on. "They're home in England for the summer."

"But you're Scottish?" I was lost.

"I am." He chuckled but didn't warm up.

"Why don't you go to Brown? Wouldn't it have been free for you to go there?" I had a friend who was doing that at Wellesley.

"Why would you assume money's an issue?"

"You took this job."

"Right, well, free or not, robotics engineering isn't exactly their strong suit at Brown." He nodded. "And I did get a scholarship for a lot of my tuition at MIT. Not all, but most. Next year is my last year, and my parents are feeling the financial strain. Hence this new makeover." He winked and held his arms out, but there was something in his tone that suggested that was not the whole story. "I feel like one of those movies where the girls are made to be hot to fit in with the popular crowd."

"Yeah." I smiled and nodded, grateful he spoke a string of sentences, even if they were somewhat mocking. "Your American accent is almost perfect."

"I was twelve when we moved here. It's been over a decade. I've had lots of time to work on it." He sauntered into the dining room, running a long finger up the table. "So, is this going to be like *Pretty Woman* where you teach me how to eat and act?"

"No." I laughed nervously at his mocking me. "More like explain who everyone is so you aren't confused or surprised by anything. You need to be able to infiltrate Fling Club and convince Cait to date you. I think it's a bit more like *Cruel Intentions*, and you're Reese Witherspoon's character." I muttered to myself, "I just don't know if I'm Ryan Phillippe or Sarah Michelle Gellar."

"What?"

"The movie. *Cruel Intentions.*"

"Never saw it." The comparison was clearly lost on him. "So, you have always belonged to this Fling Club?" His eyes narrowed, disappointedly. Like Andy's.

"I have." I reminded myself I wasn't going to let him or Andy make me feel ashamed of it anymore. It was a bit of fun in an otherwise boring summer of the same old, same old. No one got hurt. Physically, at least. No matter how I felt about it this week, I wasn't going to let them make me out to be less for it.

"Interesting," he said, like it wasn't so much interesting, though, as enlightening. Like he suddenly knew everything he needed to know about me.

"You mean *offensive*, don't you? Offensive that women would dare play the same game as guys? Or even worse, control the game?" I couldn't help myself. I'd been defending Fling Club and my own involvement in it for years. My brother was merciless when it came to tormenting me and the other "it" girls.

"No, more like why does there have to be a game at all?" His eyes sparkled the way my brother's always did when he was mocking me.

"You know the saying: hate the game, not the players. You guys invented casual and serial dating. We just perfected it," I mocked back, throwing the words he and Andy had used against me back at him. "Wearing cotillion dresses and all."

"I didn't invent anything," he scoffed.

"Well, guys like you did." I gave him that, so as not to be too impolite.

"Not guys like me, Cherry." The glisten in his eyes changed, becoming serious and making me uncomfortable again. "You've been dating the wrong kind of guys," he scoffed, and sauntered past me. "I'm going to go make a call. I'm sure we can take up lessons at dinner."

"Okay."

"Okay." He walked up the grand staircase slowly. "Dinner's at seven?"

"Yes," I muttered as I watched him walk away.

He was exactly like Andy. Smug. Smart. Quick witted. Judgmental. This was going to be a brutal summer. Two Andys.

Dialing Ella, I walked in the opposite direction and sat on the sofa in the parlor.

"Has the eagle landed?" She answered with a question.

"Yeah. He's here."

"Good."

"But we've already had an issue."

"Oh, come on, Cherry. It was simple. Get him cleaned up and pretty so that Cait takes the bait. How could you screw this up already?"

"I didn't!" I snapped, losing my cool quickly. "We ran into Griffin at the salon."

"Oh, shit! How? He had the nerve to come and find you?"

"Yeah. He tracked me. I forgot I'd shared my location with him, and he decided to treat me like a sitting duck—" I didn't even really know how to say it. "Ashley took him. Like, 'took him.'" It sounded as crazy as it was.

"À la Hugh Grant and Colin Firth in *Bridget Jones*?" Her tone lightened. We'd loved those movies growing up. Ella and I were always watching movies, talking about how we would change them or recast them or make them better.

"No. More like a single punch delivered to the face with a side serving of 'never go near Cherry again.'"

"I like him already." She outright laughed. "Did Griff fight back?"

"He didn't stand much of a chance. I don't think he saw the punch coming." I covered my eyes, not joining her in joking about it.

"Man! I wish I could have seen that. Guess I can cancel the hit I put out on him." She was still laughing, even as she said *hit* like we were in *The Godfather* and not *Bridget Jones* at all.

"Hit?" I prayed she was kidding but feared the worst. It was unwise to underestimate the power of Ella's wrath.

"Yeah. I have a couple of friends who owe me for some computer work. Big guys."

"Jesus, Ella!" I gasped. "You can't put hits out on people for cheating. That's insane!"

"Maybe. But I bet I could make him think twice about doing it again."

"Seriously, back down. Watching Cait fall off her throne will be retribution enough."

"I'm passionate. What can I say?" She was still joking, but I could tell she meant it.

"Passion doesn't need to hurt other people. That's not who we are," I reprimanded.

"Well, how are things otherwise?" she said, changing the subject.

"Not awesome. He's disinterested and judgmental. It's like being around Andy. He mocks me."

"Not falling for sweet Cherry Blossom's charm." She laid it on thick.

"I'm not trying to charm him. I still have a broken heart, ass!"

"Is he hot?" She was grinning, I could hear it.

"He's—nice," I lied.

"Nice? Cait won't fall for nice."

"We both know he doesn't have to be hot for Cait to like him. I just have to bat my lashes at him and she's interested."

"True enough. Well, I have to go. No use making idle chitchat when there are lives to ruin. Don't bore him to death. And don't forget to warn him about everyone. You suck at not wanting to point out people's worst traits. Don't blow this! I'll see you in a couple of days." And she hung up before I could defend myself.

Like our mother, Ella didn't feel the need to say goodbye. She never did anything she was supposed to. I envied her that. She might have been a hot-tempered mess, but she was free. No one controlled Ella. No one abused Ella. No one would ever cheat on Ella. Andy always joked that God mixed up Ella's and my hair color, stating that I should have been the demure blonde and her the fiery redhead.

I sat and stared at the fire flickering across the room, directing my thoughts to the summer. In some ways, I dreaded how things would play out. If Ashley would find Cait irresistible and give in, rendering my efforts and sights on revenge useless, or if he was strong enough to resist her temptation and accomplish the mission. Honestly, the more this mission shaped up, the less inclined I was to be part of it. Maybe I should call the entire thing off, forget my expectations for what summer was supposed to bring, and make myself scarce in the city.

I could take some courses or go to Europe and sit on a beach in the French Riviera. Anything but endless time spent lounging on the east shore while contemplating the infinite ways this could all blow up in my face. The worst-case scenario, of course, being my sister sitting on the wrong side of an interrogation table, explaining why she ordered my scumbag of an ex-boyfriend to be made into Hannibal Lecter's next skin suit.

My phone vibrated with a message. I glanced down to see a text from Ella: He called you a slut and put his hands on you? The hit is so on!

I sighed.

Clearly she'd spoken to Andy, who must have talked to Ashley.

Crazy Ella.

Bitter Andy.

Reactive and sexy Ashley.

Yup, this was going to be one long, brutal summer.

Fortunately Ashley didn't come down for dinner after all. I ate alone, and he had his meal brought up to him. It gave me time to reflect, specifically on the fact that I suddenly felt like the Beast at the other end of a long banquet table, waiting for Beauty to grace him with her presence.

Chapter Eleven

Morning People

Cherry

The next morning, I leaned across the counter, eating cereal and texting Erica about the first date of Fling Club. Our start of summer was a week away. The plan was scaring me, and my chicken-out personality was starting to win the battle of what I should do.

"Mr. Jardine, would you like some coffee?" Mary, our chef, asked softly over my head.

I spun, not expecting Ashley to be up yet. I was suddenly made aware that his last name translated to *garden* in French. That seemed somehow too delicate, but entirely appropriate for him.

Ashley looked different in the morning, even sexier. His dark scruff had started to come in, like a five o'clock shadow, only fifteen hours too late. And he wore a Batman T-shirt and plaid pajama bottoms. Nothing stereotypically sexy about it, and yet I had never been more attracted to a single human in my life.

"Morning." I smiled, trying to be polite and not overtly stare.

"Hmmm." He moaned and flumped onto a barstool.

"Not a morning person." I grinned and lifted my bowl of cereal, turning from the kitchen. "I'll give you your space to wake up." Desperate to put some distance between us and my obvious attraction to him, I sauntered into the solarium to sit in the sun and stare at the back garden. His rude behavior wasn't enough to rob him of his looks.

I lounged in the huge papasan near the fire and folded my bare legs in. My shorts weren't warm enough by far, but the heat from the fire felt cozy.

Chewing away on my cereal, noting the milk was winning the battle of time, I glanced out the window and got lost. There were designs on the bricks on the far side of the courtyard, shapes in the trees, and thoughts filling my head.

"Mind if I join you?" Ashley interrupted me.

"No." I tried to sit more ladylike in my short shorts.

"Didn't see Captain Crunch as a breakfast choice for you." He grinned and nestled into the oversize armchair, sipping black coffee.

"I only let myself eat crap here, when I'm home. At the beach I eat keto, and at school I eat fairly paleo. So, at home, where I rarely am, I eat whatever the hell I want."

"You have one life." His eyes met mine, and I fought the urge to sigh. I didn't know what it was about him, but something was ringing my bell. A bell I did not even want to exist, let alone have ringing. He continued, "Why waste life eating a certain way? Why not live? You never know what's around the corner. Enjoy it."

"What?" I snapped out of my ogling session. "Uhhhhh, cancer. Obesity. Society's version of what a woman should look like." Was he serious? Did he know what it was like being a young woman?

"That last thing you mentioned is all you care about. Don't church it up," he mocked.

"What?" I wanted to tell him to mind his own damn business, but it was still a bit early in this so-called friendship to unleash my inner asshole. The character trait I saved for my siblings. Not to mention I needed him. On a strictly professional basis, of course.

"Let's be honest here. Obesity doesn't seem to run in your family. Your brother doesn't have any weight to lose, and neither do you. In fact, you could stand to gain a couple of pounds. And cancer: pretty unlikely. You're twenty-one, not forty." He scolded me like I was five. "So be honest, the only reason you starve yourself is to look skinny because society tells you that's how to attract a man. You don't have to sugarcoat it for me." He laughed, possibly at me. "All you girls are the same. Hung up on what someone else tells you you're supposed to be. If I were a girl, I'd eat nothing but pizza and ice cream and stare at my gorgeous body in the mirror while telling everyone else to stick it."

I may have imagined it, but I thought I saw his eyes take inventory of me when he said the words *gorgeous body*. But it didn't save him from the wrath of Cherry.

"You know what?" My blood boiled.

"What?" He sounded unaffected by his own rudeness, making me even more irate.

"You're just like my brother." I meant it as an insult, but the jab made him beam.

"Thanks." He puffed his chest a little.

"It's not a compliment, you idiot. I don't know why I'm trying to be nice to you. Clearly, you're not nearly as nice as you pretend, Mr. Holier Than Thou. Let's not get too personal here with opinions and feelings. We don't have to be friends and share all our thoughts. Let's just get you ready for the summer. You're an employee, after all." I regretted it the moment I said it, even if he had skinny-shamed me. I hated my inner asshole for even peeking at the daylight from the dark cave where I usually hid it.

"By all means, let's keep this strictly business. I'd hate for you to have to get personal with the help." He got up. "Sorry I bothered you, madam. I'll go back to eating with the other people you keep on hand to service your needs." He bowed slightly and left.

Shit!

My cheeks flushed as I stared outside, wondering how I had come out the bad guy in this scenario. He stereotyped all women, while calling us girls, and body shamed me, but I was the one to blame?

He really was just like Andy. Good with words and even better at manipulating me.

Well, if he wanted to act like my brother, I would treat him like my brother.

I got up to storm after him, but as I rounded the corner he was there, coming down the hall at me like a freight train. I stopped short, bracing for the impact, but he didn't make contact.

He halted abruptly and hovered over me, taking up all the space in the hall—sucking out all the air—and blocking out the light from the window behind him.

"You're an asshole!" I said with more emotion than I intended, staring up at him like an ant shouting at a dog.

"I know." His voice was filled with regret. "I shouldn't have been such a dick. I'm not a morning person. And regardless of the time of day, I tend to say everything I think once I get comfortable with someone, and my humor isn't always everyone else's cup of tea."

"What?" I lifted an eyebrow, confused.

"I'm sorry. I was trying to be funny. I wasn't."

"No." I wasn't prepared for this. "I'm sorry." All the fire left my fight. "I shouldn't have called you an employee. That was rude." I lowered my gaze. "That's not how I see you. Even though we do have a job to do, together."

"Friends, then?" His hand shot into my line of sight, almost stabbing my stomach with his fingertips. He held it there for me to take.

He was so strange. Foreign. He was sorry and owned the mistake the second he made it. What was this sorcery? He was like an upgraded version of a guy like Andy.

"Sure." I lifted my stare to his, trying not to look shocked that he was apologizing even before I really had a chance to be angry. Or maybe, even better, he was nothing like my brother after all. This moment was pivotal in proving that.

"You forgive me?" He offered a hint of a smile.

"I think I can find it in myself." I maintained eye contact, not because I wanted to but because I couldn't look away, as I slipped my hand into his. I felt enveloped with warmth as he shook our hands slightly, moving mine for me. "If you forgive me."

He held my hand hostage, not squeezing, but certainly not letting go. "Can we have another crack at breakfast and coffee with slightly better behavior?"

"I would like that." I turned, still holding his hand, and led him back to the sunroom. As I approached the papasan, I realized I had to let go of him. I slipped my fingers from his, noticing a subtle tensing of his fingers as I got away, almost like he didn't want to let go.

Unless that was my imagination.

"So, why don't you tell me more about your family. Since we both know far too much about mine," I offered lightheartedly. "Yours are professors at Brown."

"Yes." He contemplated his coffee for a moment. "But maybe we should talk more about my fictional family. I don't want to get confused." He was avoiding the subject of family. Noted.

"Sure." I grabbed my phone and scrolled through Ella's texts. "Ella's come up with this whole alter ego for you. But you're a nerd. Used to living in an alternate reality and all that." I said it jokingly, unable to control myself from going tit for tat for his earlier remarks. "You're from the University of Oxford. You're English. Try not to let that offend your flaming Scottish sensibilities. You're at least given free rein to pick the location you're from. Somewhere you know and are comfortable with."

"Well, I lived in Stratford-upon-Avon before we came to America. It's about two hours to London, in the countryside where the estates are. Warwickshire." He sat in the chair he was in before, chuckling to himself.

"And that's an upscale area?" I was completely lost, starting with the Stratford thing he said, like I should have known about it.

"Yes, nice area. Good place to grow up."

"Oh." I was still lost, still stuck on the fact he'd apologized so easily, before I'd had to guilt him into it. And he didn't ignore my feelings or twist words to change my feelings. It wasn't just Andy; every guy I knew did that.

"Right. You've been, then?"

"Where?" So lost.

"The UK."

"Yeah, when I was seventeen we went for a month and toured around."

"I see. And did you like it?"

"I did. It's quaint and pretty."

"And did you stay in some castles?" He got that sparkle in his eyes, the one I suspected of mocking me.

"I did. We stayed at Thornbury Castle, near Bristol. It was creepy. I mean, it was cool but also creepy." I blushed, looking down in shame. "This sounds stupid, but I swear I could feel someone watching me when I was in my room alone. I didn't sleep at all." I laughed at myself for admitting it.

"Those old castles are totally haunted; I believe it. I've stayed in a fair few, and every time I feel bothered." He laughed with me, not at me. It was a nice change.

"Do you like it here?" I asked, imagining he must miss home. I would miss home.

"It's home now. I love exploring in the US. It's so huge and vastly different. The history is short but violent and fascinating. The culture is lacking, and yet I can't help but enjoy how real things are over here. Apart from people like you." He couldn't help jabbing me.

"Right. We're more closed off." I had to admit it, even though he meant it as a joke.

"And you have weird things like Fling Club."

"That we do."

"Tell me more about it." His humor slipped away.

"It's not as bad as it sounds. Our lives are run around functions and galas and fundraisers and dinners. So basically, we have the same guy escort us to different events all summer, to make it so no one is the odd man out. Back in the day, girls fought over guys, and of course jealousy and cattiness ensued because guys were playing the girls. So, we took back the control. We decide who our fling is; we decide what kind of fling it is. I generally hook up with someone I know will be fun and have no expectations. A few times I've had flings who didn't live nearby, so I only had to spend time with them at functions."

"Sounds so scripted. Where's the romance?"

Romance? I thought. Where was the romance? We didn't have romance in our lives. *Scripted* couldn't have been a better word. I used to imagine love as a fairy tale, like "Cinderella." She goes to a ball and meets a prince, and they fall in love. But then I grew up and realized that the prince would never have been allowed to marry Cinderella. She was a commoner, and her family brought nothing to the table. Had she been a banker's daughter or a real estate investor's niece, perhaps. But being the kitchen girl of some random family meant the prince could love her all he wanted, but she couldn't infiltrate his world.

"Our lives can be fairly scripted," I said, popping back from my little daydream. "But we still sneak some romance in. Just not in front of anyone. There's what you do for show and what you do behind the scenes. Romance isn't for show." I defended us and our weird traditions; I just didn't know why anymore.

"That, I can agree with you on. Romance is supposed to be between the two people. No one else needs to know." The way he said it made my stomach tense. "But I disagree with the Fling Club; I think a guy should ask a girl out. I think some of the older, more outdated ways of being were nicer. Having a girl pick me out of a lineup and then give me instructions for the entire summer seems a little mechanical for me."

"Well, it's lucky that you don't agree with our way of living. It will make it easier for you to avoid falling for Cait and all her charms. Fair warning, you're going to have to be made of steel to avoid that happening. Not a single man has been able to resist her in Hamptons history. Just keep telling yourself she's a stone-cold, vapid bitch who would screw your own brother if there were something in it for her. Believe me, I know." I shuddered at the thought of Cait and Andy together.

"No need to worry there. I couldn't ever fall for someone like Cait Landry." He wrinkled his nose and scoffed at the idea. "She's not my type at all." He sounded like I was offering him the most disgusting thing in the world. "Not only do I prefer honor and brains over breeding and looks, but I've grown up middle class. We despise nothing like we do the aristocracy. No, I enjoy the company of women who want to better themselves, not their family's social standing or net worth."

His words hit me right in the gut, where I could tell he meant for them to. He was blatantly telling me that I fell into the same category as Cait: distinctly not his type.

I wished to the gods of all that was holy that I would find him just as repulsive as he so clearly found me.

Chapter Twelve

FIRELIGHT

Ashley

On our last day in the mansion, our third one alone while trying to be both polite and not two young people who could possibly be attracted to one another, I was not managing my attraction well.

Cherry had finally let her guard down a little when she didn't think I was looking and relaxed some more even when I was looking. Now she was stretched out on the sofa, listening to music through earbuds and twitching her foot to the beat I couldn't hear. Her long pale legs were toned and fit, because apparently she ran to stay in shape. Which I didn't see coming. She appeared so controlled and robotic that I couldn't imagine her sweating at first, but every morning she returned home with a red blotchy face and huffing breath.

That wasn't the only thing I found surprising. Her discussion of dieting and our little fight had been all talk. She ate like she was a boxer trying to go up a weight class. I assumed her daily jogs in the park were to help with the amount of food she put away.

"Would you like a drink, sir?" Mary asked softly, catching me staring at Cherry for the third time. I was starting to think the chef was on my side, trying to protect me from myself. Or on Cherry's and keeping her safe from me.

"A coffee, please," I said politely as I sat at the marble counter. This was her domain, and as much as I wanted to grab my own coffee, I saw the pride she took in her job. She was about fifty years old and very much like my mother, saucy and stubborn and easily offended.

Cherry was more than I'd originally given her credit for, which was an issue. It was going to be a summer of temptation, forbidden fruit, and all that fun stuff.

"Some house," I offered to start a discussion, something I found myself doing with Mary a lot. It was easier than talking to Cherry, who was unknowingly destroying all my self-control.

"Some redhead, you mean." She smiled wide. "You forget yourself, Ashley." She called me by my first name because she knew my story. We'd all been talking enough about our plan that everyone in the household followed the plot. The one thing I found odd about the rich: they spoke in front of the help a lot.

"No, madam, I do not."

"There are things you avoid in this house, and she is number one." She slid my fresh Americano at me.

"What's number two?"

"The master bedroom. Number three is the Bentley. Number four is the study. And number five is the cellar, but that's because it's not safe down there. Dank and creepy."

"Any advice for the Hamptons?"

"Don't go." She laughed. "You're in over your head. Cait Landry is a terrible human being. She's going to chew you up and spit you out." Her eyes dragged over to Cherry again. "We got lucky with that one. Sweet as the day is long. Poor thing."

"Right, but some of it's an act, isn't it? I've seen her lose it. She's feisty. Not such a poor thing."

"Only when provoked. She wouldn't say *shit* if she had a mouthful otherwise, so to speak." She got back to chopping vegetables. "Not like the younger one. When you meet her, try not to stare at the things that come flying out of her mouth."

"Duly noted. Thanks." The younger one intrigued me. She sounded insanely awesome and yet terrifying.

"What are you drinking?" Cherry asked, coming into the kitchen. She was wearing those shorts again, the ones from the first breakfast. The ones I'd been mean to her in. The look on her face still haunted me. The way she'd stood up for herself surprised me. But when she called me the help, I'd lost it. I'd marched down the hall, pissed off at her and excited I'd been right, vindicated even. But then I realized what I'd actually said and how almost none of her response had been her fault. My jokes had been cruel and down putting, and telling her to free herself from society's expectations of her hadn't quite come out the way I'd intended.

"He's having coffee; would you like one as well?"

"No, thanks." She smiled and sat at the counter.

"Do you want a bun?" Mary's eyes sparkled.

"You didn't?" Cherry brightened right up.

"I had to. I've been craving them since you brought me one the other day." Mary turned and opened a silver tray that looked like something from a hotel room-service delivery. Under the silver dome was the greatest sight in the world.

Fresh raspberry buns with cream cheese frosting.

"No way!" I turned to Cherry.

She beamed a wide grin, her eyes dazzling with excitement.

Mary pulled out three plates and three forks and served us each one, delicately as if she were serving the queen. And then we sat, each of us digging our forks into the soft rolls. My stomach growled from the smell, making Cherry giggle as she lifted the fork to her perfect lips. I paused in eating my bite and watched as she did what she had done in the café. She closed her eyes and wrapped her mouth around the fork, moaning as the flavor hit her tongue. I tried not to imagine those lips wrapping themselves around me.

"Thank you so much, Mary." Cherry beamed. "That was exactly what I needed today."

"I'm going to miss you, my dear. You're leaving tomorrow?"

"Yeah, but we should be back in the city again. I'll have to keep up appearances and all that jazz." She rolled her eyes.

"Of course. And Mr. Jardine will go with you, I assume."

"Yes." Cherry glanced my way. "We have to pretend he doesn't exist until Andy comes back from the city."

"Your brother's coming back here?" Mary's cheer was lost.

"He is." Cherry laughed. "Just tell him to stop cooking. Tell him it's insulting."

"Hmm-hmm." Mary gave us both some side-eye and cleared the plates. "At least your father will be back. Your brother is a lot more manageable with him here."

Cherry bit her lip and leaned on the counter. "You're getting the better end of the stick, Mary. I have to be in the Hamptons with Mother and no Andy to run interference. Just Ella, whom she has essentially given up on."

"How bad is your mother?" My imagination had run off with me as far as this dreaded dragon lady was concerned.

"You'll be grateful you're staying at the Weinbergs'." Mary chuckled as she loaded the dishwasher.

"Pretty much. Well, we should go over the whole first night again." Cherry gave me a look as she got up. "Ella has strict instructions on how that will go."

"Okay." I scowled, allowing myself to admit my concerns as I followed Cherry and tried desperately not to notice the way her shorts hugged the curve of her ass. And of course she was a runner. Checking out her leg muscles and the way her ass tightened when she walked up stairs was not a terrible way to spend a minute or two. Though I didn't love that she ran in the park. I disliked her going alone, something she promised she'd been doing for years when I'd asked.

"So, the first night." She led me to the library and stood in front of the fire, a thing she did frequently. She wore shorts and stayed near the fire to keep warm. Not that I was complaining. We were still missing the sun in New York, regardless of it being spring.

She rubbed her arms. "I'll go to the meeting, where the girls will all greet one another and go over the rules for the new girls."

"And the rules are?" I asked again, something Andy had told me to do. Press her until she caved, which she never did.

"Not important for you or Andy to know, and I know he asked you to try to get them out of me." Her eyes sparkled. "I've given Ella enough clues that she can plot without knowing them exactly."

"I have no idea what you're talking about." I sat, acting indifferent.

"Anyway." She narrowed her gaze. "You will stay home. Then Andy and Dad will come back from the city, and we'll all go for dinner Friday night. It's tradition. Andy will bring you, his friend. You'll flirt with me. We'll pretend we've just met that week. Make sure your eyes follow me around a lot." She sounded a bit sad. "Cait will want you if it looks like you're interested in me."

"Flirt with you?" I got up, pacing in front of the fire. "Like, how aggressively?" We hadn't talked about flirting. I didn't know if I could flirt and not mean it. Giving what she looked like, I'd mean it. And once I did, she'd be mine. This was a dangerous game we were playing.

"Hard. It has to be obvious that you're interested." She gulped. "There should be no mistaking that." Her eyes twitched, fighting something, then darted away from mine.

"So, I should touch you? Put my hand on your back as you enter the room and get your chair?"

"More," she said softly, her voice almost getting lost in the fire's crackle. She stepped a little closer to me. "You should kiss my cheek and put your hand on the back of my chair, make sure you're sitting next to me. Follow me, anywhere I go."

"Kiss your cheek?" I stared at her rosy cheek, noting the way the firelight licked it. Her flawless skin glowed, reflecting the light of the flames. My insides were on fire now too.

"Yeah." She stared up at me, her eyes growing wide. She swallowed hard, her thin neck straining to look up at me. "Then after that initial meeting and dinner, all the young people will mosey over to Cait's the next night. We all bring our show dogs in to prance them about." She smiled subtly, taunting me. "I'll bring you, letting everyone know of my intentions to date you for the summer. Cait will see this, take the bait, and ask for you before I get the chance to do it. As the leader, she gets first dibs."

"That's so fucked," I whispered, still stuck staring at her.

"Super fucked," she whispered back, her eyes hooded.

The air wasn't cold or awkward anymore. It was full of something else—heat and possibility.

"I should go pack." She stepped back from me, breaking the spell. "And you should too."

"Okay." We spoke in a strange way, staring at each other, focusing on our eyes.

"Don't forget anything here; you might not be back to the city." Her tone changed a little, tightening.

"Oh, don't worry, I'll pack everything up, monkey suit and morals included." I accidentally said it bitterly, possibly taking out some unspent desire on her instead of with her. My comment made her flinch.

"Night." She turned, finally, nearly running out of the room.

I had no idea what had just happened, but I needed to focus on the job and not get lost in the eyes of the girl I was working for. Tomorrow, I would be better—stronger. I would flirt or smile or do whatever it was she asked me to do with whomever she needed me to do it with. I needed this job, but I didn't need the Cherry on top.

Chapter Thirteen

AND THEN IT GOT WEIRD

Cherry

The limo ride to the Weinberg mansion was quiet. I browsed social media while Ashley read some gargantuan email. Whatever it said, it didn't seem to make him happy, or chatty. After the strange, hypnotic way we were talking the night before, lost in each other's gaze, I'd assumed he'd be a little more inclined to flirt and laugh and joke. I was wrong; he was right back to being his judgy, closed-off self.

The last two days at the house had been better than the first few. We'd seemed to be connecting in a way I was getting comfortable with. You couldn't spend days on end with someone without eventually letting your guard down.

Or so I thought.

But the drive to the Hamptons was proving that theory all wrong.

It was early enough that the traffic wasn't bad, but the drive still took over two hours to get to the massive house facing the Atlantic Ocean. The Weinbergs, for whatever reason, had built their waterfront mansion on some of the prime sandy lots on Dune Road, only it wasn't built for the view and had multiple rounded roofs with weirdly small round windows.

It was like something from a science fiction movie.

The gardeners were working away in the cold wind, untying bushes and raking dead grass, and offered us a wave when we drove up.

Andy opened the door and greeted us like the valet. "Hey!" He beamed. "I wanted to stay and get you guys settled in. Mom knows you're here, Cherry, but she doesn't know about Ashley. So, we need to keep him under wraps until I get back on Friday. I'll say you met me here, fresh from the airport."

"Good to see you too," Ashley said with a laugh, speaking for the first time in hours as he climbed out and offered my brother a firm handshake and a half hug. Like they were old bros from a nerdy hood in Silicon Valley.

"How was the drive?" Andy asked as they stalked off, leaving me to climb out of the car on my own. Even the gardener gave me a look.

"They're having a broment," I lamented, and walked after them, leaving the gardener chuckling and shaking his head.

I gripped my purse tightly, fighting the urge to scowl as I thought of the task ahead. I needed to be stone faced and get through the next seven days.

I needed Ella. Thinking her name made me smile, so I pulled out my phone and texted that I had arrived.

Her response made me laugh. Coming!

"And you'll have to cook."

I deflated a bit as I came closer to Andy's voice.

"Likely Cherry will con Theresa into bringing you guys food so that you don't die over here," Andy joked as he gave Ashley the tour.

"We can survive for a few days, ass." I folded my arms and stood near the fire. It was colder out here on the water than it had been in the city. And this house wasn't warming; more like an old-fashioned Tudor with dark colors and cutoff rooms. No flow or modernizing.

"Here are the house keys. The car keys are all hanging in the garage; don't drive the Lambo, but the rest are fair game. Oh, and the staff doesn't live on the grounds. The maids might come during the day and work, but then leave."

"Oh, wow, the Weinbergs let them have lives. How fascinating," Ashley said, mocking our own overkept household.

"Right." Andy laughed. "No indentured servitude here."

"Don't you have to go?" I growled. Annoyed with all of this.

"Yes, Miss Cherry. I do." He bowed and turned to Ashley. "Don't let her fool you; she can actually cook a couple of things. I've seen it personally. She can make a mean PB&J, like, the perfect ratio between the peanut butter and the jelly." He laughed and patted Ashley on the back, then walked to me and wrapped me in a bear hug. "Behave yourself. Don't scare him off. We need him for the family dinner on Friday."

"Thanks, Captain Obvious." I sneered and held the door open for him, since there was no one else to do it.

"I'll text you." He waved and darted off, getting into our limo as Hans closed the trunk and waved at me. I waved back and closed the door, shivering from the cold.

When I turned around, Ashley wasn't there, but I heard his voice.

Realizing he was speaking to someone, I told myself to go to the kitchen, but my feet were pulled by the sound of his voice and the way his accent thickened as he spoke.

"Right, love you too. I'll call earlier tomorrow. I just wanted to say good night. Okay. Sleep tight." He hung up, and his shoulders slumped.

Mine might have also slumped a little.

Was he talking to a girlfriend?

Whoever it was, he seemed saddened by the short call. Feeling bad, I walked the opposite way, hurrying for the guest room where my bags were sitting. I hadn't even noticed Hans putting them away.

I sat on the bed and took in the view from the bedroom. Gloomy dunes.

This house made no sense.

Moments later my sister's voice flooded the silence, making me smile wide and rush from the room. "Cherry? Oh, you must be Ashley. I'm Ella. Nice to meet you, since we're coconspirators and all."

Wincing, I came around the corner to them shaking hands and Ella staring into his eyes.

"Might as well get straight down to business. You look the part, but why do you think you'll be able to resist Cait's charms? No man has been able to yet."

"Because I loathe rich girls and their drama and nonsense. And I don't support the elite using their influence and power to manipulate the world and get everything they want. The odds are stacked against us all a little more because everyone has to roll over for them." He tilted his head. "I mean you. You're upper crust."

"Good answer." She dropped his hand and stopped giving him the eye. Most people gave the eye in a seductive way. Ella's was more an attempt to discern if a person was lying. A skill she hadn't honed yet but refused to give up on.

I made a noise, drawing her attention.

"Cherry Blossom!" She ran at me, hugging me and losing some of her cold edge.

I hugged her and inhaled a little of the beeswax-and-honey smell she had. Her idea of makeup was lip balm. And she always bought the organic stuff. It made her smell earthy, which she was.

"I see you two have made introductions. Ashley, you've officially met the family shame."

"And proud of it." Ella beamed for a moment, then turned around to me. "I need the rules."

"No, we can work around it. I understand the gist of what you want to achieve, but I can't divulge the rules."

"Why?" she huffed.

"Because I would be breaking the rules if I revealed them, and then I wouldn't be any better than Cait. How can I shame her for breaking rules if I break them?" I glanced at Ashley, who was still staring at his phone. It was strange to see him so distracted. It made me think he really was seeing someone. I had to admit to feeling disappointed. He was insufferable in an Andyesque way, but I found him attractive even with that massive downside.

Not that it mattered. He was here for a job, nothing else.

"While that is very Gandhi-like, you're not going to hell for being a hypocrite or for ratting out some psychopath's rule book. This game is still afoot. Get me the rules." She folded her arms and gave me her best dictator smirk.

"No. Stop being evil. I'm tired. It's been a long week. And Ashley and I have to decide what's for dinner. Are you staying?"

"For takeout and convincing you to get me the rules? Hard pass. Theresa is making me a Buddha bowl with peanut sauce and chickpeas she sprouted herself. I just came for my end-of-term hug. We cool." She offered me a peace sign and nodded her head at Ashley. "See ya in the trenches, soldier."

He lifted his brow, but she was already out the door, not waiting for him to acknowledge her.

"She's smaller than I imagined."

"Bonaparte was short as well. Didn't stop him from trying to take over the world." I spun, trying to find my pleasant face through what felt like the beginning of a headache. "Is there anything you'd like for dinner?"

"That Buddha bowl sounded good." He pointed at the closed door.

"We can't risk going home. If my mother sees us, the jig is up." I took a step closer, hoping to get a feel for his situation and why he was acting so different today. "Are you all right?"

"What?" He frowned.

"You seem tense."

"No, I'm fine." He glanced at his phone again.

"Girlfriend troubles?" I smiled, trying to pry in the politest way possible.

"No, God. Father," he said, and then flinched like he shouldn't have said it.

"Godfather?" My heart paused.

"He's—um—" He paused again. "I'm sorry. I'm not really up for company right now. I think I might just go lie down for a bit. My head is pounding." He waved and stalked off. "Dinner at seven, as usual?"

"Yup." I scowled, wondering what he was hiding.

It was going to be a rough week if Ashley continued being distant. I needed his full concentration and effort in order to make it through Friday in one piece.

Chapter Fourteen

Chess, a Game of Strategy and Angst

Ashley

Lying on the bed, I mentally paced the room, going over what my mom had said.

The doctors were worried Da's cancer had gone into his bones, and they were going to be checking that this week. We wouldn't know right away, meaning his cancer could be worse than previously believed. Meaning I would desperately need to get home this summer. Meaning I really needed to do this job so I had the money to go home.

All of which really meant that I needed to not be attracted to the girl I was working for.

I changed topics in my rant and started giving myself a lecture on all the things about Cherry I didn't like. Or rather, shouldn't like.

She was rich—too rich. That mansion in the city had to be worth seventy or eighty million dollars. If not closer to a hundred.

She was spoiled—not on purpose, just by default.

She was privileged.

She was a snob.

She dated dipshits like that moron in the city, meaning she liked guys like that.

She was . . . too pretty.

I got up off the bed, nodding at that one, hitting my palm with my knuckles as I paced for real.

She knew she was pretty. Egotistical.

No.

That was a lie.

She might have known she was pretty, but her self-esteem was crushingly low. She wasn't egotistical. And if I was being honest, the only problem with her being too pretty was my total lack of self-control.

In the city, I'd eaten in my room most nights, staring at the door and wondering what she was doing. I'd spent the entire car ride out here pretending to read an old thesis of my dad's, doing everything in my power not to be nice to her. I couldn't even make eye contact. I would have reached forward, and everything would have come apart, including her blouse.

The way she leaned forward, her breasts shifting in that lacy bra I could see through the shirt, stretching the tiny buttons until it created a gap. My God. Her creamy skin was perfection everywhere, but those ample swells on her chest called me by name. The skin begged to be stroked. I imagined what color the blush would be on it, my hand lowering to my stomach, contemplating touching my erection.

"Fuck!" I glanced down at my cock, realizing I wasn't even trying. Hard as a rock and trying to burst from my pants. A cold shower; I needed a cold shower. I turned and hurried into my en suite, stripping and jumping into the tepid water.

It did nothing.

If anything, getting my cock wet was a colossal mistake.

Mainly because I resorted to a fantasy involving my new roommate as I turned the heat up in every way.

When I was cleaned of my impure thoughts and feeling less tense, I headed back downstairs to see if she had come up with an idea for dinner.

But she wasn't eating.

I paused in the doorway, seeing a shot glass, vodka, martini shaker, Grand Marnier, Chambord, cranberry juice, and limes spread across the counter. She was sitting at the bar and downing the last of a pink martini as I entered.

"Liquid dinner?" I asked, half laughing.

She nodded, looking a bit distraught. "Liquid courage."

"Is vodka keto?" I said, mocking her and her beach diet. It was clearly going well.

"Yes." She nodded again. "The Chambord isn't, though."

"Everything okay?"

"No." She shook her head. "Being back here makes it all more real. I'm super pissed off, and I want to drive to Cait's house and tell her what a fucking bitch she is. And that she is the worst friend in the history of bad friends. And that I hope she dies alone." She blurted it, exploding with rage. "Sorry." She covered her mouth, plugging the hole before more venom came pouring out. Clearly the drinks were loosening her tongue.

"Want another?" I asked with a laugh as I rounded the other side of the counter, as if I were a bartender. I didn't know another response to this type of girl craziness.

"Sure. Sorry. I didn't mean to word vomit that everywhere."

"It's fine. I get it. You're about to embark on a revenge plot. It's stressful." I tried to be like a real bartender, tell her what she wanted to hear.

"It is stressful. I mean, what if we get caught? What if she's on to me and I end up the big loser, again?" Her cheeks flushed as she grabbed the vodka. "Let me make it. I make a mean martini." She poured fast, getting up and adding ice before shaking. "It's just, she's always won, you know? Her dad is like the king of assholes."

"King shit of turd island, you mean?" I joked, making her laugh for real.

"Exactly."

Watching her shake the stainless steel container killed my decision not to get involved with her. She must have taken her bra off when she changed, because everything was moving freely, jiggling. She was wearing those fucking short shorts again, a T-shirt, some huge knit socks, and possibly nothing else. She looked like a sorority sister. Or that babysitter you always had a crush on. And she was free, and not just in the chest. She'd let her hair down and was a mess.

"You wanna play a board game?" She lifted a dark eyebrow.

"What kind of board game?" I was back to being scared of my reactions.

"I don't know." She shrugged. "Why don't you go and get one set up, and I'll make snacks?" She smiled, not flirtingly, just normally. Like she was desperate to take her mind off things. My entire body took it as that we were going to play strip poker, and then I was going to poke her.

Fuck.

"Sounds great." I offered my most churchy smile and sauntered into the other room, praying the blood stayed in my actual brain and didn't dive to my favorite brain.

I found the stacks of board games in a big chest by the two large leather sectionals in the sitting room with the huge fireplace.

I decided on chess, certain I would crush her and possibly make her hate me.

It was one of those fancy boards you saw in snobby coffee shops where the pieces were hand-carved marble and the board was some vintage mahogany.

As I finished setting up, she came in with a charcuterie board like out of a magazine. It had pepperoni, salami, mixed olives and pickles, crackers, several types of cheeses sliced up, a chunk of goat cheese that had pieces of cranberries in it, and fruit. She left it on the sideboard and went back to the kitchen, returning with a massive pitcher of martinis and two glasses.

She poured us both some of the pink liquid and handed me mine.

"Chess, good choice." She sat, her legs underneath her and her nipples staring at me, mocking me.

"You can play?" I asked.

"A bit. Andy likes it when I play with him instead of Ella; she crushes him every time."

"Whereas he beats you?" I tried so hard to maintain her stare, lifting the glass to my lips.

"Not all the time. Just most of the time." She nodded and sipped.

"Jesus, that's delicious. What is it?"

"A raspberry cosmo." She licked her strawberry-colored lips and set the drink down.

"Ladies first." I gulped. We were never going to make it through seven days. I was never going to make it.

I'd never slept with an employer before.

But I'd also never met a girl I wanted more than this one, probably because this was the first one I wasn't allowed to have. Not to mention the fact she was stunningly gorgeous and incredibly secretive. She didn't speak her emotions or lighten up easily. You had to work for it. She had to trust you. Seeing Cherry blossom was like watching one of those rare flowers bloom that needed perfect conditions to come to life—but the payoff was so worth it.

It was my own private hell.

Sitting by the fire, we played for two hours, just being us. Her laughing and me desperately trying to make her laugh so I could stare at her smile. Drinking and eating until there was nothing left on the board and nothing left in the pitcher and my self-control was hanging by a thread.

She beat me twice in chess. She played like one of those eleven-year-olds in the park, talking about nothing, twirling her hair, and crushing me like she was a seasoned battle general. I couldn't help it; I reached forward, just like it was natural, and had to twirl a lock of her shiny red hair myself.

When it was all the way around my finger and I was ensnared, both in my heart and with my hand, she gulped.

Her stare widened as she locked eyes with me, reading my dirty thoughts as they flickered with the flames, reflected in my gaze.

She spoke after a second. "We should go to bed."

"Yours or mine?" I laughed again but she didn't.

She furrowed her brow and nodded. "I need water." She jumped up, wrenching my hand with her. Without any grace, she bolted from the room, slammed the door to her room across the house, and ended the evening, just like that.

"Excellent work, Mr. Jardine," I congratulated my drunken self aloud. "This won't be awkward at all in the morning. Well done, you."

Chapter Fifteen

THE NEVER-ENDING ANGST

Cherry

My head throbbed.

My eyes were crusted over, and my heart was burning like I'd thrown—oh, right—I'd thrown up all night.

The garbage bin next to the bed confirmed that.

The smell made me gag, but I managed to get to the bathroom before anything else happened. I heaved over the toilet, nothing left in me to remove.

It lasted too long. A noise startled me and I jumped, realizing I'd passed out with my face on the toilet seat.

"Jesus," I grumped, and turned, crawling back to my bed.

"What in the seventh hell is this?" Ella shouted, coming into my bathroom.

"Shhhhh." I waved her off. "Stop shouting."

"I'm whispering, you moron. Why are you drunk? What the hell did you do last night? Ashley looks like he might be walking dead. You're a mess."

"I don't know." I made it back into the sheets as she continued yammering on. I ignored her and closed my eyes, hoping the bed would quit spinning and the sheets would reclaim me as one of their own.

I passed back out, waking to a dark room and no Ella. I felt miraculously better, and in the shadows, I caught a glimpse of why. The IV hooked up to my arm was refreshing me.

"Hello?" I called out, curious who had put it there.

"Hi. Sorry, miss. Your sister said she would be right back." A sweet-looking lady who clearly worked for the hydration-therapy company beamed at me. "You're almost done. Should be good as new in about five minutes." She left the room.

"Thanks," I shouted after her, and grabbed my phone, seeing the messages I'd sent Ella. "Good God," I muttered, and cringed at them.

I think I love Ashley.
He's so hot, would it be weird if we fucked.
Can I fuck him if we're paying him?

Who did I become when I drank? Dear God. Mom. That's who.

I double cringed when I saw the messages at the bottom of the conversation from Andy, scolding me to keep it in my pants and not sleep with the guy who was his new friend.

I'd sent the messages in the group chat. Lovely.

"Tell me you managed to keep all that to yourself." Ella waved her hands over my body.

"I think I got sick all night long."

"Oh, you did. There's no doubt. Ashley says he doesn't remember the night much. I'm assuming you went for the raspberry cosmos? I saw the roadkill on the counter. Who drinks a pitcher of martinis?"

"Oh, God," I groaned. "He must think I'm insane."

"No, I suspect he thinks something else. Like how can he get you back into that mood, minus the puking? He's being weird in that 'I almost banged your sister last night' sort of way."

"No, he isn't."

"Oh, he is. He's asked about you twenty times." She rolled her eyes. "That magic vag, Cherry. You need to learn to contain it."

"Shut up!"

"I'll see you later. Behave. Don't make me come back over here. I left you guys some lasagna in the oven. Take it out in, like, half an hour. It's from Theresa. She knows you're home and sends her regards."

"I love you."

"Not as much as you love Ashley," she teased, and left the room, waving.

The IV lady came in and unhooked me. "And you're free." She smiled and cleaned up, leaving me to my thoughts.

What the hell had happened?

I didn't recall everything.

We ate and drank and laughed and played chess. I won. Twice. I liked him. That was all I had. So why hadn't we had sex? Maybe he didn't want to. Maybe he didn't like me back. Maybe he was sick too. Maybe I got sick first. Jesus, did I get sick in front of him?

I was starving, and it was time to face the music. I climbed off the bed and pulled on a robe, then snuck out to the living room. I should have showered first, but I needed to check the lasagna. Tiptoeing, I made my way to the oven, smiling when I saw it still had twenty-three minutes on the timer.

Ashley was sleeping on the couch by the fireplace. His arm over his face.

I hurried back to my room and jumped in the shower, washing my hair and body and brushing my teeth as fast as I could. When I was done and dry, I hurried to my bags and picked the cutest set of short shorts, ivory with lace on the bottom, and a super-tight pale-pink

T-shirt with an adorable pink lacy bralette. It was casual, like I wasn't trying at all, and yet pretty.

I pulled my wet hair into a ponytail, something my stylist would kill me for, and did the fastest makeup job on the face of the earth, making it look like I wasn't wearing anything when, really, I had on tons. I had to. I needed to hide the evidence that I woke up looking like a dead fish.

Then I sauntered out, stretching and yawning, like this was the first time I'd left the room.

Ashley was in the kitchen, looking like he'd fought in the same battle I had. He was freshly showered, wearing gray joggers and a pale-blue T-shirt with a shield on it. His scruff was dark and thick, making me want to rub my hands over it. His dark eyes sparkled from behind those thick-framed glasses. "How ya feeling?"

"All right." I put my hand on my stomach. "Starving."

"So am I. That IV thing worked like a charm. You rich people don't even suffer through hangovers?" He narrowed his gaze. He looked like Superman.

"Maybe not. But we still have to suffer through each other's existence. Consider that." I grabbed two plates and twisted my torso toward him, catching him staring at my ass like he was paid to. "Want to grab water glasses?"

"Sure." He nodded, not even taking his eyes off my butt.

I put a slice of fresh bread and a huge piece of Theresa's famous lasagna on each of our plates. The smell was doing bad things to me. My stomach growled like a lion.

"Was that you?" he asked as he filled up the water, hearing me over the running tap.

"It was. I'm really hungry." I laughed and carried the food to the kitchen table.

He brought water and napkins, and we sat in awkward silence.

"So, what happened last night?" I asked, cutting the lasagna. I lifted my first bite and waited for it to cool.

"I honestly don't know." He cracked a grin, doing the same.

"We drank way too much." I placed the bite in my mouth, closing my eyes and moaning. "Oh my God," I muttered through the food with my hand in front of my mouth, perhaps relaxing a little too much.

"Mmmmmm." He was doing the same.

I wanted to kiss him and touch him, but watching him eat was almost as good. He loved food. He nodded and chewed, holding the fork and knife and letting his eyes roll into the back of his head. "Oh my God. This can't be keto."

"It's not." I grinned. "It's not even really homemade. She cheats. She uses jarred sauce from Rao's."

"Where?"

"A pasta house in Harlem. Best spaghetti in the world."

"Damn." He took another bite, performing the same dance. It was like the buns all over again.

He wiped his lips and took a huge bite of garlic bread after dragging it through the sauce.

Fuck the week. If things kept going in this direction, this was going to be an impossible summer.

"Can I ask you a serious question?" he asked after swallowing some water.

"Maybe?" The question made my stomach tense, but I knew I owed him answers. He was about to go into the lion's den.

"Why did you seem like you needed to drink last night? Did something happen?"

"No." A slow smile spread across my lips. "I was—am—worried about this week. I haven't given much thought to the fact that I'm going to be facing Cait until now. I'm panicking a bit, I guess. It's here, it's real. The weeks of us plotting and scheming are over, and it's time to implement." I sighed. "And there is a deep fear that she will still win. Because she always does."

"She won't win." He shook his head. "And even if she does, what's the worst thing that could happen?"

"Oh, well, firstly there's the possibility that I'll introduce her to you and you'll fall head over heels in love with her. She's gorgeous and good at snake charming—"

"I'm the snake?" He cut me off, sounding insulted but making me laugh.

"Yeah, but not in a bad way. More like a cute snake—a friendly snake." I dug that hole deeper, feeling my face flush with embarrassment.

"I'm a friendly snake?"

"Right." I giggled. "And she'll charm you, and then you'll betray us to her, and then she'll use you to make a trap for me. Humiliating me publicly, because that's her way of doing things. And my mother will hate me for being such a failure at life."

"This is a really extreme set of consequences for a summer of frivolities." He laughed too.

"But it's not just frivolities. It's businesses that won't hire me or my brother or sister. It's families who won't invite my family to functions. It's business connections my dad will lose. It's friendships my mother will have sacrificed. It's all connected."

"Kennedy? You think Americans are forgetting that last name anytime soon?" He lifted an eyebrow doubtfully.

"No, but that's how it works out here. Cait Landry doesn't just ruin you, she takes down everyone else with her. She's a savage."

"This sounds insane. You do see that there is a whole world outside of this place, right?" A grin crept across his lips.

"No." I lowered my fork, sitting back and shaking my head. "That's the problem. I don't see the world outside of this."

"Then maybe when this is all over, I can show you. For the sake of giving you some perspective, of course." He said it cruelly, but I'd learned enough of him to understand he didn't mean it like that. He wasn't cruel; he was real.

"Maybe." I tapped my fork against the edge of the plate for a moment. "Either way, Thursday is the big day. The first day of Fling Club, the first annual meeting." I tried not to feel the sense of dread and fear that had started within me from the moment we began this journey.

"And you are going to see it for the first time through your new frame of mind. No more rose-colored glasses," he teased. "I just hope you'll be able to sit through the whole meeting."

I smiled and continued eating, realizing I hadn't even doubted I would sit through the whole meeting. I never doubted my behavior at all. I just assumed I would suffer through all of this, toeing the line like always.

But he was right; this was the first time I was free of the taint and spin my mother had put on this world and its unacceptable behaviors that I'd always assumed to be normal. I was the one going into the lion's den, not Ashley. I was the one who was different and would have to act the part for the first time.

I wasn't so sure I would be able to toe the line this time.

I wasn't so sure I could hide the differences in me.

I wasn't sure I wanted to.

Chapter Sixteen

Vengeance with a Capital V

Cherry

Almost late, I rushed across the foyer of the old country club. It was Thursday at last, and we were finally about to be set free from the house that angst built. I should have been more excited, but I was about to see Cait—expressly not exciting. Even Ella's hour-long speech, getting me warmed up for my first time "back in the trenches" as she lovingly called it, couldn't calm me down.

"Rachel!" I called to the girl my mom had demanded I invite into the club. Not that I wanted to indoctrinate anyone else into this bitch platoon.

The cute brunette waved and hurried over to me. "Hi, Cherry. Good to see you again." We hugged. We were fake friends, having only met a couple of times.

"We better hurry in." I linked my arm in hers and hustled down the stairs to the room where we held the Spring Fling meeting every year. Only Fling Club members were supposed to know what was actually going on—not Spring Fling planning at all.

Every spring, we—certain alumnae from Paulson Academy—and our approved guests, who were still single and under twenty-two, met in the old lounge of the country club under the pretense of a committee meeting for the Spring Fling. Really it was the annual Fling Club initiation.

Out here Fling Club was everything.

It was by invite only—the most exclusive club on the entire East Coast. Nothing but a personal invite from Cait or one of the older girls got you in, and Paulson connections were everything.

You never spoke of it.

If you wanted a social life in the Hamptons, this was the only way.

"So, is this legit?" Rachel asked.

"It's so legit, you might not want in," I whispered. "It's like the *Mean Girls* edition of one of those secret fraternities." I snickered and found a seat, almost sad Rachel would have to endure a whole summer of this, but glad I was saving her and the rest of the members from a whole future of such a charade.

Glancing around the room, I saw all the usual suspects but sat away from my friends, not sure I could keep my rage under control and not in the mood to introduce Rachel with the effort needed.

"There are ten rules, ladies." Our leader started the meeting the moment the doors closed, silencing everyone. "Ten rules to a perfect summer, which of course includes your perfect summer fling." Cait Landry paced in front of us, her heels clicking on the old parquet flooring. Every step she took was another spike being driven into the coffin of our friendship. I wanted her dead. It was extreme, but it was where I was emotionally.

Seeing her for the first time, no matter how much I'd mentally prepared for this moment, made me savagely angry. And my fire for vengeance was entirely restoked.

"Rule one: If he doesn't belong to the country club, he doesn't belong in your pants. Not in public, anyway. Try to remember your breeding, girls. Select only the finest for your fling; the world is watching." Cait's eyes were filled with judgment as her stare landed on a few of the girls she was preaching to.

Silently I wished a thousand plagues upon the house of our fearless leader.

Erica's stare landed on me, checking me with concern.

I smiled, forcing my lips to lift and prove I was still okay. I pretended that I didn't feel rage.

I did.

I was sitting still and calm, but not because I was cool with Cait.

It wasn't that I didn't want to burst and strangle her; I did. But I was a professional at hiding my feelings.

I'd coasted silently for years, never stirring the pot or making waves. Being a yes-man was Survival 101 with Cait. I'd done everything she ever wanted.

And how did she repay me?

By sleeping with my boyfriend. Not a fling, an actual boyfriend.

An act I'd imagined I would eventually get over, especially after spearheading her demise.

Boy, was I ever wrong . . .

Sitting here, seeing her again for the first time since I last saw her naked body wrapped around my boyfriend, in my sheets, I could tell there was not going to be any getting over it. I had dreaded coming here tonight, but now I regretted ever second-guessing the plan for vengeance.

Andy and Ella were right.

This had to happen.

I needed blood to spill. Even if it was just metaphorical blood.

I was just grateful I hadn't acted on my feelings for Ashley. He was still in the running to be her date, and I didn't need to overcomplicate the scenario. I had bigger fish to fry.

"Rule two: never say the *L* word, unless it's *loser*, again not in public." Cait pointed her stare on another unfortunate soul. I'm surprised she didn't turn to stone.

Jenny Bassette.

Jenny lowered her gaze in dishonor as her cheeks flushed.

Two summers ago, the petite blonde had been caught saying *I love you* to her fling. An act that brought shame on us all. I myself had learned that doing such a thing only got you burned.

"Does everyone understand the first two rules thus far?"

Jenny nodded softly, still not meeting Cait's stern gaze.

Jenny's pitiful submission reminded me of who I'd been all my life. And it inspired within me a whole new sensation that I'd never felt for anyone before: hatred.

I didn't even hate Griffin. He had taken a beating, emotionally and physically, so in my mind we were close to squared. Yes, he'd wronged me in love. It was a terrible thing to do, but his betrayal wasn't the stuff Cait's was made of. Here she was, demanding we play by her rules, while she had been breaking them all along. She had defined my life while brainwashing me into being someone I wasn't.

And the worst part was that Griffin was only one line on a long list of dirty deeds. There were loads of things I suppressed in order to survive her.

But I was starting to remember.

And I was starting to see.

This was going to be a long summer filled with pain and suffering.

And none of it would be mine for a change.

"Rule three: No reheating a sister's old leftovers. So that means if he was mine last summer, or ever, you will avoid him. We don't share undergarments; gentlemen are in the same category. Part of the fun is finding fresh meat."

I nearly choked.

That was easy for her to say, but apparently hard for her to do, considering she *just* ate off my plate.

Every year, Cait would wait to see who the rest of us brought to the table and have her pick. And since she was the girl in charge of country club socializing, everyone would step back as she made her claim.

We each had to bring a guy to the first meeting, one guy who met all the club qualifications. He didn't have to be for us, just something to throw on the donation pile. Of course, this year would be different.

This year I would bring Ashley as bait. And Cait would fall right into my clutches. For the first time, I would have the upper hand. And I was going to use it. I was going to take her down, even if it meant I couldn't hook up with Ashley. Be strong my loins . . .

"Rule four: Hos before bros; whoever sees him first gets him. If I call dibs, you bitches will leave him the hell alone. As friends, we don't steal other friends' boys."

I almost rolled my eyes but managed to hold it together. I took a deep inhale and waited for my rapidly beating heart to slow down again. Sweat crested my brow as I shuddered with rage.

"Rule five: See rule four; don't try to date a brother without permission. Don't try to date my brother, or Aubrey's or Claire's or Cherry's. We saw his junk when we were kids, and we don't want to hear about your filthy summer sexcapades with him. The only exception to the rule is if you get the approval of the sister in question. None of you whores better ask me about Creston. It's a firm no."

Her eyes never even came near me. The entire meeting, she had avoided me.

I wondered if word had gotten back to her yet that I suspected what she had done. My heart didn't slow, and the sweat didn't stop. I wasn't sure I would make it out of the room, or rather if she would make it out alive.

"Rule six: Minimize couple's time. This isn't courting, it's socializing. We do not go to school this fall with the boy we let dry hump us all summer long at parties. You will not fall for these boys. The whole point of Fling Club is that it's a fling. There are no strings attached. Which means we do not get attached. This strict policy keeps the guys on their toes. We run the game. We run the show. We run the world."

The other girls all cheered like she was Michelle Obama or Beyoncé giving a speech on female empowerment.

"Rule seven: Act the part—lady in the streets and freak in the sheets. I don't think I need to explain that, and if I do, it's over your head." Cait laughed a little.

"Rule eight: We don't pay. Go Dutch and you're out. We have an image to maintain. If you can't tell a guy in his early twenties what to do, God help you in marriage." Again her eyes landed on certain people in the crowd.

I didn't like this rule. I'd never agreed girls should try to get whatever they could from the men in their lives. It was skeezy. Not to mention we all came from money. Who cared who paid with which fortune? But Cait had everyone brainwashed into believing we did this so we would be the ones dragging boys along on leashes, controlling the entirety of fun for the summer. Like we were prizes for them to vie for.

"Rule nine: Protect yourself. That means your body and your reputation. Social media is no joke, and neither are STDs. No one here needs to know your business. Try to remember who your parents are." She clapped her hands together as she reached the last rule.

Thank God.

Listening to her rattle on was annoying most summers; this summer it was unbearable.

Her smile grew wide and possibly authentic. "Rule ten: Everything has an expiration date. Playtime ends August 31. This date is not a suggestion; it's firm and set. We have a tradition to uphold. All the Paulson girls go to college single. We do not marry early. We do not have babies before it's socially acceptable." She flung her shiny blonde hair back and paced in front of us like we were her recruits in the Marine Corps, crossing her arms and giving us her intense, steely-eyed stare. "Any questions?" That was rhetorical.

After so many years of this, I finally saw it for what it was.

Bravado of the worst kind.

All along I'd missed it, believing it was more important to belong than to stand up. But Ella had been completely right about the "it" girls and this club.

It was a farce.

And our fearless leader was a dick.

I wanted my time back.

I wanted my money back.

I wanted a refund on the whole experience.

I almost laughed at Cait, but I imagined the sheeple surrounding me would attack. I would be sacrificed to the goddess of summer fun and naive girls everywhere.

That would be a sight to behold. Them running after me, all of us in our heels and little skirts. It would involve tripping and injuries. It'd be messy.

Cait's eyes finally landed on me, possibly by mistake. She winced slightly, but then maybe noticed the bitter humor on my face. "Cherry!" She spoke with a venomous smile. "Do you have something to add?"

"Not a thing." I shook my head. "I think you covered all the bases, Cait."

A couple of girls snickered at that.

Cait narrowed her gaze, then turned to the rest of the room. "You'll all be thanking me when you leave this summer without chlamydia and a clingy guy. Maybe you'll even go on to make something of yourselves that we can all be proud of."

I was so glad this was my last summer of this shit.

Cait watched us all until finally we looked down, proving how much lower we were in status.

But I didn't believe it.

No.

This was the first summer where I saw her for the fraud she was.

"Anyway, take a copy of the rules. Memorize them, burn them, never speak of them. See you all at my house for date selection for the Spring Fling Saturday night." She turned on her four-inch heel and strutted from the room, sashaying to the elevator.

Rachel glanced over at me and whispered, "Was that real?"

"Yeah," I said with a laugh. "Unfortunately."

"Thanks for bringing me. This is going to be a *super-fun summer*." The sarcasm was strong with this one. We had only hung out a few times a couple of summers ago when she was visiting her grandparents, and even with that little time spent together, she was my favorite person in the room. She didn't drink the Kool-Aid. She saw our world for what it was.

"You don't have a choice; you have to join," I whispered back, trying to repair my slip of honesty with her. "It's the only way to have a life in the Hamptons. Besides, Cait's just intense in the beginning. She gets more fun after the initial rule speech," I lied. I hadn't told Rachel our evil plan; I didn't know her well enough to divulge such information.

We stood and walked past the entrance, where she grabbed a set of the rules and followed me out of the small banquet room in the basement of the clubhouse.

Rachel leaned in as we walked up the stairs. "These are strict. Are there even enough guys to go around?"

"Yeah," I whispered back. "Fortunately, there's no actual age limit on the guys. Just as long as he's a blue blood or incredibly wealthy nouveau riche, he's fair game."

"So, he can be from a totally different town?"

"Not exactly. He has to summer out here and be connected. It used to be that he had to be from Paulson as well, but we were burning through guys too quickly with Cait's no-leftovers rule."

She wrinkled her nose. "I suppose a guy from out of town would be hard to bring to functions."

"It's easier when they have a helicopter," I muttered. "Personally, I enjoy dating a guy who lives in the city and only comes to the beach for the weekends. Then the summer is yours, *and* you don't have to worry about who is escorting you to the functions. You have free time and a date, and Cait's happy." I accidentally snarled the last words.

"She's such a control freak."

"She is."

"How bad is the club?"

"Not too bad." I struggled with whether to tell her the truth or not. "The whole secret thing gets annoying. Cait likes to think we're an underground society, but it's less secret than you'd imagine. It's just exclusive, and we don't talk about it. The guys on the shore know the club exists, that if they want to have social options, they need to be part of it in some way. But they don't know our rules. No one does. The rules and what happens behind closed doors are sacred."

"How does it kick off?" She didn't sound excited at all.

"Tomorrow night we'll have dinner here, at the country club, with our families. Everyone who is anyone will attend. A lot of guys are brought for a sort of preselection introduction. Then the next night there will be a party at Cait's, and everyone will be there. The guys will drink and have fun, and then they'll be asked to leave, and the girls will choose one. You'll ask him to be your date to the Spring Fling and a season of fun and festivities thereafter. The boys know if they want to be included in the most prestigious parties and events, they have to play along. Cait has all the power and hosts the best parties. Her dad's the most important man on the beach, and one of the most important men in the city. Careers and lives are changed in his house all the time. People vie to have a seat at his table at every function, just for a chance to catch his ear for an evening. He's always at her parties, rubbing elbows. And she keeps her parties exclusive to Fling Club."

"So guys who don't make Fling Club selection don't get invited to anything?" Rachel asked.

"Not to the Fling Club–exclusive parties. Which there are quite a few. There are other events and whatnot, parties and galas hosted by the country club or societies that everyone gets to go to. But they're never as fun. Cait's parties are sort of forbidden fruit." My answer made me feel weird now. "And the hottest girls on the shore are in Fling Club. The guys vie for a spot."

"This is the weirdest thing I've ever heard." Rachel gave me a look that suggested she was never going to be fully on board.

"I hate to break it to you, but the options are fit in or frig off, so you have to make that call for yourself. If you want a social life, this is it. Come into the fold, or get out of someone else's way."

"Holy shit." She nudged me. "This is *Mean Girls* to the extreme."

"You have no idea." I decided to level with her. "Cait makes all three of the Heathers combined look like saints," I whispered, looking around and making sure no one could hear me. "These are the worst people you will ever meet, and yet you will learn to tolerate them. Some you might even grow to like."

"What's a Heather?" She looked worried.

"The movie *Heathers*. Don't tell me you haven't seen it?"

"Okay, I won't."

"We'll watch it later. It's old, but awesome." I pulled Rachel to the foyer so we could leave and I could finally catch my breath. I was really starting to like her. She was different, and for the first time in my life, I was too.

Chapter Seventeen

WHAT HAPPENS AT FLING CLUB
STAYS AT FLING CLUB

Ashley

"Mum, you're going to have to level with me. How bad was it?" I paced in front of the massive brick fireplace that looked like it belonged in an old castle and didn't suit the nineties building scheme at all.

"He was a right ass, if I'm being honest. He told the doctor in no uncertain terms that he wasn't interested in more chemo and he would rather die with a bit of dignity instead of finish this last session." She sounded angry, but I knew that wouldn't last. She would be crushed with sadness later if he stood by this decision. She was a "cry in the shower like a winner" sort of lady. Fierce and formidable on the outside, but a delicate flower on the inside.

"Well, that's not an option. He's not even stage four, for God's sake. He needs to man up and stop this nonsense." His cancer wasn't spreading, and the chemo was working; quitting now would be foolish.

"Oh, I know that, son. He'll be round to the doctor on Monday for treatments, you mark my words. If I have to, I'll knock him out and have one of the playhouse players carry him there—he'll love that." She laughed, and for the first time in the conversation, she sounded like my mom again.

"Good. Do you need me to come home?" I had to offer it. I wanted to go home. But leaving this job behind would be batshit crazy, unless of course my father decided he was going to let something treatable kill him. Prostate cancer wasn't the death sentence it had once been.

"God, no. You've gone and gotten this amazing IT job, and you're going to be able to take care of yourself for the year. That's a huge burden off of ya, and not to be rude, but also us. Don't be daft."

"I love you both. Give him a hug for me." I hated lying to her about the job I had, but telling her I was basically a gigolo wasn't an option.

"I'll kick him in the arse for ya," she scoffed.

"That works as well. Have a good sleep." It was well past one in the morning there, and she sounded too fired up to go to bed anytime soon.

"After my brandy. Have a good weekend, darling."

"I'll try. Night."

"Night." She hung up, and I stared at the phone.

I had but a second to contemplate my father's illness and stubbornness before the front door burst open and Cherry shivered, hurrying inside.

"It's freezing out there. The car said it was sixty degrees. If this is global warming, I'm going to start funding those celebrities who make the starving polar bear videos." She shrugged off her jacket and held it for a second, like she was going to pass it to someone, before she slung it over the coat stand at the front door and came all the way in. Her heels clicked on the floor, and her lips and eyes glistened in the firelight. "Thank God the fire's going. I need to warm up." She stood too close to me, something that had been happening all week long. We got closer and closer. We sat beside each other, legs and the backs of hands touching. The sexual tension was so noticeable her younger sister assumed we were having sex. But neither of us had made the first move. A stalemate that was killing me.

"How was it?" I asked, getting increasingly nervous about the start of Fling Club and what it would mean for me, but trying to sound indifferent and cool.

"Awful." She furrowed her brow, her eyes widening like she was reliving a terrible scene. "I barely made it out alive." Her words were soft and strained like she was talking about going to war.

"But we're a go for tomorrow night?"

"What?" She blinked and glanced up into my gaze, sucking me in with her haunted eyes. "Sorry. Yes. We're good. Cait suspects nothing. The other girls have turned on the Barbie-zombie switch. And Rachel, the girl I told you about, the one my mom forced me to bring to Fling Club, is actually kinda awesome. Might even be helpful in these endeavors."

"Really?" I couldn't care less about the new girl, but I played my part, acting polite. Acting like staring at her as the flames kissed her skin didn't make me want to grab her and kiss her as well. Her pouty lips coated in gloss called to me, but I knew shitting where you ate was always frowned upon. Kissing your boss resulted in early termination. And while she would be worth it, any detriment to my dad's situation wouldn't.

"Yeah, she didn't like Fling Club at all. She thought Cait seemed like a tyrannical bitch. And she sounded like—" She tilted her head, toying with a grin. "You, actually. She sounded like you. She was sort of bitter and funny and not at all like me." The grin won, spreading over her face and making my stomach tighten.

"Weird. Will she fit in?" I asked it in a hypnotic tone, stuck again staring at her.

"No." She smiled wider. "She won't at all. She seems like she would rather hang out with Ella than spend one more minute there. I might even tell her about our plan, see if she can help."

"You should wait and make sure Andy thinks that's a good idea. He's fairly focused on getting even. And Ella doesn't come across as the sort of girl who would take lightly to you introducing a wild card."

"I'll wait and make sure she's not one of them, bought by the limelight of being an 'it' girl and the subculture the club provides." She stepped forward. "I want to thank you for this. I know it's weird and unconventional and immature and twisted." She laughed at herself, blushing and glancing down. "Tomorrow, you'll see what I'm talking about. You'll see all of it. And it will be shocking to you, but you need to try to blend in and take it in stride."

She lifted a small hand to my arm and her gaze to mine, not realizing I could feel heat from her thin fingers through my shirt building in my entire body. "When you see it all playing out, please don't think less of me." She pressed her lips together, like she might even cry. "I really saw it all tonight for the first time, and I can't believe what an idiot I've been." She blinked, and a single tear left her glossy eye.

"Cherry." I didn't know why I said her name, but I did. I stared at that tear, wanting so badly to lift my hand and wipe it away, cup her porcelain face, and press my lips onto hers.

"Just promise you won't judge me. I've done enough self-critique lately for the both of us." She wiped her tear and looked at the fire, lowering her hand. "I should go. I need to shower and pack for home tomorrow. No help here and all."

"Okay. Night."

"Night." She turned and left, going to her room even though it was only a little after nine.

Cherry was a problem for me.

She was too beautiful to not want, so adding the human qualities I'd seen all week and the intelligence and humor to her cold exterior was like being tormented by forbidden fruit.

I closed my eyes and exhaled for the first time in at least a minute, trying desperately not to let myself fall for the broken rich girl.

Chapter Eighteen

Bathroom Breaks and Bravado

Cherry

Friday night, Andy, Ashley, and I made our way to my parents' table at the country club. My parents and sister were meeting us there.

When we got to the table my mother smiled, glowing and laughing. She was clearly on her second bottle of wine, typical for her.

Rachel and her family were also seated with us, her dad becoming my dad's new favorite person.

Glancing around the room, I saw them all, all my friends. I waved at the ones I should, including Cait. She smiled wide from her father's table, acting genuinely excited to see me. I did the same, although I was smiling because I was imagining bludgeoning her with my Louboutins. The blood-red shoes wouldn't even get ruined.

Griffin's parents were at a separate table, but Griffin was notably missing. I had hoped he wouldn't show his face, but was scared he would be here. It was my lucky night.

"Mother, Father, Mr. Swenson, this is Ashley Jardine, a friend from Oxford who is over for the summer. He and I met a few years ago when I was on the debate team freshman year." Andy introduced him to the table. "Ashley, this is my sister, Ella; my mother and father; and our friend, Mr. Harold Swenson, and his daughter, Rachel, and son, Ryan. And you met my other sister, Cherry, in the limo on the way over."

"Nice to meet you, Ashley." Mr. Swenson stood with my father and Ryan as I sat, and Ashley pushed in my chair, lingering over me. Mr. Swenson nodded at Ashley. "We were just in Oxford last summer. Lovely town."

"Quite. The campus is stunning, and the heritage is truly unique," Ashley said with perfect British form.

Ignoring them all, I leaned into Rachel, whom I'd chosen to sit next to. "Hey."

"Hey, yourself." She smiled wide. "So Cait is totally a Heather," she whispered in my ear, making my beaming face glow. "I watched it last night, and I was dying. This is us and our life for the summer. And I seriously think your sister is Christian Slater."

"I know." I winked at Ella, who was scowling at Rachel and I whispering in each other's confidence. "Rachel watched *Heathers* last night," I said to Ella, who instantly started to snigger and glance about the room.

"I see," she said, giving Rachel a scrutinizing stare. "I suggest you watch *Cruel Intentions* next."

"Maybe we could all watch it together." Rachel laughed.

"How was your semester?" My mother glanced my way, interrupting us. I'd avoided seeing her since I'd been back.

"The usual." I shrugged.

"Excellent." She sipped from her glass coyly while lightly resting her hand on Rachel's dad's forearm. "Cheryl goes to Wellesley."

"How nice. Another school with a lot of heritage." Rachel's dad smiled at me, not taking notice of my mother still lingering in his private space as they both turned back to my father and Ashley's conversation.

"Oh, God. My mom's making a play for your dad," I whispered to Rachel.

"What?" She sounded worried. "For real? She would do that? He's not ready for that kind of thing."

"I'm kidding." I laughed. "She's flirting, but don't worry. She only sleeps with guys who are under thirty and do manual labor for a living. It's gross."

"Your mom has affairs, and you know about them?"

"Welcome to the Hamptons. Affairs are a way of life."

"Seriously." She gulped. "I miss Europe more and more every day. They have affairs, but at least no one talks about them."

"And how was last night?" My father beamed. "Your first spring prom meeting?"

"It's the Spring Fling dance, Dad." I grinned at him. I was always going to be his little girl.

"Excellent." He glanced to where Cait was kissing her dad on the cheek. "Well, if Caitlyn Landry is handling it, you know it will be magnificent."

"Of course." Ella rolled her eyes with him. She and our dad got it. He saw the Hamptons for what it was: a lot of bravado. I used to think he was cynical, but now I saw he was correct.

"What's the Spring Fling?" Ashley cocked an eyebrow and pretended to be new.

"Spring Fling is the start of event season here, a party to kick things off. It's like the gun going off for the beginning of summer. The Landry family always plans it. This year the elusive role of queen of clubs is Cait's. Before her, her older sister ran it. Before that it was an aunt. And I think her mom did it too. I know her grandma was in charge. Her dad's the chair of the club," Ella explained quietly. "She and her family think they sit at the top of the food chain around here. Her dad's a drunk tyrant and a bit pervy. He lets Cait and her siblings use his name to throw their weight around, while her mom is a vase."

"Vase?" Ashley sounded lost.

"Very pretty to look at, but don't ever touch it. It's fragile and price-less." Ella laughed.

"Creepy and entirely accurate." Andy nodded along.

"Ella!" my mother snapped. She usually ignored what we said until Ella went too far. Then she gave a slight wave to someone as she mut-tered to us, "The Landry family is a perfect example of what we should all strive for. And the Spring Fling committee is important. Paulson Exeter Academy has a reputation to uphold, even for its graduates. You ladies don't want to break tradition."

"Of course not." I lifted my glass of wine at Ashley, hoping he was following along. "Never." My mother gave me a shocked look. I never spoke up about this sort of thing. But having Andy, Ashley, Rachel, and Ella seated around the table made me feel like I wasn't alone in this anymore. Or even more importantly, like I didn't care.

Ryan narrowed his gaze. "You sound like you don't approve, even though you play along." He hit me right in the stomach. A brutal blow by a newcomer.

"To be honest, I was fully invested for the past six years." I could see him judging me. "This season, I'm more invested than ever, just in a different capacity. What's everyone having for dinner?"

Andy folded his arms across his chest and tilted his head dubiously at me. "Cherry, stop trying to change the subject; the young man has questions. You know you have always loved being one of the 'it' girls, being part of something bigger than you. You aren't a stranger to sac-rificing self-worth for a place at the table next to the high queen, just like all the other good girls."

Ella defended me, her eyes darting to our mother. "Survival of the fittest." I could see this was an act, everyone doing and saying what they normally would, and as usual I was the butt of the torment.

Rachel's father frowned. "Is it that cutthroat here?"

"Ask Rachel what her first meeting was like." Ella glanced at her.

"Absolutely." Rachel nodded, sipping her wine. "We are talking first-class assholes and arranged-marriages status."

"Arranged marriages?" Her father made a face. "Did we make a mistake? Is the school horrible too?"

"It's not so bad." Ryan shrugged. He was the same age as Ella, a senior in high school. "Everyone's been nice to me so far, but I've only met kids outside of school. Maybe it'll be different when classes start again in August."

"Don't listen to my family." My mother had joined in again. "This is the best school on the Eastern Seaboard. Ryan will benefit immensely from the year he will have here. And even the three months Rachel has in town for the summer will be of some help. The influence of the people in this very room can move mountains. Look around and you'll see the future staring back. Leaders and their wives are seated around every table."

"Their wives." Ella snorted. "Mother, easy on the 1960s speech." A bitter smile lingered on my sister's face. She was never going to fit in here. I wished I didn't.

Ella was like our dad, through and through. He might have grown up blue blooded, but he tried to be a regular guy in every way. When he stayed in New York during the week, he went to games, ate hot dogs, and wore jeans. His life was simple and real. The weekends here were the work.

And like him, Ella was hard and soft in all the right places. She would be a challenge for any guy who ever wanted to get close. She made boys work to get to know her.

Not that I'd seen many try. Most were scared. She was brilliant, honest, and humble. No one was ever prepared for that combination here. Especially the humble part.

My sister was one of the leaders sitting at a table. Just not the sort that fit the mold. Here, men took the lead and women looked pretty.

And that was the mold I had always shaped myself in accordance with.

I had been a follower to the extreme. I always made it look like I was my own person, but I wasn't.

I even gave it—*it*—up sophomore year of high school because Cait had pressured me. She'd said virginity was passé, and if I wanted to be in the club she was forming, there was a strict no-virgins rule. I did it with a drunk boy I didn't like at a party I didn't want to be at.

Dad smiled at Ella before turning back to Rachel's father. "Honestly, the school's amazing. The opportunities it provides for the kids are top notch and incomparable to the other schools. Some years I've seen the worst student here get picked for the best colleges, entirely based on the academy." His voice dropped down. "You just have to keep your inner Democrat hidden under the table. No one likes to see it out in public."

"Phillip!" Mom leaned forward, shaking her head slowly at my father. "That's a lie. There are several Democrats out here. They came out at the last election." Her eyes narrowed. "You will recall."

"I do." He nodded and took a gulp of his whiskey. He was one of them; my mom was just in denial about it.

"Left an impression, did it?" Ashley laughed. His cheeks flushed when my mother glared at him.

"Indeed." My dad winked.

Ashley pressed his lips together and raised an eyebrow, lifting his glass at the rest of us. "Good luck to us all fitting in." His eyes flickered to me again. When he stared at me, I noted tension before his eyes darted to Rachel. "You sure you want to be involved in this world?"

"No," she laughed. "Not after that first meeting. And I'm glad I didn't go to school here. Sorry, Ry." She glanced at her brother. "I hope they keep being nice to you."

"I hate Paulson." Ella popped back into the conversation. "It's the worst school ever. I'm so glad I don't go."

"You don't?" Ryan asked.

"Not a chance." She shook her head. "I'm a senior in New York. Our dad stays Monday through Friday for work, so I come and go with him. We have a house there."

"She goes to Trinity," I said proudly, hoping he saw that she was so cool.

"Really?" His eyes widened. "Wow, that's a good school."

"Yeah." She gave him an odd look. "I know. And the city is much more diverse. Obviously."

"Paulson is not so far from the city." Ryan laughed, hinting at something.

"And I come home on the weekends." She blushed, and I was puzzled.

Had I missed an important part of the conversation?

Was my sister actually flirting?

Is this what it looked like?

"Speaking of the Spring Fling club." Andy turned to Ashley. "You're probably going to get dragged into going."

"Are you going?" Ashley asked. I hoped the question didn't sound scripted.

"He can't. He's not an option," Ella answered.

"Says who?" Ashley turned to her.

"She did." She tilted her head at me. "No exes allowed. He dated Cait."

"You choose who can go to parties and who can't?" Ashley's eyes narrowed as a wry grin screwed up his lips. He was playing this part a little too well, making me uncomfortable. I wished the dinner conversation didn't turn to this, but I knew my parents needed to be played and convinced.

"I'm glad I can't go. It sounds like too much work anyway. From what I hear about some of the girls, it's a lot of formality and not a lot of reward. Bunch of girls who just want to play at dating but don't know the first thing about it. Why all the games?" Andy's words hit home, attacking me without calling me out.

Only now I had no defense of the club—not a real one. I could joke all I wanted, but the reality was that I was ashamed of it and all my years spent belonging. I hated Cait, the club, and even being here, watching my mother wave her arms around and dazzle and play into the whole charade. I wanted to go home and pretend none of this had ever happened.

"Excuse me." I stood and walked to the bathroom. I needed a minute. A minute of no more club or guy talk. It might have been an act, but it hurt nonetheless.

I leaned into the mirror, considering my own soul, and decided that this summer was going to be different. This summer I was going to get my revenge and possibly redeem myself in my own eyes. Prove I wasn't a silly girl who played silly games.

Just then, the bathroom door shot open, and Cora burst in. "Cait's on her way in here. She said she needed to talk to you. I thought I should give you a heads up." She hurried into a stall and closed the door.

I clenched everywhere as I waited for the attack.

A second later Cait stormed in. "Cherry, how's it going? I haven't heard from you for weeks." She gave me that fake smile, the one that I saw through now.

"Oh, just busy. Wrapping up the year was a bit more time consuming than normal." I glanced at her in the mirror.

"You were spaced out at the club meeting. Is everything all right?" Her eyes narrowed, daring me to accuse her of sleeping with my boyfriend. Daring me to be ballsy and stand up for myself.

"I'm just drained from the semester. I'm sure I'll be feeling more myself in no time." I bowed down to the queen of clubs.

"Hmmm. I heard about you and Griffin breaking up." She leaned against the counter and then turned, looking at herself. She was beautiful in every way, except on the inside. "I was in France when it happened. Sarah messaged me. I was sad to hear the news, but glad you'll be part of the club again this summer." Her smile widened, like it was real. "I was worried he might throw a wrench in the situation."

"France?" I almost twitched and screamed that she was a lying bitch.

"Yeah. Just for the week. I needed a break. School was actual work this year, ya know?" She winked a lush set of lashes at me.

I fought the urge to rip them off.

"You still look tired and funky. You better snap out of your haze and look alive for the selection party at my place. As one of the seniors, it's your job to step up your responsibility and set an example." She took charge again, pushing me down so I remembered my place. When she turned back to look at herself, she dropped the act. "What's with the new girl, Ronda? Her brother is gorgeous. Who is he?" She got Rachel's name wrong on purpose. She did that.

"Rachel? Her name's Rachel, not Ronda," I muttered, desperately holding back all the murderous things I wanted to say and do. But killing her in the bathroom wasn't going to ruin her, just me. "Not a clue about the brother." It was the truth. I knew nothing about him. "He's only a senior at Paulson."

"Oh, he's young." She sniffed. "And the other guy at your table. He's not related to her?"

"No, that's Andy's new BFF. Ashley Jardine. He's from England. Kind of a dick, like Andy."

"Hmm." She primped her hair. "He's not my type anyway."

"No." I smiled, mocking her in my head. He wasn't someone's boyfriend, so of course she wouldn't be interested. "Of course not."

"But he is hot. You should convince him to come. See you tomorrow night."

She walked out and that was that.

She would claim him.

Ashley would be hers for the summer.

How did I feel about that?

Staring at my reflection in the mirror, I had to be honest with myself. I liked Ashley. A lot.

Him dating her was not something I wanted to think about. It was everything Ella and Andy wanted, but he wasn't one of us. Even for money, he didn't deserve this.

And what if he fell for her?

That might break my heart a little.

But it wasn't like I could even acknowledge my attraction to him. I couldn't very well pay him to be my fling and then really date him without the whole thing turning out like the plot of *Pretty Woman*.

All of that meant he would be dating her. She'd take the bait. Andy and Ella would win.

And I was going to get my revenge.

But it didn't feel good, like it should.

"She is such a liar. She flew to France the day after you caught them." Cora slipped from the stall, interrupting my mental crisis. "I think Cait knew they got caught and fled."

"You think she knew I saw?" I wondered if all my friends knew that it was Cait. How humiliating, everyone talking about it behind my back. No doubt Cait was laughing about it and me.

"I think so. She won't own it; you know how she is," Cora whispered. She was always so quiet. She rushed forward, hugging me. "Please don't let her get to you. She's disgusting."

"I won't." I hugged back, gripping tightly to my friend.

"Three months and we're back at school, and we never have to hang with her again. This is our last summer. You can do this." She sounded like she was telling herself that as much as she was convincing me.

"You're right." A slow, disappointed sigh slipped from my lips as we left the bathroom. "I'm going to get some fresh air for a minute." I squeezed Cora's hand and slipped from her grip, turning left as she turned right.

I hurried to the deck, pushed the door open, and almost stumbled out into the fresh ocean air. I gasped my breaths, heaving as the rage and fury dissipated.

How had I thought I could handle this, seeing Cait acting so smug and lying her face off?

The door burst open behind me.

Through my rage-filled rant, I saw a face and hands that pulled me into a warm body, wrapping itself around me.

Ashley.

He was warm and comfortable and familiar in a way he shouldn't have been. "You okay?" he whispered.

Ashley held me in the cool breeze, letting me lose the anger as a subtle awkwardness crept in. Here I was hugging him when I'd technically just sold him to the devil.

I cleared my throat and gathered myself, pushing back a bit on his chest. "Sorry. I was just so mad. I didn't even realize I was crying." I wiped a tear and laughed bitterly at myself. "Andy says it's because I'm a ginger and the evil rage makes its way out in tears because I so rarely get angry. It has to come out somehow."

"While Andy is an idiot, that actually sounds plausible." He laughed with me, but his eyes were full of concern. "I saw that girl follow you to the bathroom. Are you okay?" His concern was killing me.

"Yeah, she was just full of lies and passive-aggressiveness. And I was filled with an uncontrollable rage. It took every ounce of self-restraint not to kill her." I glanced at my trembling hands. They shook with unspent desire.

His hands lifted and closed around mine. It was the simplest act ever and yet maybe the most sensual thing ever done to me. He held them until the trembling stopped. "You've got this, Cherry. We're going to take her down."

"She's already asked for you to come to the selection night." I said it so softly that the wind almost carried it away. I wished it had.

"Wow, I haven't even turned on the charm yet."

"Oh, please." I sniffled and laughed.

"She's already taken the bait. It just got real, didn't it? Maybe you're right, maybe we should bring Ryan and Rachel into the fold. This doesn't seem like their cup of tea either." He sounded like Andy. Only, standing here in the dim lighting from the lanterns around the deck, in the dark, crisp air, he was obviously something else.

"Yeah, we could use the help. I'm feeling like we're way out of our league."

He lifted a hand and brushed my hair to the side. I shivered, but not from the cold.

"Let's go back inside. You're freezing." He held my hand and led me back to the door. I wanted to go home. I'd had enough excitement for one night. Crying at the country club was so basic, it made me want to scream.

"Does my makeup look okay?" I lifted my face in the light by the entrance.

"Perfect." He sounded conflicted, but his eyes weren't. They were screaming that he was going to kiss me, convinced this was their moment. He paused, staring, as if having a wrestling match with his conscience over whether to do it or not.

The angel on his right shoulder won.

He blinked and lost all the emotion.

Which was probably for the best.

I'd just given him away, so of course I shouldn't go kissing him.

Ashley opened the door and led me back inside, still holding my hand.

As we walked back, as if on a timer set to go off the moment I was even close to interested in someone, Cait's eyes darted to where we were. They narrowed into slits, like she didn't know I saw her plotting. A smile crested her bright lips as she nodded at the person speaking to her, but her eyes followed along with whatever I was doing and wherever I was going.

"And us holding hands just sealed the deal. Cait will make her play for you," I whispered.

"It's what we want, right?" He glanced back at me and squeezed my fingers lightly.

I forced a grin to my lips. "Yeah. It's what we want."

He squeezed a little harder, as if needing me to steady him this time, while Cait eyed him like he was part of the spring lineup at fashion week.

It was exactly like Ella had planned.

Except as much as I wanted Cait to go down, I really didn't want Ashley to go with her. Holding his hand, I couldn't lie anymore. I wanted him for myself. I was just being honest about it now that I couldn't have him.

Ashley pushed in my chair as I took my seat, desperately ignoring the glare coming off my mother. She would no doubt be researching who Ashley was and confirming his identity by morning. Fortunately Ella had prepared for this moment.

Ashley sat and stared at me, possibly still checking to make sure I was all right.

I wasn't.

I'd never been so conflicted in my life.

"Everything okay?" Rachel asked in a soft whisper.

"Yeah, just had a chat with Cait." I acted like it was nothing. "I think she wants Ashley to be her summer fling."

"Really." She swallowed hard. "I sort of got the impression he was more interested in being yours."

"No." I took a huge gulp of wine. "I was asked to put in a good word by the queen bee herself."

Rachel glanced her way. Cait lifted her glass, grinning. We were playing into her hands as much as she was playing into ours.

"And how does he feel about that?" Rachel asked, giving Ashley a look.

"The whole Spring Fling formal is a joke. No guy wants to be asked out by a girl." Andy puffed his chest a little.

"No, indeed," Ashley agreed. "We like to hunt."

"Oh, there will be hunting." An evil smirk played upon Ella's lips. "It just won't be you doing the chasing."

"I'm not interested." Ashley said it like he was serious, but when he glanced back at Cait, his stare suggested otherwise. He played his part perfectly.

Between the vile grin on Cait's lips and the hateful one on Ella's, I was beginning to fill with dread.

Chapter Nineteen

THE END OF ANGST

Cherry

The ride home was unbearable.

He'd come to my rescue again.

He'd hugged me and comforted me.

He'd held my hand and looked into my eyes like he was going to kiss me.

And I was selling him to the wolves.

If I stared out the window and let the conversation he and Andy were having become nothing but white noise, I could still feel his arms around me and his hands over mine.

Making it all worse, I watched him in the reflection of the window, catching his eyes darting toward mine.

As we pulled up to the Weinbergs' house, I sat up straight and readied myself for the next ten minutes of final packing and getting back into the car. I would need a plan for handling Mom when I got to the house. I hoped she continued drinking at home after dinner.

At least I would have Ella.

Ashley popped open the door and stepped out, holding it open for me. Andy jumped out next, not seeing the gesture for what it was.

But I did.

Our eyes met as I climbed out. "Thanks."

"Of course." He grinned and offered his arm. "When we get in, can we go over what I have to do tomorrow again? Seeing everyone in action tonight made it more real."

"For you and me both," I mumbled. "Rachel and I are going to meet you and Andy at Cait's house," I began. "Ella wants Andy to come; she thinks it will unnerve Cait a bit that I'm throwing him in the pile. We'll all go inside, pretend to mingle. You will flirt with me mercilessly so everyone thinks you're interested. Cait will bully me into letting you be her date like she has every other summer."

I didn't stop talking as we passed through the front door. "You and Andy and all the guys will leave, and we girls will choose our dates. The tradition goes that Cait will then show up on your doorstep with a small gift and ask you to be her fling. You say yes, because you're not allowed to say no, let's get real. And then you and she will go to the Spring Fling, and from there, we commence our plan of forcing her to break all her own rules." I took a breath.

"Okay." He nodded. "I think I can manage that." His lips toyed with a grin as Andy stalked off to one of the bedrooms and we walked to the fireplace and stood there.

"Just remember not to fall for her." I said it with a hint of warning. "As you've now seen for yourself, she's gorgeous and sneaky. She has those womanly wiles people talk about."

"She's not my type, Cherry." He stared straight into my eyes, making my breath hitch.

"My mother was in peak form tonight," I said, changing the subject. "Did you see the way she kept touching Mr. Swenson?"

Andy came into the room, pulling on a sweater and sitting down.

"No," Ashley gasped sarcastically.

"You joke, but you should be on the lookout. She'll be putting the moves on you next." Andy laughed. "It can get a bit ridiculous here."

"She'll come on to me?" Ashley lost his grin, checking with me.

"She might." I shrugged. "You're fit and handsome and tall and toned, and your eyes—" I stopped myself before I started describing more personal details.

"That would be embarrassing." His cheeks flushed with color.

"Don't you have a home to return to?" Andy turned to me, making it clear that he was ready to finally have Ashley to himself.

"Yeah." I gasped. "Shit! Hans is still in the driveway."

"No, he left." Andy got up and sauntered to the front door.

"Okay, I'll call him to come get me."

"Nonsense. I'll drive you," Ashley said quickly. "I can take you now."

"Oh—" I tried not to react to his wanting me to go. "I'll get my things." I turned and left the room, feeling incredibly uncomfortable. I'd already packed my bags myself, since the house was almost entirely devoid of help, so grabbing my things took but a moment.

When I arrived at the front door, Ashley wasn't there, but Andy was. "Don't worry, Cherry. She's going down."

"What?" I asked, dragging my own bags.

"You acted weird tonight, and I know it's because you're worried about this scheme not working. But you don't need to. We'll be fine. We got this." He said it casually as he sauntered back over to his chair.

"Right. See ya later." I turned and left, dragging my bags outside to where Ashley was with the car.

He hurried forward. "Hey, let me get those." He grabbed my suitcases and brought them to the trunk.

"Thanks!" I turned and climbed into the car, feeling anxious.

He got in and smiled at me. "I haven't ever driven a car this nice before."

"Well, get used to it." I smiled and stared at my hands.

"I wanted to tell you, you were right."

"About what?" God, was he about to tell me how gorgeous Cait was?

"I wasn't mentally prepared for how awful it all was. At all. I don't think I've ever met such dreadful people. Your dad seems great, and Mr. Swenson is cool. But your mother and everyone else in that place were terrible. Those movies you made me watch were accurate."

"Yeah." I wrinkled my nose. "I did warn you. *Heathers*, *Cruel Intentions*, *Valmont*, and *Dangerous Liaisons* are my sister's favorites. She made me watch them over and over. I thought she wanted to be like them, but then I realized she was trying to give me some perspective."

"Yeah, I was unprepared for the level of peacocking and the fake everything. Smiles, breasts, lips, cheeks, hair, tans, kindness. There were very few genuine people, and you could see it instantly."

"It's pretty bad."

"Where am I going?" he asked after a second. "I got so excited to be leaving the house after our movie marathon week, I forgot to get directions."

"Oh, shit, right. Sorry." I started to laugh after I realized he was driving the wrong way. "It's the opposite direction. I'm so used to—" I shook my head and stopped myself from sounding pretentious. "It's about ten minutes down the road. Stay right along the shoreline."

"You're so accustomed to people driving you that you didn't notice we were going the wrong way?" His tone was mocking.

"I just assumed you knew where you were going, like everyone does." I didn't want to own to what he'd said.

He chuckled and turned around, and the weird silence that we always seemed to end up in took over the car.

After a few minutes, I glanced at my phone, trying to look like I didn't mind the silence. I had handfuls of texts asking me about the cute guy at my table tonight and if he was coming to the fling meeting. My insides clenched as I contemplated what to say. Of course he was coming; he was bait.

"So, who will you end up with if I get paired with Cait?" He asked the question I hadn't even given any thought to in days.

"I don't know. I guess one of the others at the party." I shrugged, acting like I wasn't dreading all of this now.

"Will he be your date for real?" He glanced at me.

"I don't know," I answered again, feeling too many emotions. "It's two houses to the right." I pointed just ahead of us.

"Oh." He sighed.

"Will you be able to find your way back?" I realized how weird it was that he was driving me, and that he didn't know the Hamptons at all. For a minute, I'd been able to tease myself that he'd been part of the tapestry here all along.

"Yeah, I think so. I have Andy's cell number if I can't," he muttered, sounding down as he pulled in. "Holy shit!" he said at the gate as one of the guards saw my face and opened it for us. "This is your house?"

"My parents' house." I didn't understand the question.

"It's bloody massive!" He leaned forward as we drove up. "It's like five of the Weinbergs' house in one."

"Right." I nodded, thinking it was probably closer to six or seven of it.

"Oh my God. I don't think I've ever seen a house this large," he said as he parked and Hans rushed over to open my door. "It looks like a hotel."

"I guess." I tried to downplay his surprise, suddenly feeling self-conscious of the unnecessary opulence.

"Miss Cheryl, I didn't realize that you had wanted to come back," Hans said, sounding upset.

"No, it's not your fault. I changed my mind and decided to come home. Sorry, I should have said something." I smiled and patted him on the arm as he grabbed my bags. "Thank you, Hans."

Ashley got out of the car but stood by its open door, staring at me.

I walked over to him; I didn't know why, but I did. "Thank you for the ride."

"So, you'll stay here then, from now on?" he asked.

"Yeah." I exhaled the word awkwardly.

"Okay." He stared, and I stared, and we were awkward, and it sucked. "But I'll see you tomorrow?"

"You will." I smiled, stuck on him in every way I could be. I'd never felt like this with anyone before. I stood on my tiptoes and placed my hands on his chest, pressing a soft kiss on his cheek. I lingered; it might have been inappropriate, but I couldn't stop myself. It was horrible that we were about to be apart for the first time in two weeks.

"I don't know what I'll do without you," he whispered, pressing his face into the kiss. "I just don't see Andy making cosmos or charcuterie boards with the same flair."

"No, it'll be a lot of nachos and beer, I'm afraid." I smiled.

"Just not the same quality."

"I'll miss you," I admitted boldly. What did I have to lose? We were alone, and this was his last night to possibly be mine.

"Not as much as I'll miss you and the entertaining way in which you win chess." He swallowed a lump in his throat, or words he shouldn't say. Either way, we stood, staring, speaking in glances and clinging to each other.

"Cherry!" My dad's voice broke the moment. "Ashley, come inside. Have a drink."

"Say no," I whispered, so my father couldn't hear.

"Thanks, Mr. Kennedy, but I have to get back. I left poor Andy at the Weinberg house, and they don't even have cable. I don't want him getting himself in trouble. Idle minds and all . . ."

"Well, you boys make your way back here for dinner tomorrow night before the big party at the Landrys'."

"Thank you, sir." He waved as my dad went inside, then looked once more at me. "Good night."

"Good night." I squeezed his hand and left. Every bit of me was colder than I'd ever been.

Chapter Twenty

The Queen of Clubs

Cherry

Lying back in the chair, I fanned myself lightly. The heat had come out of nowhere. We'd woken up and summer was here, skipping spring completely.

I glanced over at Ella in her black skirt and tank top and wrinkled my nose. "You must be sweating."

"I am." She shrugged. "It's good for you. I read sweating is the body's natural way of cleaning and cooling. So technically I'm cleansing."

I chuckled, but Mom lifted her head and scowled. "That is the most ridiculous thing I have ever heard. Why don't you swap out reading for more important things, like a social life? Maybe Cheryl could get you into the club, even if you're not a Paulson girl."

"No way! Ella's too cool for the club." I winked at my sister.

"Cheryl, darling. Don't argue. It's a good idea and about time she joined. It's your final year; you have sway. And her joining will keep us connected."

"Not likely." Ella rolled her eyes and ignored Mom, who was still carrying on.

"What a lovely event last night. I adore your father, Rachel. He's a wonderful man. And your brother is a sweet boy. Very handsome. I thought for sure he was older than seventeen."

"Yeah, Ryan's cool." Rachel nodded along, fanning herself as well.

"He sure is, isn't he, Ella?" I narrowed my gaze, certain I hadn't been mistaken.

"Who?" she asked through a huge grin.

"Ryan, darling. Rachel's brother. He's a nice boy, isn't he? And your age." Mother hinted as subtly as a car crashing into you.

Rachel watched Ella for a second before blurting, "My brother is crazy about you, you know!"

Ella's cheeks instantly flushed. "What—that's impossible." Suddenly it was Ella who was sputtering, awkwardly too. "He can't possibly already—"

"It's true." Rachel sighed. "He didn't sleep last night. Just don't make him suffer. He doesn't believe me that you're not into guys, so you'll have to tell him yourself."

"What?" I burst out laughing because people always assumed Ella was gay.

"You know, being into girls and all." Rachel was serious.

"Who?" Ella looked up casually. "Me? Oh, no, I'm—"

"Into girls?" Mom started some kind of sputtering-and-spilling-her-drink act. "Ella—honey—you aren't into girls? Are you? Is this why you asked to go to that school in Manhattan?" She started shouting. *"Ella, for God's sake, stop laughing! Cheryl! Will you both stop laughing? Someone explain this right now! Are you coming out?"*

I was cry-laughing and trying to explain, but I couldn't get the words out of my mouth.

Finally, through her own laughter at our mother's dramatics, Ella managed to spit out one statement: "Not gay."

"Oh, shit!" Rachel's jaw dropped. "Oh, God. I just thought—someone said—"

"No!" Ella was waving her hands, trying to stop laughing at Mom.

"Oh, thank God." Mom sighed, showing a little too much homophobe in her hemline. "Oh—um—not that there's anything wrong with being gay, sweetie." Mom downed her entire drink and wheezed a little as she poured herself more. She honestly was one of the worst people ever.

Rachel's hands still covered her mouth, but she managed to speak through her fingers. "I didn't mean to assume. I hate it when people assume."

Ella snickered more. "It's whatever." She wiped some of the smudged mascara off. "Seriously, that was awesome. Did you see Mom's face?" Ella laughed right at our mother. "Mom, you turned purple. I thought your head was going to explode."

Mom fanned herself and took another big drink. "Stop making jokes out of it."

As we all calmed back down and Mom stopped twitching, Ella glanced over at Rachel and smiled. "So, I guess that's why Ryan asked me out for dinner. We're going for a burger down on the boardwalk later."

Mom gasped. "You're going out with a boy? Wear pretty underwear, just in case."

"Okay, stop making a big deal about it. It was funnier when you were just being insane." Ella sighed as she got up and left us.

Rachel's face was still bright red.

"Stop feeling bad. Being assumed to be homosexual isn't offensive." I tried not to look right at my mother while saying it. "Her best friend's gay. Ella gets it all the time, just not in front of our parents. She hangs with a herd of chicks and does roller derby for fun. She goes to gay clubs. She's—"

"She does?" Mom looked like she might start the exploding thing again.

"Yeah, like I said, her friends are gay. She goes to be a wing woman."

"What?"

"Nothing." I waved my mom off.

Wincing, Rachel got up and poured herself a glass of iced tea, but only got half a glass before the pitcher was empty.

"Leah." Mom gave the maid a heated look. "Didn't you see that the pitcher was nearly empty?"

Leah rushed over.

"We can get ourselves drinks, Leah. It's cool. Actually, it's hot. Go take a break inside. Get yourself a drink. Take a load off. It's too hot to work out here." I forced a smile while taking deep breaths. Being around Ashley all week and doing things for ourselves had been nice. And I appreciated the break from constant watching.

Not to mention my mom drove me nuts, and rarely did I let it get to this point, but her outward mistreatment of others was where I drew the line. Ella was good for her. She made her have the uncomfortable conversations she tried to avoid. To accept that being gay or a feminist or a democrat weren't things that people had to keep private.

"She's right, Leah, dear. It's hot as sin out here. Go inside." Mom got up from her chair, staggering slightly as she walked inside. She came back with a full pitcher of iced tea, tiptoed her way over to us, and filled everyone's glasses. As if it were her idea all along.

I held my glass up. "Cheers."

Mom lifted hers too. "Cheers, girls. To the very best summer of your lives. The last free one you're ever going to have." She sounded bitter and dreamy.

Rachel nodded toward the pool. I shrugged back, but before I could suggest a swim, Henry walked out onto the deck. "Miss Caitlyn Landry is here to see the young ladies." He barely got the words out before the devil herself sauntered over.

My mother stood up. "Caitlyn, how wonderful to see you."

Cait walked over in her prim little dress and perfect hair. She and my mother exchanged fake kisses. "Thank you, Mrs. Kennedy."

"Have a seat, dear." My mother pointed at the lounger across from us. Leah ran and got it and put it next to ours.

"Thank you." Cait sat down, taking a spiked iced tea. "Cherry, how are you?"

"Fabulous. And yourself?" I tried not to snarl or throw my glass in her face or jump on her and choke her out.

"Excited about tonight." She glanced at Rachel. "Hello, Rachel." It was funny to watch her be nice for the sake of winning over a boy. It made her mortal for a few seconds. "Did you have fun last night?"

"I did. It was interesting." Rachel chuckled. "Thanks again for letting me join."

"Oh, it's my pleasure, isn't it Cherry? We always try to invite the girls who are new to the area. Welcoming arms and all." That was a lie.

"Very thoughtful of you."

"How are you liking it here?"

"It's stunning. My mother always liked it here, so Dad thought we should come and stay, experience a small part of her. My grandparents have a house here, so we bought near them. Since my mother died, they've been a bit sentimental." Rachel answered the question like she was talking about a pair of shoes she'd bought, not a parent she'd lost. I didn't know how to take that.

"I noticed you have a younger brother."

"Yeah." Rachel swallowed hard. "I do."

"Will you be invoking the fifth rule?"

"Yeah, he's only seventeen."

"That's good." Cait nodded. "Anyway, part of the reason for my visit is to talk to you, Cherry, and make sure you're planning to bring that guy from your table last night."

Rachel looked horrified. I was hardly shocked that Cait was going for the throat and not pussyfooting around a little more. But she could do whatever she wanted.

"I wasn't planning on it. When I asked him last night, he said he wasn't interested if Andy couldn't partake in the festivities."

"Oh, how disappointing. Well—" She paused, like she needed this moment of thought. "Why don't you bring Andy then. The more the merrier." She flashed that winning smile.

My blood boiled as my mother patted me on the knee.

"What an honor to have the queen of clubs personally invite my baby boy." She winked at Cait.

I threw up a little in my mouth.

Rachel gave my mother a dire look, not aware of our evil scheme.

"Of course." I grinned back, doing the dance. "I know that would make Andy happy. And Ashley would like to meet new people; it's hard being in an unfamiliar place. What better way for him to make genuine friendships than by introducing him to genuine people." I might have sounded like a vise grip was around at my throat. Really it was an evil python who had me in her clutches. Only I had to remind myself I had a secret weapon this time.

My mother clapped her hands. "Excellent. What an excellent match. Ashley is a wonderful young man. Just last night when we were dining with him, I had thought he and Cheryl had taken a liking to each other. But being chosen by the queen of clubs is a far better prospect than that."

That being *me.*

Me being the lesser prospect.

For the guy I actually liked.

I wanted to tell my mother that I might as well date Ashley first, as Cait was such a fan of my sloppy seconds. I wanted to rub that in Cait's slimy face.

But I didn't.

Not yet.

Not yet.

I whispered that mantra to myself over and over and over.

"I actually was asking Ashley to come to be my date," I said weakly. I had to like him so she would know she was stealing him.

"Oh, interesting. We'll see, I guess." Cait reached across, moving with elegance and an unhealthy amount of confidence, to place her hand on my arm. "Good luck." She put her iced tea on the table and got up. "See you girls tonight at my house." She smiled at my mother. "Have a lovely afternoon, ladies, Mrs. Kennedy."

"Yes, I will." My mother beamed at her. "You as well, dear."

Cait left, and I contemplated screaming.

Rachel and I sat there, equally as frozen and angry as my mother was elated.

"It really is exciting that Cait is showing such an interest in our family," Mom said. "That means as long as Ashley does right by her, we'll all be in good graces with the Landrys. They really are one of the most influential families out here. You make sure you let her have him. It will be better for everyone in the long run, dear. But on that note, I need to take my leave as well. It's too hot out here." She got up and staggered into the house, humming to herself.

"I don't understand. He was all over you, and you barely fought for him?" Rachel sounded disgusted. "She's insane. The balls on her."

"Yeah." I decided it was time. "Why don't we get in the pool and sit in the shade. I have a story to tell you."

"Okay." Her eyes widened. "Why do I have the worst feeling in the world about this story?" Rachel asked.

"You have sharp instincts." I sighed. We got in the pool, and I started at the beginning: my first year in Fling Club and losing my virginity at a party, drunk and being slobbered on by an equally drunk guy. I told her about the pressure and the misery that I had lied to myself about, all for the sake of fitting in.

And finally I told her about my recent experience and the plan concocted by my evil-mastermind siblings.

Her eyes narrowed and widened in horror and then delight.

"Wow, Cherry. Things just got a whole lot more interesting around here. Count me in. I know you're not asking me to help, but I want to."

"Thanks." I was relieved. "I haven't told any of the other members, since I can't be sure if they'd be on my side of this or not. Everyone fears Cait. She's vile."

"I can't believe she slept with your boyfriend. This isn't high school anymore. That was a real relationship, and she ruined it."

"She only gets fifty percent of the blame, and how real was it if he was also willing to cheat?"

"At least Ashley punched him in the face. I wish I'd seen that."

"Yeah." I pressed my lips together and relived the moment. "It was pretty satisfying."

"So, this Ashley guy?" She wrinkled her nose. "I really thought he was British. He's a good actor."

"Well, he's from Scottish descent. His parents live in England now, and he did, too, until he was twelve. I don't honestly know. He's cagey about his family. Something's wrong with his godfather. He's sick or something."

"I see. You two seem fairly cozy for this all being a ploy, though," she pried.

"He's nice."

"You're such a liar. He's gorgeous, and I saw you last night. And I saw him. He likes you too. The moment Cait left that bathroom, he was worried. He was watching the door like a hawk." She nudged me. "You should make him be your fling."

"I'm paying him, so in that case, I would literally be forcing him to date me."

"So, don't pay him. Tell him you like him and dating you is worth more than money." She snickered.

"But I think he's counting on the money for school or something. I already hired him. He's not from a wealthy family like we are."

"Yeah, that's awkward. Makes it a little seedy. Well, when this is all over and he's paid in full, you should totally go out with him."

"Yeah, maybe." I pretended like the thought hadn't already crossed my mind. "Except he's going to fake date Cait all summer. Might ruin it a bit for me."

"I guess so. She's wretched." She swam across the pool and hopped out.

Ella came walking out on the deck. "Why was the queen of the bitches here?"

"Cait came to tell us that Ashley is going to be her summer fling, which I used as leverage to get Andy in tonight."

"Excellent. Look at you go." Ella started laughing. "Poor Ashley. He won't know what hit him."

"I told her about the plan." I pointed at Rachel.

"The more like minds in on this, the better. I'll gather Andy and Ashley too. We'll have a proper meeting about how this is all going to go down this evening." She almost did the maniacal cackle. Almost.

Chapter Twenty-One

NEW RULES

Cherry

"No more skirting the issues here." Andy gave me an annoyed look with Ryan, Ella, and Ashley looking like his henchmen. "Tell us all the rules. Don't hold anything back. If we're going to make Cait break them, you have to give us all the information."

I wavered, wanting to lie about this. I'd never betrayed the actual rules or any of my so-called sisters.

"Here." Rachel pulled out a piece of paper from her purse and passed it to him and Ashley. Ella and Ryan read it over their shoulders, looking disturbed for the most part. My entire body tensed seeing them read and judge.

"Oh my God." Ashley cocked a dark eyebrow after a couple of minutes and gave me a bewildered stare. "Is this for real? Are you shitting me? When you said Fling Club had rules and we were going to make Cait break them, I had no idea they were this screwed up. You've been doing this every summer?" His disgusted face was back.

"You can't tell anyone you saw it," I said, concerned about maintaining some semblance of secrecy around the club. I didn't want to be the one who outed the rules.

"If I were you two, I wouldn't tell anyone you belong to this." Ryan shook his head slowly. "It's disgusting. Imagine if guys had a club like this? We'd be outed on TV and have harassment charges filed."

"This is what happens when people don't spend their free time constructively. A few more evenings spent in homeless shelters, helping the less fortunate, and maybe we wouldn't be so concerned with getting our rocks off at some fancy-shmancy parties," Andy added.

The four of them read the list over and over, judging us—well, me.

"I just can't believe this," Ashley said after another gander at the piece of paper. "You're right, Andy, this needs to go down."

"So, you aren't part of this at all?" Ryan asked Ella carefully.

"Not a chance. Not my kind of crowd." She winked at me. She didn't see what their reactions were doing to me.

"Okay, let's get down to brass tacks then." Andy folded his arms, his eyes doing the evil sparkly thing again. "Ella's original plan didn't include Rachel and Ryan or a complete breakdown of all the rules. Just ideas on how to make Cait shame herself and slum it a little. Now we'll make sure it incorporates all of us and takes each rule apart at the seams."

It felt like I was making a deal with the devil.

Ella laughed. "This is going to be fun to watch."

Andy folded his arms. "Give us an hour to draw up a new set of plans so everyone gets a part of this." He shook the paper in our faces. "For the record, this is disgusting, and you should be ashamed. It's much worse than I thought." He turned and stalked into the house with Ryan, Ella, and Ashley next to him.

"That was rough." Rachel gave me a grave look. "I wish I'd never gone to the stupid meeting."

"Sorry I brought you." It was the truth. I was sorry.

"It's not your fault. Your mother was never taking no for an answer. I get why you're a part of it."

She said it as I stared at the house, wishing Ashley thought that way. But his expression was breaking my heart.

"At least if Andy and Ella are involved, there's a good chance Cait will go down. They're both geniuses when it comes to maneuvering. It's all evil, though. Especially where Cait is involved." I sat back in my chair, closing my eyes.

We lay in the sun, worrying, until finally Ryan came back out with Ella, both of them completely oblivious to the level of stress I was facing. But it was nice to see Ella having fun. I'd never seen her like this with anyone. It was weird and unnerving. I was waiting for her to turn on him, maybe go full-on blood-sucking vampire while spouting dark poetry.

Instead, he seemed to soften her.

It was like insta-love.

She saw me watching them and flipped me the bird. And there she was, regular Ella.

"Ladies." Henry strolled out to the patio. "The young men wish to speak to you."

We followed Henry into the house to my father's library. The coolness of the house was shocking against my sun-kissed skin.

The guys were seated at my father's mahogany desk, reading over a piece of paper when Rachel and I walked in. Henry left the library, closing the door.

"Hey." We strolled over.

"Hey," Andy answered without lifting his face from the paper. Only Ashley gave us a look, and it wasn't the one I wanted.

"You done?" Rachel asked. "We have to get ready for this party soon, so we need a full plan."

"Yeah. We just need to discuss some of the things we want you to do. We'll start at the beginning and sabotage the club from the inside, as was Ella's idea. Rule one: if he doesn't belong to the country club, he doesn't belong in your pants." Andy nodded his head at Ashley. "He's her MIT fling of shame. Once she's knee-deep in him, we'll out him on a chosen date."

"Okay." I hesitantly gave Rachel a look.

Ashley's eyes sparkled as he spoke. "Rule two: never say the *L* word, unless it's *loser*. I particularly like this one. I'll get her to tell me she loves me. I'll record it. Simple. Easy."

I stifled a laugh.

"You doubt my mad skills with women?" He scoffed at my doubt as a slow smile crested his lips. "Trust me. I've got this one."

"Okay." I put my hands up. "Whatever."

Rachel gave him a look of uncertainty. "You did see her, right? Blonde hair, cold blue eyes, *bitch* written all over every inch of her, including her Louis Vuitton heels?"

"Anyway . . ." Ashley sighed and continued. "Rule three. No reheating a sister's old leftovers. That one is easy. Andy being a fling guy now and Cait's ex means whoever gets him is reheating. And Cait allowed it."

"Rule four: hos before bros; whoever sees him first gets him. Obviously her stealing Ashley from you is a violation of that code." Andy spoke loud and clear in my direction.

"Rule five: see rule four. She's allowing someone to date me. We just have to act like it was blackmail so she could have Ashley." Andy sounded too excited about this. "We'll have Ella and Ryan doing most of our surveillance. She won't even see them."

"Okay," I agreed, getting less and less comfortable with the idea.

Andy cleared his throat. "Rule six: Minimize couple's time. This isn't courting, it's socializing. That's easy. You spend as much time just the two of you as you can, while we record it. Between me, Ella, and

Ryan we shouldn't miss anything. I want her fawning over you to win you over. Grumpy guy at the bar." He winked at Ashley, who wrinkled his nose as Andy continued.

"Rule seven: act the part, lady in the streets and freak in the sheets. I think we should try to catch her with whomever she cheats on Ashley with. Ruin her that way."

As Andy finished that sentence, my entire body went pins and needles. "This is too mean." I was losing my nerve, even after seeing her and how rude she was to me. Catching her cheating or slumming meant photos or video. I didn't think I could invade someone else's privacy like that.

"Stop being a baby, Cherry." Andy scoffed and continued, "Rule eight: We don't pay. Go Dutch and you're out. Ashley is going to start the constant Dutch treat on their first date. Or just forget his wallet and let her pay. We'll record it."

"Right, I won't pay for a single thing of hers and try to get footage of it," Ashley agreed.

"Rule nine: protect yourself; that means your body and your reputation." Andy grinned up at me. "Oh, her reputation will be blown to smithereens, you can guarantee that. Last but not least, rule ten. Everything has an expiration date. Playtime ends August 31. By the end of this mission, there won't be a single relationship left intact."

They were sadists.

Cait, and all of her minions, my friends, didn't stand a chance. I just hoped I did.

Chapter Twenty-Two

Rule One

Cherry

As the guys left the house, I felt sick.

My stomach ached, not just from the setup of the plan, but also from the lack of eye contact Ashley and I had made. From the moment he'd seen the rules—rules I'd lived by for summers on end—he'd cooled off. He never even said goodbye.

I hated that I'd been so cocky and callous about the club before, laughing about the rules with my friends. Playing the guys instead of being played was how we saw it. We justified our actions with that.

But it hadn't saved me from heartache in the end. In fact, it had brought it on full force.

And now I felt both broken and ashamed.

The guys climbed into their car and drove off, both of them visibly disgusted.

"Is it just me, or did they all seem really harsh suddenly?" Rachel leaned against the doorframe and watched them go.

"Yeah, they're grossed out." I sighed.

"Your brother gave you the most epic of horrified looks. I don't know if a guy has ever glared at me like that before," Rachel muttered.

"My brother is a shithead. So, I don't take that personally." But Ashley was a whole other matter.

"I'm gonna go get ready for tonight. I'll meet ya there?" She offered me a look.

"Yeah. I'll wait outside for you so we can go in together."

"Okay." She swallowed hard. "This is the right choice; seeing that mean-ass queen bee on her throne was painful. But watching her waltz in here, asking for the guy who visibly likes you, was a whole other thing. We need to crush her."

"I know." I tried my best to wear my crush-other-girls face, but I didn't really have one, so I had no idea how it appeared.

She waved and walked out the front door, leaving me here alone and more than a little scared.

I texted Andy constantly, ensuring he was completely ready for the cocktail party that was actually more like a cock-and-tail party. The guys would come, drink, socialize, and then leave. Girls would decide who their fling was. And the summer would begin.

Andy was in charge of getting himself and Ashley ready at the Weinbergs' house before picking me up on the way to Cait's. He'd canceled dinner with Dad, saying they needed time to mentally prepare for the party. Which I was certain Dad got.

I finished dressing and hurried downstairs.

"You look wonderful." Mom hurried over, beaming. She was also dressed up.

"Thanks. Where are you guys off to?"

"Since your brother canceled dinner with us, your father and I are going to dinner with the Ramirez family, from his office."

"Nice." I smiled politely, wondering how much of all of this she actually liked and if she was ever real. Like, did she take her earrings off at night and the persona with them? I'd never really seen anything but the act. I assumed it had become who she was. Even with the lights out. It made me sad. Especially now, seeing it for what it was. It also gave me the weirdest feeling in my life. Like this was the future I had wanted before Ashley. This was the woman I could have grown into. Maybe Griffin had done me the biggest favor of my life by cheating on me that night and saving me from myself. I should be thanking him instead of loathing him.

A knock at the door saved me.

Henry opened it, revealing Ashley.

"Hey." I was nervous in front of him again.

"Hey." He had lost the light and the sparkle. But he looked handsome—more than that. He was perfect. So perfect he made every inch of me ache with a need to fix things between us. It had seemed so easy at the Weinbergs' house, but now it was like he was back to being the guy I first met. Maybe it was for the best. It would be easier to ignore each other than own to the validity of his opinion of me or watch him and Cait all summer.

"You guys ready?" I asked.

"Yeah." He didn't sound ready.

"Well, you kids have fun tonight." Mother smiled brightly. "And remember what I said about the queen of clubs," she said, nodding at Ashley.

When she waltzed out of the room, Ashley paused and stared, like maybe he was going to say something, but he didn't. Instead, he glared. His eyes spoke the words, telling me how disappointed he was. Telling me that he couldn't believe I was ever a part of something so despicable. He said everything he needed to without ever parting his lips.

"We should go," I whispered, already conflicted enough to last a lifetime. I didn't need more disapproval.

I had enough of my own.

He offered me his hand, not like he was the light, but like he was my pretend boyfriend and we were going to rock faking it enough so Cait would for sure want him. Being a sucker for punishment, I took it. I let him envelop me with warmth and awkwardness.

He led me to the car where Andy was hanging out with Hans, laughing about something.

Ashley sat up front, and the guys joked the entire ride over. Neither of them seemed as if they were nervous about how this was going to go. Or like they gave a shit about me at all.

My whole body was a ball of nerves and tension.

I was a mess and wanted it to be over.

Revenge wasn't nearly as much fun as I had imagined it would be. It was stressful.

When we got to the party, we were second to last to show up and met with Rachel in the driveway.

The guys hung back as we hurried inside. "Cait looks pissed," Rachel muttered as we grabbed drinks.

"Ignore her. She'll just rub it in that we should have been here earlier, but she won't risk being mean to me. Not until she has announced that she's claiming my guest. Then she'll attack. We're safe for one night."

I greeted everyone and made my way over to the girl I intended to see: Sarah. "Hey!"

"Hey!" She hugged me; it was more fake than normal. Cait was no doubt watching us, and Sarah knew. She was Cait's minion when she had to be.

"How's it going?" I smiled wide, batting my lashes.

"Awesome. Excited for the start of Fling Club. What about you?" She nudged me.

"Good. I have my guy all picked out. He's a friend of Andy's who's over for the summer from Oxford." I pointed at Ashley, even pausing to appreciate him.

"No way. Awesome. Griffin who?" She laughed.

"Exactly." I laughed, too, like a Stepford Wife. "And Andy is the guy I brought for donation."

"What?" Sarah's eyes widened. "Holy shit, but isn't he one of Cait's exes?" She furrowed her brow, losing her cool exterior. "And your brother."

"I know. That's the cost of entering Ashley in the mix. And I really want him in the mix." I said everything Ella had told me to.

"Well, shit, if your brother is in, then he's mine!" She winked and sauntered off, heading straight for Andy to claim him. She had always had a massive thing for him.

I strolled back to Rachel, nudging her. "The bait is set. Sarah is going to pick Andy, and she now knows I want Ashley for my own. Which means that when Cait steals him, it's actually stealing. I have a witness. Besides you."

"I can't believe she's such a hateful bitch." She sounded disgusted but managed to smile through it.

"She is."

"Okay. What next?" She didn't sound so sure about being here.

"Now we pick our guys." I started scanning the room.

We ambled around, saying hello and introducing Rachel to people until Cait tapped her glass delicately, drawing the attention to herself.

When we all stopped talking she smiled wide and couldn't have looked phonier. "Welcome to Fling Club! As everyone has finally arrived, we can get to the business at hand." Her gaze drifted to the men all standing at the back of the grand room. "Gentlemen, you will have an hour to introduce yourselves to the ladies, show interest if you will. Then we'll ask you to leave while we make our final decisions. Don't forget to try and win that lady over. If you aren't picked as a fling, you won't be able to come to the functions this summer. Let the games begin." She half curtseyed and sipped from her champagne.

"She's such an attention whore," I muttered, and turned, noticing Ashley staring at me. My insides clenched as I sighed. "I'm going to go and chat him up so it looks like he's mine." I wished I sounded more excited.

"Yeah, I'm coming. I don't want to be alone here. It's creepy." Rachel followed as I made my way to where Andy and Ashley were eating and drinking and laughing with Sarah, like this was a fun night.

"Hi." I couldn't be casual if my life depended on it. Not tonight.

"Hi." Ashley grinned, but he was still cooled off. "I guess it's time to get into character, huh?" he whispered. "Let's go outside to chat." He slipped his arm into mine, overwhelming one whole side of my body with warmth from his, and led me to the deck doors. We strolled to the pool deck and gazebo like this was a romantic encounter.

I had seen him dressed up already—I'd picked dress clothes for him myself—but seeing him in action wearing them was so much better. He was beautiful in the garden lights.

Leading him away from everyone else to a dark corner of the deck near the exit to the side yard, we sat down and I leaned in, whispering. "Can we talk about this?" I asked, wishing this weren't how things had turned out.

"Which part of this?" He sounded annoyed.

"The part where you're suddenly treating me like the worst human being you've ever met?"

"Worst?" He shook his head. "I never thought that. Weakest, maybe." He maintained the cold stare.

"Weakest?" My voice cracked as I got up. "That's what you think of me?"

"Well, explain that list of shit to me in a way that doesn't make you look like a spineless follower. I mean I knew it was bad, but seeing the list changes things." He was angry, visibly so. "Do you have a string in the back I can pull to make you say all the things you're supposed to?"

My tense stomach lurched as the verbal blow struck. Trembling, I stepped back. "You know what, we don't have to do this. She saw you and I together. It's good enough."

"You're right, I'm just the help." He got up too. "Just like you said."

"Have a fun summer. I hope you enjoy all of it," I seethed, looking up at him. "That goes for the twenty grand you have no problem taking to get laid by a knockout, Mr. Upstanding Morality."

"Are you upset? Did I actually offend you? Do you offend? Is that one of your preprogrammed emotions?"

"You're rude. You go around acting like you hate me because you're so much better. Well, *I* hate to remind *you* that you're not so innocent in this game. Last time I checked, you had free will."

"Hate you?" He followed me. "Why do you care what I think of you or what anyone thinks of you for that matter? Why can't you be your own person and choose for yourself how you're going to be? Why do you have to follow that stupid list and pick guys out of a lineup?"

"Because I'm stupid. I'm a selfish, pathetic girl. Isn't that what you want to hear? I'm so bored and spoiled that I can't help but be silly?" I spun and glared. "Don't you see? You win. You're right. I'm a pathetic loser who never formed her own identity or made her own decisions or had her own ideas. I let my friend, who isn't really my friend, run my life and make me do terrible things so I wouldn't be shunned. I dated a jerk who mistreated me because he was the right fit. That relationship wasn't me deciding anything; I was a lemming. Are you happy?" I said everything I'd ever wanted to and burst into tears. Not sad tears, angry ones. I ran around the side of the house and headed for the car.

Realizing I didn't have a clue which car belonged to us and I didn't see Hans, I groaned and continued past the vehicles lining the massive driveway.

The valets appeared confused, but I kept going. I texted Ella to come and get me and kept walking, kicking my shoes off onto the side of the road and carrying on barefoot.

"Cherry!" Ashley called.

I started running again.

"Cherry! Wait!" He was gaining on me.

I would have sped up, but being barefoot made the running harder.

"Wait!" he demanded, gaining on me enough to grab my arm and spin me. "Wait!" He was huffing the same way I was. "What are you doing?"

"Go away. I don't need your judgment. You think I don't feel stupid enough already? You think I don't see what a moron I am? Thank you for so kindly pointing out all the things I'm doing wrong." I backed away from him. "Go back to the party and claim your prize so you can dance for my brother the way I do for Cait." I waved him off and spun around again, breaking into another run.

"For God's sake, can you please stop running?" He grabbed me again, spinning me yet again, hurting my feet. "I'm not judging you. I mean I am, but not the way you think." He stepped closer. "I like you. A lot. I like the you I think you are. The you at the Weinbergs' who plays chess and makes strong drinks and laughs until two in the morning."

"Leave me alone." I moved back, but he stepped closer, closing the distance between us and pulling me into him.

"No." He held me tight. "I won't leave you alone. I don't want to. I want you to see the potential I see. Yes, you're spoiled and bored and lacking motivation, but that doesn't make you silly or stupid or pathetic. It makes you young and confused and lost. It means you're unsure of yourself. All your life you've clearly had the wrong people influencing you." He brushed my tears away from my eyes and stared deeply into them. "And I want to be someone who helps you correct those things."

"Why?" I tried to pull back, but he held me too tight. "You don't even know me."

"Because I think you're amazing. And you're wrong; I do know you. The last two weeks have been the weirdest time in my life. But getting to know you has been the best part. You're funny and sweet and easygoing. You're a worrywart and obsessed with dessert even if you pretend you only eat keto. More than dessert, you're obsessed with everyone else's opinion, when the only opinion you should consider is your own." He lit up as he spoke. "And maybe mine."

"I don't like your opinion of me." I blinked another tear down my cheek.

"You don't know my opinion of you. From the moment I met you, I thought about you. Watching you stare at that bun like it was going to be your last meal was hilarious. A girl after my own heart, I thought. A girl who eats whatever she wants and does whatever she wants. But then I saw you at your town house, and I realized the girl I saw was stifled by the world of the rich. This you, this one here on this stupid fucking shore, is fake. It's an act. This isn't you. That girl contemplating eating both those pastries: that was you. The girl who got mad that I skinny-shamed her: that was you. You were funny and sarcastic, until you got home with your mom, and you've hardly shown your face."

"Why would I, when all you've done is act like you're disgusted with me?" I pushed him away.

"If you saw I was part of a secret group of guys who misused women and treated them like property, how would you feel? Assuming you have feelings for me the way I do for you? How would you feel?"

"I—" I paused, stuck on what to say after his confession. He liked me.

"It's terrible to play games like this, Cherry. The girl who invented this club is clearly a selfish and damaged person. She's so obviously jaded. Why would you want to be like that? Why would you ever let that girl determine who you are?"

"I don't know." It wasn't a lie. I just didn't have an answer. And I didn't need one.

Headlights saved me.

My sister was speeding down the road to me. Her headlights flashed on us as she slowed.

"That's my ride," I said, trying to mask the emotion in my voice.

"You're leaving? What about selection?" His eyes widened.

"I can't do this. You're right. The girl I am here is fake, and I don't think I can put on an act anymore." I pulled away from him and hurried to the car, then climbed in. "Good luck with Cait!" I said, before slamming the door.

"Do I dare guess what just happened?" Ella muttered.

"No. Drive, please." I lowered my head, unable to meet his gaze as I left him in the middle of the road, in the middle of a conversation, possibly in the middle of him confessing feelings.

I didn't know how to take any of it.

I should have been angry but my rational mind whispered that his worst crime was seeing through my bullshit and my phony-ass act.

He called me out on it.

He scolded me like he knew me, and I wanted to say he didn't, he couldn't. But it felt like maybe he did.

He was real, but a type of realness I didn't know how to react to.

"Are you being a weirdo again?"

"What?" I turned, offended, not just by her, but in general. "No." That might have been a lie. I didn't even know myself anymore.

"You are!" She glared back. "You're doing that thing where you flip out in your head and don't know what to do, and don't tell anyone what you're thinking or feeling. And it makes you look nuts. Your eyes are darting around the car, and you're sweating. You look like the bomb is about to go off any second and you're bracing because you planted it."

"I literally feel like that," I admitted, defeated. "It feels like I'm waiting for the attack, always. Waiting for the bottom to drop out."

"You have anxiety, Cherry. You always have. For whatever reason, being on your own, making your own choices, stresses you out. Like Griffin. You can't tell me you loved him, that you loved that he was everything and you were on his arm, taken care of. And now that guy back there, Ashley; he seems into you, but you can't see that because he would give you too much latitude to be yourself. And God forbid you tried to find out who you really are."

"I can't do this right now. That's not it. Just stop."

"Why?" She laughed at me. "Am I triggering your sensitivities? Is this traumatizing you? You need to stop and take a whiff of the reality in the air and harden up a little. You're not Mom. You're not Dad. You don't have to be like anyone else. You can just be you."

"*I don't know me! Okay! I don't know who I am or what I want! Fuck!*" I screamed, pounding a hand on the dashboard.

"Well, hello, sister. Look who just woke up from her dream state." Ella grinned. "Did the computer running your system finally short-circuit?"

"Fuck you, Ella!" I jumped out of the car as she stopped for a stop sign and ran away from her.

But Ella wasn't Ashley. She didn't follow me. She just shouted, "Get lost, Cherry. It'll do you some good to have to solve something on your own!"

I hated her.

I hated everyone.

My feet ached as I slowed to a march and then a stroll, defeated. Eventually I ended up sitting at a bench in a neighborhood where the yards were smaller, staring at the concrete because I couldn't take another step.

It was too early for a midlife crisis and too late for a temper tantrum. So, what the hell was going on with me?

The bench wasn't comfy, and the air wasn't warm anymore, but I started to relax, staring up at the sky.

His words drowned out everything else.

He was so right.

I was faking it here.

This wasn't me.

I contemplated who I was at all my different houses.

At school I was fun and yet controlled. I ate a certain way and acted a certain way. I didn't gossip about other people, and I sure as hell kept my own name out of the rumor mill.

At the beach house, I was a fun party girl, but still controlled. I ate a certain way, and while I partied, I never rocked the boat or caused any waves. I was fun, but never too fun.

At home in the city I was a little freer, lost in the crowds.

I ate what I wanted.

I did what I wanted; no one was looking.

I realized that was it.

No one was watching me in New York.

And even better, at the Weinbergs' house, I was relaxed. There had been no expectations.

My mind blanked, and I tried to find the moment it went wrong. Where I went wrong. But if I was being honest, my life from the start, the very beginning, had been off course.

Even worse than Ashley being right, Ella was right too.

I hated that.

But she was.

I didn't like making choices or having to be alone.

Even now, here in the middle of the road, I felt the need to find a herd to belong to.

Me being alone made me vulnerable and unsafe.

But the truth of the matter was that where I was sitting couldn't have been safer. It was a patrolled neighborhood with guards and police and security like nowhere else in the world. I might as well have been in a gated community.

The lack of safety was inside of me.

The lack of decision-making skills was where the fear came from.

I couldn't be trusted to protect myself.

What the fuck was that?

Why did I feel that way?

I needed to see my shrink again.

Overanalyzing and tracing my insane behavior back to my mother in a Freudian way made my eyes heavy.

My head tilted to the side, jerking back upright every time it felt like maybe I was losing the war on staying awake.

I blinked rapidly until the blinks grew longer and longer, and then grew too long.

I wasn't sure if I dreamed or if I just lay there, sort of sleeping like a homeless person in an area that had no homeless people. Unless you counted metaphorical homelessness as a state of desperation, and in that case, I was definitely in need of assistance.

Chapter Twenty-Three

THE SELECTION

Ashley

Frustrated with the girl driving away and desperately contemplating running after her, I found my train of thought interrupted by Andy shouting.

"Ashley!" he called out.

"Yeah?" I spun, feeling dragged in two directions. One meant I got to see my dad and could afford to spend whatever was left of the summer with him. The other meant I could take care of my heart.

"Selection is starting in, like, fifteen minutes. We have to put in one more appearance. Where the fuck is Cherry?"

"Gone." I sighed, defeated.

"Gone where?" Andy scowled as he got closer.

"She's done, mate. She's not cut out for this kind of thing. She's a mess. Ella just picked her up. She's on a tear."

"Oh, great. She chooses this moment to lose her fucking mind and come out of the Stepford coma? Really?" He grunted and started walking back. "Well, the plan still works if you and I go back. We'll tell Cait that Cherry wasn't feeling well."

I followed him back to the party, past the drivers and valets who were gathered, laughing and smoking in a circle. I almost wished I were headed toward them and not the lion's den that was Cait's house.

Rachel was glaring at us both from the opposite wall when we got back. Two guys were talking to her. She excused herself and hurried over. "Where is Cherry?"

"She's gone AWOL," Andy said in a hushed tone.

"Great, what do we do?"

"You go tell Cait she's had to leave, that she's very sick. Cherry will have to make her selection tomorrow."

"And that will give Cait a better reason for grabbing me." I shuddered. The blonde was gorgeous, no denying it. But she had the craziest eyes I'd ever seen. She was downright awful. And her skin-deep beauty was showing. Not my kind of girl. In fact, I was half tempted to walk and not take the money. I could finish school a little slower and work a couple of jobs. I could delay working for NASA. I could do all sorts of things. And every ounce of my being screamed for me to leave and go find that crazy redhead and kiss her until she understood what I felt for her.

"Andy, introduce me to your friend." The blonde spoke from behind me. Her shrill voice clawed at my flesh as she talked; I'd know her voice anywhere.

"Ashley Jardine, this is Caitlyn Landry. Ashley's an old friend from Oxford. And Cait is an old ex from a time when I was sexually confused and thought I liked soulless girls."

"Andy." I scowled, trying not to laugh while defending the horrible person who was feigning hurt feelings, like she had any.

"That's fine, Andy and I go way back." She offered a tiny manicured hand. "Cait." She smiled, batted her lashes, and acted demure.

"Ashley." I shook her hand, not kissing it. I could tell from the way she had it out, she thought she was the bloody queen.

"English. Where from?"

"Warwickshire. Stratford-upon-Avon."

"Oh, near Shakespeare's birthplace?"

"It is his birthplace," I corrected.

"Right." She laughed delicately. What a phony. Like she had me convinced she was a flower petal with all her silky femininity. As if I couldn't see the claws and fangs and horns.

A blind man wouldn't even have found her attractive. Maybe especially not.

She was a man-eater.

The worst kind of person.

I was never going to be able to keep this up. My only saving grace was that Andy said she would love a grumpy-guy-at-the-bar act, and if I could pull off one impression in front of this girl, it was that one.

"And you're here visiting the Kennedys? Are you a relation?"

"No." I gave Andy a look as he slunk off with the Sarah girl we were talking to earlier.

"How long are you in America for?"

"The summer. I decided sort of last minute to come. Andy said he was housesitting and would love the company."

"Oh, right, the Weinbergs. Yes, of course. So cold and dark, that house. Don't you think?" She slid an arm into mine, prancing me around the party, talking to me hypnotically, like she wanted me not to notice that I was on display. She was showing everyone she'd claimed me.

But I noticed.

"It is a weird house. The view is bizarre. No view from the main floor. Just dunes."

"Exactly." She smiled wide and laughed like I'd said something funny. She slapped my chest lightly, leaning in. "You're funny."

"Not really." I shrugged. I had to date her, but I didn't have to be nice to her. In fact, the more like dry toast I was, the more likely she was to cheat sooner. Maybe even slum.

"Cherry left," I mentioned. "Did Rachel say anything to you?"

"Yeah, said she was feeling awful. Poor thing. Cherry is such a funny girl. I adore her. Poor thing just got dumped by her boyfriend," she lied. "She really needs this selection." She acted like she was doing Cherry a favor, pointing to a guy I assumed was a male model. He was jacked. And handsome in a way that could make me sexually confused. The blank stare on his face as he spoke to three girls said a lot about him. He was bored, or he was forced to be here, like me.

"I'm going to give Cherry him, since she's sick and missing selection. He's amazing. Total gentleman. Handsome. Wealthy. Well connected. All the things Cherry's looking for in a man." She smiled coyly. "I mean, aren't we all?"

"I guess so." I was boring myself.

She giggled again as an alarm went off in her pocket. "Oh, time to pick." She opened her eyes up wide, staring into mine, like she was again hypnotizing me.

"Okay then." I patted her on the arm and walked away. Andy was dying laughing, pretending to be talking to Rachel, but I knew he heard us.

"Gentlemen, it's time for you to leave. Thank you so much for trying out this year. I wish you all the luck in being picked. Good night. Ladies, please stay for selection." She pointed to the door of her massive mansion, offering me, specifically, a little wave.

I followed Andy out, desperate to get to the Kennedys' and find Cherry.

"Oh, man, that was amazing. She was really working you, and you looked like you might die any second."

"I was dying. She's crazy. You can smell it on her. That's the kind of girl who cuts your balls off in the night because you wronged her in some small way. Can we go to your house? I think we should go see if Cherry's okay," I said as I found Hans and jumped in the car.

"Of course," Andy agreed.

We waited in a massive backup for the limos to leave the party, and when we finally got onto the main road leading to the Kennedys', I was desperate to get to the house.

"Cherry was a mess tonight." Andy lifted an eyebrow. "I want to be pissed at her for almost ruining the plan, losing it. But at the same time, I'm pumped she's finally getting angry and losing her mind. She needed to. She's been like a ginger zombie Barbie for a long time."

"I just hope she's okay." I tapped my foot.

As Hans pulled to a stop, I dove out, rushing for the house.

Ella was walking with her phone and a cookie, dressed in pajamas and sporting a weird look when I burst in, not even knocking. "Where is she?"

"How should I know?"

"You picked her up."

"I left her on the road. She was being nuts."

"Seriously?" I turned and ran back to Hans. "Can you drive me around? Cherry's out there somewhere." My heart was racing. She was upset and likely all alone in a dress on the side of the road.

"Of course."

I jumped in the front seat, giving Andy a look. "I'll meet you back at the Weinbergs'. I need to make sure she's all right."

"Okay, man. I'll take my car over. Thanks, Hans!" He waved and walked inside.

They were so nonchalant about the fact Ella had left Cherry on the side of the road.

We drove for hours up and down the road until finally we came upon her.

She was sleeping on a park bench. I hated her brother and her sister for a whole minute as I leaped from the car, gripping her to me and lifting her delicately from the cold bench. She looked intact. No wounds or blood or signs of a struggle.

What kind of family did that sort of thing to each other?

Who were these people? Maybe it was a good thing I was here. Cherry needed someone to care about her and get her through this. I couldn't justify taking twenty thousand to teach some rich bitch a lesson, but I could justify it to help another one learn to see herself the way I saw her. This girl—she was worth it.

Chapter Twenty-Four

An Indecent Proposal

Cherry

I woke to warmth. It surrounded me, wrapping around me as breath tickled my cheeks. I snuggled into it, expecting one thing but getting another.

I thought for sure I was in bed with Griffin and he was spooning me.

Instead someone else whispered, "Cherry. You have to grip my neck to sit up."

My eyes shot open, and I saw a face I didn't know, not at first. My body went to pins and needles. My lips parted to scream. His hand covered my mouth, and he pulled back, shaking his head.

"Don't scream. You'll wake your mom up," Ashley whispered. "And I really don't like your mom."

"Where are we?" I glanced around, seeing the interior of a car. I was in a car. Whose car?

"We're at your house, parked out front. Hans and I have been looking for you for hours." He sounded annoyed, which was worse with his accent.

"You don't have to keep talking like you're English." I yawned and wondered what kind of dream this was.

"Well, thing is, this is my actual accent. I sound American because I make myself talk like that. You're sleepy. I already told you, I do it to try to blend in. This *is* my normal relaxed way of speaking. So, I hope you don't mind that I'm going to continue talking naturally after just saving your bloody arse from the middle of suburban hell."

"Whatever." I blinked and tried to get my bearings. I gripped him and sat up, eventually standing on shaky legs and waiting for my body to get signals from my brain to walk inside.

"It's not whatever. You were sleeping on a bench. You're lucky it was me who found you. Your family is insane. They left you out there." He paused on our walk to the house. "We need to finish our conversation. I think you're misunderstanding me."

"I don't want to." I rubbed my eyes, regretting it the moment the sting of mascara filled a watery eye. "I want sleep." As far as I was concerned, I was still sleeping.

"We will later then. Let's get you inside." He led me to the house.

At the front door he tapped lightly, still holding me. I let him. Not just because he was warm and I was freezing, but also because there was a chance I might sway and fall over. I was practically sleeping on my feet.

"No one's up, except poor Hans. The man must be exhausted." I glanced back at the sun just starting to lighten the day. It had to be five in the morning. I reached forward and opened the door. "We don't lock it."

"That's nuts."

"We have a gate and a guard, and we live in the safest place on earth." I gave him a weird look. "Thanks for the ride."

"You mean rescue." He softened, and the worried stare changed to relief. "Have breakfast with me."

"I'm sleeping through breakfast."

"Brunch."

"No." I didn't even know why I was saying no at this point. I was being difficult on purpose. I hated that he was right about me, and I was punishing us both like a child.

"Dinner. Coffee. Snack?" He cracked a sleepy smile.

"Just come inside," I relented, speaking with a frog in my throat; likely he'd jumped in during my park bench nap. I grabbed Ashley's hand, leading him into the house. I closed the door and crept across the great entrance to the rounded double staircase. We hurried upward, him tugging slightly, like he wasn't sure about this at all.

When we got to my room, my wing of the third floor, I pulled him in and closed the door. Light filtered in by the sides of the curtains, giving us just enough to see each other's faces.

"Just stay with me. I don't want to talk about it all. Just stay," I whispered.

Today, I would start making decisions for myself. And it all started with taking a brooding, pain-in-my-ass, sexy-as-hell, Scottish-English-American god to my bed.

He scowled, like he had things to say, but he kept them to himself.

We stared at each other, the tension so thick I could taste it. It was aftershave, beach air, and attraction that had started the moment two sets of eyes met in front of a pastry display.

"I like you too. And you're right about me." I dared to take this a little further. He moved like he was going to kiss me, but I turned and pulled him to my bed. He kicked off his shoes as I dragged off my dress and climbed into the cool sheets in my undergarments. He slipped his pants and shirt off and climbed in after me, wearing his underwear and nothing else. I rolled away from him, letting him drape himself over me, and closed my eyes.

The pillow and the sheets and the comfy bed were nothing compared to the warm body pressed against me.

Sleep came hard and fast, probably because I was already sleeping.

This had to be a dream.

There was no way I'd said he was right about me aloud.

Chapter Twenty-Five

HOOKER

Cherry

I didn't dream, or remember dreams, and I didn't toss or turn. I fell asleep with Ashley pressed into me, and I woke that way.

I recalled dragging him in here, half-asleep and not wanting to be alone, not wanting to be away from him after the weird conversation we'd had. I felt differently about him being here now.

It wasn't that I didn't want him in my bed, pressed against me. It wasn't that I didn't like the feeling of his arm draped across me or the way his breath felt against my ear. It wasn't that I was disappointed in my decision.

It was that I needed more.

I liked all of this, but I wanted so, so much more.

Feeling brave or stupid or adventurous or a combination of them all, I trailed my fingers up his muscled arm, noting he'd placed his hand in front of me on the bed and wasn't actually touching me except where our bodies met.

He was a gentleman, and it made me smile.

I'd invited him into my bed.

I'd taken most of my clothes off in front of him.

I'd essentially given him permission to touch me.

And yet he didn't.

Maybe because he hadn't gotten actual spoken permission.

I liked that too. It was as if I had some control over what he did and didn't do. It was a new feeling for me.

Reaching down, I lifted one of his thick fingers and pulled his hand back, not leaving the embrace but dragging the hand across my body, forcing him to touch the soft skin of my ribs, right below my bra.

I made him rub my skin until he did it on his own, caressing me in a place where people didn't often touch. Guys our age always went for breasts and ass and areas of stimulation. But feeling the fiery touch of a half-sleeping guy on a delicate spot like my bare ribs was magical.

His breath quickened as he pressed himself against me more, his exhales tickling my ear and the firmness of him crushing against the back of me. His fingers dug in, needing more from the tiny place I allowed him to touch, trembling as they fought against the cage they were trapped in.

I pushed my butt back, meeting firmness I'd already noticed. He woke the way most guys did, jacked with testosterone.

He groaned, rubbing himself on me as his fingers made a daring journey south, tiptoeing to my stomach, before he placed a hot, flat palm there and pulled me back into him even more.

His breath became grazes as he ventured from my ear to my neck, blanketing the curve with kisses and warmth.

My breath changed as I opened the space for him, allowing his face in fully. A soft moan escaped my parted lips as his hand continued to creep lower. He didn't dare go under the clothes; maybe that wasn't what this was about. Maybe we were just touching and teasing, and it wasn't going to lead to anything else.

I moved my legs a little, allowing him access, granting him permission to touch the place I suspected he desperately wanted to put himself.

He traced the soft area, gently massaging and tickling until I was the one moving, I was the one forcing his fingers to touch and rub faster, firmer.

My eyes didn't open, my mouth didn't close, and his fingers never entered me, but I was already close. Close to being louder than I should have been at my parents' house. Close to taking the rest of my clothes off and letting him ravage me. Close to saying things I couldn't take back, dirty things I had never said before.

He pressed a little harder, rubbing my clit like he had one too and knew exactly how it needed to be touched. As everything in me pulsed, I tensed and rode the waves he was making, creating heat and pleasure.

Sweat popped from my pores as gasps became moans and breath became words, whispers of *more* and *faster* and *push*.

I finished orgasming and landed back in reality and awkwardness, twitching and shaking my head in disbelief. What was I doing? We hadn't even gone under the clothes yet. We hadn't even kissed.

We hardly knew each other a week, and here I was having better nonsex than the actual sex I'd had over six months with Griffin.

I contemplated turning over, facing Ashley, rectifying at least the kiss.

But he whispered something and did the last thing I ever expected. "Say yes." He dragged my underwear down as he spoke. I didn't turn over or kiss him or move.

Instead I whispered back the thing he requested. "Yes."

He pressed his body against mine again, only slightly altering our position, dragging my butt back more.

My heart fluttered as I wondered what I'd just said yes to. His cock answered the question as he dragged it between my lips, lifting a leg to gain better access, testing the lube I'd made—that he'd helped me make. He pushed himself inside of me, feeling like too much for a second. I clung to my pillow, trying to relax against the invasion and exploration until we were both comfortable.

My pussy clung to him, stretching as he slowly dragged himself in and out, making room for all of him. He didn't speed up right away, so I felt every ridge and detail of what I imagined was a beautiful cock. A huge, beautiful cock.

Never in all my years of having sex, limited experiences at best, had I ever done anything like this.

He gripped my leg and hips, moving us both with gentle strokes, the sort a girl did to herself with a toy. Long and steady, holding himself inside of me for a moment before pulling out again, leisurely.

Ashley kissed my shoulders and neck, groaning into me, whispering sweet everythings. "You feel incredible, Cherry. You're so wet." His breathy words became a soundtrack to the moment. "You're beautiful."

His fingers dug in as his strokes grew faster, harder, and his words became muddled. I couldn't understand them, and eventually I lost them as our grunting and groaning matched. He rolled me onto my stomach, spread my legs wide, and lifted my ass up.

"I need you." I moaned it. "I want you inside of me." I writhed as I said the dirty thing I'd never said before but had always wanted to. "Fuck me."

And he did.

He fucked me hard, pounding himself into me, spanking my ass with his hips.

My eyes shot open as instant pleasure overwhelmed me. "Oh, God!" I shouted, and lowered my face into my pillow, shouting some more. My body convulsed around his, and my breath and moans got stuck in my mouth, unable to leave as everything became about the wave of pleasure overwhelming me.

When I finally did break the seal over my mouth, I moaned into the pillow, certain I didn't know what sex was until this moment.

This geeky, weird, English-Scottish dude I didn't even really know was rocking my world.

And he kept going.

He fucked me like a warrior, like a Spartan. It was camera worthy, and even when he came it sounded savage. I was sorry I missed the show as I shouted into my pillow some more.

His fingers had to be leaving bruises and his hips had to have left welts, but I didn't care. Everything was right in the world.

I fell as he landed on top of me, unable to hold us both up.

"Oh, fuck, Cherry," he whispered breathily into my ear. "Oh, fuck." He kissed the side of my face, kissing me for the first time. His sweat rubbed against mine, and I nodded into it, not even slightly caring about anything in the world.

"Well done," I muttered, not even really sure what to say. What did one say to life-altering sex? Did I clap and offer a tip? Did I thank him?

"You're so beautiful." He kissed my cheek again, nestling in my hair that was everywhere, lingering and inhaling me.

I had nothing to offer back.

I wanted to ask if he was a professional fucker.

I wanted to laugh at myself for even thinking that, but I'd also forgotten the word for fuckers. There was a word, wasn't there?

I wanted to turn around and kiss him, but I was worried he wasn't looking for that. He didn't want kisses and snuggles. He wanted to fuck me from behind and call me out on my shit and then maybe leave.

"Do you have a bathroom in here?"

I nodded against him, noticing my breath was calming, though my heart wasn't.

I was scared of what his next move would be.

If he got up and left, I might die. I might never make another decision again.

Only when he finally pried himself from me and crawled off the bed, he glanced back at me over his muscled shoulder. "You coming?"

"Where?"

"To the shower." He turned around and offered me his hand. "Come on."

"Hooker." The word popped into my mind and out of my mouth.

"What?" He squinted, confused.

"Nothing." I took his hand and let him lift me off the bed.

"Did you call me a hooker?" He laughed and pulled me along.

"No." I shook my head, feeling the heat on my cheeks. "I couldn't remember the name for—" This wasn't improving the situation. "Nothing. Anyway, yes, I am coming to the shower," I answered after briefly panicking, thinking about the fact that I'd never showered with another human being before.

But when he stared in the light of the bathroom, it was the kind of staring a girl wanted, right in my eyes. At one point, while the water was heating up and we were standing awkwardly waiting for there to be something to do beyond not look at each other's bodies too obviously, I thought I heard him sigh.

He opened the large glass door wider and stepped in, offering me a hand again. I took it like we were going to dance in a Disney movie, not that Disney would ever consider making a movie based on what we'd just done.

The warm water poured down on me, drowning me and hardly getting him wet. I hadn't realized how tall he was. I covered my breasts, shyly. It felt strange being naked in the shower, being stared at by him after he had stripped me so bare in conversation last night.

I stepped to the side so he could get in the water; there was no way I was washing the important stuff in front of him. He wasn't modest about that, though. He started soaping up, using my flowery body wash, cleaning what I confirmed to be a beautiful cock right in front of me. He lifted his arms and washed his hairy armpits and possibly even the crack of his ass.

There was no response for someone cleaning himself in front of you.

So I stared, watching the way his muscles flexed. He wasn't ripped like a body builder was, but he was fit. Very fit for a nerdy engineering student.

"Do you work out?" I asked, blatantly staring at him.

"Yeah." He laughed. "Everyone works out to some degree. You have to. Robotics engineering can be a lot of sitting. Do you?"

"Yeah. I do yoga and of course run in the park."

"Yeah, I noticed last night. You're a great runner."

"Keeps me skinny," I said, cracking a grin.

"Shut up." He laughed harder. "I meant weights."

"I don't lift weights; yoga only."

"Well, whatever you're doing, it's working."

"You're really good at—" The words fell out, and I paused, scared of where I was taking this. Was I complimenting his fucking? Was I that weird? My eyes darted to the bedroom the same moment his did.

His cheeks flushed, maybe the same color as mine. "So are y—"

"Don't say that." I lifted my finger to his lips, both of us staring at each other, drowning in the shower. "I didn't do anything but lie there."

"You said yes." He tried to be cute, but we were past that.

"Do a lot of girls say no?" I was being serious. I couldn't help it. I took sex seriously.

"No." He shook his head, losing the charm and gaining more blush.

It was late for modesty and reminders that we were in the real world. We were in my parents' house. My childhood bedroom.

"I already told you, I wanted you the moment I met you." He leaned closer, and his eyes got that look, the one that suggested he might kiss me. Finally.

"Well, I picked you."

"But what you hadn't realized at the time was that I picked you too," he whispered as his hands lifted, cupping my face and tilting it up to meet his. The showerhead hit the back of him, and that protected me from the water as he lowered more, his eyes locked on mine as our lips met.

He became a blurry, beautiful mess in my vision, but I stopped seeing with my eyes. I started seeing with my lips, imagining with my mind, and tasting with my tongue.

The kiss was more—more than being fucked, more than being stroked into oblivion, more than being possessed.

It was he and I dancing in the shower, sealing our fates in the downpour of everything. Water. Emotion. Seduction. Bliss.

Kissing him finally was too much.

I wanted more of everything I'd just received.

I hadn't even washed off the last sexcapade and I was ready for round two. So was he. He pressed himself against my stomach, making my body ache for more.

His hands left my face, lowering to my body, cupping my ass and lifting me into his arms. I wrapped my legs and arms around him, clinging to him as he entered me again, pressing my back against the shower wall.

This time was different.

Our mouths never left each other.

They didn't speak words.

We didn't grunt or jerk.

We moaned into each other, dancing, filling each other up at the same time that we took everything the other person had to give.

Kissing him for the first time was better than any other thing I'd ever done in my life.

I wanted there to never be enough.

I wanted it to go on forever.

For a minute I believed it would.

We stumbled into my bed again, wrapped in each other and ready for more sleep.

"Won't your parents come in?" he asked.

"No." I laughed. "My dad's in the city today until Friday night, and my mom doesn't really come in. She sends for you if she wants you."

"What about the staff?"

"They won't tell," I whispered, and kissed him again. "I've never spent a Sunday in bed before."

"Me either." He nuzzled my neck. "Not the whole day anyway."

"I wish we were at the Weinbergs' weird house and we were able to just go into the kitchen and make food."

"That is the best part of not having a staff of fifteen roaming the grounds, ready to pop in on you at any moment."

"I suppose being poor has its benefits." I giggled, tormenting him.

"It does." He knit his brow. "We've kind of broken the rules of Fling Club already."

"Maybe so." I grinned wide. "But if Cait chose you last night like she was supposed to, then this is my first time ever, stealing her fling."

"Does it make it sweeter?"

"No," I answered honestly. "You already made it sweet enough." I laughed at my own cheesy line and closed my eyes.

I was half-starved, half-asleep, completely satisfied, and a lot smitten.

It was a fabulous way to fall back asleep.

Chapter Twenty-Six
New Checklist

Cherry

Waking up Monday with him gone and my bed cold sucked.

But Rachel texted and asked me to come over for brunch. Not feeling like being alone, I said sure.

She smiled wide when I arrived. "Hey!"

"Hey. Sorry about selection night. I bailed. I couldn't do it." I was embarrassed. This girl didn't really know me, and I was flaking on her hard.

"That's okay. I mean we were all kinda worried when you left and didn't come back. And then Ashley left, and we all sort of assumed maybe—"

"Maybe what?" I tried to sound like I wasn't reliving every second of it.

"Maybe you left together." She bit her lip and raised her eyebrows. "Went and had a quickie before Cait got her grubby hands on him."

"Oh." I couldn't lie, so I lowered my face, hating that my expression was giving me away as we walked into the front room to sit. "Yeah, no. I left with my sister."

"I got that story. Ashley came back to the party. That was awful, watching him and Cait talk. He looked like he wanted death." She wrinkled her nose. "So, Ashley got picked by Cait." Rachel's eyes looked like my insides felt. I hated it.

"I knew he would. She's so predictable. And how did selection go for you?" I asked, trying to be present. It was rough after being stuck in a ball of pleasure for a day and a half. I was on a routine from the bed to the shower and back to the bed again. I was lost in noises and sensations and whispered words.

I was hung up on feelings that I hadn't even known were possible.

There were also the feelings I didn't want. Feelings like remorse and confusion over everything Ashley had said to me at the party. Things we still hadn't discussed.

"I don't know. It was weird." She sounded worried. "Felt like buying a farm animal at an auction. I got some guy who seems nice. I picked him 'cause he sort of looked like he didn't want to be there. It doesn't really matter who we're stuck with; Ashley and Cait is the important stuff."

"Right. Ashley never mentioned it, so I assumed it all went according to plan."

"You spoke to Ashley? Did you see him last night? Fling Club hasn't even started yet, and you're already hanging out behind Cait's back?" For a new friend, she was a bit intense. But she was real, something I was working on.

"No." I tried so hard to be cool about it. "I mean, it wasn't like that. I was upset. I'm having a tough time being around Cait. And just wearing this fake skin I've always put on here. It's rough being back to a place where nothing changes, while I desperately want to be someone different."

"Did you guys hook up?" she blatantly asked, going for the jugular.

"No," I lied.

"Liar, liar, panties on fire." She tossed a pillow at me. "Just tell me it was half as amazing as I assume it would be."

"What?" I gasped. "Why do you think it would be amazing?" Jesus.

"I don't know." She grinned like a cat. "I guess 'cause he's so confident and yet nerdy and comfortable with his nerdiness, like he knows he's better than other people but wouldn't dare say it. Those kinds of guys are always so unsuspecting and freaky. Like female librarians. Freak flags a mile long."

"Shut up!" I tossed the pillow back at her.

"Well?" She caught and hugged it. "Spill. I know you hooked up."

"It was nice." I cracked a grin, fighting so hard not to be that loser who kisses and tells.

"Niiiiiiiiice." She said it like Joey on *Friends*. "I could use some *nice*, just personally. So, if he turns out to just be the kind of guy who's down to fu—"

"No." I lost my humor.

"Ha!" She pointed. "I was testing you. You like him a lot, you filthy liar. He's amazing, isn't he?"

"Amazing." I wanted to gush and release the hounds, my emotions and truths. But I stayed calm and collected. "I mean, he calls me out on my shit, which is weird for me. You know what it's like being with someone like my mom; it's all plastic." I wondered if I was making sense.

"Oh my God." She widened her grin. "So jealous. I need some of that. Maybe not someone to call me on my shit, though. I have a brother for that."

My phone buzzed, drawing my eyes down. It was a text from Ashley.

Morning.

I grinned and texted back. Morning.

So, day one of Fling Club, and I'm already her little whipping boy. She made me come for breakfast and flaunted me all over the country club. I can't do this.

What should we do about that? I laughed.

Go back to New York and forget about the Hamptons completely? You can be my chubby little pastry girl and I'll be your daily dose of reality.

I grinned at his response. "Asshole."

"What did he say?" Rachel asked.

"Who?" I asked.

"Please, like I can't tell it's him by that grin."

"He hates Cait." I laughed again. "He wants to run away and pretend none of this ever happened."

"Poor guy. I mean, I feel sorry for him even if you're paying him to be here and date Cait."

I parted my lips to argue, but she was right. Jesus. I'd technically just paid Ashley to have sex with me. Correction: my brother technically had paid him to have sex with me. I shuddered. I hadn't handled the money aspect, but that changed nothing.

Rachel winced, no doubt seeing my simple math adding up on my face. "That's not what I meant."

"Right. Of course." I cringed.

"I didn't mean you're paying Ashley for anything. I mean you aren't. It's not like that." Rachel tried to reason with me, no doubt seeing the twist in my stomach on my face. I was certain my pallor had turned green. I felt green.

She tried again. "Ashley isn't like—"

"It's okay." I cut her off. "It doesn't matter. You're right. Ashley's here for a reason, and it's not to frolic about with me all summer. He has a job." I swallowed down the nausea and got up off the sofa. "I should go, though. I have to figure out who my fling is. I'll see ya later." I waved.

"Cherry, don't be angry with Ashley. He likes you, and you got him into this mess."

"Yeah, I know." I nodded, still queasy over the fact he was being paid to fake-date Cait but ended up screwing me.

For money.

Jesus.

This was what came of me making decisions.

I couldn't even be trusted with a simple thing like sex.

I drove home with the window open, desperate to shake the icky feelings, but nothing helped.

Not even seeing him, Ashley, when I got there.

Not even seeing him in a swimsuit by the pool, laughing with my dad and brother.

Not even seeing him holding a drink and wearing sunglasses, being casual like nothing in the world was wrong.

From the living room I watched them all outside, remembering the feel of every inch of him, inches I couldn't see but wouldn't ever forget.

"You're so screwed." Ella sauntered in eating ice cream from a bowl with cat ears on it. "You're so into him."

I glanced at her, not speaking, and stole the spoon to take a large bite.

"What happened to your keto home regime?" she mocked.

"Not a word, Ella; not a single word." I took her bowl, too, scooping a huge bite and shoving it in my mouth. Pushing my feelings down with some Cherry Garcia.

"So, are we talking love or lust? I know it's only been, like, two weeks, but I'm struggling to tell exactly what that look on your face is." She nudged me, taking back the bowl.

"Conflicted mess is what I would label it." I stared, unable to break away from watching him.

"You look like a creeper."

"I know." I nodded. "I am a creeper." My words hushed, becoming something not fit for the world, not fit for my sister's ears or my lips, but I couldn't hold them back. Even here in the Hamptons I couldn't hold them back. "We had sex. Andy's essentially paying him to have sex with me. Who's the rule breaker now?"

"Oh, wow." She handed back the bowl. "Yeah, that's aggressive."

"He made a joke about this being like *Pretty Woman*, and I laughed." I turned to her. "I don't feel like laughing now."

"Maybe Andy can write you into the contract as part of his payment." She burst out laughing, nodding and taking a step back. "So you're the hooker, not him."

"Shut up, Ella," I snarled, and went back to the ice cream.

She had her laugh, then stepped close again, speaking with a smile. "He likes you. You like him. That's bigger than getting revenge. I want you to get revenge, but more than that, I want you to find yourself. I want you to forget old you and try to embrace new you. Being with him, even if it's just sexual or fun, seems like a good start. He's not like us. Like this bullshit."

She held her arms out. "He's normal. He can take you home to meet his parents and go to movies, and you can make out in the car, and no one will be watching or comparing him to anyone else. He doesn't have to sneak around, pretending to be something he isn't. Just pay out his 'services' for the summer, because you owe him the money, and end it there. End the contract so it's done, and you can both start fresh. What the hell do we care for money anyway?"

She was so smart. "Do you think I could just go pay the tuition and not tell him and just leave it at that, or do you think he needs the money? Andy's giving him, like, twenty grand."

"Wow. To tolerate us all summer, that's not enough. That doesn't even cover tuition." She grabbed my arms and turned me as I was midbite, staring me down with her bright-blue eyes. "Honest to God,

I thought you were a goner for a long time. You got together with that shithead last winter, and I thought, okay, she's going full Stepford. We've lost her. Andy and I had a funeral."

"Dicks."

"Right. But the point is that you're back. You're lost, confused, crazy, and unsure about your future, and yet this is the brightest I've ever seen you. Your eyes are clear. So maybe it's Ashley. Maybe it's just seeing how much of the Kool-Aid you've been drinking over the years. Maybe it's getting some distance from Cait and all her poison." She stepped closer, hugging me, something she rarely did. We were a non-touching family. "Whatever it is, don't let it get away. If you have to pay Ashley to be with you, whatever. It'll make a fun story for when you're old."

I sighed into her embrace, hugging back. I loved how she smelled, like rose oil and self-assurance.

"I'll let you get back to staring like a pervert. Try not to touch yourself while you're doing it. Mom could walk in, and it would end her. On second thought . . ." She patted me on the arm and stalked off after taking her ice cream back.

"You could have left the ice cream," I said.

"Not a chance. I'm not wasting it on you. You're not even tasting it, just eating your feelings." She lifted a middle finger and rounded the corner, leaving me with her wisdom. It was a half solution, but she was right. What did I care about the money? Or the revenge?

I was over it.

I'd found something better. Something that had the chance at being real. He didn't check a single item on my list.

He was a new list.

Honest, check.

Funny, check.

Outgoing, check.

Self-confident, check.

Gentlemanly, check.

Smart, check.

Self-sufficient, check.

Amazing in bed, check.

I wasn't done with the list, though.

There were things I still had to learn about Ashley. Things like loyalty, respect for his parents, and plans for the future.

But for the first time in my life, I wasn't worried about those things. I wasn't trying to get too far ahead.

I wanted the journey to last a little longer. I wanted to be sure before I was anything else.

But Ella was right about another thing: I needed to say goodbye to the old me, the one who was part of the Fling Club.

Did I walk away and forget my revenge, or did I finish what I started?

Maybe taking down Fling Club once and for all would be the final nail in the coffin that held the old me, now buried six feet underground.

Chapter Twenty-Seven

STRIP CRIB

Cherry

Getting ready for bed the next day, I was startled by a knock at my bedroom door.

No one in my family knocked. My brother knock-opened. Ella opened. My father didn't come in here. And my mother sent word that she wished to speak to me.

So the knock was foreign.

When I opened it, I was surprised by the coy smile of a cute guy waiting outside my door.

"Hi." His eyes said far more than his words.

"Hi." I pressed my lips together. It was weird seeing him here. I wanted to grill him about his dates with Cait and see if he'd fallen for her, but I needed to trust that he was what he said he was. It was hard.

"Can I come in?"

"Yeah." I opened the door wide and stepped back, letting him in.

"I spent the entire day having drinks on a yacht with the worst people I've ever met. It was awful. They passive-aggressively mock everyone.

They're rude in ways I haven't ever seen before. I need a shower." He had on pajama pants and a shirt with some nerd symbol front and center.

"Did you change into jammies and then come here?"

"Yeah. I couldn't wear my boating clothes. They smelled like sunscreen and sleaze."

"So, you spent the entire day with Cait in a bathing suit?" My heart cracked a little.

"Yeah. Which is a bit of a sin. 'Cause I got a good look at her, and I will say, for being the worst human on earth, she has that extra five pounds I was talking about before." He winked.

"Dick!" I shoved him, but he caught me and pulled me in, kissing my smile.

"I'm kidding. You're perfect. And she's evil," he muttered against my mouth. "Never change from being the girl I know you are." He kissed me again, sealing all the sweet things he said into me.

His hands ventured, cupping my ass and lifting me, but I wiggled free.

"There's something we need to discuss." I pulled from his octopus arms.

"You wanna play hard to get?"

"No." I tilted my head, contemplating that. "Maybe. But not right now. First we need to talk about the finances part."

"No one wants to talk about finances. Especially in your bedroom."

"Right, but we need to consider the fact that as of now, it looks like my family is paying you for sex, and that's—"

"Creepy." He took the word from my mouth.

"Precisely." I folded my arms, trying not to notice the way the groin area of his pajamas was bulging.

"What are we going to do?" He cocked an eyebrow, cooling off.

"Be friends and coconspirators for the summer until the transaction is completed. Take it slow and see if this is genuinely what either of us wants. I could use the time to get to know myself, the real me, and break free from the conformity of my family's expectations." I'd practiced this part a lot.

"You want me to hang with you, date your awful friend, watch you date some male model, and not touch you all summer long?" He sounded dubious of the whole thing and completely ignored most of the points. "After I've already had you?"

"Yeah." I gulped.

"No." He said it without even thinking. "Not a chance. I want to be here for your spiritual and emotional growth, like a shaman. So maybe I'll quit. It's that simple. It'll be volunteer work." He stepped close again, pulling me into his arms and kissing my neck. "I'm putting this on my resume, though. So I expect you to answer questions about the level of effort I put into my volunteer work."

I giggled as he kissed my neck and then lifted me into his arms, carrying me to my bed. "Seriously, stop!" I laughed and squirmed.

"Are you playing hard to get now?" He tossed me on the bed.

"No." I waved my hands. "I was thinking maybe we should get to know each other better before we—I mean, maybe we could go on a date or play another board game. The slow-it-down part of the story."

"Another board game." He nodded. "I like it. Not chess this time, though. You cheated."

"I did not!"

"Let's play cribbage. You have a crib board?"

"No." I folded my arms.

"No, you do. Every family has one. You're just the wrong person to ask." He held a finger out. "Don't move. I'll be right back." He turned and left the room, leaving me smiling and yet worried. It was a natural state for me.

How was he going to pay his tuition if he didn't have a summer job?

Likely he would have to get two summer jobs to even come close to helping his parents with tuition and bills. Instead he was having fun here on the shore, just to be near me.

He was dedicated, I had to give him that.

He returned five minutes later with a weird-looking piece of wood that had pegs sticking out of it and a deck of cards. "What a score. Your dad has this old vintage one." He showed me the wood carving, displaying the funny-looking shape. It took me a second to recognize it was New York State.

"You seriously have never played this before?"

"No." I didn't know what he was talking about.

"Well, we're playing strip crib. I don't know that it's been done before—might be a bit of a sacrilege—but I don't care. I'm throwing caution into the wind."

"Strip crib?"

"Do you wanna put on some layers? 'Cause this is going to be a serious ass whooping. And once you're naked, the game's over, and I win. And I get to pick my prize." He winked.

"Beginner's luck is kind of a thing of mine," I lied.

"We'll see." He sat and explained the game to me. I liked listening to his half-American, half-English accent with weird Scottish inflections every now and then. He was such a mix of everything. Worldly. The opposite of me. I traveled the world, but I never took any of it with me, not the way he did.

Half an hour later we were playing our first real hand after several practice rounds.

He won, gloating with a grin. I stripped my pants off first, sitting in my boy shorts underwear. I decided to try to play to my advantage and rolled over onto my stomach, displaying my ass. The way his eyes darted there, watching less of the game and more of me, was amusing.

I won the second hand, and he pulled off his shirt, displaying his freshly tanned skin.

I took a deep breath, trying not to let him distract me.

He won the third hand, and I pulled my underwear off, flinging it at him. He caught them and took a deep inhale of them.

"You're weird."

"And you smell like honey." He tucked them in his pocket. "For now. In half an hour you're going to smell like me."

"You're being too cocky. That's bad luck." We played the fourth hand, and I won. He removed his pants, sitting in his underwear.

I sat back on my butt, spreading my legs just slightly.

He cleared his throat, his gaze stuck between my legs and his cock getting hard in his underwear. "Looks like we both have a single article of clothing."

"Nope." I lifted my shirt, revealing a bra. "I have two." I spread my legs a little more.

He whooshed the air from his lips, pursing them and trying to focus on his cards.

We played the fifth hand, and he won. I slipped my bra off from beneath my shirt and tossed it to the side of the room. He was rocking a slight erection in his gray underwear until I slid my free hand down between my legs. I started swirling my fingertip, rubbing and making myself breathe faster.

"Come on, Cherry." He inhaled sharply. "That's cheating."

"Is it?" I slid a finger inside of myself, closing my eyes and moaning into it.

"Fuck this." He threw the cards to the side, grabbed me, and lifted me into his arms. He carried me to the bed again before laying me down savagely and jumping on top of me. He kissed my neck, lifting my shirt up and burying himself in my perky breasts, inhaling them one at a time.

He didn't waste time. He dragged his underwear down as he crawled between my legs, shoving himself into me, desperate. Never before had anyone been this anxious to get inside of me. No one had ever wanted me more.

We both cried out with the first thrust, carrying on through the next and the next until we were moaning into each other.

His mouth found its way to my face again, sucking my lip and biting gently as he rocked us both.

"Cherry," he whispered into our kiss. "I'll never get enough of you." He fucked me this time. Not like in the shower where we'd made something resembling love, without the love.

This was savage and desperate, answering an animalistic call in us both.

When we finished I didn't know my name or the date. Just that the guy clinging to me was mine.

He lifted me, carrying me with him to the bathroom before starting the shower yet again. I didn't know when I'd ever been this clean. He carried me inside before the water was completely warm, but I didn't mind.

I clung to him the way he did me.

We held each other, kissing and caressing as the water washed over us.

He grabbed a washcloth and lathered it with soap, then paid attention to every inch of me, massaging as he went.

When he got between my legs, he cleaned gently and rinsed before bending a knee and placing a kiss on my inner thigh.

"I never knew redheads were red everywhere." He lightly grazed my landing strip. "I mean I heard the drapes matched the carpet, but I wasn't sure it was true."

"All my body hair is reddish."

"Is your family Scottish too?"

"No." I took a knee with him, sitting down and letting the water pour all over us. "My dad's family is Irish, obviously: Kennedy. My mom's family is Romanian."

"Your mom's Romanian?"

"Yeah. My great-grandma came to America before the Second World War, fleeing the Nazis. My grandma was a little girl. She didn't know what was happening. Just that they were leaving before things got bad. My great-grandma worked three jobs to put my grandma through Wellesley to make certain she was spending her time with the right sort of people. When she finished school, my grandma married into a wealthy East Coast family and lied about her heritage. Being Romanian wasn't good enough for my grandfather's family, I guess. So, my mom isn't from some rich, old-money family. Her dad was, but the rest of her family were normal people. Poor, actually. Had my grandma not been friends with my great-aunt Karen, my grandpa and grandma wouldn't have ever met."

"And yet your mother shuns the normal people the most?"

"Trying to cover up the fact she has old-fashioned red blood like the rest of the population. But my dad—the true blue blood, the true old-money family—is the cool one. He lives in the city most of the time, away from her. He and his brother are super casual. He volunteers and does tons of pro bono work."

"But they want you to be a snob like them?"

"My mother does. She's got expectations about me marrying well. You heard her speech about the leaders and wives. She actually believes that shit. We've had to give her multiple lessons on humanity as far as the staff are concerned. She still considers them the help."

"Jesus."

"You have no idea. If she knew we were in here and you were a regular guy with scholars for parents, she'd lose her mind. We would have to medicate her," I joked, kinda. "Meanwhile she coasted through college, taking only easy courses, and can't even tell you where Romania is on the map."

"What is she going to say when she finds out you're dating a mere mortal? Like at the end of the summer?"

"Is that what I'm doing?" I teased, still scared of the revenge plot we'd already put in motion.

"Yeah. It's what you're doing, Cheryl Kennedy. We're dating. You're my lady." He flashed me that grin, the one I liked. "And you're going to have to slum it and come meet my parents."

It was just like Ella said it would be. "It's not slumming. I'd be happy to meet your family. Why wouldn't I?"

"'Cause I'm not Griffin what's-his-nuts."

"No, you are not." I'd never laid a better compliment on him. I leaned into him, taking a deep inhale as the rain showerhead poured down on us.

"And I acted terribly toward you. The other night. I was upset, and I shouldn't have said any of that."

"You were right." I pulled back and stared him in the face. "You called me out on my shit and demanded more from me, for myself. You were right."

"No, I don't know what it's like being out here, being one of these people and having those intense expectations placed upon you. I have no idea how hard it is." He was giving me too much leeway, and for once, I didn't allow myself the extra rope.

"I had choices." A slow, humble smile slipped across my soaking-wet face. "I didn't have to be this girl or stay here. You know, when my sister had to start high school, she went straight to my dad and demanded a different school."

"She did?"

"Yeah. I didn't even know that was a possibility. I'm three years older than her; by then I was already a senior. It never even crossed my mind that I had other options, whereas she demanded them. She saw what Andy and I went through, trying to fit in at Paulson, and she said 'not a chance.'"

"Your sister has got some brass balls."

"I know. And smarts. I mean Andy and I, we never even considered going against the grain. But Ella never considered going with it. I could have been like her." I said things I'd never said before, never felt safe to say before. But the shower was like our own personal safe place, a pod no one else had access to. "I wish I'd been more like her."

"I don't." He reached up and cupped my face. "This revelation makes you more beautiful."

"Thank you for seeing me." I blinked and wished for tears, but I was touched, and that wasn't what my body used tears for. So my chest and throat burned with no release.

"You're welcome." He didn't try to explain it or talk himself away from the awkward feelings I'd forced on us both.

He'd seen me. We both knew it. As uncomfortable as that fact was, it was the truth.

I cleared my throat and changed the subject, asking the dreaded question. "What's your plan after college?" I didn't know enough about him. We'd skipped all the beginning stages of a relationship and dived headfirst into the good part. But now there was backtracking to be done.

"Work for NASA at the Ames Research Center in California. I already have an internship. I start in June next year after I graduate." He pulled me back. "What about you?"

My lips parted and words wanted to come out, but there was nothing. How did I explain that I had essentially hoped I'd marry and have kids and take care of other people, which was ironic now, judging by how well I was taking care of myself? I'd always told myself that considering who my mother was, I was doing okay. I should have been a bigger mess. But maybe I just wasn't looking hard enough at how messy I actually was.

"You have no idea, do you?" He laughed, brushing my wet bangs away from my face. "Well then, I fear you'll have to bartend in Australia or Ireland and possibly take the train through at least four countries in Europe before the answer will hit you."

"Four specifically?"

"Yes. Or you could just settle for working at Starbucks and end it there. I mean, they have benefits."

"Starbucks?" He was randomly precise.

"Yes, or you could go waitress in LA and pretend you're going to be an actress." He lifted my chin. "You have the looks. And I know you're good at acting."

"Shut up." I pulled back. "I don't know how to act. There's more to it than pretending to fit into one aspect of society without completely offending all the others."

"Aspect, instead of class?" he asked.

"Your word, not mine." I couldn't fight the giggle.

"It's your last year, Cherry. You have time. And you're rich, so you have some YOLO room."

"Are you mocking me?"

"Yes." He leaned forward, pressing his wet face against mine. "Always."

"You're a jerk."

"I know. It's part of my charm." He kissed me again.

We kissed, and I tried not to overanalyze everything.

I suddenly had the feeling this was going to be an amazing summer.

My first true one ever. And I didn't even need the club to guarantee that.

Chapter Twenty-Eight

T. REX

Ashley

Decorating with rich people meant supervising the staff of the country club as they decorated.

Being Cait's lapdog for the summer meant I got to help supervise.

And that meant I got to listen to her berate the staff and treat people poorly as fuck. I'd joked about quitting with Cherry, and after the last week with Cait, I was serious. This wasn't worth it. It was painful.

She smiled over at me, waving all cutesy, before she turned and lost it on a man for bringing the wrong chairs upstairs.

As she ranted and shouted and stomped around the massive ballroom like a *T. rex*, I started to text Cherry, begging her to put an end to this charade before I put an end to my life.

But Cherry was too busy with her friends—the girl squad she hung with from here—so her answers were short.

My phone rang midtext.

"Hiya, Mum." I smiled, talking low so Satan's mistress couldn't hear me.

"Hi, darling, I just wanted to update you. Dad's doing much better. His cancer has reacted well to the treatments, and the doctors confirmed it hasn't gone into his bones so he's going to be right as rain in no time."

"Fantastic news. So he's been going steady then?"

"Aye, he finished the last set yesterday, pissing and moaning like a child, but it's done. He's sleeping now. He'll be sick for a couple of days, miserable old codger, and then he should be good. If you wanna visit, any time after this week works. The sooner you come, the weaker he'll look. But he bounces back fast. Doc says that if he's mending well, he can go back to school in September of next year, only missing one more year of work."

"Oh, that's great news. Made my morning." I sighed, half lying. My dad missing another year of work would be awful for my family, but I would do everything I could to help. I certainly couldn't quit this job. I needed the money, which meant I couldn't volunteer for this position.

"Where are ya? What is that terrible racket?" I could imagine her face as she said it, scrunching up her nose and all.

"The job, Ma. That's the devil-boss," I whispered.

"Sounds right mad!"

"Oh, yeah. You have no idea . . ." I laughed. "Give Da a kick in the shin for me."

"I'll do just that. Love ya."

"Love you too. Bye." I hung up, feeling at least one positive thing from the day, week, month.

Staying meant I would be able to afford to go see my dad. Maybe I could bring Cherry. Andy was moving this little plan of his along fast, with Ella and Ryan recording everything to ensure he gleaned what he could from the time I spent with Cait. I was making a video of her being a twat every chance I had. I had a camera hidden in the sunglasses on my head. I wore them everywhere I went. On my head. On my face. Sticking out of a pocket. I looked like one of those idiots who wore their sunglasses indoors and at night.

But it was working.

When we slow danced at a bar, the recorder was rolling.

When we ate, the recorder caught her entire meal, or lack thereof. She ate like a bird.

And someone was watching us at all times.

His fling was Sarah. A match that seemed a little off at first. She didn't seem his type. And yet as the days moved along, they actually got on quite well. She didn't demand a lot of his time, and she really only wanted to hang out when they had functions. So he had time to monitor and obsess.

Cherry's guy was the same. His name was Josh, and as much as I was sure he was a model, turned out his parents wouldn't allow it. He was also gay, which as an odd turn of events, made me quite relieved.

Cherry commiserated with him because he was forced into the closet and out to the Fling Club. She could relate to another person who couldn't be who he truly was as a member of this society.

Poor lad.

Him being so easygoing meant all my free time was spent with Cherry, in secret. The rest of the time was spent like this, with me and Cait and her craziness. She didn't even mind that I never paid for her. I didn't hold her hand. I didn't pull out her chair.

I literally spent the first two weeks doing the opposite of what my mother told me to.

It felt wrong.

But the results worked. The less I did, the harder she tried. She was desperate for me to like her.

I could see it in her eyes. She faked harder and tried harder. Her level of phony reached new heights. As did her bashing of other people.

She cackled with her friends over how brutally Cherry was dumped by Griffin. She loved the fact that Sarah was dating Andy, her leftovers. Breaking the rule didn't even bother her. Everything was about her desperate hate for Andy and Cherry. And we recorded it all.

And being the silent observer, I could see how much they bothered her. The more Cherry smiled, the worse Cait got. And thanks to our secret affair, Cherry was smiling more and more. She made my world brighter, and I clearly made hers more real.

Sort of the opposite effect I had on Cait.

The whole thing was intense to watch.

I imagined some pinnacle of disaster was coming, an impending-doom moment.

Cait was spread thin, running such a tight ship and working so hard to be perfect for all the moments when anyone who mattered was looking. She only relaxed with her closest friends, of which she had few. The flaws were starting to show. The seams were splitting, and I could tell it was just a matter of time before she cracked.

Chapter Twenty-Nine

SPRING FLING

Cherry

Spring Fling was a success. Everyone was dancing and drinking and socializing, and the drama seemed to be kept to a minimum. But it was still early.

Rachel was even hitting it off with Laura, Cora, and Erica. She was fitting in beautifully.

Andy danced away with Sarah, looking a bit too into his role. They were getting along better than Sarah and I ever had. I hadn't seen that coming.

More predictably, Cait seemed smitten with Ashley, working double-time to garner his affections. His cold-shoulder routine seemed like just the ticket. The less he tried, the harder she did. I realized then what his mad skills were. Indifference. Indifference was the key to all girls. Mean or grumpy guy at the bar. It was a thing. Girls were fixers. We liked the idea of making that grumpy guy smile. We wanted people to be happy. An indifferent guy drove us crazy. Just like Ashley was doing. He was the grumpy guy at the bar, and Cait was desperate to please him.

God, we were easy to play.

Josh, my date, and I danced, chatting civilly and acting more like friends.

"May I?" Andy cut in, like I wanted to dance with my brother.

"Sure." Josh stepped back and let him take me into his arms. "I'll go get us some drinks, Cherry."

"Thanks!" I winced as my brother stepped on my foot. "What's up?"

"Just wondering if maybe you girls would be into some deep-cover work?"

"Deep cover?" I was lost.

"Yeah. Can you possibly tear yourself away from here, even with lover boy clinging to Cait, to go do something for the cause?"

"I could. He's not clinging or my lover boy, by the way. You can't possibly care that I'm secretly seeing Ashley?"

"You mean besides the fact he's being paid to sleep with you?" He went there.

I was quick to Ashley's defense. "He said he was going to quit. He said he isn't taking the money at the end of the summer."

"What he says and what he does might be different. Just be cool until he proves you mean more than money." He sighed. "But, back to the plan, I want you girls to go to Cait's and snoop while everyone else is distracted. We're not having an easy time coming up with the kind of dirt I want. I need more to seal this."

"Okay." I nodded. "I'll assemble a team." I sent a text to Rachel and Ella and walked to the bathroom, hoping Rachel would come to Cait's and Ella would meet us there. Ashley's eyes followed me across the dance floor.

When I got to the bathroom, I closed the door and stared at myself. Two weeks earlier I'd been in this same bathroom, staring at myself.

I'd wanted my revenge.

I'd wanted her to hurt Cait the way she'd hurt me.

But things had changed in two weeks.

I'd changed.

Could I actually go and break into her bedroom and snoop in her shit? More importantly, did I care enough to do it?

"Cherry?" The door opened, and Griffin came strolling into the girl's washroom, looking a little tipsy. "I thought that was you." He leaned his back against the door. "We need to talk."

"Griff, you can't be in here. It's the women's washroom." I'd hoped he wouldn't come; the whole Ashley-and-Cait thing should have been enough of a reason for him not to come. His parents were members of the club, but I truly didn't think he would risk the scandal by showing his face.

But here he was, drunk and needy. Idiot.

"I came to see you." He staggered forward, reaching for me.

"No." I pushed his hands away. "You blew it."

"I miss you." He grabbed me, mauling me like a bear. "I miss the way you smell." He draped himself over me. I pushed and wiggled, trying to escape, but he was too big.

"Stop!" I shoved harder.

"Just give me another chance." He staggered and tripped, pushing me into the wall with him crushing me.

"*No!*" I heaved him again, this time making him lose his balance the other way. He staggered back, almost like he was tap-dancing.

"You miss me, too, admit it."

"I don't." I snorted, straightening my dress and folding my arms. "I don't miss you at all. In fact, I haven't thought of you since it ended." That was a lie.

"I think about you all day." He said it like he was sober. Or in pain. I didn't care which it was. He continued, "I think about you all day and all night." He slumped against the counter, leaning on the wall. "Give me a second chance."

"No." I might have succumbed to this moment had I not met Ashley. Had my sister not left me on the side of the road. Had I not had a slight mental breakdown and slept on a park bench. Had I not seen

Cait and the club and my life for what they really were. Had I not realized I had low self-esteem and possibly a couple of personality disorders.

But all those things had happened.

"Please," he pleaded.

"Never. It's not going to happen. So you need to go back out there and find someone else to trick into falling for you. You shouldn't even be here. Cait's with that guy who punched you in the face, and I'm sure he'd take pleasure in doing it again."

"Just tell me the truth about one thing. You really did fall for me? The way I fell for you?" His eyes tried to seduce me, like a snake charmer. Only he was the snake, and I was the mouse.

"I did." I told the truth. "But then you broke my trust and my heart." I admitted it for the first time, not just to myself but also to another person.

"I'm sorry, Cherry," he said, seeming truthful. "I fucked up so bad. She came to the flat, said she had something to tell me. I was still drunk from the party the night before. She crawled in my bed and said you were dating some guy behind my back, that she had proof that you were going to break up with me and have a final fling, and then she stripped naked and started sucking me off, saying she was a better fit than you—"

"I don't need to hear how it happened." My face and insides lit up, burning me from within.

"But she didn't mean anything to me. She was just a whore. That's all. She just didn't want us to be happy. She can't stand anyone being happy, because she isn't." It was the most profound thing he'd ever said. "I'll never be as sorry as I am now."

"Good." I nodded, trying not to cry with rage. "Then you won't ever do that to someone else again."

"No." He stared me straight in the eyes and whispered, "I won't ever break someone's trust again." He turned and left, leaving me with a pounding heart and angry tears in my eyes.

I turned and looked at myself in the mirror. I now knew the answer to three questions: Did the punishment fit the crime, was I willing to stoop this low, and was I willing to become as bad as Cait was?

The answer was yes, to all of them.

I stormed from the bathroom, clicking my heels across the floor as I went to the ballroom where Rachel was and pulled her aside.

"We're going to Cait's to break in and snoop in her shit and see if we can't find something damning. Andy's not having much luck with his nonsense, and I've had enough dragging out Cait and Ashley's honeymoon from hell."

"Okay." Rachel sounded excited. "Finally, something worth doing around here."

I was terrified. I'd gone from not just agreeing but now spearheading the whole thing?

Anger was a funny emotion.

And I was at my boiling point. Ex-boyfriends and ex-friends with a cheating streak had a tendency to bring that emotion out, I guess.

Chapter Thirty

THE BURN BOX

Cherry

I parked the car on the side of the road a block from Cait's parents' house.

"We used to sneak out when we were younger, like fourteen. We used the service gate over there. There's a gap in the hedge." I climbed out, glancing down at the flip-flops I was wearing with my dress. "This was a good idea." I wiggled my toes.

"Yeah. I can't imagine sneaking around with heels on." Rachel gave me a look. "You sure the entire family is at the party?"

"Yeah. I saw her parents and her brother right before we left. Andy said he'd text if she left." I swallowed hard. "Ready?"

"Kinda. I feel like we're on an episode of *Pretty Little Liars* or something."

"Except they never wore flip-flops. They ran around in those huge heels." I lifted a foot.

"That's what stunt doubles are for." She rolled her eyes. "Let's go."

We closed the car and locked it as we snuck along the road to the hedge. The lights from her house were visible from the road, but the hedge had to be twenty feet tall.

I went straight to the gap, recalling it too well. Cait and I'd had fun when we were young. She was always bossy and mean, but I was on her team. I was protected by the friendship I never abused or squandered or even questioned.

The same couldn't be said for her.

Something changed in her when we were fifteen.

Whatever it was, she got meaner and more bitter as the years went on. Pushing the limits of what we'd do.

Holding my body tight, I slid through the gap, hoping my dress didn't snag. It led to the service gate, which was easy to climb from this side. I tucked my dress into the top, flashing my underwear at Rachel as I climbed over and jumped to the ground below.

"Wow. You're practiced at this."

"We snuck out a lot," I whispered back as she hopped over too. We were at the service garages, behind the house. I hurried along the path between the buildings to the backyard where the pool house and guesthouse were. The back door by the bar was always left open; the Landrys were known for their summer parties and guests for weeks on end.

I crept through the door and glanced around. "Now we have to look like we're supposed to be here. There're no security cameras, just lots of guards. Her dad doesn't like anything he does filmed."

"Sounds like a nice guy."

"Oh, he's the best," I muttered, and walked like I owned the place.

I avoided the main hall and took the staff stairs, hurrying up both flights without making a single sound.

We came out on Cait's floor, and I opened her double doors. Her bedroom was off the charts. It made mine look like a little kid's or a guest room.

Her parents gave her the better of the four master bedrooms in the mansion. Something I doubted they had much choice on.

"Holy shit," Rachel gasped. "I've seen some nice rooms in my life, but this." She spun in a circle. "This is amazing."

"Yeah. She's spoiled." I nodded and hurried to Cait's bedside table. I pulled open the drawers, rifled through them, not even sure what we were looking for. I went to the other side of the bed, searching, but nothing. "Check the bathroom," I whispered. "Look for USBs or a diary or even an iPad or something."

Lights flicked on as we searched high and low for something to use against her.

Then I spun in the room, staring at the walls and noting how they'd changed. Where she used to have signed posters, she now had artwork. Where she used to have a candy stand, she had what appeared to be a tranquility area.

We'd aged, and if you looked at her now, judging her by her room, you'd think she was a well-balanced young woman.

But I knew how unstable she was.

Going to Griffin's house and lying about me dating someone behind his back was a sick and calculated move. He was right. She didn't want anyone else happy. She didn't want me to miss out on Fling Club, her chance to control me one last time. Until she figured out how to control me as an adult.

But we were too old for these games.

I was too old to be snooping in a bedroom. I had turned twenty-one a couple of months ago, two weeks before Cait. We were both too old for these antics and yet, here I was, wearing dollar store flip-flops and a four-thousand-dollar dress while sneaking into Cait's room to sabotage her.

"Uh, Cherry?" Rachel walked toward me holding a small box.

"What?"

"Pretty sure operation Destroy Cait needs to stop." She lifted her gaze, horrified by whatever was in the box.

"Why?" My heart raced, curious and terrified of what she could have possibly found.

"She has blackmail material on all of you." She handed me the box and turned to the computer.

I started combing through the dusty old box, finding ancient photos of everyone I knew in compromising positions, including me, from when we were much younger. "Holy shit, this is like *Mean Girls*, only it's a burn box. Where'd you find this?"

"The back of the closet behind a bunch of other shit. Old luggage and some shoeboxes she clearly hasn't opened in ages."

"What the hell?" I stared at it.

"Dude, we need you. Now!" Rachel spoke into her phone; I hadn't even realized she'd called anyone. "Cait's bedroom computer—we need in. You have seconds to get here."

"Who was that?"

"Ella."

"Oh. She didn't answer my texts when I sent her a message about coming." I didn't ask why we needed Ella; I was stuck staring. A photo of me losing my virginity, drunk and scared and uncomfortable, was staring back at me. The picture wasn't the only one of its kind. In fact, every girl I knew had a similar one. Everyone except Cait. "This is disgusting." I noted the picture had a time stamp. It had come from a video. My skin crawled as I tried to recall the moment.

It was hazy, but I didn't remember Cait being there, or there being much light.

We were in a bedroom at a party.

I stared at the picture more closely, realizing there was a slot in the wall or wood or something alongside the photo; Cait had been hiding behind the wall or in the closet, filming us.

It had been her idea.

She'd set me up.

I started to feel a little sick, a little disoriented. She'd filmed me having sex? I lost my virginity with some random guy because she wanted a movie of me doing it?

I slumped to my knees, cradling the box.

I knew she was sick and twisted and weird and a complete bitch.

But this was something else.

I'd just thought about how we were so past this.

And here, all along, was proof that I hadn't even gotten started on my revenge.

But *revenge* wasn't even the right word now.

I didn't want that or vengeance. Now I wanted something else.

I wanted to be away from her, deleted from her life and free from her brand of crazy.

Ella came bursting through the door, wheezing and nodding. "I'm here."

"She filmed me," I whispered.

"What?"

I lifted the single picture up, flashing my naked teenage body at my sister.

"What the fuck?" She grabbed the box and started rifling through. "Oh my God, what a sicko. Oh, that's Andy; I can't take back seeing that." She dropped the box and squinted her eyes like there was acid in them.

"The computer. I think those images are from recordings. They have time stamps like they're screenshots." Rachel spoke with urgency in her tone.

"Okay." Ella hurried over, plugging something into the computer and typing like a mad woman. I grabbed the box and held it tightly, not sure what to do or where to go from here.

I watched her typing and cringing, and then she was done, too fast.

"I left myself access to this computer, so I can do what I want remotely. Let's get out of here before they come home." Ella pulled the thing from the computer and hurried to me, lifting me up.

"She filmed me, Ella." I wanted to cry. I wanted to burst into the biggest ball of emotions. But I was sad. I wasn't angry enough to cry.

I was heartbroken.

"I know." She dragged me from the house, trying to take the box, but I refused to let it go.

As Rachel took the keys and we drove away with Ella following us, Rachel gave me a look. "You okay?"

"No." I clung to the burn box and thought of one thing and one thing only. "You have a fire pit at your house?"

"Yeah."

"Okay."

After she pulled into her driveway, I jumped out and hurried to the side of the house. Her dad was home, not a fan of the club, the Spring Fling, dances, or formal anything. He was more casual about life than anyone I'd met. But fortunately he wasn't around to see me in the state I was in.

I rushed to the backyard and dumped the box of pictures into the pit. I stared at it, not even really sure what to do with it now.

Rachel came up behind me a few minutes later and dumped liquid on everything, then tossed a match onto the damp pictures.

They ignited instantly, bursting into blue and yellow flames.

We backed up, watching the images burn.

"It's like a box of kiddie porn," Rachel murmured.

"Yeah, it is."

When every image was gone and all that remained was ash and some coals from the logs that had already been in there, I turned to her. "Please don't tell any—"

"I wouldn't. Ever. I'm sorry this happened to you." She hugged me. My eyes burned with the need to cry, but I wasn't angry enough. Not yet.

Chapter Thirty-One

Camerawoman C

Cherry

"What have you found?" I paced behind where Ella was typing away on her computer.

"Cait has videos of everyone we know having sex or in some precarious situation; even if it's just a flash or a couple of minutes, she ensures she gets a good face shot. It's apparently a creepy fetish of hers. Not one you'd expect from a girl like her. After we show your friends the videos, I'll remotely delete them all from the computer and set her back to default. She's going to think the computer crashed. Then I'll erase ever being there, but it's likely that she backed that thing up. I bet there's a flash drive somewhere. One good thing is it didn't look like she'd logged on to the computer in weeks."

"Great. We have to find that USB or hard drive?"

"Yeah." Ella sighed. "She's disgusting. I can't believe you were even friends with her."

"Me either." I wanted to defend myself and suggest that maybe we weren't ever friends to begin with, but the truth was, we were. It was a demented friendship. "I messaged Sarah, Cora, Erica, and Laura and told them to sneak out of the party. I sent Hans with the car to fetch them. He's bringing them over now."

"We both know they need to see this."

"Yeah, they deserve to see their videos." As I said it, the door opened.

"Some young ladies for you, Miss Cheryl," Henry interrupted.

"Thanks." I left my sister and followed our butler downstairs to where my friends stood.

"Hey!" Sarah smiled wide, looking a little too fresh faced. I wished I weren't about to ruin that as she said, "Are you all right? Cora and I saw you two leave so suddenly. You looked upset."

"I ran into Griffin in the bathroom," I growled. "It doesn't matter now. I have something to show you guys." I didn't pretend to be happy. I didn't bother pretending anything.

"Everything okay?" Laura asked cautiously.

"Nope." I turned and walked back up the stairs, expecting them to follow. I wasn't okay, and they weren't going to be okay either.

When we got to Ella's room, I held the door open for them.

"Hey. Maybe just come over one at a time." Ella spoke softly from behind her desk. "Erica, you first."

"What's going on?" Erica gave everyone a look as she walked slowly to my sister's desk. She stood facing us and the computer, which had its back to us. Her eyes widened, and her cheeks lost all color for a second before it rushed back in. "How—where did you get—"

"Cait's computer." Ella spoke softly.

"What the fuck?" Erica burst into tears, covering her face.

"What the hell, Cherry?" Sarah lost all that fresh-faced joy.

"Sarah, you can come look next."

Erica ran to me, wrapping herself around me.

"There's one of me too." I hugged her, wishing my tears would show up. My eyes were burning, and my stomach was twisting into knots. I held my friend as another one learned the terrible secret.

Sarah started to cry, shaking her head. "No one was there. That's impossible. No one was there!" She covered her face like this was her shame to carry.

"Laura," Ella whispered, clearly disgusted.

"I don't wanna see." Laura shook her head. "I don't wanna know what this is."

"Yes, you do," Erica sputtered, wiping her eyes so the mascara didn't smudge.

"Fuck." Laura held herself tightly, clinging to her own hands for strength. When she saw the computer screen, her brow furrowed. "Holy shit. I thought it was something else."

"She filmed you getting it on?" Sarah gasped.

"Yeah, it's weird, but it's not where my mind was going." She sighed, taking a knee. Clearly she had other things on her conscience. I didn't even want to know what they were. If this didn't disturb her, God knew what did.

"I honestly thought you had some sick and twisted murder video or something. Like *The Ring*. Oh my God." She was heaving her breath.

"Cora." I nodded at the computer, still embracing Erica.

"I already know." Cora didn't take a single step.

"You knew!" Sarah sounded like she might go off the deep end.

"Cait showed me." Her cheeks flushed, and her eyes lowered to the floor.

"She blackmailed you already?" Ella arrived at the truth before the rest of us.

"Yeah." Cora winced, her eyes twitching like she might cry. No. Sob. Like she might lose the hold she desperately had on herself. "She made me do things." She whispered the next part. "To you guys." And then it happened. She dropped to her knees, heaving and sobbing, covering her face.

"Oh, God." Sarah took a step back, scared to be too near Cora.

"Cora?" Laura narrowed her gaze. "What kind of things?"

I defended her. "Give her a minute."

"It could have been any of you," Ella reminded us all. "I've deleted all the files and remotely set her to default." Ella closed her laptop and sat back in her chair, looking like maybe she needed a drink and a vacation from this.

It took several minutes before Cora got control of herself. We sat around her, trying to be supportive with our bodies because our words couldn't be. Not yet.

"She made me take pictures of you when you were drunk." She glanced at Sarah. "You started making out with that guy Beverly's dating."

"Oh, shit." Sarah grimaced. "Scott? They're engaged."

"I know." Cora continued, "She made me film you eating a sundae off of Corrine's stomach." Her eyes darted to Laura.

"She fucking dared me to do it. I had to."

"She lit the candles and told me to pretend to go to the washroom during it, but I went to the window. From that angle it looked like you and Corrine were alone."

"So what?" Laura scoffed.

"She thought your parents would be upset you were having sex with a girl." Cora said it so quietly I barely heard her.

"My parents don't give a shit about that. They act the act, but my mom's best friend's gay. She's been married for a while, and my mom was maid of honor." Laura cracked a grin. "My dad agrees with the bullshit out here when people are looking, but he doesn't think that way. So fuck you, Cait. Guess she doesn't know everything."

"Guess not." Cora didn't smile. She didn't sound relieved even. Her eyes darted to Erica. "I have pictures of you stealing. Shoplifting."

"Oh." Erica's cheeks brightened. She lowered her eyebrows, maybe angry with herself a little.

We all knew about her condition. When school got hard or life became too stressful or she had a fight with her mom, she stole. It wasn't something we judged her for.

We all had things.

Sarah had battled with maintaining weight, bordering on an eating disorder and binge drinking. Cora had cut a few times; her reasons had been her own. They were making more sense now, though. Laura smoked too much weed, clinging to false reality instead of ours.

And I was a doormat.

I said yes.

I hid flaws.

I buried feelings.

I told myself I was weak and pathetic and I needed someone else to lead me. My self-esteem was in the toilet, and Cait was ruining our lives. Or maybe she was living hers by tormenting us.

Cora started to cry again, but this time she spoke through the tears with a shaking voice. "She set you up. She wanted you to see." She didn't look at me, but I knew she was talking to me. She'd tried to tell me that in the bathroom at the club, and it didn't make sense until this moment. "I told her when you got on the train to come to Griffin's. She went there, knowing you'd come. She didn't know you had a key. She thought you'd knock and she would answer."

"She wanted to see my face when I realized?"

Cora nodded her answer with a whisper. "I'm so sorry."

"I don't blame you. This could have been me. Honestly, she's pushed us all so far, look where we are. We've been friends for years, and yet not one of us trusts the others. She has us on edge. Alienated. She wants us this way; it's easier to manipulate us." I leaned forward, taking her hand in mine. She tried to pull away, and I saw it, a fresh line covered with tattoo makeup, hiding the wound. I grabbed her arm harder, turning it over. "You're cutting again?"

Her eyes didn't lift. She didn't try to defend herself.

I pulled her to me, surrounding her with my arms. "Cora, would you have done anything to any of us on purpose if Cait hadn't made you do it?"

She sobbed. She didn't answer.

The other girls leaped at us, crushing us with shaking hands and trembling fingers that dug in too hard, needing too much.

We cried, they cried, and we hugged until I was cramping and struggling to breathe.

"What does she have on you?" Ella asked after we started to calm down. "Cora, what does she have on you?"

"Nothing. Just a sex tape," she lied. It was painfully obvious.

"Tell them the truth," Ella said, indicating she knew that there was more.

She shook her head in tiny twitches, begging Ella not to tell.

"What is it?" Sarah's eyes narrowed. "Tell us. You know all our shit."

"Do you want me to tell?" Ella asked, not threateningly, but genuinely caring. Cora nodded and Ella spoke. "It was Cait's dad. Second year of college."

"What do mean, Cait's dad?" Sarah cocked an eyebrow.

"Her video is of her and Cait's dad in the guesthouse." Ella spelled it out for the slow ones.

"Gross," Laura blurted.

"Jesus, Cora." Sarah shuddered.

"Why?" Erica wrinkled her nose.

"He tried it on me too." I admitted a truth I'd never told a single soul.

"What?" Sarah gasped. "No!"

Even Ella appeared shocked.

But Cora gave me a look, relieved.

"Yeah. Cornered me, said some skeezy shit, and propositioned me. I managed to escape, but not because I was being strong. I was fast."

"He goes for the weak ones." Ella shamed me, but nothing she said was a lie. It never was. Ella didn't lie.

Cora nodded. "I was drunk."

I felt sick.

And all our friends stayed silent, traumatized by the revelations of our formative years spent in the company of someone who wanted nothing but to punish and torture us.

"And now comes the fun part of the night." Ella switched to cheerful again—vindictively cheerful. "Cherry and I have something else to tell you." Her eyes avoided mine in case I was against bringing them into the fold.

But at this point, I wasn't against anything that would destroy Cait.

This was going to be the summer we took back our power and got our freedom from the club. Not just me anymore, but all of us. Together.

Chapter Thirty-Two

INTO THE FOLD

Cherry

"I can't believe you brought them all in," Andy growled at me the next day, folding his arms and pacing our massive rec room between our bedrooms, tapping a finger on his bicep. "You sure they won't out us or change teams?"

"Yeah." Ella didn't tell him why yet.

Andy gave me and then Ella a look. "You trust those girls?" He stared her down, like he was reading her mind, until she nodded. He placed such trust in my sister that when she said something had value, he believed it and vouched for her.

"Okay then." He and I wouldn't ever have the same relationship. "So what's next?"

"We need to tell you something," Ella added.

"Or we can just—"

"No." Ella cut him off. "We need to talk before anyone else comes here or interrupts. This changes everything."

Even if it made my stomach ache to do it. I told myself that ending Cait's reign was more important than any of us, even my trust issues. Considering she'd been the one to give them to me, I owed her this.

I owed her so much more than this.

"She has sex tapes," I whispered to my brother.

"What?" The color left his face.

"Of all of us, when we were younger."

"And now until we take her down, most of us have something to lose." Ella's eyes darted to our brother. "Which means we need to bump up this plan. Fling Club is sort of weak in comparison to where we're at now. We need to change the plan."

"Holy shit." He sat, but it looked like he fell into the chair. "Sex tapes?" His voice cracked.

"She's been using Cora to do her dirty work: record people and trick them into doing things, or spy on them. Blackmailing her into blackmailing others."

"Blackmailing her with her sex tape?"

"Yeah."

"Does anyone else know?" he asked.

"No, just us and the girls. Hence the reason they won't betray us," Ella added.

"That psycho!" He sounded weird. "Have you seen them all?"

"No," Ella scoffed. "I can't handle that much kiddie porn. And anyway, I don't care about the porn. All I need to know is, where are you with your own data? Has something come from recording her?"

"No. She hasn't strayed from Ashley once. She hasn't been getting it on with anyone. She seems crazed, actually. She talks shit about everyone who isn't there and she's been treating people terribly when she thinks no one is looking. She's stressed. She's cold as ice when she doesn't think he's paying attention, and sweet as honey when she thinks he's noticing. She actually cares that he doesn't like her."

I broke in. "Well, we need something else. We need a plan. Ella's right, you guys and this crazy list of rules we were gonna break, it's not working. Yeah, she's slumming with Ashley and acting like a giant bitch, but that's about it. Besides letting your ass into Fling Club this year. She's broken, like, two rules. Big deal." I was starting to come undone.

"We can't do anything too rash until we get the USB or hard drive from her. There's no way she's had all those videos for all these years and never backed them up. Her computer isn't as old as the oldest videos, so we know she uploaded them. Those files got transferred somehow." Ella started pacing.

"We need a new plan. We can't worry about the stupid rules; we need to figure out something worse than what she has, in case she ever tries to use it."

"Great." Andy sat, staring at the wall. "We're so screwed."

"Hey!" Ashley came up the stairs into the room, smiling but looking unsure about interrupting us.

"Hey!" Andy said bitterly, and left with Ella hot on his heels.

"All done with your date?" I asked bitterly, too, kinda hating that he'd been out with Cait again today after seeing her last night at the Spring Fling, kinda hating her for existing, and kinda hating life.

"Yeah." He sighed and sat down. "She's exhausting."

I snuggled into the arms of the one person I didn't want involved in this plot. Especially now that videos and photos and other disturbing moments had surfaced.

Ashley kissed my cheek. "I've missed you lately."

"I know." I'd been avoiding meeting with him in my bedroom a bit. I needed to deal with my icky feelings of betrayal before I could really enjoy being alone with him again. Not to mention his constant dates with my archnemesis. They were driving me nuts. Whenever he was with her I found myself with Andy, huddled over a laptop, watching the live stream of boring bullshit Ashley suffered through.

"Have you missed me?" he whispered as he kissed up to my ear and bit my lobe. He was different with me. Real. With her it was more like he was being forced to breathe to stay alive.

"Yeah." It wasn't a lie, and it wasn't the truth. I missed being fun and the ease with which we did everything. Instant connection. Instant attraction. Instant relationship. But the hard part of being in that instant everything was being real. I was hurt and crushed and a little withdrawn. I didn't know him well enough to be all those things around him when I wasn't calm. I didn't doubt he would be there for me like he was before, but it wasn't the same as those other moments, like Griffin needing a punch out or me hating Cait. This was something else. This was me being filmed while having sex as a teenager. Losing my virginity. I really didn't want to talk to him about it.

"You don't sound like you missed me." He scooped me into his arms and got up. "Which means I have to remind you what there is to miss." He threw me over his shoulder and carried me to the hall that led to my bedroom.

"Ashley!"

"Don't Ashley me, missy." He turned and headed for my bedroom, slapping me on the butt. "This has all gotten too serious. I think you need to remember this was supposed to be a fun summer. As far as I recall, you sold it as fun."

"I lied." This was never going to be a fun summer, but having a few moments of fun spread among the chaos wasn't such a bad idea.

He walked the long hall, not speaking, not joking. He'd switched to serious Ashley, the one who took sex to a place I hadn't ever gone before meeting him.

When we got to my room, he closed the door and put me down, making me dizzy as the blood rushed back into my body. I swayed and he caught me, like an old-fashioned movie.

He held me, staring into my eyes, telling me everything he was about to do with just a look.

A slow smile crested my lip as he took a knee.

"Can we just snuggle?" I whispered, breathily.

"No." He lifted my skirt, making the rush of soft air on my thighs give me goose bumps.

He leaned in, tracing his nose over my cotton underwear, giving me more chills.

Sliding his face up and down my cloth-covered slit, he made me forget everything. I became insanely aware of only the moment I was in.

He pulled my underwear to the side, leaning in, his soft breath tickling me as he lazily licked his way into me. I spread my legs slightly, giving in to the promise of pleasure I wouldn't regret. I never did.

My hands slid down into his hair, gently touching his head as one of his fingers, my favorite one, slid between the folds of my pussy. He pushed in, making me nearly buckle, but my fingers gripped his head harder as his tongue flicked my clit, forcing my breath ragged and my eyes closed.

I got lost in the buildup of pumping fingers and flicking tongue and the warmth of his mouth covering my most delicate places.

My hand shot out, grabbing the doorknob behind him, working at holding me up better as he drove me to bliss.

He pushed me over the edge, fingering and sucking and caressing until my head dropped back and my breaths became moans and my body became his again.

I came with shaking legs and a trembling body, jerking and moaning until it ended. He lifted me up and carried me to my bed, laying me down and dragging my body to the edge of the bed to tear my underwear off and spread me, sliding his cock into my desperately ready body.

He didn't give me the slow strokes or the time to welcome him into me. He pushed in with force and fucked me, lifting my ass off the bed. I countered, pressing my feet on his shoulders and positioning myself to maximize pleasure.

We didn't even undress; we fucked. He gripped and thrusted and grunted until we found the height of pleasure together, me clenching and him pounding until he collapsed on top of me, resting his head on my chest.

"I missed you." I smiled, forgetting all my troubles for a moment.

"I knew ya did." He nodded, kissing my shirt.

He took the shame from sex. He made it so I felt like I was owning my place in this coupling and not just consenting, but wanting. Something I so desperately needed after experiencing Cait's proverbial mind fuck.

He cleared up the murky water I saw life through by taking away all the shit that clouded it. He was real, and this physical relationship had no ulterior motives. Our emotional connection was still building, but I had faith, for the first time, that this was the right choice.

He was mine, and Cait Landry couldn't take him if her life depended on it.

She wouldn't stand a chance.

He was mine and I was his.

And when he pulled out and climbed onto the bed, curling himself around me, I relaxed into him. I relaxed in everything.

Chapter Thirty-Three

Lip Crack

Cherry

The pool party at Cait's the next day was surprisingly fun. Mostly because I knew we were about to do some serious damage. Who knew that notion could be so calming and uplifting?

Sarah sat next to me, laughing and joking with Andy, who seemed like he was actually having a good time. Or he was faking it better than ever.

"Stop being such a worrywart." Sarah nudged him but gave me a look. "Andy thinks the moment he goes back to the city next week with your dad, a certain evil queen is going to trick us all into eating poisoned apples." She rolled her eyes.

"He does have a point." I actually agreed with him. "We've all had our fair share of rotten fruit."

"Maybe. But we're in this together. I've got your back, and you've got mine." She lifted her glass. "And for the first time I feel like we're really meeting each other. All of us."

"Cheers to that." I clanked my glass to hers and smiled, feeling the exact same way. Tragedy had brought us together.

"And we need to make sure we don't fall back into those old patterns of being fake and lying." Her eyes dazzled.

"Never again." It was the truth. I drank to her weird toast, hoping we could all live by those words.

"So, Ashley is hanging out with Cait still." Her eyes darted over there. "I can't believe you tricked her into picking him."

"It was easier than it should have been," I scoffed. "She's so predictable."

"You should go talk to Cait. She'll suck up to you extra, try to flaunt Ashley at you. Get a feel for what she's doing this week. She hasn't said anything to Ashley about her plans. But she'll gloat to you." Andy whispered to me as he took my drink in his hand, as if he'd leaned over to talk to me just to steal it.

"Hey!" I pretended to glare. "Guess I need a new drink." I winked at Sarah, who nodded knowingly. I got up and stalked over to the bar, leaning on it right where Cait and Ashley were talking. His eyes darted to mine. "A mojito, please." I smiled sweetly at the bartender, letting the alcohol I'd drunk make me appear a little more radiant.

"Hey!" Cait leaned my way, offering a fake smile and side hug. "How's it going?"

"Good." I spewed fake me all over her. "The party's a hit. Everyone seems to be having a good time." As I pulled back I noticed her bright-red lipstick didn't smudge on the wine glass. "What are you wearing on your lips?" I leaned in again a little too far, as if I were drunk. "Is it lip stain?"

"Yeah. It's called LipSense. It's one of those home-shopping things. A friend at school told me about it. She got it from the set of a TV show she was working on as part of her degree. They use it 'cause it doesn't smudge or come off. Works like a hot damn." She pulled a tube of it from her purse. "It's all I use now. I've thrown out all my old lipsticks. I can hook you up." She said it like we were besties again. Like this wasn't even slightly uncomfortable. We'd share lipstick like we shared guys, and it would be cool.

"Awesome," I said, playing along. I could be cool with it. I could be cool with the fact that she believed she was kissing my ass. She was sweet and kind to my face, all the while laughing on the inside, because she banged my boyfriend. Well, this time, I was laughing too. Because I was banging her fling.

"I don't want red; it would clash with my hair. And pink would be too girlie." I twirled my hair like a moron. The moron she believed me to be. "I'll let you pick for me."

"I'll have it tomorrow. My girl keeps a huge stock. I'm telling you, you won't ever go back to regular lipstick again. My friend is dealing it all over the Upper East Side, like crack. We actually call it lip crack." She laughed, so I laughed too. We were having fun. We were friends. Her being so nice suddenly was incredibly confusing and exactly what my brother had said would happen.

I started to see the patterns in it all.

The times she gushed and fawned over me, all the while knowing she was doing something seedy in the shadows I didn't see.

"What are you guys doing all week?" I asked, changing the subject.

"Oh, we have the regatta. Don't tell me you forgot," she scolded me.

"Regatta?" Ashley's eyes narrowed.

"Yeah." Cait's cheeks flushed as she tucked some of her pale hair behind her ear. "You have to come, obviously. I'm going. It's going to be a blast. Every year we host a massive party at the club."

"Sounds like fun." He didn't sound like he thought it was fun. He also didn't sound like he'd known about the regatta at all.

"And we're doing dinner tomorrow night with Liz and her fling. My parents are hosting a small gathering of close friends on the beach." She said it with the usual zest and flair. Trying to sting me.

"Awesome. I guess I'll see you guys later then. I need to find my date." I took my drink, but she grabbed my free hand.

"See ya later." She slipped a hand into Ashley's. Tormenting me.

"Sounds good." I waved and sipped my drink, acting oblivious. It wasn't anything new for me. In fact, it was my go to for most occasions. It was the calm on the surface while the storm brewed underneath.

And underneath I was pissed off and hating her hands being on Ashley, but I chanted that it was for the greater good. Keep Cait happy and distracted while we put this shit to bed once and for all.

I sauntered over to Rachel, Laura, Cora, Sarah, and Erica. Smiling wide. "Well, she took the bait," I said in a low tone so only they would hear. "Spent the whole time telling me about the lip stain she uses now instead of lipstick. Like I gave a shit. Then I went for the kill. They're doing dinner here on the beach tomorrow." I flashed my eyes at them.

"Okay, good." Rachel wrinkled her nose as she spoke. "And I don't know what's up with her, but she's all over Ashley tonight. He's going to need a bleach bath before you kiss him again."

"Yeah." I sighed, not so interested in kissing him suddenly. I hated Cait. I was tired of this show. "I want this over, like now. I want to end this—"

"But if we don't do it carefully, all our sins are going to come tumbling out," Sarah said, cutting me off.

We glanced over at Cait and Ashley as his eyes met mine, but I couldn't hold the stare. I couldn't stand to watch this anymore.

Cait slipped her fingers into his and led him around the side of the house to the guesthouse.

"Oh, shit," Sarah gasped, and my heart landed with a thud on the ground.

"He won't do anything," I whispered, not even convincing myself. This was my worst nightmare coming to life.

As much as I wanted every detail of what was going on with them, I didn't actually want to know a thing. I'd never felt so disgusted—not in him, but myself. Not even staring at my own dirty pictures or video.

Renting out the guy I liked was disturbing, and I was reaching that threshold, the one where I would end this and never look back.

Ashley and Cait never returned from behind the shed for the rest of the night.

My heart was pounding, and my fake fun was over. There was no way I could contain the hurt or rage I felt.

I wanted to trust him that he wasn't doing anything back there in her little sex house, but I couldn't. Too many burns from the same spark had taught me to fear this.

I hurried to my brother, interrupting his conversation with Josh and some other guy. "We need to talk." I dragged him away.

"I saw." He nodded, letting me know he didn't want to talk about it here. "I'll see you at home, and we'll go over everything there." He meant footage.

We would watch the footage of Ashley and Cait in the guesthouse.

I wasn't so sure I would be able to handle that.

In fact, I didn't think I was able to handle much more of anything.

Chapter Thirty-Four

THE SNAKE CHARMER

Ashley

"She's so pretty, don't you think?" Cait asked me as we watched Cherry and her friends.

"She is." I shrugged, trying to maintain the indifferent act as I reached into my pocket to find my sunglasses. Shit. They weren't there. I winced inwardly as I realized I'd left them in the car. I remembered taking them off when the sun went down.

"I heard a funny thing about her." Cait leaned in, whispering in my ear. "Wanna know?" Her tone changed, and her vicious whisper told me I didn't, but it also scared me into finding out what other vitriol she was about to spew about my girl.

"I heard she likes you. And that she was going to choose you for her fling." She sounded so strangely savage.

Now that news, I could handle. "Yeah, I know that." I said it with all the attitude in the world.

"And you care for her?" she pried, her eyes analyzing everything.

"I was looking forward to getting to know her, until you chose me for your fling. Now I'm trying to be a gentleman." I wasn't so sure that was the right thing to say.

"I have something special to show you." She slipped her hand into mine and pulled me around the side of the house, her fingers gripping tightly like this was nonnegotiable.

She led me to the guesthouse in the back, the one Andy said was a place for naughty things to go down during parties. Sort of like a dirty room. I didn't like where this was going. I was about to see just how dedicated I was to the whole mission.

Cait grinned like the evil stepmother on "Cinderella" as she led me inside and closed the door.

In the dark we stood, alone and uncomfortable. I parted my lips to tell her I needed to go, but she opened a laptop that was on the bed.

"Exhibit A." She clicked a link and brought up a picture of me from the MIT robot wars. "Ashley Jardine, the son of two scholars who work at Brown." She glanced back at me. "The jig is up."

My stomach tightened.

"You aren't some rich European. Your parents are poor teachers. The way I see it, either you're Andy's idea of a funny joke, or you're weaseling your way into the Kennedy family. Which means, if that's the case, I need to go see the Kennedys and tell them there's an imposter in their midst."

"What makes you think they don't know who I am?"

"There is no way Mrs. Kennedy knows who you are and lets you roam the grounds of her estate." She pulled out a lipstick. "But if she does, there's also exhibit B." The case glinted in the dim lights coming in the window. She pulled the cap off and plugged it into the computer; it was a USB drive. "Right now, this is private; no one can see it. It's just a stored file of mine."

She clicked a link, and a video started to play.

It was like amateur porn, except in the dim lighting I could see the red hair and pained expression of a much younger Cherry. I closed my eyes, desperate to get that image out of my mind.

When the noises stopped I opened my eyes, seeing the frozen image of Cherry and some drunk kid.

"Not a very flattering video of her, I'm afraid." She smiled like she was brilliant, even if she was missing a huge part of the plan. Thank God. 'Cause what she had on Cherry was enough to destroy her. Cherry would be crushed if anyone saw this.

"You're a sick bitch," I replied quietly.

"You have no idea. And if you don't leave, tomorrow, and never come back, I will publish this on YouTube and every porn site in the world. And then I will go visit the Kennedys and make sure they know exactly who you are. And maybe I'll even speak to my father's friend, the dean at Brown, and ensure your parents never find work at a reputable university again."

"Why are you doing this to her?"

"I know she likes you. She's trying to hide it, but I've had a lot of experience with Cherry. She's not great at keeping things from me. And I would like nothing more than for you to break that little heart of hers. You see, one of the employees at the Weinbergs' mentioned you two were hot for each other. Quite hot. So, you leave town tomorrow. Go and tell her goodbye. And then if I ever catch you two together again, even just saying hello, I will publish this video. Don't force me to do it."

"Fuck you."

"Oh, believe me, that's what she thinks is happening in here. And you will let her think that. You will not tell her we didn't fuck. You will not break things off with her with some romantic speech. You'll just go and act like you don't want to be with her and leave." She had a knack, I had to give her that.

"Make your way through the back gate and go home and pack, lover." She lifted a hand to my hair and stroked it. I jerked away, but she just cackled, evil and sick and twisted-like.

The sound of it would haunt my dreams forever as I turned and left, crunching along the path to the backyard and leaving through the gate.

I had one job in all of this. Protect Cherry and my parents.

I would leave. I would let Cait think she was winning. And then when Andy took Cait down, I would come back and help ruin her for good.

Until then I needed to make Cherry think I wasn't interested in her anymore.

But how could I do that?

How could I break things off with her?

How could I do to her what all these people did—betray her and make her think she was the one in the wrong?

How could I stay?

That video alone would humiliate Cherry and crush her image. Her parents would be devastated. She was already so fragile. Not to mention my parents' jobs and reputations.

No, I had one choice.

I walked faster, conflicted and desperately upset.

When I got to the Weinbergs' I wanted to find the employee who spoke to Cait and beat the piss out of her, but she wasn't there. It was night. And I didn't hit girls.

I paced like a tiger, spending my time the way I had when I first arrived. I told myself all the things I needed to hear.

Reasons why it was better to cut Cherry off now.

She was too rich.

She was too pretty.

She was going to have to marry someone better than me.

I was never going to match her mother's expectations.

Her parents would hate me when they met the real me.

This was never going to be more than a summer fling, if I was really honest with myself.

And my parents needed me and their futures intact.

By the time I was done, I'd convinced myself the water was tea and the sky was purple.

I knew there was just one thing left to do.

I just didn't think I could do it.

Chapter Thirty-Five

HE'S OUT

Cherry

The knock at my door came the same moment my cell phone rang. The call was my brother. I answered as I got off the bed. "Hello?" I wondered why Andy was calling me so early.

"You alone?"

"No, I'll call you back. Someone's at the door." I hung up the phone and opened the door, flinching when I saw Ashley standing there. "Hey."

"Hey." He furrowed his brow. He looked different. Or maybe I saw him differently, and it wasn't altogether Cait's fault this time. I'd tainted this one myself.

"I just came to say I'm out. I can't do this. I didn't sleep last night." He sounded weird, cold and angry. I didn't blame him.

"Come in." I grabbed his hand to pull him in, but he pulled back. "I didn't sleep either. I was racking my brain, imagining what Cait made you do. You didn't answer my texts or calls, and I wasn't sure what happened." That was a lie. I was sure, and I was sickened by it. But how did I blame him when I made him do this? I fell for him and let him fall for me and still rented him out.

"No, I'm leaving now. Right now. I just wanted to say bye." His voice cracked ever so slightly.

"Bye?" My heart crumbled, not even close to ever-so-slightly. "Like 'see you in the city' bye?"

"No." He swallowed hard, his eyes not meeting mine. "I can't do this. Any of it. I have to go." He stepped back. "I have to go." He repeated it, but quieter. He turned and left, walking down the stairs quickly, pretty much running to get away from me as fast as he could.

I slumped in the doorway, gripping the frame and trying to rationalize what was happening.

He was leaving.

He was leaving me.

Why?

The answers came flooding in.

I hadn't even thought about what it was like being him here. What it was like for someone outside of this world to step in and see the horrors under the rugs.

I tried to tell myself it wasn't me, it was this world. He'd gotten creeped out. He was disgusted and disenchanted and needed out.

But no matter how much I tried to tell myself it wasn't me, I knew it was.

I'd done this.

I'd driven him off.

I'd loaned him out.

I went back to bed, unsure of what to do or where I went from here. He was the piece of the puzzle that fit, the one part of my life I liked.

Sleep evaded me. I lay there, awake and upset.

Cait had won again. Only this time I'd helped her win. I'd helped her crush my heart myself.

The rest of the morning was filled with lonely hours of contemplation and despair and regret. I knew I should have done what Ella said. I should have left. I should have taken the second chance that Ashley had become for me and ran with it.

I should have escaped this batshit-crazy world and walked away, blissfully happy and unaware of what scandalous things Cait was up to next.

I couldn't hate myself for staying completely.

Even if I'd wrapped myself up in the scandal and drowned in it.

And I'd drowned Ashley too.

And he left, choosing sanity over this.

He'd played a good game; he'd acted like he didn't care that I was making him do this.

Up until that moment when he was pushed too far and had to take Cait to the dark corners of the party.

I hadn't wanted him to have to do it; maybe that was why I didn't go after him today.

I let him leave; I let him walk, because it was easier than facing the truth of what I'd done to him, what he'd done to himself, and what we were doing to each other.

This game was ruining everyone.

"Ashley's gone." Andy poked his head in my door. "Did you know?"

"Yeah." I nodded slowly, not sure if my brother was really there or not. Or if I was hallucinating.

"This whole thing was a mistake. Us trying to trick other people into doing what we wanted. We were always playing with fire." He strolled in, sitting on my sofa by the window with the blinds closed, even though it was midday. "I'm so sorry, Cherry. Ashley—" He sighed. "You were right. This was stupid. We sank to Cait's level and toyed with people."

"Hate made us blind." I offered us a pathetic excuse.

"We made ourselves blind." He wasn't going to excuse us anytime soon. I didn't blame him.

"So now what?"

"I was thinking, Cherry—" He pressed his lips together for a second, leaning forward. "What if you girls went to her place tonight and found and destroyed the evidence, and we ended it here? No more games or rules or blackmail—or even Cait. We just walk? Heads held high and self-respect intact, and then forget this ever happened?"

"You don't need any more revenge?"

"I'm way too old for this. It's not fun like I always imagined it would be. I had plans for getting her back, smearing egg all over her face, but those are lingering fantasies from when I was seventeen. And the reality is that it's been nothing but stress and bullshit, and I can feel it consuming me. And it's real now, ya know? We're not kids. It's real feelings and real people and real everything. I don't want to play anymore."

"Me either," I confessed.

"You and Ella go over, find the USB or hard drive we know she has, destroy it, and we end it here." He stood up and walked to the door. "Oh, and Ashley took the money before he left. He thought you should know." He didn't look back at me as he left the room.

I sat on my bed, clutching my stuffed bear, as my throat and eyes burned, but nothing would come out.

Numbness clung to me. My heart ached in a way I didn't know it could.

I resigned myself to the pain I was in. I lay back in the bed and closed my eyes, praying for sleep or tears or some equally satisfying release.

Instead I got my sister loudly walking into my room with a knock. "Andy says we should go to Cait's house now; he just checked down there. Her family's still having that clambake on the beach, the catered dinner. No one will be in the house for a while."

"I don't want to go."

"So you want her to have all those recordings of everyone having sex?" She paused. "You want her to release those videos to embarrass you?"

"No." I groaned and got up, staggering after her.

"What's your problem?"

"Nothing." I pushed her away emotionally and followed her from the room.

"Are you going to get dressed first?" She stopped at the top of the stairs. "Or just going over in your jammies?"

I glanced down, realizing I was still in pajamas.

"I'll wait in the car. Be fast." She sighed and left me there.

I didn't hurry. I also didn't try to look cute. I dragged on shorts, a T-shirt, sandals, and sunglasses and pulled my long red hair up into a ponytail.

I didn't give a shit if we saw anyone.

Ella wrinkled her nose as I got into the car. "You look like you smell bad."

"I do." I nodded.

"Wanna talk about it?"

"Nope."

"Good." She didn't sound relieved; she sounded like she didn't give a shit. Not even half.

Chapter Thirty-Six

A Color for Every Season

Cherry

Cait's bedroom was too big to search every tiny nook and cranny with just the two of us in the limited time we would have while Cait's family ate on the water, so we brought reinforcements. Sarah, Rachel, and Erica joined us in taking sections.

Rachel took the shoe and bag closet, the one she'd found the burn box in. She was also on the lookout for maids or other staff.

I took the bed and dressers and the drawers near the bed, searching and trying not to think about Ashley or the aching in my chest.

Ella took the clothes closet with Erica.

Sarah took the bathroom.

We searched high and low, but to no avail.

"How much makeup does one human need?" Sarah muttered. "She has to have seventy-five shades of lipstick, and they don't even match all the nail polish. And, like, whoever does their own nails anyway?" She strolled into the bedroom and slumped on the bed.

"Oh, you know Cait: if it's the best, she has to have it, even if she won't use it."

"Including all my boyfriends," I mumbled bitterly.

"True that," Sarah groaned.

I finished looking under the bed and touching every part of the frame, as if Cait were a spy and a part of the bed would come apart to reveal a secret stash of information. Some on us, some obviously about her time spent spying on the Russians.

I inserted an eye roll into my own thoughts about how larger-than-life I'd made her.

"Did you say she has tons of lipstick?" Rachel asked as she came out of the closet wearing a funny look.

"Yeah." Sarah shrugged.

"Lipstick." It took me a second, but I caught on. "She says she doesn't use it." I jumped up and rushed into the bathroom with Rachel and Ella. We grabbed at the tubes, pulling them apart. Each one was actual lipstick, never used before. "Shit. Why'd she lie about throwing them away?"

"She didn't." Rachel's eyes widened as she pulled the other side off. The lipstick worked; it was just shorter than it should have been because the other side was the tiny USB port.

"Holy balls." Erica grabbed one and pulled the bottom off of it. "I wonder how many are authentic?"

"Check the nail polish too. She's way above painting her own nails." Sarah grabbed one, pulling off the lid to find a USB stick in the handle.

We all hurried, pulling them apart, finding thirty-five USB sticks hidden in Cait's cosmetics. All were ironically labeled with shades such as Tight Lipped and Never Kiss and Tell. I rolled my eyes for real this time.

We dumped them into Sarah's handbag and put the bathroom back the way it looked before.

Erica looked like she might kill someone.

I felt the same way.

But we didn't kill anyone.

We sneaked from the room, leaving no trace of ourselves behind.

We hurried behind the guesthouse and left, acting like we had a million times at Cait's house. We were supposed to be there. Guests of the clambake, no doubt.

On the drive to pick up everyone's laptops and then go to my place, I texted Cora to meet us there and told Ella to head for my bedroom.

When we got there we separated, each with laptops and USB sticks, each with tingling stomachs and uneasiness.

"Corrine," Laura called out, and Rachel wrote the name on the whiteboard we'd brought in.

"Haley Dawson," I shouted as I turned off the video after a couple of seconds, then labeled the USB.

We each shouted out names until every USB was identified and labeled. Griffin didn't show up on any of them. I was surprised.

As I loaded my last one, I cringed, seeing it featured Liz, Cait's bestie. She walked into the guesthouse at Cait's, looking confused or drunk. Cait's dad came in after her, closing the door. I turned the video off when I noticed the way they made out and how they acted like this wasn't the first time. Cait knew this and was her friend still? Jesus.

"So, thirty-five people, all people we know well. All members of Fling Club. Whatever Cait's problem is, this is insanity," Ella said, contemplating.

"But why?" Rachel joined her, tapping her finger on her lip. "Why do this?"

"Like Mom says, that room is filled with all the future leaders," Ella added.

"And their wives," I said. "So, sex or incriminating videos of them as teenagers and early twentysomethings to use as bribery for later?"

"Jesus. She has a sickness. What do we do with them all?" Sarah asked.

"I'm fifteen in that video. I want it destroyed," I said flatly.

"Me too." Cora nodded.

"I kinda want to keep mine, the sex tape part is meh. But the other part is kinda awesome," Laura joked. "Makes me look kinda badass. Corrine is a complete score. She's totally out of my league."

"I want mine burned too." Erica ignored Laura.

"Mine too." Sarah nodded.

Laura folded her arms. "I am so done with Cait Landry. I'm done with Fling Club. I'm done with the whole thing. I might not even tell people I went to Paulson. Fuck that."

"Yeah, I'm out too. I won't be attending any other functions," Sarah agreed.

"Nope." Erica followed along. "I already broke it off with my fling. He's a douche Cait made me pick."

"What if there're other copies?" Cora sounded worried.

"Then I guess Cait's dad gets humiliated too. He was an adult, and you were nineteen. Sleeping with your kid's friends is gross. Cait Landry is dead to me." I got up.

"Let me deal with this." Ella folded her arms, looking the part of tiny evil dictator. "You guys keep your videos; I'll take care of the rest."

"Okay." I glanced at my friends. "I love you girls. And I am so sorry for being a bullshit, fake friend for the last decade. Longer." I sniffled, but the tears still wouldn't drop.

"Me too!" Sarah ran at me, and it snowballed until everyone, even hateful little Ella, was in the hug.

We clung to each other, and for the first time in my life, I was grateful I had them.

We had become the real friends we'd always pretended to be.

Tragedy had brought us together, but strength would bond us for life.

Chapter Thirty-Seven

ROBOT WARS

Cherry

I watched the scenery fly by as I drove to MIT. I didn't know where else to go. I didn't even tell anyone I'd left. I just took my car and drove until my ass hurt from sitting in the car for so long.

I was a bit exhausted and a lot stressed. But I needed to find him.

What was I going to say when I found Ashley, assuming this was where he'd gone?

Why was I going to say it?

He didn't want to be with me.

He'd left.

He'd even taken the money.

Why was I chasing after him?

It felt like a strange thing to do, going after him, possibly because my mother had brainwashed me into thinking that women were made to be chased. Men hunted women down, and women coyly feigned disinterest.

There was also the issue of where I would find him. MIT was a start, but not a great one. It was midsummer. Would he be there? I didn't think so, but I hoped someone would know him and give me a hint. Brown was my next stop.

I pulled in and parked, heading across campus to the one place I knew here: the Post-it note wall.

When I got to the wall, I sighed, seeing how sparse it was.

There was still a gap in the middle, where Andy had pinned the note that Ashley responded to. The note that set off this whole crazy chain of events and changed my life in the most unexpected and necessary ways.

Nervously I glanced over at the stack of sticky notes and the pens tied on strings, contemplating what to write.

I closed my eyes for a second and thought of Andy bursting in behind me, like last time. I imagined what he would write as he called me a pussy and scribbled.

Invoking that spirit, I grabbed a pink Post-it note and wrote, speaking it as I got it down. "In search of a guy who got paid to date a girl in a plot to ruin lives and destroy society. I need you. I miss you. I'm sorry. Email imightloveyou@gmail.com."

I glanced at it and then placed it on the board, where the empty spot was.

It wasn't exactly what Andy would say, and definitely not what I wanted to say, but it got the point across. I wanted to be wordier. I wanted to ask questions, like those brave souls who bared themselves on the other pieces of paper.

I stepped back, seeing movement next to me. A couple of guys walked in, both glancing at me. "Excuse me—" Another idea popped into my head. "Do you know where the engineering building is?"

"Yeah." One guy nodded. "I'm in engineering. I can show you the way." He pointed like his finger was magically answering this for me.

"Thanks."

"It's this way." He led and I followed, not saying anything.

It was an awkward and uncomfortable silence, so I broke it. "I'm looking for a friend. I know the campus is massive and there's not much chance you'd know him, but, Ashley Jardine." If that was even his real name . . .

"No, I don't think—wait. Robotics engineering?" He scowled. "Tall guy?" He said it like maybe there was a chance.

"Yeah. Dark hair. Looks like Clark Kent."

"Sure." He didn't agree. "I think I remember him making a robot last year for the robot wars that was awesome. It had a lobster claw—"

"Do you know if he's here now?" The robot wars? Jesus.

"No." He scowled. "I don't know. Maybe. We're not that close." He furrowed his brow again. He was a confused sort of guy. Or awkward around girls. He held a hand out. "This is the building. See ya round." He waved and stalked off.

What an odd guy.

Or maybe he was the norm here.

I'd heard students at MIT could be more intense in school and less versed in human interaction.

But maybe that was a stereotype too. God knows, the stereotypes that once defined me no longer meant anything.

My phone rang as I climbed the stairs.

I smiled seeing Ella's name. "Hey."

"Where are you? I'm in the middle of my takedown, and there's no one to appreciate my brilliance," she said in her usual brisk manner.

"I'm actually in Boston for the day—a couple of days if I have to go down to Brown."

"Boston?" She sounded confused. "Brown?"

"Yeah, at MIT. I'm trying to find him."

"You went to Ashley's school to find him in the summer?"

"I didn't know what else to do!" I snapped, pacing in front of the building.

"You didn't think to ask me?" She sounded insulted.

"I did, but then I thought you might try to talk me out of it. Like leave the poor boy alone."

"Cherry." She sighed. "He's the best thing that ever happened to you. Let me help you. What have you done so far?"

"I'm at his school building. Sort of hoping I could find someone who knew him. He doesn't have Facebook or Instagram. I couldn't find any Jardines in the phone book. His parents are listed at Brown, but I can't find a number for them, just an email."

"Give me a minute." Typing filled the background noise. Her fingers flew over the keyboard. "He's in England, you hammerhead. His parents are in Stratford-upon-Avon at some festival. His mom posted a picture eight hours ago, and guess who's in it?"

"England?" I grimaced.

"I'll meet you at JFK with your passport and book you on the next fight out. I'll arrange a car and keep tracking him as long as his mom keeps posting."

"Thanks, Ella."

"I can't believe you drove all that way without asking me for help. I'll try not to be offended this time, but never underestimate my powers again." She hung up, and I stared at the phone, wishing I could defend myself, but there was no chance.

What did one say in defense to that?

I jumped in the car and started the long journey back to New York, contemplating everything that was about to happen and whether or not I deserved the second chance I so badly wanted.

Chapter Thirty-Eight
THE WOLFINGTON BROTHERS

Cherry

I stared at the passport and the British pounds Ella had brought.

I almost wanted to ask if this was real. I was so exhausted from all the driving and panicking and desperate pain in my chest. I hadn't slept since he left.

"Don't screw this up. Be the person he thinks you are." She hugged me again, a third hug in one summer. Things were changing. "Text me when you land." She turned me and pushed.

I glanced back as I stuffed the pounds in my purse and dragged the carry-on she'd packed me. God only knew what was in there.

She waved and I waved back.

"Don't be a dipshit!" She smiled wide and watched me leave, as if she were the big sister and I were the little one. It was always this way.

I hurried to the security checkpoint to go through, flashing my ticket she'd emailed me.

By the time I was on the flight, I was lost in thought and exhausted. I stretched my pod out and made a bed, closing my eyes.

But I couldn't sleep.

I saw his face, heard his voice, and felt his arms around me.

For the first time in my life, I began to glimpse what real heartbreak was.

I wasn't feeling it yet.

I knew it was there on the horizon.

It was hovering, waiting for its moment to blanket me in sadness.

There was a chance he would tell me to get lost, that he genuinely didn't want to be with me and my heart was wrong.

The blanket would fall, then, smothering me.

The heartbreak would be profound, and I might not recover. I would know real agony.

I dreaded and oddly enough welcomed the feelings. They had to be better than this, this limbo. I didn't want to face reality in England, fearing the worst, and yet I didn't have the strength or ability to fight it. It overcame me, dragging me to it.

By the time the flight was over, I was cramped and uncomfortable. I sat the seat up and tried to stretch it out.

"We're making our descent, Miss Kennedy. If you could straighten your seat, please." The flight attendant spoke with a beautiful English accent, the kind you thought all English people had.

The way she said Miss Kennedy was the exact way my name should always be said. Like it was coming from Mary Poppins's own lips.

We landed, and I hurried to customs, staring at the officer as he asked me the purpose of my trip.

"I'm here to tell a guy I love him." It wasn't a lie.

"Well, he's a lucky lad then. On with ya. Good luck, miss."

"Thank you." I grabbed my passport after he stamped it, and hurried from the airport.

It was four in the morning UK time as I staggered through the arrivals gate, seeing my name on the card held by a driver.

"Miss Kennedy." The driver recognized me.

"That's me." I let him take my bag. I still didn't know what was in it.

With my luck, Ella would have packed nothing but lingerie and Ashley would turn me away, and I would end up in a hotel in London, eating sheet cake and crying in my skimpiest clean clothes while drinking champagne from the bottle.

"We're headed to Stratford-upon-Avon. Your sister said that the man you're looking for is staying there."

"Okay." He led me to the Bentley.

I climbed into the back, feeling a little sleepy but mostly terrified of what I was about to do.

The last time I surprised a guy my heart was crushed.

The image of Cait and Griffin in that bed and the noises they'd made still haunted me.

Fucking Cait Landry.

She'd ruined so many things in my life, with my help of course, but this one was tops. I couldn't. I pushed away those negative thoughts and believed that deep down, there was a chance Ashley would forgive me. That we were more than stupid games played by some stupid rich kids over some stupid videos.

My driver started the car, moving away from London toward Stratford-upon-Avon. I didn't know where that was, just that it tied into Shakespeare in some way.

The countryside was stunning.

I stared out the window until the car was parked between two red brick buildings. The sun was completely up, and yet I knew it was still early.

No one moved outside.

I was barely able to move, so exhausted and stressed that I was starting to come round to the other side and get energy again. Or maybe it was being here, in the town where he was.

"Your rooms are ready, miss." The driver opened the door, letting cool air take over the car.

"Thank you." I carried my purse and followed him up the stairs to the lobby.

"This is Christopher. He's the valet and your personal butler. He'll take care of you from here." My driver smiled. "Here's my card, if you need anything. I'll come straight away." A slip of a grin toyed with his lips, like he was hinting at something else. Who knew what Ella had told him?

"No, I shouldn't need you. But, thanks?" I said, unsure of what I was really thanking him for. I tipped him and followed the butler. The room was on the top floor with two rooms and a large bathroom overlooking the village and river. It was a stunning view. I had the impression this was the best room they had—maybe the best room in all of town. I'd have to thank Ella for hooking me up, especially since the trappings weren't her personal style.

"Is there anything you want at this time?" The butler drew the curtains and turned on the lights by the bed, then opened the zipper to my bag.

"No, thank you. And I can unpack that. Thanks." I cut him off, handing him ten pounds. "I think I'll try to get a bit of sleep since the village is likely doing the same and the person I'm looking for won't be awake yet."

"Who is it you're here to see, if you don't mind my asking? I might be able to find them for you."

"No, that's okay. My sister is already on the case. She's quite the detective, actually," I joked, even through my exhaustion.

"Well, I'll leave you to it then." He pocketed the money and left with a slight bow.

I sighed and locked the door, then headed for the bathroom to wash my face before getting into bed.

When I was finally lying down, wearing nothing but underwear and fatigue, I tried not to imagine how this was going to go.

Fear suggested one way it might end, perhaps protecting me from being too optimistic, but my heart was desperately trying to stay positive.

I closed my eyes and snuggled into the crisp sheets, sleeping too easily. Almost as if my body knew he was nearby—sensed him.

I slept like I did that first time he held me in his arms.

I woke that way too. Well rested and sated.

I glanced at my phone and grimaced. It was one in the afternoon.

Hurrying, I got up and opened the bag, dreading what I would find. I was pleasantly surprised to pull out shorts and T-shirts and flip-flops and sunglasses. She'd packed me a couple of bras, a few pairs of underwear, and a bathing suit. There was even lip gloss, mascara, and a few key items I couldn't really live without.

I was amazed. And then I recoiled.

A huge purple dildo greeted me, still in its wrapper. It had a Post-it note stuck on it. "Just in case you don't find him. Also fun for security," I read aloud. "I hate you, Ella," I whispered, and pushed the huge thing back in the bag, thanking the gods I'd been cautious with the personal assistant. I dragged my underwear off and jumped in the shower, leaving the dildo behind.

When I was clean and dressed and semiready for the day, I hurried downstairs, disappointed it was already two.

I hadn't even blow-dried my hair. I was desperate to find him. After a bit more primping, I dialed Ella and walked out the front doors.

"Hey." She sounded sleepy. It was only ten, and she was much more of an eleven girl in the summer.

"Can you locate them?"

"Maybe," she grumbled. "How was the flight?"

"Fine. But I'm anxious. I have work to do."

"All right, all right. I get the hint." Keys tapped over the line. "The last time his mom posted, he was at Shakespeare's house. There's a garden there. His mom posted a picture half an hour ago. They're watching plays in a garden or something."

"Thanks. Go back to bed."

She hung up before I had a chance to respond, as usual.

I stopped the first person I found. "Can you tell me which way to—"

"Shakespeare's house?" They laughed. They were American too.

"Yeah." I chuckled along with them.

"Go that way, turn left on Bridge Street, and then stay right at the roundabout. It'll be on your right. There're signs the whole way. You honestly can't miss it. They're obsessed." The man pointed.

"Thanks." I waved and hurried off.

I walked so fast I was nearly running by the time I got to the house. It looked like something out of "Hansel and Gretel." I bought a ticket to tour the entire house, making my way past art and artifacts. One side of the old house was actually quite a modern museum.

I tried not to stare and get lost in the writing and newspaper articles. It was fascinating to be here, especially having studied Shakespeare in school. I'd never been the scholarly type, but I'd always enjoyed literature. It was the easiest part of school. Reading a book and discussing it; how hard was that?

I made my way through the garden into an area filled with people. It was beautiful. There was a crowd surrounding a woman speaking. She wore a beige cloak and a pale cream-colored dress, all of which was old fashioned.

I recognized that she was reciting *Hamlet*, not because I'd read the book. The Mel Gibson movie was my Paulson English teacher's favorite.

I paused, listening to her perform, all the while scanning the crowd for the one face I was seeking.

But he wasn't there.

The garden and the performance my sister spoke of were all in place, but no Ashley.

The actress finished her dramatic set, and we all clapped as I headed for the other part of the museum, the house tour. I got inside as a lady started speaking of glove making and tanning leather.

She spoke of life at the time, the hardships and styles of living. My heart was racing as I listened impatiently and waited for her to stop.

Her monologue lasted several minutes before I was freed to go about the house myself.

I stopped looking at the tiny beds and small dressers and started searching faces.

When I knew he wasn't here, I sighed, defeated, and left the homestead, heading back out onto the street.

It was a busy place, filled with small artsy shops and streets you couldn't drive down.

I wandered down the road, smelling coffee. Good coffee.

Following my nose, I ended up in a cramped little café. I sighed. Glancing up at the shelves I saw "Monsoon Coffee" printed on all the plain brown bags. A name I didn't know.

"Help ya, miss?" a tall man asked as I stared at the coffee bags.

"Yeah, I'll get a cappuccino." I glanced at the pastry case. "And, oh shit. Is that custard pie?" I smiled. "I'll get a big slice of that."

"They're precut quite small." He winced.

"I'll get two slices, please." I beamed, not even caring. Ella was right, I had an unhealthy relationship with eating my feelings. And I was going to eat the hell out of them right now. I handed him the cash, leaving a tip in the jar with the witty joke pasted to the side.

He made the espresso, giving me a weird look. "Do I know you?"

"I don't think so."

"You from that TV show, with the wolves? The man wolves, werewolves? My sister watches it, and I always call it the Wolfington Brothers, but that's not quite right."

"*Teen Wolf?*" I chuckled. I'd been mistaken for Lydia too many times not to know the show. I'd never watched it, but I had looked up the actress and agreed we were incredibly similar.

"That's the one! You that girl?"

"No." I shook my head. "Not her."

"Related then?"

"I don't think so." I tried to meet his eyes politely and not stare at the street obsessively.

"Here ya go." He handed me the coffee in a small mug and grabbed the pie from the dish, plating it with some whipped cream. There really was nothing better than whipped cream in England. Except maybe butter.

"Thanks." I took my pie and coffee and sat in the window, staring out at everyone.

My first bite almost made up for the fact I was a complete failure in nearly everything. The second bite healed old wounds and filled up dark shadows with light. I closed my eyes and sighed into the bite, savoring the custard.

I lifted the coffee to my lips, sipping and moaning.

But as soon as I turned back to my pie, cutting off a huge bite and lifting it to my lips, I saw the eyes staring at me through the window.

They were his.

He was wearing his glasses again and one of those T-shirts I knew was dripping with irony, only I didn't know how.

He said nothing, just stared, confused, and maybe angry. I didn't know what to think of his response to seeing me. Nervous, I stuffed a huge piece of pie into my mouth as he wandered into the shop, taking up the entire doorway.

I waved, chewing and nearly choking on my pie.

"Cherry?" he finally said, still not nearly as pleased as I might have hoped.

My throat got thick with fear and tears I wouldn't cry. I could barely swallow the bite of pie, wincing as it tried to kill me and ached the entire way through my esophagus. I took a gulp of coffee to push it down.

"What are you doing here?" His eyes narrowed behind the glasses. Mine burned like they wanted to fill with tears, but that wasn't going to happen.

"Eating," I answered, not knowing what else to say.

"You came all this way for a slice of pie?"

"Yeah," I lied.

"Well, you picked the right spot." He hated me. It was so obvious I actually thought I might die.

"Appears so," I whispered. I couldn't speak.

His eyes darted to the people standing out front, older people. They were watching me through the window. "I'm here with my parents."

"I know," I whispered again like a frigging idiot.

"Did your family come?" He was just asking random questions now, maybe not sure how to break this off.

"No. I came alone." I blinked, wishing a tear left my eye. "I'm staying at the Arden Hotel."

"On Waterside?"

"Sure." I nodded, not sure.

"Well, have a lovely time, Cherry. You should really go to Warwick Castle while you're here." His eyes spoke words he didn't. They told me this was done, even if it was hurting him for whatever reason. He didn't want it to end. He wanted to say things that he wasn't going to say.

He walked away, and when his parents asked him who I was, he glanced back, and he lied. He said no one.

I was no one to him.

My throat burned, aching for release. I got up, leaving my coffee and my pie behind. I thought the man selling the coffee called out to me, but I might have imagined it. I couldn't hear anything.

I turned away from the direction Ashley had walked, and wandered off.

My heart cracked again. This time the damage was substantial. I blinked and something changed. The fire in my throat didn't subside, but my vision blurred and my eyes burned. I blinked again and they flooded, filling with tears. I sobbed slightly, staggering down the busy road as tears of sadness came for the first time in a long time, at exactly the wrong time.

I got lost for a while, wandering aimlessly and crying, but eventually found my way back to my hotel, tired and unsure of what to do next.

So, I called my brother.

"Cherry?" he answered, sounding jovial.

"Hey," I whispered.

"You okay?"

"He hates me, Andy. He hates me. I came all this way, and he won't even see me."

"What did you think was going to happen?" He gave me that honest brotherly truth, stinging me everywhere. "We fucked up."

"But I thought—"

"What? That he was cool with you letting him go off and hook up with Cait for money? He's a real person. I told you that we fucked up." He sighed. "I'm sorry. I know how much you liked him. I wish we could take it all back. Even if Cait's currently going off the deep end."

"I don't care. I hope she jumps straight in and drowns." I hung up. I didn't say goodbye. I didn't want to hear another thing about Fling Club. I wandered up the stairs to my room and pressed my back against the closed door when I got inside.

I slid down the door and sobbed again.

Some of the tears were angry. Some of them were filled with self-hatred. Mostly they were tears of longing. How wrong and naive I'd been.

Here I was again: back at the worst summer in the history of summers.

Chapter Thirty-Nine

THE DO-OVER

Cherry

A noise startled me awake.

I blinked and checked my phone. Eleven at night. I'd fallen asleep and missed dinner. My stomach grumbled about the disservice I'd done it.

Certain I'd heard something, I got up, searching for the noise as it happened again. A knock at the door.

I assumed it was the butler, wondering if I wanted something to eat. They were probably used to Americans with jet lag.

I opened the door, stepping back when I saw Ashley standing there. He grimaced when he saw my face. "You okay?"

"No." I burst into desperate tears again. He rushed forward, pulling me into his arms. I closed my eyes and cried. "I'm so sorry," I sobbed.

"Cherry," he muttered, pushing me back and closing the door. "Why did you come here?"

"Because I fucked up. I fucked up everything."

"No." He pulled back, staring down at me, wiping my tears from my eyes. "You didn't. I mean, it wasn't your fault." He walked to the bed, sat down, and pulled me into his arms. "You can't be here, though. We can't be together."

"Why?" I was ready to beg. I was ready to plead. I would have done anything for him to take me back. I realized I wanted the same thing Griffin had wanted: I wanted a do-over. I wanted a fresh start. I wanted a second chance at something new with the person I couldn't get over. I understood Griffin's desperation. Being in his shoes was hard, even if he'd wronged me. "Please, please don't do this. I can change. I can be better."

"No. Don't say that. I'm crazy about you—you have to know that? I didn't leave because I don't have feelings for you." He sounded emotional for a moment, then sighed and spoke as if revealing a terrible secret. "I left for a couple of reasons."

"Such as?" I asked.

"Firstly, Cait figured me out. Somehow, she recognized me from my MIT robot wars articles in the newspaper. She was going to ruin my parents' jobs and reputations and go tell your parents who I was." He took a deep breath like he was struggling. "And secondly, Cait's got something on you. I had to leave or she would let it loose for the world to see. I left to protect you."

"What?" I hadn't seen this coming. At all. I should have but I didn't.

"I don't know, she showed me a tiny clip of some dirty sex video on her phone. And if I didn't leave, it was going viral on top of my parents losing their jobs."

I reached into my purse, pulling the lipstick out and snapping the back off. "This USB?" It felt foreign in my fingers, my numb fingers.

"I don't know. Is it? How the fu—did you know all along?"

"No!" I gasped. "Of course I didn't know she filmed me losing my virginity when I was fifteen." I said it a little harsher than I intended.

"Jesus, Cherry. Why do you have it? Where did you get it from?"

"I stole it from her when I found her stash. She had over thirty of them."

"What? She was filming all her friends having sex? What the hell kind of shit is this?"

"I don't know." I shook my head; it was the truth. "Andy and Ella are still working on ruining her. I don't care anymore. When you left, you broke my heart," I whispered. "I didn't realize how much of it I'd given to you. I'm an idiot and I will change. I promise you, I am so angry with myself over it."

"I shouldn't have taken the money, but I knew if I did you would think I was only there for the money, and you'd leave me alone. It was the only way I could think to keep you safe. I wasn't prepared for the threats she made. And I've never been so out of my league. Your world is shiny and glitzy, but it's terrifying too. No one's ever blackmailed me before."

"Well, you haven't spent much time in the Hamptons. I still can't believe Cait chased you off. Why does she care so much about me being happy?"

"I was starting to think she's in love with you. When you were with the girls, sitting and drinking that night, and she dragged me to the guesthouse and showed me the clip on the laptop. She had it all set out. She said there was a lot more to it, and if I didn't leave, she was posting it on the internet. She said I wasn't allowed to see you or come back to the Hamptons or tell you anything. And that if she ever saw us together, she would post the video. She wanted you to think something happened between us."

"So, no-nothing happened?" I gasped, realizing I was willing to let it go if he told me what I wanted to hear.

"Fuck no!" He was insulted again. "I'm not like you people. I don't function like that."

"I'm so sorry. I just assumed—"

"Assume one thing about me, and that's all. One thing. That I'm crazy about you and would never do a single thing to hurt you. Unless it was in the name of protecting you."

"So, she took you there to make me think you hooked up and then drove you off. It's like she's obsessed with making me miserable."

"I don't know. I tried to stay, but the day I left, she sent me a text threatening me again. I didn't even know how she had my cell number. I left. Took the money and told Andy to tell you so you'd hate me. It would protect you until I could fix this." He brushed my hair from my face, dragged his thumb under my eyes where I no doubt had tons of mascara. "I'm so sorry I didn't tell you. I hate that I hurt you."

"I get it." I nodded, disgusted with the entire thing but not really as shocked as I ought to be. "I'm just sorry I dragged you into this."

"You Hamptons girls have a weird idea of summer fun."

"I have something important to say, though, like super important."

"Okay." His confusion turned to discomfort.

"I really am so sorry for dragging you into this, paying you to pretend you had no morals, and for making you act like one of us."

"Cherry—"

"Let me finish." I took a deep breath. "I'm also sorry for not introducing you to my parents as you were, for lying and making you something you weren't to impress them, like you aren't already impressive on your own. Because you are. You're smart and funny and sexy and real. And I know being real doesn't sound like much, but it is." I blinked, hoping for tears to soothe my burning eyes, but apparently I was done with sad crying again.

"I honestly don't care—"

"No." I lifted my hands to his cheeks. "Please care. It's important to me that you know you're more than any of that other shit. You're not some fling; you're the exception to every rule I was ever given. And I don't care about those. Not the way I care about you." I bared my soul. All of it. I pulled open my ribs and exposed my heart.

"Then I forgive you. If you'll forgive me for ever leaving instead of staying and fighting Cait."

"I do." And it was the truth. I forgave him for hurting me. His actions had been at least honorable. He'd wanted to protect me. I didn't have the same reasoning.

"I missed you."

"I missed you too." I sniffled again even though I was tearless. I couldn't believe Cait had done that to me, and that bothered me more than anything. How could I not believe she would screw me over this badly, after everything else she'd done? I was an eternal moron, always doubting how far she would take things or how dark her cruelty could turn.

But even with her efforts, her twisted games, I was here with Ashley. She hadn't stopped anything. If anything, my feelings for him were stronger from having thought I'd lost him.

I snuggled in, letting his fingers trail up and down my back, rubbing.

It should have been a sexy moment, being reunited.

But it wasn't.

I grabbed his hands and pulled him to my bed, stripped off my clothes, and dragged him into the cool sheets. I wrapped myself in him and the blankets and slept.

I was getting my second chance. My fresh start. My do-over.

There was still a half summer of fun to be had.

We'd wasted a lot of it, and I was going to cherish every second of the rest.

Chapter Forty

Meet the Parents

Cherry

I rolled over, groaning when I saw the time. It was five in the morning.

"What are you doing?" he moaned, pulling me back into his arms. "Why are you awake?"

"Jet lag. I've been sleeping at weird times. Now I'm wide awake," I grumbled.

"It's five." He snuggled back into a comfortable position. "That doesn't even make sense in New York. It's, like, one in the morning. Sleepy time."

"Is it?" I rolled over, facing him. He kept his eyes closed as I slid my hands down his torso and grabbed his rigid cock. "Seems like maybe you're awake too."

"No, that's my kickstand. Keeps me in bed." His lips cracked into a grin.

"Fine." I leaned in, kissing him softly as I squeezed a little. "I'll let you sleep." I let go and turned away, climbing out of bed and standing.

"Cherry," he moaned. "You can't squeeze it like that and then leave. It's bad for it."

"Is it?" I giggled.

"Yeah." He held the blankets open for me to get in. "Come back to bed, and we'll sort this out."

"No." I took a step away from him. "I think I'll leave you like that. I like this look on you." I hurried to my bag and pulled on shorts and a tank top. When I got to the door I slipped on flip-flops and sunglasses and grabbed my purse, fleeing before he could get up.

"Cherry!" he shouted as the door closed.

I laughed too hard at it all as I hurried down the stairs.

The sun was rising and the sky was reddish when I got outside. I wandered along the cobblestone road, checking out the red brick buildings and the Shakespeare center. The whole town was a combination of modern and ancient.

The renovations and new buildings carried the old ones, holding them up, like a great-grandparent dancing with a small grandchild.

It was beautiful.

I found a bench and sat, wondering if this was suddenly becoming a thing for me. Sitting on benches, confused and lost in life.

I thought about finishing my degree and where it was going to take me. I'd always assumed I would work in marketing until I married. That had been something of a plan.

My whole life goal had been to marry.

To chicken out and take the easy route, accomplish the things I was supposed to, whether I wanted them or not.

But sitting here in the cool morning air, in a foreign country filled with sites I hadn't ever noticed, even as I walked past them, I realized how young I really was. How immature I was. Ashley was worldly and driven. He knew what he wanted in life; he was striving toward that goal, working for something. He had a job lined up a year away. And here I was, stagnant and standing still.

He was right.

I saw it then and there.

I needed to bartend in Ireland.

Ride a train through foreign countries.

Find something that lit me up inside the way robot wars did him.

He hadn't even told me about the robot wars, and yet I knew that the moment he did, he would look ten years old and more excited about that than anything.

"Why do you look like you're plotting something?" He staggered down the road, interrupting my moment of contemplation.

"Tell me about robot wars and the lobster." I smiled, waiting for it.

And as I predicted, his eyes lit up. "How do you know about that?"

"I met someone who says you're famous in the robot world for a lobster pincher—?" I tried to recall what the guy had been yammering on about.

"Oh, man, that was the best one yet." He came and sat beside me, his hands coming to life, mimicking the robot's movements and the battles it had won. He said things like *hydraulics* and *turbo*, and I got lost in the details. He made weird noises, and for a second I felt like I was watching another *Star Wars* movie with Andy.

Seeing Ashley so excited about something confirmed everything I'd been thinking before he came and sat.

I needed to find what made me feel that way.

Not a guy.

Not a marriage.

Not someone else's dreams.

Not a plan made up by my mother when I was a kid.

I needed a real, solid idea of who I was before I made this decision.

We spent the sunrise on robots and breakfast on NASA, and we strolled along the river talking about his parents. They sounded amazing. Not what I expected, but amazing nonetheless.

He walked us to a small cottage, holding a hand out. "And if you want to meet them, they're in there."

"In that shack?" I gasped.

"It's our house from when I was little." He laughed. "Mom was finishing her PhD, and Dad was commuting between here and London. He had to stay in a flat in London so this was all we could afford here." He wasn't embarrassed; he was just so genuinely honest about everything.

"We should invite them to the hotel." I didn't go to people's houses uninvited, and I usually conducted business on my own turf. Where it was safe and I was in control.

"No." He shook his head, almost giving me a look like he felt sorry for me. As if in this I was the one who was roughing it. "They wouldn't want to have some formal meeting. Come inside." He took my hand and pulled, and that was the moment I panicked.

"I look awful. I'm not wearing makeup, and my eyes are puffy—"

"You look fine. They won't notice. They're not like that." He dragged me to the door. "It's not about that for them." He opened the door, smiling wide at a pale small man at a little table with a pencil behind his ear and a paper in his hands. He lowered the paper and grabbed the pencil, circling something.

"Finding many mistakes today, dad?"

"Oh, aye, ya know those editors couldn't—" He turned, pausing. "My word. The young lady from yesterday." He slowly got up. His bushy white eyebrows and frizzy gray hair didn't match Ashley at all, but the rest of him was an older version. Ashley was almost identical to his dad. I hadn't noticed it when I saw them yesterday; I was in such shock, I hadn't paid much attention to them at all.

"Welcome. I'm Ashley's da, Martin Jardine." He sounded like he'd lived in Glasgow his entire life. He was as Scottish as they came. He was even wearing a plaid shirt with his dress pants. I was surprised not to see a kilt. He pushed his glasses up and held a frail hand out for me.

"I'm Cherry. It's nice to meet you." I took his hand, shaking both our arms for him. In his eyes and skin I could see weakness and a sickly pallor and realized Ashley hadn't been calling him a godfather. He'd been saying *God, father*. Like "God no, my father is ill." And he was. My chest ached for Ashley as I realized what the money was for.

"The American girl who broke his heart, I assume?"

"I guess so?" I glared at Ashley, thinking he had broken my heart, but whatever.

"Aye, about time we meet you. We were starting to think ya were a figment of his imagination. Or he'd made a robot lady friend. That was a bigger concern." He winked at me and jeered at Ashley.

"Dad, I told ya she's real."

"Hmm-hmm." He scrutinized me, narrowing his eyes. "You're not of English heritage, are ya?"

"Romanian and Irish." I didn't mention my mom being half English. He didn't need to know that part.

"I suppose it's not so bad. I told his mother moving him ta England as a wee lad would ruin him." He scoffed. "Well, come on in." His accent was intense. It mesmerized me.

"Dorrie'll be home in a moment." He hobbled over and held out a chair for me. I tried to take the small house in as I walked to the table and sat.

"So, tell me about your family."

Ashley cringed, like I needed to keep some things to myself.

"They're not very interesting," I lied.

"Her brother goes to Harvard; he's in law. Her sister's a computer genius."

"And what about you?" he grilled. Even sickly, he was ten times more frightening than anyone in my family. "What are your plans?"

"Bartending in Europe for a while." It might have been the truth.

He paused, like he was waiting for the real answer, then burst into a laughing fit, coughing from it.

Ashley gave me a weird look, as if asking me why I was sabotaging this. But I couldn't tell him that I had no plans, and lying to his dad felt wrong. Like he might be able to tell. Like he knew teenagers and young people better than they knew themselves.

"Don't listen to her, Dad. She's going to Wellesley and finishes this year with a degree."

"In what?" he barked.

"I was hoping to work in marketing." That was the truth, but it was an old truth. I didn't want to work in marketing now, or at least not the kind of marketing that had me pumping more products to the über rich while I continued to lose my soul.

"Marketing." He nodded. "So you're lost is what you're saying?"

"Dad!"

"No." I smiled at Ashley. "He's right. I'm totally lost, Mr. Jardine. I'm not like Ashley or my brother or sister, who're set in what they want to be and so skilled toward those goals. They've known who they are all along."

"And you haven't?" He sighed and sat back. "I know this story. I see it loads at Brown. But I also lived it." He grinned, maybe remembering. "A hundred years ago when the Earth's crust just cooled, I was a wee lad working at my uncle's newspaper. I thought I would be a newsman. I saw that for myself." He chuckled a hearty laugh. "Then I went to college, and I met this girl."

"Mom?" Ashley sounded confused.

"No, ya dafto. Muriel. She was beautiful, inspiring. I ended up taking some of her same classes, following her and hoping she might see me too." He winced. "I didn't realize she wasn't my type, or rather I wasn't hers. She was in love with our professor, Ms. Tealing."

"Dad!" Ashley said that a lot.

"Oh, don't get your knickers in a knot, the story has a happy ending. I met your mother in those poetry classes I'd followed Muriel to. By then I'd found my passion; Robbie Burns had lit me up with Scottish pride. Made me feel things I never imagined I would. And certainly not for an old, dead codger. But your ma fancied me for it. Even if she is a traitorous—"

"Dad!" Ashley sounded exasperated. "First time meeting someone. Not the right moment."

"He's a lot like his ma. Overly excited and all. Emotional people." He winked at me, making me laugh. "Not like you and me."

"I hadn't noticed that side of him until I asked him about robots."

"Oh, aye, don't ask about that."

"Why did I think this was a good idea?" Ashley asked himself aloud.

"Shall we get out the albums so your mother can get it over with when she gets home?"

"Not the albums," Ashley pleaded.

I relaxed, laughing even more.

His house wasn't how I'd imagined it. I'd pictured scholarly snobs who knew they were smarter than everyone else and rubbed it in your face.

This was far better.

Messier, but better.

I'd also imagined something perfect, pristine, and super domesticated. I didn't know it would be shelves of books and half-written works and lamplight over desks and clutter everywhere.

I didn't see creative chaos as how it would look but now it suited. Like Bilbo Baggins's hobbit hole.

It was better this way. They were real. Frighteningly real.

The door swung open, and the woman I'd seen in passing yesterday smiled wide. "Oh, the market was crazy!" She came in like a tornado, with bags of groceries nearly falling on the floor. She paused when she saw me. Her eyes darted to Ashley and then her sick husband.

"Ma, this is Cherry." Ashley put his hand out to me, like I was on display.

"Of course." She sounded less Scottish but still had an accent. Hers was more like Ashley's, mixed and Americanized. "I see you found each other." She winked. "He was all sorts of worried about you being here." She sounded unimpressed.

"I didn't tell him I was coming." I stood and held a hand out. "Cherry Kennedy."

"Kennedy?" She cocked an eyebrow. "As in the great family?" She lost all the joy she'd had a second ago.

"No," I lied. I didn't know why I lied to her, but it seemed like the right move. We were cousins of the great family, our family also rich and connected. I wasn't sure what she felt for them, but whatever it was, I didn't want to chance it.

"You're not related to them?"

"I mean, super distantly. Like maybe some cousins in common." My siblings and I were the cousins in common.

"Interesting. And how did you two meet?" She was not friendly. Her eyes spoke volumes about the level of dislike she had for me or maybe my family. People she likely didn't even know.

Sweat popped from my skin as my anxiety started to grow.

"School. Her brother's a friend of mine from school," Ashley covered. It was a half-truth.

"He goes to MIT?"

"Harvard, law. But he comes to the robot wars," he lied. "Cherry goes to Wellesley."

"Harvard law and Wellesley?" Her look of disdain was overwhelming. "So you must come from money?" She said it as if money was the worst thing possible.

"Oh, now, Dorrie. Don't get on that again." Mr. Jardine tried to lighten the moment, but there was no lightening it.

"Mom," Ashley scolded.

"Where are my manners?" She forced a smile over her face, one I recognized right away. "You'll have to excuse me. I have to put these groceries away. It was lovely meeting you, Cherry. Enjoy your trip here."

She forced herself to say it and then left, walking to a room in the back and closing the door.

"I should probably . . . ," I said, and got up. "It was nice meet you." I hurried from the house, leaving the door open and rushing down the road until I broke into a run. My flip-flops weren't great for escaping, but I managed. Even with Ashley yelling my name as he ran after me.

I hurried back to the bench, not really sure where else to go. I slumped down and covered my face, wishing I'd never gone to the house. The way she looked at me was still burning holes in me.

She was exactly how I'd imagined her.

She did think she was better than me. In fact, she knew it. And for the first time I understood how it was for Ashley to be in the Hamptons. He'd done remarkably well for someone so out of sorts and his league, as I was here. I'd never struggled to fit in before. It was a terrible feeling. One I didn't even have a reaction to.

"Cherry?" Ashley walked over quickly, heaving. "Look, I'm not much of a runner." He wheezed and sat down next to me. He started to joke. "So that was awkward. I'm going to guess that's how it'll be for me with your parents?"

"What?" I dropped my hands and turned to him.

"I'm sorry about that. My mom hates rich people. She hates the blue bloods and rich elite. She thinks American royalty is the biggest joke in the entire world." He laughed bitterly. "And I know how your family is—"

"Mother," I corrected him. "My dad's nonchalant, like yours. He'll think NASA is the coolest thing ever. My mom's not going to be like that." I pointed in the direction of his house and laughed. "She's going to be much worse. Much. But I wouldn't have done that to you. What the hell was that? Why would you take me there without warning me?"

"I didn't know. I've never seen her strike at anyone before." He grabbed my hands and kissed them. "I am so sorry. I didn't know she would act like that toward you. I thought maybe meeting you would win her over. Like seeing you weren't some spoiled brat bent on ruining and corrupting me—"

"Oh my God," I gasped. "I did try to do that! She's right!"

"No, you didn't." He leaned in and kissed my cheek. "And trust me, my dad's going to give her a firm tongue lashing. She won't get away with treating you that way."

"I can't believe your mom hates me because I'm rich," I said with a groan. "She didn't even give me a chance."

"Just like your mom won't give me a chance once she finds out I'm not rich. Do we care?"

"Yeah?" I turned and faced him, staring into his eyes, clearly saying the wrong thing. "No? No, we don't care. When you meet my mom for real, I promise I won't care what she says."

"And I don't care what my mom says." He smiled peacefully with the statement. "If she wants to be unreasonable, she can do it when I'm not around. And she will be apologizing to you."

"No, please. Don't. I honestly want to forget it ever happened." I sighed and leaned into him. "I never imagined your mom would disapprove of me."

"Yeah, well, she can be crazy."

"So can mine," I agreed. It was extra baggage we didn't need. I'd already made enough drama to last us our lifetime.

"So, did you mean it, what you said about bartending?" He got serious.

"Maybe. I honestly don't know what I want to do." It was shaping up to be a crappy morning.

"Want some custard pie to go with this conversation, since I ruined yours yesterday?" He nudged me.

"I do." I glanced up at him. "You did ruin my pie."

"I'm sorry." He laughed. "I was just so shocked. I couldn't believe you were sitting there, eating. I'd worked so hard to not go back to the

Hamptons and to you, and then there you were, casually having some pie three thousand miles away from home."

"I think we both know I've got an unhealthy obsession with dessert."

"Movies and dessert." He stood and took my hands, pulling me up.

"What do you mean?"

"You relate everything in life to movies. It's bizarre. Everything reminds you of a scene in a movie. You're obsessed. And you've seen everything. You bring up quotes from movies I've never heard of. And you remember them better than any details in the real world."

"No, I don't."

"You do. You love movies. Admit it," he joked.

I realized he was right about that. I did love movies. I escaped through them. "Everyone loves movies," I said, defending myself.

"No. Not many people love movies the way you do. Your love is the kind that, I don't know, directors have. Taking the moment of reality and capturing it for film. Taking the realness of this life and creating art from it. I told you, you should be an actress."

"I'm not actress material," I muttered, and let him drag me along the street until we got to the café from yesterday.

The tall guy was behind the counter again. "Hey! I was worried about you when you ran out of here yesterday. The food couldn't have been that bad!"

"It was delicious, actually." I went to the counter. "In fact, I want more custard pie and a cappuccino, please. And I'll buy some of your beans to take home. This Monsoon Coffee is incredible." I turned to Ashley. "What do you want?"

"I'll share yours," he said absently.

"He'll have the same." I smiled at the barista as I paid, then frowned at Ashley. "I don't share."

"Fine."

We sat and waited for our coffee and dessert, staring out the very window I'd looked out yesterday, wondering what my fate with this man would be. We watched people as the shop got busy and the food was delivered.

I took my first bite and moaned. "Oh my God." I chewed slowly, savoring the taste and creamy texture. "I could live in England, never go home again, and be three hundred pounds heavier from all the desserts I lived on."

"No, you couldn't." He ate slowly, too, clearly enjoying his. "You like dessert, but you don't love rain or cold. You complained about spring all the time. You were ready for summer and heat and running. Running in the rain is miserable."

"It's warm here," I corrected.

"It's been freakishly warm here this summer. Normally there's a lot of rain and cold weather. And fall, spring, and winter are all cold and wet. You'd be depressed in no time."

"Okay, well, I could open a bakery in New York where they only use traditional English recipes."

"That would be amazing. I'd be into that. A little taste of home in my new home." His eyes danced with pleasure, staring at me like maybe I was home to him in the way I suspected he was home to me. Carrying around my delicately mended heart in his pocket.

"I guess." I sipped my coffee, trying not to overthink anything. "Maybe I could be a barista here and just do summers and try to find myself, then go to Australia for winter."

"Or you could finish your degree and try some new things, new hobbies. Venture out of your comfort zone and see if something lights you up."

"You mean the way you do?" It was cheesy, but I had to say it. He was the light. He made me brighter. He made me want to be brighter.

"Do I light you up?" he mumbled in my ear.

"You do." I leaned into the sweet embrace. "You make everything better."

"And you make everything worthwhile." He kissed my cheek. "Want to go back to the hotel room?"

My cheeks flushed as I nodded. "We need to get my coffee beans first."

"Okay. You go wait outside, and I'll grab the bags." He kissed my cheek again and wandered over to the counter.

As I headed outside, I tried not to get distracted from the promise of what was about to happen, battling with the differences between our families.

I told myself it didn't matter.

That no matter what the future held, I was confident we would always find a way to be together. Even if it was just him and me and playing house with no view of the outside world. We could find happiness anywhere. We made it everywhere we went.

Chapter Forty-One

Et Tu, Andy?

Cherry

We strolled around the gardens, listening to the tour guide as he led us and explained everything. Warwick Castle wasn't what I'd expected. It was really touristy. Like an English version of an amusement park.

Ashley kissed my hand and led me after the man.

"Is your dad going to be okay?" I asked the question that had been sitting with me since meeting him.

"Yeah, sorry. I should have said something. I know he looks god-awful right now. Just finished his last chemo. Doctors say he will be right as rain in no time. That was why I needed the job so badly."

I understood. "It's why you stayed?"

"No." He grinned. "You were why I stayed. He was why I started. I have morals and ethics and a conscience, and I let you and your brother sell them so I could afford school and not rely on any money from my parents this year. My dad isn't working."

"If you need money, can you just tell me? My monthly allowance is more than your entire year at MIT. Money means nothing to me. At all."

"I can't, Cherry." He scowled. "You're not my sugar mama."

"No, I'm your girlfriend, and if I needed something stupid like money, you'd do anything to give it to me. I know that. Look what you did for your dad."

"Keep your money. What I want from you is far more precious." He kissed the side of my face as we strolled.

We were in the middle of listening to a battalion discussion when his phone rang.

"Yeah?" he answered. I'd never heard him answer the phone before. It was a strange way to answer. No hello? I assumed all English people said hello. And goodbye. I assumed their manners were better than ours.

He scowled and lowered his voice; I caught nothing but one word: *guess*. Was he guessing something or asking the person to guess, or was he saying *I guess*?

I was nosy, but that's all I learned from the conversation until he hung up.

"It was my dad. He wants us to meet for dinner. Suggested eating out so Mom doesn't have a chance to cause a scene." I parted my lips to say no, but he stepped closer, kissing my mouth and whispering into the embrace. "Please do this for me. Please. She's being unreasonable, I know that. She's judging you for no reason. It would mean the world to me if we tried to patch this up."

"Eating dinner with someone who hates me isn't going to patch things up, but I guess it's a start," I agreed.

"I'll owe you." He cracked a grin.

"You mean you'll eat with my mother and endure whatever bullshit she tosses your way?"

"Precisely." He kissed me again. "Did I mention you're the best girlfriend in the world?"

He'd said that word a couple of times before. But this was the first time, to my face, since the incident, that he'd called me his girlfriend.

It warmed my face and melted my heart and made dinner with his mom sound like a walk in the park.

"They're going to meet us at your hotel at five."

"We should call and make a reservation," I said.

"Allow me." He lifted the phone again, only this time when someone else was on the line, he spoke in a friendly way. "I think you might have a table open; it's for Miss Kennedy in room four-oh-seven. Right, that's what I thought. For four. See ya then. Cheers." He hung up and grinned. "Your name really does do a lot. Do people ever say no to you?"

"You. My mom. My sister. My brother." I contemplated for a second longer. "This one teacher at Paulson. He was a bit of a jerk. Though now that I think about it, I suspect he just wanted more from us. We hid behind our parents and their names."

"He might have helped you out more than you realize," Ashley chided. "Might have brought a little dose of reality to an otherwise unrealistic world."

"Maybe," I admitted, allowing for the fact I grew up spoiled and lacking conviction.

"And I think you're mistaken about something." He pulled me to the side of the tower, away from where our group was walking, and pressed my back against the rough bricks. "I've never said no to you."

"You kinda did. You rejected me." It was the truth, even if it hurt him. I regretted saying it and causing the look that came over him. "You told your parents I was no one when you saw me."

"Oh shit, you saw that? I'm so sorry for that."

"But I understand. Believe me. I've spent my life controlled by Cait. Well, my last six years anyway."

"So it all changed when she was fifteen?"

"Yeah. She was always bossy and rude and uppity. She expected things handed to her. But when we turned fifteen, she got mean. The videos and pictures seem to start then, too, by what I've seen."

"Did they start with you?"

"I don't know." I contemplated it for a second. "I guess so. I was the first one of the group to be forced to lose my virginity by her. Erica was second by a couple of weeks."

"What changed at fifteen?"

"She and my brother broke up." I answered honestly, but my brain got stuck there, curious about that.

We wandered the sites and ventured through the castle, and the guide spoke a lot of what he knew about the era the castle had been built in and the changes that had come over the centuries since it was built.

And while I tried to be a good listener, I was stuck.

I didn't recall it all that well, but I knew Andy and Cait had broken up right before she started Fling Club, and it was then that she became vindictive.

Contemplating it all, I texted my chat with my brother and sister.

You guys recall anything special about the time Cait created Fling Club? It seems to me that she went from dating you, Andy, to cheating on you with that guy from Italy, to dating Brom Wendell, him cheating on her, and then she created Fling Club and became the meanest bitch of the east. But why?

Andy answered first: She was embarrassed. He'd cheated on her with that townie. Made a fool of her.

Then why make a fool of me? I was the first person she attacked that summer. And the only link to her and me was you, Andy. Did something happen?

Ella answered next: You telling her or am I?

My insides tightened. What did Ella mean? Tell her? Tell me?

"You okay?" Ashley asked.

"Yeah." It was a lie.

I couldn't blink—I could barely breathe—as I waited for the answer. But it didn't come in a text. It came in a call.

Andy was calling me.

"Hello?" I answered nervously.

"Hey." He sounded weird, hesitant.

"What did she mean?" I closed my eyes, terrified of what was about to come out.

"That Fling Club didn't start because of Brom Wendell." He sounded hollow and yet remorseful.

"What does that mean, Andy?" I shouted. "What are you not telling me?"

"Don't freak out!" he warned me. "After Brom and Cait broke up, she and I hooked up again. I begged and pleaded with her to come back to me, said I was angry that she'd cheated on me."

"Oh my God, Andy, what did you do to her?" My entire body was on pins and needles.

"I recorded us," he muttered. "Recorded her with me. That's what's on my video. It's why I wanted it destroyed. I didn't want you to know. Anyone to know."

"Fuck, Andy!" I whispered. "How could you do that?" Disgust sat like a slug in my throat.

"Because I was pissed off. Because I hated her. Because I wanted to have the upper hand. I wanted to ruin her for cheating on me with the Italian. I wanted to show her that I could be sneaky too."

"And then she bullied me into losing my virginity—bullied me and filmed me to gain the upper hand on you?" I gagged. "And made Fling Club as a means to do it all?"

"Yeah. Only she didn't stop there. She did it to everyone. I didn't know, Cherry. I didn't know she was making stockpiles of movies of everyone we knew." His voice cracked. "I thought she made up Fling Club to fuck me over, so no one would ever date me again. So she could control the summers and the fun. To cock block me. It was revenge, but I didn't see how deep it went."

I hung up the phone without saying goodbye. I couldn't listen to his excuses. I called Ella.

"He fucking started this?" I gasped.

"Yeah." She sounded as disgusted as I was. "I recently suffered through the old videos, trying to find a clue or a motivation. Then I remembered Andy had been so crazy about destroying his video. But I hadn't given it to him yet, and he was being a dick about it. So I made Ryan watch it for me, and he said Andy kept looking at the camera, like he had orchestrated the whole thing."

"What do we do with this?" I didn't even know what to say or how we went about fixing this mess.

"I don't know. I was thinking maybe you should tell the girls. Tell them what happened, and then you could all talk to Cait. Together. Tell her you know what Andy did to her and how this all got away from her. Be on her side a little, even if she did sacrifice you to the plan."

"Confront her? Be on her side?" That didn't sound like a good idea at all.

"Yeah. Our brother filmed her losing her virginity and tormented her with it."

"I'll talk to them." I didn't want to, but I knew I had to. Ultimately Cait had been a victim of this as well. Her being fifteen, she knew how I felt. Yes, she'd made me the same sort of victim she had been, but in the end this all fell back on my brother's lap. He started it. He lit the fire that burned all of us. "I'll call you after I talk to them."

"I didn't want you to know about this until after you got home. I wanted you and Ashley to figure things out first."

"We did." I nodded, glancing his way. "We're good."

"Okay. Call me later." She hung up.

"What was that all about?" Ashley sounded worried.

I took a deep breath and began to relay the entire conversation back to him, filling in the gaps that he didn't hear.

As it went along, his expressions matched my words and I wondered if these looks of horror had been the ones I'd had.

How could my own brother have done something so terrible?

It was a question I wasn't so sure I would ever have the answer to, or want to have the capacity to understand.

Chapter Forty-Two

MEET THE PARENTS, PART DEUX

Cherry

We walked into the restaurant, and I tried really hard not to feel nervous. The weird story about my brother and the fact that Ashley's mom hated me weren't going to undo me. I wasn't letting this shit happen to me anymore. No more victim Cherry for everyone's garbage.

But I refused to let my brother and his bullshit ruin one more thing for me. And winning over Ashley's mom was going to happen.

I sat and folded my napkin on my lap, waiting for them to show up.

"They're always late," he said nervously.

"My mom too. It's part of the power play," I said shortly. I took my wine in hand and chugged back half the glass, then followed it with a deep inhale. It did nothing to calm me, though. No, I was at DEFCON twelve for discomfort and betrayal.

My own brother. Responsible for six years of hell and brainwashing. Responsible for the creation of a club that he himself said was full of sick, twisted control freaks and vapid sluts. Well, how would he defend himself now?

No. No, Andy.

I needed to focus on dinner.

Ashley's mom hating me was solvable. I could do it.

He reached over and took my hand in his, kissing the back of it as his parents walked around the corner. His mother's cold eyes narrowed on the kiss, her disapproval laid on thick.

His father was jovial, though, maybe enough for the both of them. He wrapped an arm around her waist and forced her forward.

"Dad, Mom!" Ashley stood and kissed his cranky mother on the cheek.

She closed her eyes and leaned into the kiss, relaxing for a second.

"Cherry, lovely as always." His father took my hand and kissed the back, reigniting the fire in his wife's eyes.

"Nice to see you again." I offered a smile, forcing it to stay on my lips.

"I'm starved. What's good here?"

"Everything." Ashley helped his mother into her seat and sat back down.

"I see they have lamb on the menu. Wonder if it's Scottish lamb?"

"Maybe." Ashley laughed at his dad. "I have to tell you guys something. Cherry and I are heading back to New York tomorrow." He broke the news we'd both agreed on after the Andy discussion. He knew I had to get back and put an end to the madness, once and for all. As much as I wanted to avoid it, it had to be done.

"Oh, aye, we figured you'd be off doing your own thing soon enough." His dad winked at me, but his mother tried to kill me with her laser eyes.

"I'm having some family issues," I admitted. A truth I wanted to keep hidden, but offered to her as a sacrificial lamb. An American lamb.

"Really?" Her eyes widened.

"Yeah."

"Well, did ya like Warwick Castle then?" his dad asked, not at all subtle in his attempt to change the subject.

"I did," I said, willing to keep the conversation safe and friendly. It was different for me.

"I hate it," he blurted. "Too many people. Too busy. Give me a quiet castle, or even some ruins, any day of the week. But that bustle of clueless turds is too much to take."

We all laughed, and he took it from there, entertaining everyone.

Even Ashley's mom smiled and shook her head at her comical husband. He charmed me with his unassuming nature and unapologetic tactlessness. A man passionate about poetry and his country and yet real and funny could entertain anyone. He was a gem.

Even my mother was going to like him. I smiled at that. I realized I wanted Ashley's family to meet mine. I wanted us to date. I wanted a future with Ashley. Not the future I'd always planned on, but something not so set in stone but instead something new and fun. It had to be new, since he didn't fit into the mold I'd been sculpted by—not by a long shot.

After we ate, I made my way to the bathroom. I washed my hands and was reaching for a towel just as she came in: Ashley's mother. She stood in the doorway and blocked my escape.

"Look." She sighed. "I've sat through this whole dinner and put on a good face, but I can't figure it out. What do you want with my son?"

"What do you mean?"

"He isn't one of your fun party boys. I know all about you Hamptons girls. You rich blue bloods who think you're better than everyone else. But Ashley isn't a pawn in a game. He's going places. He's going to be a—"

"I just want to love him." I blurted my truth, interrupting her fear. "I want to help him accomplish his dreams. I want to be his friend and his lover and his girlfriend. I want to watch him succeed in everything he tries, because he just seems like that type of person. The kind who gets what he wants."

"And he wants you?" Her eyes narrowed again.

"He does. I don't know why, but he does. So that makes me the lucky one. Something I realize; don't worry," I said, serving up a little attitude of my own.

"All right then." She nodded after a minute, stepping to the side and letting me pass. "Then I guess I have to give you enough rope to hang yourself on."

"Challenge accepted." I tried to not smile, which was hard. This was by far the weirdest conversation I'd had in ages. I passed her and left the washroom, certain I'd failed in making her like me. But hopefully I'd gained a bit of her respect in making her see that I wasn't a threat to Ashley's happiness or future. I didn't ever want to be that for him.

When I got back to the table, Ashley and his dad shared an expression of worry. I smiled wide to reassure them.

"Did she attack you?" his dad gasped. "I checked her bag for sharp objects before we left the house, but she might have snuck a table knife away." His eyes darted around the table, maybe counting knives.

"You okay?" Ashley asked with genuine concern.

"She didn't attack me. She asked some pointed questions." I glanced to where she was, coming this way but still across the restaurant. "I think we understand each other."

"Dear God," his dad muttered, and gave Ashley a grave stare.

"Stop looking so serious, you two." His mother sat and nodded. "Cherry and I had a lovely conversation, and I think we're on the same page." She winked at me, losing all the anger and meanness.

They were so weird, this family. They talked about everything, even the uncomfortable things.

"Don't say it like we have no reason to be worried. Ya recall the woman she 'spoke' with in the bathroom last time we were home in Scotland?" His father used finger quotations for the word *spoke*. "Never saw her again, poor lass. Rumors swirled that she was last seen in the Highlands . . ."

Ashley and his mother laughed, but his father sounded serious. I feigned a laugh for a second until she gave me a wide smile.

"Don't listen to the old goat."

"Old goat? I, who has never strayed nor loved another? And how could I? 'But to see her was to love her; / Love but her, and love forever.'" He took her hand and kissed the back of it.

She blushed and pulled away. Feigning annoyance when it was obvious she loved him. They loved each other. It was the kind of love my sister would have. The kind Rachel would have too. And had I not met Ashley, the kind I would have always wondered about.

But he was real, as real as his dad spouting poetry in the middle of a restaurant. I assumed the poetry was Burns, which was likely frowned upon considering this was Shakespeare's home.

"Now, tell us why you're going home. What are these family troubles?" Ashley's mom was prying, fully prying.

I considered lying or making something up, but they discussed the hard stuff, so I did too. "My brother is an asshole, and his stupidity is coming back to bite all of us." I glanced at Ashley, knowing it had even affected him.

"Brothers can be stupid," she admitted. "I have two, and neither of them has a clue about life. Or women. Daft bastards." She nodded. I wanted to stop talking about it, but it was progress.

"Women troubles are my brother's issues too."

"Oh, it's the same old story, no matter the age. I always end up cleaning after their messes. They break the hearts, and I end up pouring a glass of wine for the poor thing and listening to what a cad I'm related to. Even now with their wives."

"Then you know my struggle."

"I do." She narrowed her gaze, maybe not believing we had this in common.

"My sister is the smart one," I owned. "She's a genius. Solves all his issues. Catches him in his lies." I sighed.

"And yet you're the one they all turn to. The leader in the group," Ashley said. I wasn't sure it was true or a compliment.

"Some leader." I laughed and took another drink.

"Well, here's to a safe flight at least." His father lifted his glass of wine.

I lifted mine and clinked it, touching everyone's glass before taking a sip. "How long will you be staying?" I asked.

"We aren't certain. We try to get back every year, but we haven't made it the last couple," his father owned. I knew he meant Ashley's school costs were weighing them down. He continued, "We have a lot of repairs that have built up. So a few more weeks at least before he can travel back to the states."

"And then back to America to prepare for the new semester for me and lots of rest for him," his mom chimed in. "It's lucky Ashley won that money with the robot wars. We were able to still have enough for his last year of school with Martin off. I'll be grateful when this is over. I love you, but you're expensive." She leaned in and kissed Ashley's cheek.

His reddened cheek. Red because he'd lied.

But he didn't need to make eye contact for me to play along. His story was much better than how he got the money. Much.

"Yeah, his robots are pretty cool. I'm not a gadgetry sort of girl, so I get lost pretty fast. But if my brother is willing to bet on him, then it's got to be good." I smiled proudly. There might have been some lies mixed in with the truths, but no matter what, I was proud of the truths.

"I'm the same, Cherry." She said my name for the first time since I'd introduced myself. "I haven't a clue what he's talking on about, and I don't pretend to, not like this one does." She pointed at her husband. "The fool doth think he is wise, but the wise man knows himself to be a fool," she said, possibly paraphrasing Shakespeare. I sort of recalled that one.

All of us laughed but his dad.

"If we weren't in his birthplace, I'd have some fresh words for you, missy." He leaned in.

"Dad, you're out of your league on this one." Ashley patted his father on the shoulder. "They've made friends. Even just two women win against a hundred men if they're each other's ally."

"Ah, true, son, very true." He pretended it didn't make him happy, but it did.

It made us all happy that I had somewhat won her over. I'd been skeptical, especially in the bathroom. But my bit of attitude in the bathroom had earned her respect. Or maybe it was my vulnerability. Either way, I seemed to be growing on her.

In a day of losses, this win was everything.

Chapter Forty-Three

FORGIVE AND NEVER FORGET

Cherry

I sat in the limo staring at Cait's house. I hadn't come through the gate this time. I wasn't sneaking up through the back door. And I wasn't alone.

I turned and looked at my friends, asking if they were ready with my stare.

"Let's do this." Laura got out first.

Cora and Erica climbed out behind her, leaving me and Sarah to climb out last.

"No matter what, we stand together." Sarah reached for me, wrapping her hand over mine.

"No matter what." I turned my hand over and squeezed her back.

We got out and hurried up to the house, knocking.

The butler answered, appearing a bit grim. "Sorry, Miss Cait isn't home," he lied.

"Yes, she is." I knew she was because her Instagram had a photo from fifteen minutes earlier of her in her room. I pushed past the butler and marched up the stairs.

"I'll have to ask you to leave, ladies. Don't make me call the authorities. Or worse, your parents."

I ignored him and ran up the massive staircase to Cait's floor. We burst through the double doors, catching her in the middle of a hissy fit. She was shouting and tossing things from the closet. The burn box closet. She was looking for something.

"Cait!" Sarah spoke loudly, interrupting her fit. "You won't find it."

Cait emerged, her eyes glowing like the wicked stepmother in "Cinderella." "What?" She was a mess. A scary mess. Her blonde hair was everywhere. Her mascara streaked down her cheeks, running along a huge pimple. She wore a thin tank top with shorts and a silk robe that was untied. Her nails were broken and chipped.

I'd never seen her like this.

She looked like the girl from *The Exorcist*, her skin mottled and pasty and her eyes filled with venom.

The black-and-white Instagram photo had been of a sunlit flower in her room. That flower was smashed on the floor now.

"You won't find the pictures or videos. We took them," I admitted.

"What did you do?" she screamed, continuing to scream for a full minute. "What did you fucking bitches do?" She spit the words, letting spittle fly from her lips. "Fuck!" she raged. She'd lost it completely.

I did the only thing I could think of. I rushed her and pulled her into my arms. I held her tight and whispered, "I know what Andy did to you. I know why you did this."

She crumpled, not losing the rage, but losing the fight. She dropped, taking me with her until we lay on the floor together, and she sobbed.

She cried so hard that the girls behind me started to cry too.

They encircled us, pulling us in.

We group hugged as she rage-cried until she finally lost that too. She calmed to a simple whimper and shook, heaving still with the state she'd put herself in.

"I hate you." She lifted her gaze. Her eyes stuck on me. "You and your entire family."

"Okay." I let her have that. I didn't need her to like me. The water might have been under the bridge by now, but it had wiped out the town along the way, and I couldn't look past the things Cait had done. But I wasn't going to spend my life hating her. I was going to get past this, as past as I could get. I also wasn't going to forget the last six years.

She'd made my life hell. I now knew why. I understood her motives. But I too was an innocent bystander in this.

"I forgive you, Cait. For all of it." It was a lie. I wasn't fully ready to forgive, but I was close enough that I could make myself say it.

"Don't." She winced. "You need to hate me."

"No. You need me to hate you. You need me to be as miserable as you are. You need me to suffer so my brother pays. But I'm done paying for the terrible thing he did to you. My brother is a douche; I won't ever take that from you. He acted like a pig. But you took this way too far." I glanced around at the girls surrounding us. "And you hurt them. None of us did anything to you. We were victims in this too. We didn't deserve this, the same way you didn't deserve what Andy did. You owe us an apology, which I suspect we'll neve—"

"I'm sorry." She said it too easily and too fast.

"No." Sarah shook her head, leaning in. "You just want your videos back. And that's never going to happen. You made them. You alone. Andy didn't do that. He might have been an asshole, but you tortured and tormented us and made us do terrible things because you wanted revenge. You took this way too far, Cait. Way too far. And like Cherry said, I forgive you. Because carrying this around is only hurting me."

"I forgive you too." Laura nodded. "It was sick and twisted, but I never thought you were anything but. Even when we were little, before the Andy thing. So this honestly comes as no surprise. But hopefully, you can let it all go and change as a result, Cait. You have a lot of work to do before you come even remotely close to being a decent human being, but you can't possibly go on living this way. Spiteful and full of vengeance, using other people without empathy. That shit won't fly in the real world."

"I forgive you." Erica said it through bared teeth. "But I never want to see you again. We are friends off. Forever."

"I don't forgive you." Cora sat up on her knees, her eyes welling with hate and tears. "I hate you, Cait Landry. I will hate you for the rest of my life." She leaned in and slapped Cait hard across the face. She got up and ran from the room.

Cait's cheek swelled with the handprint, but she hadn't even flinched or recoiled. She took the hit. As she sat there, stunned and pathetic, the girls trickled out of the room. Abandoning their fearless leader. Until only I was left.

The queen bee sat across from me on the floor, dethroned and missing her crown, with her cheek bright red from the handprint she hadn't even touched yet.

"I just wanted to get even." She blinked tears down her cheeks. "I liked him so much. He dumped me because I cheated, but I was drunk, and I didn't mean to. I kissed another guy, an Italian guy. I told everyone I dumped Andy—I think even he believed it—but he dumped me. I wouldn't have sex with him, and then I kissed that guy and he lost it. I hooked up with Brom to make Andy mad; I still loved him. And then he told me he wanted me back so badly." She started to sob. "Or I thought he did. Turns out he just wanted to make that video and harass me."

My stomach turned over, imagining my brother doing that to her. I hated him, not just for her but for me too.

"He showed me a copy of it. He laughed and said that we were even. I'd broken his heart, and he'd robbed me of my virginity. And no matter how much I lied to everyone, he had proof." She looked down. Her mouth moved and whispers came out, but I didn't hear them. She was lost, cracked and broken and not going to be put back together anytime soon.

I stared at her, trying to understand how she had possibly gone this far in it and not noticed. How had she done this to herself and everyone else around her and not seen the end in sight?

Surely there had been moments of warning screaming at her to back off or stop.

But no, she'd pressed on, scheming on top of old schemes to cover the mess she was making. No matter what she did, she was always digging that same old hole for herself.

She twitched and whispered, and I realized she didn't know I was there anymore. I didn't know if she knew where she was. I got up and walked down the hall, seeing a maid and pointing. "You need to call her parents. She's a mess." As I glanced back one last time, I wondered if I would ever see Cait Landry again. If anyone would ever see her again. Or if that shell of a human her evil deeds had created was all that was left, like my mom and her fake joy.

I returned to the girls, huddled in the lawn like survivors of some epic battle. We'd lived through the reign of Caitlyn Landry. We were beaten and battered, but we were alive.

We got up together and climbed into the limo.

Those faces, those tear-stained faces and swollen, puffy eyes, were evidence of what this mess really looked like.

The limo filled with girls was my new everything. Them and Ashley.

As Hans drove away from the house and left the gates, none of us looked back.

We looked at each other; seeing each other this summer for the first time had sealed us as friends.

I wrapped an arm around Cora and kissed the side of her sweaty face. "We're going to be okay." It was the truth. "Better than okay."

Sarah nodded, reaching over and squeezing my knee. "Better than okay."

In the back of the limo, riding with my best friends, we created a new motto for our lives.

A motto we would need every day we had to spend out here.

The ocean and beaches and people vacationing from the real world tricked you in the Hamptons. They made you think this was a place where the rich came to play, but the truth was that we didn't play around.

And I hoped deep down that our generation would be the end of that.

I hoped that the girls in this car would find truth and reality and end the games with me.

It all had to start somewhere, so why not with us?

Chapter Forty-Four

Second Fiddle

Cherry

Two weeks later, I held my hand up, grinning like a moron because I had no poker face, even if this wasn't poker.

"That good, huh?" Ashley grimaced. He looked adorable in his underwear and nothing else, holding the cards in his huge hands.

"That good." I winked. I still had my underwear, shirt, and bra left. I didn't tell him I'd gotten a cribbage app and was playing nonstop.

"Eight."

"Fifteen." I moved my peg two.

"Seventeen."

"Nineteen for two." I pegged another two for the pair of twos.

"Twenty-nine," he said smugly, assuming I didn't have another two. He was right. I didn't.

"Thirty." I laid an ace.

"Go." He narrowed his gaze.

"Thirty-one for four." I giggled and moved my pegs the final four spaces I needed to win the game.

"Dammit!" He threw his cards down and got up on his knees. He tugged off his boxers as he stood, naked and gorgeous and all mine. "And what does milady demand of me this time?"

I'd won twice now. The last time he went down on me and delivered three orgasms, back-to-back. I could barely sit at the end of that night.

"I think this time I wanna see something a little different." I got up and knee-walked to him, taking his cock in my hand. I squeezed slightly and leaned forward. I took his semihard erection in my mouth and began sucking, slowly stroking and making suction with my lips. I reached back and grabbed his ass as his hands slipped into my hair, wrapping his hands up in it.

"I thought you won?" He said it throatily and turned on, pushing my head to meet his gentle thrust as his cock doubled in size.

I would have laughed if I could breathe, but I really couldn't as I worked his cock, getting him to the point he was pulling my hair a little.

Just as he began pumping, I pulled back, leaving him exposed to the cold air. He shuddered in the air-conditioned room. "Don't stop."

"Oh, but I won." I got up and walked to the bed. "So I say how it goes." I patted the bed. "Come lie down."

He grinned like this was going to go far better than it was.

"Close your eyes," I said as he lay flat on the bed.

When he did I tiptoed to my things, grabbed them, and headed for the door.

"Cherry?" he muttered, feeling with his hand into the air.

"Yeah?" I said as I slipped my shorts back on.

"What are you—" He sat up, opened his eyes, and then glared. "This again?" He shot up and ran for me as I shrieked and darted for the door, flinging it open and hurrying out into the hallway.

He didn't consider that anyone walking past the little beach house we'd rented for him might see him or anything else; he ran into the hall chasing me, erection bobbing and all.

I was giggling and screaming as I headed for the stairs, trying to do my pants up.

He grabbed my arm and dragged me up the two stairs I'd made it down, lifting me into the air and hauling me over his shoulder. "I didn't like it the last time we played this game." He smacked me on the butt and stalked back to the bedroom, closing the door. He tossed me on the bed, his eyes filled with humor. "I'm gonna get a complex if you keep trying to escape my hard-on."

"I like it when you're hard and desperate." I giggled more.

"You're really gonna like it in a minute." He dragged my shorts down, tearing my underwear from me, and dropped to his knees. He buried his face, sucking my clit and sliding his tongue in and out of me. I moaned, taking my turn to wrap my fingers up in his hair.

He pushed me to the point of orgasming, then stopped. He pulled back, doing exactly what I'd done to him. "See how it feels?" He wiped his mouth. "You're just lucky I'm not you." He dragged my butt to the edge of the bed and spread my legs, dragging his cock's head up and down me. I shuddered from the contact with my clit, so ready to come.

He pushed inside of me, rubbing his thumb on my clit as he slid in and out slowly, driving me crazy.

I closed my eyes, wiggling into his thumb until the feelings rushed back in and I came. He pressed down, massaging ever so slightly but pressing hard until the waves of bliss passed. Then he grabbed my feet and placed them on his shoulders, lifting and cupping my hips and pounding into me. I cried out, moaning.

He pounded again.

"I'm going to fuck you so hard." He gripped me and did just as he promised.

When I orgasmed again, I felt it everywhere. I got lost in it, letting him consume me and force words and sounds from me like no other person ever had.

It might have been the best orgasm I ever had.

He collapsed on top of me and sighed. "I think I might be in love with fucking you." He said it exactly the wrong way. But then he lifted his head and stared me deeply in the eyes. "I mean, I know I love you as a person. But we might have to have more sex for me to be sure about the love of fucking you."

"You suck." I laughed at him, even if I was kinda swooning a little. "You can't say you love a girl right after sex, firstly. And secondly you can't say you love fucking her. Or love her as a person. That was terrible, all of it." I laughed at him again.

"You want poetry?" He cringed. "I only know one by heart." He cleared his throat and spoke in a perfect Scottish accent. "Not the bee upon the blossom / In the pride o' sunny noon; / Not the little sporting fairy, / all beneath the simmer moon; / Not the Minstrel in the moment / Fancy lightens in his e'e, / Kens the pleasure, feels the rapture, / That thy presence gies to me." He winked.

"You think Robbie Burns is what I want to hear?" I teased.

"You want real poetry?" He wrinkled his nose, looking handsomer than he ever had. "I'm afraid I haven't got any of that. I save all my best verses for the robots. My true loves."

"You shit!" I pushed him off and crawled up the bed. "You suck."

"I mean, you'll always be second fiddle to them. I think you should know that going in." He tried to sound serious.

"Sort of like how you'll be second fiddle to whomever my mom makes me marry?" I asked, being a cheeky ass back. His meeting my mother was still being delayed. I wasn't ready to show us to the world. We were the fish and the bird that fell in love, and currently we were living in a world we made our own. One we could survive in with no outside influences. A safe place.

"Right. Being second husband is going to be rough, but I understand." He crawled up the bed and slid his arm under my neck and cradled me to him. "But being serious for a moment, there's something we need to discuss."

"No." I shook my head. "I don't want to be serious. We were serious all summer. I just want to goof off for these last couple of weeks and pretend we aren't who we are and life is easy and nothing matters."

"But this is going to be a busy year for me, school wise, and then I'm going to have my internship, and I'll have to move, and I don't want any of that to get in the way of this." He glanced down at me. "So promise me right now, if you ever feel like things are going wrong or I'm not giving you enough attention or I'm too busy with school, you'll remind me that I love you almost as much as I love robots."

"Whatever." I rolled my eyes. "You love me way more than that."

He positioned us so I had to stare him right in the eyes. "I do." He gave me that look, the one I loved. "I love you way more than I love robots. More than anything in my whole life. I love you, Cheryl Kennedy."

"I knew it." I kissed him, pressing myself against him. "I mean I suspected as much."

He kissed me and whispered, "Though it might have been weird, this was the best summer of my life." He kissed me again.

He made everything right in the world.

Almost everything.

There were things neither of us could fix. That would be left to time, which was working on mending injuries all across the shore. But she worked so slowly.

A knock at the door made me nervous until I heard Ella talking to someone outside.

There were a few people who knew we were here.

"Time for an Ella invasion?" Ashley asked. Fortunately he liked my sister, a lot.

"Yeah, put clothes on." I dragged on my yoga pants and a sweatshirt and headed down the stairs. "Hey." I opened the door, smiling at Sarah, Ella, and the girls.

"I have a surprise. I texted you we were coming over, but you didn't respond." She pushed past me and hurried inside, grabbing my laptop.

"I was busy." I chuckled and let everyone else invade our sacred space.

Whatever Ella was doing made her nervous. She paced in front of my computer on the counter as it loaded. She had been coy, secretive even, for weeks.

Rachel gave me a curious glance, but I shrugged. I honestly didn't know where this was going.

The clock on the main floor started to chime five o'clock, and Ella sprang to life, typing a bunch of things into the computer and pressing one last button. She sighed and stepped back as the computer screen began to play a video.

"*Who are the rich elite?*" A man we couldn't see asked as a picture of a bunch of girls at cotillion flashed. They looked pretty and normal and sweet in the photo. Like any of us at a fancy party. "*Or rather, what dark secrets are the rich elite hiding?*"

My stomach started to hurt. "Ella?" I whispered.

Images began to flash of partying teenagers and important faces I knew.

"*Several years ago, an exclusive club was created in the Hamptons—a club every girl wanted to be part of. It was a secret society of young women determined to humiliate young men. A group of girls who bullied and tormented young men as payback for years of imbalance in the elite society. What does this all say about the upper crust, and does this imbalance trickle down into the lower echelons of society?*"

"Oh, dear God," Sarah whispered as an image of the rules of the club flashed, no doubt the copy Rachel had taken and not burned.

"*Here are the rules of the secret society. As you can see, it's labeled 'Fling Club.' A fun name for a dark purpose.*"

I swallowed hard, scared of what was about to come out. Ella was doing exactly what she had been born for; I just never imagined I would also get taken down by her.

My insides were on fire, but I stared.

"What does it say about society that young women are making up these dating clubs and controlling the young men? What does it say about girls going this far to the other side of feminism? How much is too much? Tonight, we will explore the secret society inside of the Hamptons' very own Fling Club." The announcer said it like he was talking about something dreadful. Not summer frivolities.

Ella closed the computer and stared at us all for a moment before speaking. "I took down the club and the rich elite. I didn't name names. I got statements from groups of guys who belonged and some of the girls. I protected my sources. I used the flash drives, pixelating any images of nudity or faces."

"Jesus." I swallowed that down like a bitter pill. "Everyone is going to know Cait created the club and that this is about her. You went this far?"

"I did." She nodded, no regret on her face.

"Even though you knew what Andy did to her?"

"Yeah. Andy made a single mistake, a disgusting mistake. She hurt him so he hurt her. But she made the choice to spend the next five years hurting the rest of you and tormenting you. It's not the same; you see how it's not the same, right?" She was always the voice of reason, but I was also having a tough time swallowing the simplification of Andy's crimes.

"I guess I don't." I glanced at the other girls. "As someone who had sex because of peer pressure while someone filmed it and used it against me, I understand her madness and rage. He let her trust him and then did that to her. I can't downplay what he did, any more than I can what she did."

"I'm not downplaying his actions. He lied to us for years, knowing all along how Cait got this crazy. I'm just saying, she took it that extra step." Ella sounded impassioned. "It's done now, though. Her Fling Club and rules and twisted games are outed for the entire world to see. The program *60 Minutes* has a series of shows about this, all leading back to the abuse of women and the misdirection of feminism against a patriarchal society."

"Wow." Sarah nodded. "Guess we're going to be under the microscope a little."

"Maybe it isn't a bad thing, Sarah," Ella added.

"I agree." Rachel shrugged. "We all know it needs to end, the arranged marriages and fake love and leaders and their wives."

"Exactly." Ella clapped her hands together.

"You are one badass bitch, Ella." Laura shook her head. "I thought you might make a web page and out Cait for her bullshit and her lies. But this, this might actually change a few things."

"And if it doesn't change them, it doesn't matter; the whole thing has changed us." Rachel gave us all a smile. "This summer has changed me."

"Me too." Cora spoke up, louder than normal.

"How's Andy?" Sarah asked, like she might actually care.

"Sick with himself," Ella said flatly. "Like he deserves to be. He's holed up in Boston, back on campus early, avoiding everyone. I don't know that we'll see him before Christmas at this rate. I'm okay with that."

"Me too." I wasn't really. I hated him for the moment, but he was my brother, and I would miss him. Eventually.

Maybe.

Or maybe I wouldn't ever forgive him.

Or maybe I already did but didn't want to admit it to myself.

A lot of maybes.

"This has been the weirdest friggin' summer I've ever spent. You girls know how to party." Rachel laughed.

We all laughed.

Some of us even sounded like we thought it was funny.

Ella's use of the USBs had been a ballsy one.

"Where are the USBs now?" I was not okay with any of this.

"I hand delivered every single person's USB to them with an explanation that Cait's well-timed nervous breakdown was because she was caught," Ella answered, completely justified in her actions.

She'd done exactly the thing she had wanted to from the start. She took down Fling Club. She took down Cait. She was savage and ruthless and outed Cait for all her bad behavior. She took the secrecy we thrived on here and outed everyone.

My brother suffered silently along with Cait, though never named as the reason she'd started it all. The shore was going to be lit with rage and gossip and a fire Ella had started, all based on assumptions. Ella was determined to take down the patriarchy and the old blue-blooded way of doing things, and she'd started here in her own backyard.

Had anyone known who was really behind it all, the ramifications would have been dire.

My mom would have been devastated.

Dad would have been concerned about the results it would have on business.

I would have been proud.

As it stood, I was proud. Quietly proud.

Ella would always hate it here.

And Andy might not ever come home again.

But he'd made his bed, and I had to let him lie in it. Another thing time was working on.

"Want something to eat?" I asked my friends.

"Yeah, I'm starved." Ashley came down the stairs and kissed me softly. "And I imagine Ella is starving after all the work she's been doing." He winked at her. "I like it."

"Thanks." Ella beamed. "Who cooks?" She glanced around, worried.

"I do." I smiled back, still recovering from the shock of Ella's revelation. "That's how we've lived here. No service. No staff. No one but us."

I didn't know that about myself before, but it was how I preferred to live.

I was more like my dad than I thought. Luckily.

And I was grateful for Ashley showing me that too.

Epilogue

Cherry

My dad leaned in, speaking softly over the sound of the family Christmas we were in the midst of. "Ashley's mother just called your mom an antiquated relic, and your mom thought it was a compliment."

We chuckled. Ella gave us a look from where she was sitting, then got up and sauntered over to us. "Why do you look like you're laughing at us all?"

"We are." My father nodded. "I've never seen your mom laugh as hard as she has." He said it like he was enjoying the night. "Ashley's father has to be one of the funniest men I've ever met. Highly intelligent as well. Much smarter than he lets on with his jokes."

"Yeah. He lets his wife win a lot." I folded my arms and watched Ashley chatting up Rachel and Ryan. "Where's Andy?" I asked.

"Hiding in his room still," Ella scoffed. "He's such a child."

"He hasn't come home in months, and when he does he hides up there. He left early this summer. Do I dare ask when you two will forgive him?" Dad asked. Ella had eventually revealed to our parents what had happened, I suspected as a means to torment our mother.

"No," we said at the same time.

"Fair enough. I won't make an excuse for his behavior." He nodded, not pushing. That was our dad. He kissed us both on the cheek and headed back into the snake pit, where Mr. Jardine clearly needed some help.

"How're things with Ry?" I asked, as if I didn't know the answer. My sister was dating; that meant it was going well.

"Meh." She shrugged but smiled, her eyes twinkling.

"Liar." I nudged her.

"And things with Ashley?" she pried, giving me a nosy look.

"Meh." I stole her answer, also lying.

"It's okay for real? With him being so busy with school and you being so busy finishing a degree you don't want?"

"Shut up. We spend almost every night together. He sleeps in my apartment or I in his dorm. It's getting a bit pathetic. The train employees are recognizing me, calling me by name. I brought coffees the other day for the morning crew and knew everyone's order."

"Wow. That's bad."

"Should we forgo the small talk and go ahead with attacking Andy?" I gave her a look.

"I was waiting for you to bring it up." She linked her arm in mine, and we headed up the stairs. "It's time to finish his punishment so we can allow him into regular society again."

"Sounds good. But you better come up with something fitting the crimes." I was being serious, where she was joking.

When we got upstairs he was sitting on his bed with his laptop. He looked bad. He had a beard, and he was thinner. The cocky brother we'd always known was a shell of who he used to be. His eyes darted to us as we walked in, and he flinched. It dawned on me that my brother didn't need punishment, he'd had enough. He needed an intervention now.

"Can we talk?" I asked, taking the lead.

"I'd rather not," he said bitterly.

"Well, too bad. We are willing to listen to you grovel now." Ella folded her arms.

"What can I even say?" He lifted his gaze, his eyes glistening. "Have you ever made a mistake that you knew was off the charts bad, but it was done and you couldn't take it back?"

"No." Ella sounded cold.

"What Cait did—what we did to all of you and each other—is inexcusable. I don't want your forgiveness. I don't deserve it." He broke, heaving a little as he sobbed, but only once. "And I am so truly sorry. I've been doing things to try to right these wrongs—"

"We don't care about that," Ella interrupted.

"I know. And all I can ask is that you give me a fresh start. Please. Let the things from the past stay there. Give me a chance to be the person I am trying to become. The person I'm trying to find through this mess." He sighed and nodded. "I fucked up. I own that."

For the second time in my life, someone was asking for a second chance. I felt better odds in the chance I'd denied Griffin than this one, but I said something I hadn't thought I could. "Okay." I only agreed because there had been a time in my life when I needed a second chance. And I wouldn't be where I was now, as happy as I was, without it.

I'd convinced myself second chances were possible, even if the unlikeliest of second chances was staring me in the face.

"Thank you." Andy sounded genuinely sorry. My brother truly needed my forgiveness. So I gave it.

"I forgive you. For real."

"Me too." Ella broke, her crusty exterior flooded with remorse. We ran at him, attacking with hugs and tears.

He sobbed, shaking in our arms.

We held each other for a long time, him crying until there wasn't anything left.

Then I wrinkled my nose. "What is that smell?"

"It's me," Andy said softly.

"Dude, you need to start showering again." Ella wrinkled her nose. "You get cleaned up and come downstairs. Everyone wants to see you. It's Christmas."

"You sure?" he asked, scared of us or what everyone would think.

"Yeah," we said at the same time.

He smiled, and I swear for a second I saw a glimmer of my brother in the homeless looking guy on his bed.

"I'm glad you're back." I smiled and left him there to change.

I needed a minute, so I turned for the back door and headed outside.

It was cold and frosty, but I was in need of some of that real-world intervention I'd learned to find in the solitude of silent benches.

I sat on the cold bench and stared up at the clear sky.

It was vastly different from New York or Boston here in the Hamptons. Here you could see stars.

I shivered and watched them all twinkling as I debriefed from my harrowing last ten minutes.

"And that's our good deed for the next ten years?" Ella muttered, coming out to see me. "I feel like we rolled over way too easy. But honestly, what should we have demanded as repayment?"

"I don't know. Blood?" I offered weakly.

"He's been publicly humiliated. Everyone out here knows Andy's and Cait's involvement, or at least suspects them. They don't have any friends left. She missed the first month of school after she spent that two months in the center."

"It wasn't a bad thing." I recalled the way she'd looked the last time I saw her.

"No, and it was some fancy place where people like us go to chill for a month or two. Not like she suffered."

"I can't imagine the kind of baggage they both have from this." It was too much for me.

"Yeah. Me either. Did you hear her mom kicked her dad out, after his freak show with Liz was outed?"

"No, Jesus. Gross."

"Super gross." She nudged me. "Hey, but on a brighter note, I have big news. I got accepted to MIT. Ashley and I are going to take over the world!"

"No. Oh my God! You're going to break tradition again?"

"Uh, yes. I'm not going to friggin' Wellesley finishing school."

"It's a good school." My cheeks reddened.

"Maybe, but it's still weird. And I'm not down for all that girl-on-girl action, despite popular belief."

"Shut up." I pushed her.

"It's cold out here; you ready to go back in?" she asked.

"No. I'm gonna stay a couple of minutes longer. You go on in." I smiled.

"Fine. I'll stay. But I need amusements." She took my phone from my lap and started playing on it.

"Whoa! When were you going to tell me about this?" Ella held up the screen so I could see my acceptance letter.

"Oh, that." I laughed at how efficient she was at snooping, considering I'd just changed the password.

"Seriously? That's all you have to say for yourself?"

"I'm going to grad school for filmmaking." I nodded. "I'm starting in June with a summer program." Even saying it aloud didn't make it feel real.

"Tisch? Seriously? Martin Scorsese went there. How the hell did you even get in?"

"Luck," I lied.

"Lucky you were born a Kennedy." She laughed too. "I'm proud of you, maybe for the first time. Like, really proud. This is huge." She kept my phone and walked back to the house. "But I'm still telling on you," she shouted as she got to the door. "This is going to save me for my betrayal for going to MIT!"

I got up and followed, pausing at what I saw. In the window, I watched my family as snow softly fell on and around me. It was like a movie. The window was frosty, and the scene inside was warm and filled with a brightly decorated tree and a bunch of nuts.

They laughed and let their crazy out of the bag. Ashley's family brought out the real in mine.

I wrapped my arms around myself and sighed, watching them interacting. Rachel, Ryan, and their dad had become permanent fixtures at our house and in our life. We'd adopted them, and whether they liked it or not, they were family. I felt sorry for them a lot.

Ashley had been a hard-fought battle by my dad, forcing my mom to not be a giant bitch. I managed to avoid the entire scene, being at school when I finally broke it to her.

It was a tough one for her. But she was nicer to him and his family than his mother originally was to me.

Andy came down and joined everyone, getting hugs and pats and handshakes. He looked so different.

I thought about myself eight months ago and knew where he was. He was lost. He needed some tough Ella love and to find himself again. He would be okay again. Not the same—better, but scarred.

I knew this story too well.

I had the guy.

I had the life.

I had the money and the fancy clothes.

I had the opportunities.

But up until recently I was missing so much more inside of me.

And my life was about to change for the better because I started to figure these things out.

I had a new checklist, and it didn't revolve around a guy. It was my own.

Motivated, check.

Happy, check.

Focused, check.

Living with purpose, check.

In love, check.

And as if on cue, love came strolling out, eyes twinkling and smile wide. "She's outing you in there." Ashley chuckled. "Ella just told everyone about Tisch."

"Oh, God. My mom's gonna lose it."

"Yeah, she's flipping out. Said she wasn't paying for your education so you could be a waitress in LA." He sauntered over, wrapping me in warmth and light. He pressed his lips to my forehead.

"It's okay. She just needs a minute to come around and she'll get over it." I pulled back. "Are you having fun?" I asked, laughing.

"I am, are you?"

"Yeah. I talked to my brother, so that's something."

"He's a human being, Cherry. He makes mistakes. Granted that was a bad one, but he's paid an awful lot for it."

"I guess. I don't really want to talk about it, if it's all right."

"That's okay, I have something serious I want to talk about anyway." He pulled back and brushed the snow from my hair and cupped my face. Then he dropped to his knee and pulled out a small silver box, almost giving me a stroke. "Cheryl, Cherry Kennedy, from the moment I saw you, I knew I needed you. I knew that nothing in my world was ever going to be the same. You were a different breed of human than I was used to, but I decided early on I would form myself to fit in around you."

My insides tightened, and my fingers crept to my lips as everything in me felt like it was about to burst.

"And then you showed me the weirdest summer I have ever spent or imagined possible, and I knew right away, this was it. We had some ups and downs, and during a particularly bad down, I realized I can't actually live without you. I was at my parents' house, meant to be fixing the roof, and all I did was hack my mom's Instagram and refresh yours and wait for a clue as to where you were and if you were okay. I spent hours staring at your face. Being apart from you was the worst I have ever felt."

He cracked open the box, pulling out a single Post-it note. He handed it to me, stunning me. There was no ring, just the Post-it note I'd left on the wall for him when we had broken up, so to speak.

"I need you too. And I love you."

I took the Post-it note, not sure what this meant. But then he pulled out an old ring.

"It was my grandma's. My mom would be honored if you'd wear it, and I'd be honored if you'd wear it, as sort of a promise to each other of where this is going. It's not an engagement ring, not yet."

Tears flooded my eyes, and he became nothing more than lights and twinkling stars in my vision, but I nodded and let him slip the ring on my finger of my right hand, not my left.

He stood and pulled me close, kissing me and whispering into the embrace. "I think my mom's on my side because she wants us to hurry up and get engaged for real and then married so you can be rid of that last name. Of course I joked I was taking your name."

We laughed, and I shook my head. "You ruin all the good moments."

"It's part of my charm." He kissed me, and as much as I wanted that to be a lie, it wasn't. It was part of his charm.

I loved him, weird romantic-moment destroyer and all.

We kissed some more, with the snow falling down on us and our family watching from the inside of the house, my mom no doubt trying to see what the carat was on the ring.

It was just like a scene from a movie.

In fact, I contemplated using it in at least one of my own Christmas films.

One day.

This guy, this summer fling, turned out to be the exception to every rule.

ABOUT THE AUTHOR

Author photo © 2015

The international bestselling author of *Roommates* and the Puck Buddies series, Tara Brown writes in a variety of genres. In addition to her comedic Single Lady Spy series, she has also published popular contemporary and paranormal romances, science fiction, thrillers, and romantic comedies. She especially enjoys writing dark and moody tales, often focusing on strong female characters who are more inclined to vanquish evil than perpetrate it. She shares her home with her husband, two daughters, two cats, an Irish wolfhound, and a Maremma Sheepdog. Find out more about Tara by visiting www.TaraBrownAuthor.com.